Brattleboro Retreat, Joseph Draper

The Vermont Asylum for the Insane

Its annals for fifty years

Brattleboro Retreat, Joseph Draper

The Vermont Asylum for the Insane
Its annals for fifty years

ISBN/EAN: 9783337368210

Printed in Europe, USA, Canada, Australia, Japan

Cover: Foto ©Andreas Hilbeck / pixelio.de

More available books at **www.hansebooks.com**

THE

VERMONT ASYLUM

FOR THE

INSANE.

———•••———

ITS ANNALS

FOR

FIFTY YEARS.

BRATTLEBORO:
PRINTED BY HILDRETH & FALES.
1887.

CONTENTS.

CONTENTS.

CONTENTS. v

ILLUSTRATIONS.

INTRODUCTION.

WHY this book? *First*, because the Vermont Asylum is one of the oldest institutions for the care of the insane in the United States, and has in some respects a unique history that has not been fully told in its published reports; which latter, moreover, are now so scarce that for many years it has been impossible to obtain a complete set.

Second, the completion of a half-century of its chartered work warrants the compilation of its results, for the benefit of the specialty in its statistical elaborations and generalizations.

Third, as here presented it affords in a single volume a complete résumé of the fifty years' work, in such form that it may take a place in libraries along with kindred literature, and be conveniently referred to.

Fourth, it has seemed to the compiler a work that could not be longer delayed without loss of much of the material which now goes to make up its annals, and which has been gathered to a considerable extent from those already deceased.

Besides the records of the Trustees from the beginning, and the published reports, the early correspondence of the Trustees with men prominent in philanthropic work a half century ago has been drawn upon to some extent, as also the verbal history derived from those early engaged in the work, who, within the time of the writer, have borne testimony to many unrecorded facts. It has been our endeavor to show, as far as possible, the yearly life, with the accomplishments of each annual period; also, the ideas underlying the general policy of management and the professional conduct of the establishment, as evidenced by numerous and extended quotations from the Trustees and Superintendents, and in some instances from published reviews in contemporary Journals.

The writer is aware that some typographical errors exist that might have been avoided had a professional proof-reader been available; but which he trusts will be overlooked by the general reader. Absolute exactness has been aimed at in respect to the facts. All statements made may be relied upon, and all comments have been made in the spirit of fairness, with strict regard to truth.   J. D.

THE

Vermont Asylum for the Insane.

ITS ANNALS.

RECORD OF 1834.

Mrs. ANNA MARSH,

Ⓓ Ⓙ Ⓔ Ⓓ

Oct. 14, 1834, Aged 65.

Consort of

Dr. Perley Marsh.

THIS monumental stone, in the old burial ground in Hinsdale, N. H., beside that of her husband, Doct.r Perley Marsh, who died Sept. 18, 1807, aged 41, attests the resting-place of the founder of the Vermont Asylum for the Insane. The will containing the bequest for this purpose bears date June 3rd, 1834, and reads as follows: "I, Anna Marsh, of Hinsdale, in the County of Cheshire, and State of New Hampshire, being weak in body, but in my own apprehension of sound and disposing mind and memory, considering the uncertainty of this mortal life, have thought it best to make, and accordingly do hereby make, this my last will and testament in manner following, that is to say, as to all my worldly estate, I dispose of the same as follows:

"I give unto the town of Vernon, in the County of Windham, and State of Vermont, two thousand dollars, the principal to be kept at interest as a permanent fund for the support of preaching in said town, the principal to be kept entire, and the interest only to be used.

"I give unto Samuel Clark, John Holbrook, Epaphroditus Seymour, and John C. Holbrook, all of Brattleboro, in the County of Windham aforesaid, and their successors, ten thousand dollars in trust, for the purpose of erecting and supporting in the County of Windham, near Connecticut River, a hospital for the relief of insane persons, and in case of the decease of one or more of said trustees, the survivors shall from time to time fill all vacancies; and the said trustees, being four in number, shall forever hereafter have the sole superintendence and direction of said insane hospital; and it is my will that the said trustees procure an act of incorporation, as soon as may be after my decease.

"I give unto my cousins, Cynthia G. Arms, Sarah Tilden, and Helen Hunt, all residing in the State of New York, five hundred dollars each.

"I give unto Fanny Blake, wife of Dr. Blake, of Northfield, and Sally Pomeroy, wife of Medad Pomeroy, of Warwick, all my household furniture and wearing apparel, to be equally divided between them. And as to all the rest and residue of my estate, whether real or personal not otherwise herein disposed of, I give, devise, and bequeath the same to Hunt Blake, of Vernon, in the County of Windham, and State of Vermont, to hold to him, his heirs and assigns, forever.

"And lastly, I do hereby constitute and appoint John Nevers, of Northfield, Mass., and Asa Keyes, of Brattleboro, Vermont, executors of this my last will and testament, hereby revoking all former wills by me made.

"In testimony whereof, I the said Anna Marsh, have hereunto set my hand and seal, and do declare the above to be my last will and testament, this third day of June, in the year of our Lord, one thousand eight hundred and thirty-four.

"Signed, sealed, and declared by the said Anna Marsh to be her last will and testament in presence of us, who have witnessed the same in presence of the testatrix and in the presence of each other. } ANNA MARSH. (L. S.)

ADELINE RICHARDSON,
ORRIN SNOW,
SALLY KEYES,
ASA KEYES.

RECORD OF THE YEAR 1834.

" Proved at Keene, first Tuesday of January, 1835, Sally Keyes and Orrin Snow witnesses. Notice previously published. Copy filed in Marlboro Probate District, last Wednesday of March, 1835. Notice previously published. John Nevers and Asa Keyes, executors, [appeared] and gave bonds in $25,000. Inventory to be returned in three months. Inventory returned first Tuesday of April. Property appraised March 7, 1835, by

> JONATHAN BROWN, ⎫
> OBED SLATE, ⎬ Appraisers."
> TIMOTHY A. BASCOM, ⎭

The inventory of the estate exhibited a total of $21,720.49, which was largely invested in notes of hand. The first action of the trustees was to apply for a charter from the Legislature, in accordance with the request of the founder. This was granted by the General Assembly of the State of Vermont in the same year in which the testatrix died, and the following is a *verbatim et literatim* copy:

AN ACT
TO INCORPORATE THE VERMONT ASYLUM FOR THE INSANE.

SEC. 1. It is hereby enacted by the General Assembly of the State of Vermont, that Samuel Clark, John Holbrook, Epaphro' Seymour, and John C. Holbrook, and their successors, appointed as hereinafter directed, be, and they hereby are incorporated, and made a body politic and corporate by the name of "The Vermont Asylum for the Insane," with all the powers and privileges incident to such corporations, and by that name may sue and be sued, plead and be impleaded, appear, prosecute and defend in all suits and actions, and shall have and use a common seal to be by them devised, altered, and renewed, at their pleasure.

SEC. 2. It is hereby further enacted, that the said corporation may take and receive, hold, purchase and possess, of and from all persons disposed to aid the benevolent purposes of said institution, any grants and devises of lands and tenements, in fee simple or otherwise, and any donations and bequests, and subscriptions of money or other property, to be used and improved for the erection, support, and maintenance of an asylum as aforesaid, provided the income of said corporation from its real and personal estate does not exceed the sum of ten thousand dollars per annum.

SEC. 3. It is hereby further enacted that said corporation, may from time to time make and establish such by-laws [and] regulations, for the internal government and economy of said asylum as they may think proper, not repugnant to the constitution and laws of this, or the United States; and may at any meeting thereof duly warned, choose all necessary and convenient officers, who shall have such power and authority, and be elected in such manner and for such period of time as the said corporation by their by-laws shall limit and direct.

SEC. 4. It is hereby further enacted that it shall be lawful for said corporation at any meeting duly warned for the purpose, to alter or change the name of said corporation by substituting or adding the name of any distinguished benefactor who may make liberal contribution to the funds thereof, and upon such change or alteration as aforesaid, the said corporation shall have a right to assume and take such name, and shall have, hold, and enjoy all the powers and privileges given by this act, notwithstanding such alteration and change.

SEC. 5. It is hereby further enacted, that the said Samuel Clark, John Holbrook, Epaphro' Seymour, and John C. Holbrook, and their successors, not exceeding at any time four in number, shall be a Board of Trustees, and shall have the sole superintendence of said Asylum, and in case of the decease, resignation, or removal of one or more of said trustees, the survivors shall from time to time, fill all such vacancies.

SEC. 6. It is hereby further enacted that after the organization of said corporation, the said trustees shall keep, or cause to be kept, just and true books of account of all the transactions of said corporation, and shall therein enter all the funds, income, donations, receipts and expenditures thereof, which said books shall at all times be open for the inspection of the Board of Visitors, nominated in this act, and the said trustees shall make an annual report to the General Assembly of the amount of the funds of said Asylum, the receipts and expenditures thereof, the number of patients admitted and discharged, the number cured, the state of others discharged or remaining, and such other information as may be necessary to show the effects and operations of said institution.

SEC. 7. It is hereby further enacted, that the Judges of the Court of Chancery for the time being, be, and hereby are, constituted a Board of Visitors of the said Asylum, with authority to visit the same annually, and oftener if they think proper, to inspect the said establishment, and the actual condition of the patients thereof, to examine the by-laws and regulations enacted by said corporation, and generally to see that the design of the institution be carried into effect, in a careful, tender, and effectual manner; and the said Court of Chancery shall have full power to correct any and all abuses of trust, done, suffered, or permitted by said corporation, or the officers thereof.

SEC. 8. It is hereby further enacted, that the said Samuel Clark, and upon his neglect, any other member of said corporation, may call the first meeting thereof, by giving notice of the time and place of holding the same, in some one of the newspapers printed in the County of Windham, at least six days previous to said meeting,—and all other meetings of said corporation shall be warned and holden in the manner provided by the by-laws thereof.

SEC. 9. It is hereby further enacted that the estate both real and personal, and all other, the funds of said institution, shall at all times hereafter be exempt from all taxes.

SEC. 10. It is hereby further enacted, that any future legislature shall have power to modify, alter, and amend this act, so far as to provide for the more perfect and effectual accomplishment of the objects of this act.   [Approved Nov. 3rd, 1834.]

Thus was the Institution established, upon the foundation solely of this legacy. The circumstances attending the bequest we have from Asa Keyes, Esq., who drew up the will, and who subsequently became one of the Trustees of the Asylum. In testimony given before a Legislative Committee in 1878, he thus gives an account of them: " Mrs. Marsh sent for me, and requested me to come to her house; the messenger told me she wanted to make a will. I went over there, and she said she did. I called for paper, and asked her to whom she wanted to will her property, and she said she would give ten thousand dollars for an Asylum for the Insane. It was new to me and I tried to divert her thoughts to other things,—suggested the Bible Society, and other things of that nature,—but she refused every one of them, and said she was determined to have an Asylum for the Insane. So I took the minutes down, and told her I would go home and write them out, and come over in the course of a week and have her will executed. When I went over there, I found that she had still the same mind about building an Asylum. Then I asked her where she would have it situated ? She said over there in Windham County, near the Connecticut River, you can find a good place. Then I told her it was necessary to have some trustees; and she wished me to name some, and I did so, and she chose them. The trustees were Dea. J. Holbrook, Epaphro' Seymour, Samuel Clark and John C. Holbrook. She died sometime in the fall after, and I was named as executor, proved her will, and went on and administered her estate, together with John Nevers, of Northfield, Mass. We settled the estate and paid over to these trustees the amount of ten thousand dollars."

The home of Mrs. Marsh was four miles below Brattleboro, on the New Hampshire side of the Connecticut River. There yet stands the square hip-roofed two-story mansion (see frontispiece), now 122 years old, typical of the better class of residences in the early part of the present century, from which during the twenty-seven years of her widowhood she dispensed a liberal hospitality, and connected with which was an estate of 400 acres, which she managed with signal ability. The place itself would have been entirely suited to the purposes of the institution which she endowed, had she chosen thus to devote it; but in determining the location of the Asylum she was decided in her preference for the Vermont side, declaring "she had already done enough for New Hampshire,"* where she resided. It is probable, however, that her preference was determined by the fact that Vermont was the home of her ancestry, as well as her own birth-place.

In making her bequest to the town of Vernon (directly opposite her place of residence) for the support of preaching, she remarked: " They are a very godless people over there, and never go to meeting; I want to do something to get them together on the Sabbath."

When other objects were urged upon her notice as worthy of charitable consideration, as stated by Mr. Keyes, she remarked that, " Everybody gave to missionary objects, and educational interests belonged to those who had children (she had none living), but nobody cared for the poor insane; they were neglected and shifted about, and she wanted to provide a home for them."

These fragmentary reminiscences derived from Mr. Keyes in verbal conversations, go to show that her last will was the result of much deliberation upon the matter, and—coupled with the fact that Mr. Keyes was solicited by a nephew of hers to whom she had in a previous testament bequeathed the bulk of her property, to scruti-

---

*Besides many contributions to worthy objects during her life-time, she gave to the town of Hinsdale, in 1828, a bell weighing 910 pounds and costing several hundred dollars, which was placed upon the first church in that village, and remained there as long as the building stood. It was then hired by the Universalist society, on condition that it be rung regularly three times a day, at 9 A. M., 12 M. and 9 P. M., for the benefit of the town. This church was subsequently leased to the Methodists, and while in their charge the bell became cracked. In 1873 it was sold by the town for old metal at 13 cents per pound, and the avails, $118.30, were turned into the town treasury.

nize carefully her testamentary capacity when making the alterations she might suggest—go to show that in this document she had determined to set aside considerations of relationship, and carry out, so far as she was able, her philanthropic views, which clearly were not the result of any sudden or unaccountable freak of benevolence.

The author of the History of Brattleboro, published in 1880, cites the case of Hon. Richard Whitney, who died in Hinsdale in 1806, under unfortunate circumstances, as very probably having suggested to Mrs. Marsh the need of a hospital for the insane. Mr. Whitney, who had been a man prominent in political life, became mentally deranged, and was obliged to be placed under restraint.

At that time little if anything was known in regard to the proper treatment of insane persons. The faculty were vainly groping in the dark for a potent weapon with which they could meet this mysterious enemy of human happiness, called insanity. Many, especially the devoutly religious classes, attributed this malady to supernatural causes. Therefore they considered all remedial efforts vain, and nothing could be done but to confine the unfortunate victim, and wait for death.

A council of physicians [Dr. Marsh believed to have been one] decided upon trying for the recovery of Mr. Whitney a temporary suspension of his consciousness, by keeping him completely immersed in water three or four minutes, or until he became insensible, and then resuscitate or awaken him to a new life. Passing through this desperate ordeal, it was hoped, would divert his mind, break the chain of unhappy associations, and thus remove the cause of his disease. Upon trial, this system of regeneration proved of no avail, for, with the returning consciousness of the patient came the knell of departed hopes, as he exclaimed "You can't drown love." But the failure of this experiment seems not to have convinced the physicians that they were upon the wrong track. Some accounts say the repetition of it terminated the life of the patient; others, and the most reliable, state that in the subsequent trial opium was selected as "the proper agent for the stupefaction of the life forces," which was essayed with a fatal result.

The head-stone over the grave of Mr. Whitney, in the same burial ground with that of Dr. Marsh, bears the following inscription:

"Here rests
the mortal part of
Richard Whitney Esq,
Counsellor at law
of Brattleboro' Vermont,
Who departed this life
Sept. 9th A. D. 1806,
Aged 39 years."

"Those who knew him not may
Learn from this Monument stone
that his virtues have rendered
his memory precious to his
bereaved friends—the sight of it
will exite a tender recollection
of his worth, in the bosoms of
those who knew him, and a tear
of regret at his early and
Untimely departure.
Let us humbly hope he is gone
where those virtues will be
fully appreciated."

No likeness of Mrs. Marsh has been preserved, but she is represented as a large, rather plain, but kindly woman, of extremely hospitable feelings. She added a wing to her house, which she fitted up as a drawing-room, with arched ceiling, and furnished with costly furniture, where she was accustomed to entertain socially invited parties from Brattleboro and vicinity. In the management of her estate, as already mentioned, she was singularly capable, and her grounds gave evidence of an appreciation of the æsthetic; her fine garden and beautiful flowers, in diamond or heart shaped beds, being the particular admiration of the neighboring children, as the accounts of those now old, but who personally remember her, attest.

Two years before her death she leased her farm, reserving to herself all the privileges she desired, including the use of any four rooms she might choose in her house, and of her horse and chaise, which were to be kept at her disposal. Later, in 1833, she surrendered the farm upon a life lease to herself. She was most probably led to this retirement from her active business life by the premonitions of that malady, a renal affection, of which she died after a short final illness,—and not because of the infirmities of age.

Mrs. Marsh was not identified in membership with any church, but every act of her life bears witness to her Christian character. In her several donations and public bequests her unsectarian spirit found expression and bore testimony to her large-heartedness. The bell upon the first meeting-house in Hinsdale village was not given by her to the church, but to the town, as is shown by the fact that when finally broken the proceeds of its sale went into the town treasury. So, also, her bequest for the maintenance of public preaching in Vernon was not made to any church organization, but to the town, and for the purpose of gathering the people together for religious exercises, thus to controvert what she observed to be a laxity in the religious habits of the people there. And, in her larger gift, for the founding of a public institution, her philanthropy was likewise unrestricted. In the spirit of the Master she humbly sought "to provide a home for the poor insane."

E LEVEN months elapsed after the passage of the Act of Incorporation, before the Trustees received the legacy of Mrs. Marsh. Meanwhile, however, they were not idle. Nor were they alone interested in the untried project. A lively interest was manifested by the press of the State in the establishment of such an institution within the borders of Vermont.

A letter from E. C. Tracy of Windsor, then proprietor and editor of the Vermont Chronicle, to Mr. John C. Holbrook, bearing date February 28th, 1835, is preserved, showing a personal enthusiasm in the matter, and which indicates a previous correspondence upon the subject. He says: "I have just received a letter from Dr. Julius [a German psychologist then in this country] who informs me that he shall be in Boston at the end of May, and will be very happy to meet you there. He thinks it probable that he may be able to visit with you the institutions at Worcester and Hartford, should you be able to do it then. You will find him an open-hearted philanthropist, and one able to give you a great deal of information. I hope for the good of our State, you will not fail to make arrangements to have an interview with him. He is now at Washington, but about leaving for the South, to return by way of Albany, where he will be about the 15th of May. I will copy for you so much of his letter as relates to the Insane Hospital: 'According to what you mention, there is an objection to a grant of the Legislature arising out of the circumstance that the new institution will be under the Trustees of the legacy, and not under the control of the Legislature. This apparent obstacle, might, I think, be converted into an advantage. In Germany, where I am sure lunatic asylums, by the reflective and philosophic mind of the nation, are better than in any other country, we divide all such institutions into two classes, sometimes entirely separated and in different places, sometimes in adjoining localities, and united under the same administration. One of these classes consists of curable lunatics, under which denomination I would comprise all cases not older than two years' standing. After this time, if the physician of the institution should [judge] them affording still reasonable hopes of restoration, they might be removed to the other institution or class, containing incurable lunatics.

" ' The first class, certainly the most interesting to the feelings of the public, and that which is most wanted anywhere, and therefore also in Vermont, requires greater expense from the variety of means of restoration which must be provided.   But it is more useful to provide first of all an institution for this class, because the increase of lunacy is thereby stopped in its source, and because there is reasonable hope that public sympathy would be awakened, and liberal contributions flow in from all sides, to the fulfilment of this philanthropic enterprise.

" ' By this division of the two classes, the newly-erected corporation might limit its narrow means to the first, leaving the second to be provided for by the State.   Both institutions standing under a separate or joint administration, might be erected one near the other, connected by the gardens whereby they are surrounded, and thereby taking away the unfavorable impression which in some rare instances might be made on the friends of the patient, by his passing from the curables to the incurables.   For this last class of unfortunate beings a milder name has therefore been adopted in Germany, and we call the houses where they are kept Pflegeanstalten,—institutions for taking care, for nursing, or nurseries.   A similar expression might be easily found in Vermont.

" ' Relating to the situation of the Asylum, it must be high, healthy, not destitute of water, at some distance from any public road, and from the curiosity of passers-by, and with as much land as possible for gardens and fields; laborious exertion in cultivating them being one of the principal means of restoration.   Fifty acres would be the smallest extent of ground which I find desirable.

" ' According to my ideas relating to the treatment of the insane, a mad-house ought never to be one large building with different stories (an objection which applies to the Asylum at Worcester, and I believe also to that at Hartford) but it ought to comprise different small houses, each with a small garden, according to the different varieties of the diseased.

" ' As the means of the institution are so small, I propose therefore to erect first a house whose center building might be thirty feet long and have two wings each fifteen feet long.   The center building would be two stories high, serving as a dwelling-house for the physician, who must live in the institution, and as the seat of the administration, and of the offices; both wings one story high, the one for new-comers, to be under the physician's uninterrupted observation, and the other for convalescents.

" ' Besides this large building, which might accommodate from eight to twelve patients, I would erect two small one-story cottages, one for maniacs, and one for melancholics; the first for four and the other for eight patients. All these three buildings might easily be enlarged as the means increase, by building in the same direction in which they stand. All the one-story buildings ought to have a cellar for securing the patients against dampness, and for warming their rooms by hot air. The relative position of the three buildings, so that they all may be under the occular inspection of the physician, I must reserve to indicate when I shall perhaps have the pleasure of an interview with Mr. Holbrook, and the advantage of seeing a ground plan of the place where the Asylum is to be erected.' "

Mr. Tracy concludes as follows:

" If desirable I can communicate with Dr. Julius again before he reaches Boston. I must repeat my hope that if practicable you will arrange your business so as to be in Boston at the end of May, for I feel very anxious to have the proposed institution become a model."

The smallness of the bequest was from the first a matter of grave consideration by the Trustees. It was a current remark by citizens and business men, that a failure would be the most probable result of an undertaking so slenderly endowed. There is evidence that the three older members of the Board doubted the expediency of attempting to carry out the conditions of the will. To Mr. John C. Holbrook (the junior member) is undoubtedly due the credit of assuming at this juncture, in earnest, the work necessary to the inauguration of the enterprise, which his energy and sanguine temperament fitted him especially for.

The organization of the Board took place September 28, 1835, pursuant to notice signed by Samuel Clark, and published in the Vermont Phœnix of September 11. The first meeting was held at Col. Chase's stage-house in Brattleboro. The meeting was called to order by Samuel Clark, and, after reading the Act of Incorporation, the corporation was organized by choosing Samuel Clark, chairman; F. Seymour, treasurer; John C. Holbrook, secretary—to hold their offices until others were chosen. The meeting was then adjourned to meet at the Bank of Brattleboro on the third of October ensuing.

The Trustees met pursuant to adjournment. Asa Keyes, Esq., one of the executors of the will of Mrs. Anna Marsh, appeared, and stated " That he was ready to deliver over to the corporation ten thousand dollars, according to the directions in said will, provided the Trustees would take such notes as were on hand belonging to the estate, to draw interest from this date. That there was not so much money on hand collected, and unless this proposal was accepted the donation could not be paid until the money was collected, and then be paid proportionally with other legacies, with the risk of there not being enough realized from the estate to pay the whole."

"After consultation by the Trustees, and considering the above remarks, and taking into view that if the notes were not taken (which they deemed to be all good) the interest would be lost until the money was paid, which otherwise would accumulate on these notes, it was voted to receive them in full payment of the legacy, and a receipt was accordingly given to Mr. Keyes signed by all the Trustees, and the notes [thirteen in number, together with a cash check for balance due], were deposited in the Bank of Brattleboro."

At the same meeting it was also voted to pay Mr. Keyes the amount of his charges for time and expenses at Montpelier, in procuring the Act of Incorporation in accordance with the stipulations of the will, and that the location of the Vermont Asylum for the Insane be fixed in Brattleboro in Windham County. It was further voted to loan the money on hand, with good security, and that the officers chosen at their last meeting hold their offices for one year or until others were chosen; also, that the secretary be authorized to call future meetings, on application of any member of the Board of Trustees, by notifying each member personally, or by leaving a written notice at his dwelling.

The question now uppermost was upon what scale the institution should be started. Should it be in any way commensurate to the needs of Vermont, or should it make no aim to serve the State, but be merely a family home for a limited number, wholly independent of any relation to the State?

At the time of the incorporation of the Vermont Asylum, there were but ten such institutions in the United States,* and of these but three were in New England. The McLean Asylum at Somerville, Mass., was the oldest of these. The Connecticut Retreat at Hartford had been ten years in successful operation. The hospital at Worcester, which had been recently erected as a pioneer estab-

---

*Besides proprietary plants, institutions exclusively devoted to the care and treatment of the insane had been established as follows: At Williamsburg, Va., 1773. Frankford, Pa., 1817. Somerville, Mass., 1818. Bloomingdale, N Y., 1821. Hartford, Ct., 1824. Lexington, Ky., 1824. Columbia, S. C., 1827. Staunton, Va., 1828. Worcester, Mass., 1833. Baltimore, Md., 1834.

lishment under the auspices of the State of Massachusetts, naturally attracted popular attention, and awakened in the neighboring States a desire that similar ones should be opened to their own citizens.

Recognizing this, and sharing in the popular feeling, the Trustees determined to present the matter to the consideration of the representatives of the people in their report to the General Assembly then about to convene.   The following is this document in full:

To the General Assembly of the State of Vermont now in Session :

The Trustees of the Vermont Asylum for the Insane, agreeably to the requisitions of their Act of Incorporation, respectfully

REPORT

That they have lately received of the executors of Mrs. Anna Marsh, deceased, ten thousand dollars, the sum bequeathed by her for the foundation of an institution for the insane, and that they have proceeded to fix its location in Brattleboro, the terms of the will restricting them to some place in Windham County near Connecticut River.

The Trustees also take this opportunity to remind your Honorable Body of what must be obvious to every one, that the sum of ten thousand dollars is far from being adequate to the establishment of such an institution as shall be commensurate with the wants of this State, and in which the most approved and scientific treatment can be adopted.   Thirty thousand dollars at least are required; and as this is a subject of general interest and one which commends itself to every benevolent mind, the Trustees cannot but express their hope that your Honorable Body will take some measures at your present session for supplying such additional sum as may be requisite for the accomplishment of an object of great importance to a large and interesting class of our fellow citizens.

The establishment of Insane Hospitals has for several years past occupied a prominent place in the thoughts of Benevolent individuals, and in the deliberations of several of the State Legislatures. In Massachusetts it is well known that an Insane Hospital on an extensive plan has been erected entirely at the expense of the State, in addition to a large one already in existence [Somerville] under private control.   In Connecticut, also, an Insane Retreat has by its great success and happy influence been demonstrating the advantages of such institutions; while Maine, New Hampshire and New York have taken effective measures to extend the benefits of similar establishments to the insane within their respective limits.

Vermont alone, of all the New England States, has made no provision for the relief of this afflicted class of her citizens.

Should it be said that nothing is required of her in addition to what has been done in the adjoining States, and that their institutions will be adequate to the wants of their own and our citizens, it may be replied that Vermont ought not surely to be indebted to her neighbors for the advantages of all these institutions for the relief of the unfortunate. Besides it has been found by actual examinations in the three adjoining States, that the number of the insane is one in every thousand of the inhabitants ; giving to New York about one thousand, to Massachusetts six hundred, and New Hampshire between two and three hundred, and in the same ratio to this State, nearly three hundred. It is apparent then that the public wants require an institution for the insane in this State ; and the Trustees indulge the hope that on such a foundation as is laid by the generous donation entrusted to their hands, a superstructure may be raised which shall prove at once an honor to the State, and an inestimable blessing to her citizens. The vast advantages of such institutions, and their great importance to the community, are now established beyond dispute. Formerly, insanity was not only deemed an incurable disease, and consequently neglected, but an idea prevailed that its subjects were unconscious of bodily suffering. Hence recent examinations in adjoining States have disclosed an amount of misery endured by its unfortunate victims almost unparalleled and almost beyond belief. Cases of equal severity and aggravation in this State have also come to the knowledge of the Trustees—one, they cannot forbear to record. It is that of a man now, or until lately, confined in a cave by his ignorant not to say inhuman father, for the crime of insanity. The lateral dimensions of his apartment were such as scarcely to admit of a change of position, while its height utterly forbade its miserable inmate to stand erect. The floor was of stone, through which, by means of fire beneath, was communicated what little warmth was admitted to this cheerless abode. Here the victim was condemned to prolong a miserable existence, until at length his body assumed a frightful deformity, while from his mind was erased probably the last remaining trace of reason, which haply better or more kindly treatment might have restored to its original vigor. Indeed it seems on reading the well-authenticated statements of similar discoveries in other States, as though the human mind had been racked to discover modes of torture for this· afflicted class of people, more terrible than those of the Inquisition itself. To use the language of the commissioners of the Massachusetts Lunatic Hospital, "From the absence of suitable institutions the insane have been visited with a heavier doom than that inflicted on the voluntary contemners of the law," and from comparisons made by the commissioners they "cannot entertain a doubt that the aggregate of the terms of the confinement under the poor debtor law, has been much less than that of the imprisonment of the insane."

At the present day, and in communities otherwise highly enlightened, there is reason to fear that a lamentable degree of ignorance prevails upon the subject of insanity, an ignorance which, could it be once dispelled, some of the most painful records in the history of human suffering might be closed immediately. It is now abundantly demonstrated that with appropriate medical and moral treatment, insanity yields with more readiness than ordinary diseases. This cheering fact is established by a series of experiments. A few individuals justly entitled to a conspicuous station among the benefactors of their race, have exploded the barbarous doctrine that cruelty is the proper antidote to madness, and "self-devotion to the welfare of the insane is the only efficacious means of their restoration." In the principal institutions the proportion of cures varies from forty to ninety per cent; while it is believed that in seventy-five out of every hundred cases, as usually treated, the disease has become permanently fixed.

The Trustees of the Massachusetts Lunatic Hospital, in their second and last Annual Report, after stating the fact, "that almost from the first moment of its being opened, the building has been filled with inmates, and during the preceding year one hundred and nineteen patients had been received, and a large number refused admission for want of room (93 applications being made in five months, and 46 of them rejected), the cures being fifty-five and three-fourths per cent," go on to remark as follows: "The experiment of this institution has abundantly and happily shown that there are very few cases of derangement or obliquity of intellect, which may not be ameliorated by the kindly influences of humane treatment. In this respect the bounty of the Commonwealth has not been misapplied." The result, in the opinion of the Trustees, has entirely exceeded the most sanguine expectations, and this alone is a consummation which can neither be weighed nor measured by any pecuniary considerations whatever.

"The Trustees cannot therefore but believe that this object will commend itself to the favorable notice of your Honorable Body, and that the importance will be felt of procuring an institution for

the relief of the insane, convenient for the citizens of this State,—
that they may be able and induced to place all cases of insanity,
while yet recent, under proper treatment, in which event it is
believed nearly every patient may be restored to soundness and
usefulness.   To accomplish this highly important and most desirable
object, the Trustees respectfully pray your Honorable Body to
appropriate the sum of twenty thousand dollars, with such provisions
as shall seem necessary and proper.   All of which is respectfully
submitted.

SAMUEL CLARK,   ⎫ Trustees of the
JOHN HOLBROOK,   ⎬ Vermont   Asylum
EPAPHRO' SEYMOUR,   ⎭ for the Insane.
JOHN C. HOLBROOK,

October 7, 1835.

In furtherance of the proposition urged in the foregoing report,
for the State to aid in extending the capacity of the institution
already established within its borders, so as to enable it to meet
to a recognizable extent the probable demands of the insane of Vermont, Mr. Keyes was employed to present the matter, in behalf of
the Trustees, to the Legislators and the Council.

The result of this mission is found in the following letter from
Mr. Keyes to the Trustees, which has been preserved :

"I have just got the enclosed Act through the Council, and
although it is somewhat clogged with provisos, I am perfectly satisfied no other act could have been carried, and I believe this ten
thousand dollars will be a handsome addition to that already on
hand.   I do not consider the repealing proviso as any objection, for
such provisos are customary here, but a future legislature will not
avail itself of it.   *   *   *   *   *   *   Owing to the
confined limitation of the will, as to the sole superintendence of the
Hospital, it was a difficult thing to get any appropriation here."

The following is the Act passed November 9, 1835, and referred
to in the foregoing letter:

" AN ACT directing the Treasurer to pay to the Trustees of the
Vermont Asylum for the Insane, the sum therein named.

" It is hereby enacted by the General Assembly of the State of
Vermont, that the Treasurer of this State be, and he hereby is,
directed to pay to the order of the Trustees of the Vermont Asylum
for the Insane, the sum of two thousand dollars annually, for five
successive years, out of any money in the treasury not otherwise
appropriated, to enable the said Trustees the more effectually to
promote the benevolent designs of said Institution.   Provided, that

the said Trustees shall take no, benefit from the provisions of this Act, until they have so far erected the buildings and organized said Asylum, as to receive patients therein. Provided also, that any future legislature may alter, amend, or repeal this Act."

In the procurement of the Charter, as well as of the foregoing Act, Mr. Keyes was the accredited agent of the Board, but it does not appear by the records of the Trustees that he was charged on either occasion with any propositions other than were accomplished by the passage of the Acts mentioned.

Yet in his testimony before the Legislative Committee in 1878, before referred to, he says, "After the money [the Marsh Legacy] was paid to the Trustees, I went to Montpelier and got an Act of Incorporation. I remember very well some members objected to it, on the ground that the Legislature had nothing to do with it ; we were a separate corporation, and controlled ourselves entirely. I then told these individuals that they might appoint four trustees to act with our four trustees, and have an equal voice. I was advised by Norman Williams, the Secretary of State, and others, not to let the Legislature have anything to do with it. He said if it got into the hands of the Legislature they would ruin the institution ; there would be so many parties they would always quarrel about it."

It is probable that Mr. Keyes, who was ninety-one years old when the above testimony was given, was somewhat confused in respect to the time when this matter was discussed, for in notes taken upon some of the early points of the history of the Asylum, five years before, he stated clearly that "with Mrs. Marsh there never was an intention that her bequest should become in any manner connected with any other bequest, or public appropriation. It was not contemplated by her. The question of associating with it State aid was not debated nor considered at the time of the incorporation of the institution, by either the Assembly or the Council," before whom Mr. Keyes urged the Charter. It was doubtless at the time that the first Legislative appropriation was asked for, that these individual views were expressed, and that the appointment of co-trustees was suggested by Mr. Keyes.

Immediately after the passage of the foregoing Act, the plans of the Trustees began to crystallize into definite shape.

At a meeting held December 21st they *Voted*, "'To proceed to purchase land for the location of the Asylum, and to erect a building or buildings for the reception of patients."

At another meeting, held December 26th, "several propositions were received for purchasing land for the location of the Asylum."

THE beginning of this year was devoted to the important work of selecting a suitable site, and meetings, formal and informal, were held for the consideration of this very vital question.

Among the propositions submitted was one including ten acres of land at $200 per acre, embracing an area north of the line of house lots on the north side of High street and west of the line of house lots on the west side of Main street, as far north as the Unitarian church, thence running west parallel with High street, to what is now Highland Park, then owned by Wells Goodhue; and another of seventeen acres on the east side of the Putney road, then owned by Messrs. Minott, Keyes, Bradley and Pettis, for about $70 per acre, together with about nine acres on the opposite side of said road, then owned by Judge Whitney, if desired, at about the same rate.

A third proposition embraced what was called the Kingsley farm, which was then owned by Francis and Joseph Goodhue, afterward by Nelson Crosby and Newman Allen, and which was finally added to the Asylum estate in 1858.

This property embraced at the time it was offered as a site 285 acres, in which half the area of the meadow was included. Two houses, six barns, a cider mill, 150 feet of sheds, one chaise house and one corn barn were located thereon. This was offered for a total of $14,500, or something over $50 per acre on the average.

The foregoing are all the proposals that seem to have been definitely made and submitted to the Trustees in black and white ; but other sites were considered by them, particularly the plateau west of the village cemetery, and the tract now known as Mechanics' or Forest Square, west of Highland Park. The proposition for the ten acres north of High and west of Main streets was probably rejected on account of its limited area. That on the Putney road, now the fine estate of Mr. Richards Bradley, was decided against because of the difficulty of procuring water supply, although the Trustees were strongly inclined toward it.

The Kingsley farm exceeded the means at the disposal of the Trustees, and besides had no building plateau of sufficient size, at a desirable elevation.

On the 25th of May the Trustees met, all being present, and after duly considering all the propositions for sites, which they had carefully examined, *Voted*, " To purchase the situation in Brattleboro village, owned and occupied by Mr. Nathan Woodcock, about six acres, and the meadow-land adjoining, owned by Ebenezer Wells, consisting of about forty-five acres, on the best terms possible."

They then proceeded to make a bargain for the same, and finally agreed with Mr. Woodcock for his premises, at $3,500, and with Mr. Wells for the meadow-land at $62 per acre, or $2,700.

A few rods of land lying along the east side of the Newfane road, a narrow strip between this road and the forty-five acres of meadow purchased of Eben'r Wells, was bought of Houghton Pike, near the close of this year [December 10th] for a nominal consideration of $8.

The original purchase of Nathan Woodcock embraced about two acres only on the westerly side of the road ; but here was situated the mansion house, a two-story wood building, which was subsequently known and designated as the " White House," until finally giving place to the brick building now known as the " Marsh Building." On the opposite side of the road, on the same plateau,— now the site of the main buildings,—were four acres more, then used as a garden. The meadow land was contiguous to the garden on the north, and after the purchase of the narrow intervening strip of Houghton Pike, was bounded by the county road upon its westerly side.

A letter bearing date, Boston, May 27th, to Mr. John C. Holbrook, from Rev. Louis Dwight, at that time secretary of the Prison Discipline society, and an active philanthropist, attests his view of the fitness of the location thus secured, as follows: "I received your letter of the 25th inst. this morning, and reply without delay. I have no doubt you have decided wisely in regard to your location for the Asylum. I never supposed that the place which you describe could be purchased at any price. I understood, when I was in Brattleborough, that it was owned by a man of fortune who had retired from the busy scenes of life to enjoy that beautiful retreat, and as I saw it was fitted up in a style of taste and beauty which is not surpassed, in my judgment, by any country seat in the environs of Boston, New York, or Philadelphia, and had such a profusion of flowers, shrubs, and fruits, why ! of course — as I supposed, no man of fortune would sell such a place. I should always have preferred that house, and that location, to the farm-house location [the Kingsley farm already noted] but I consider it more of the perfection of beauty of nature and art to unite that house and grounds, with as much of the meadow as was wanted, than could be aspired to by any man. It appears now, from your last letter, that you have secured this house and grounds for the insane, and can have as much of the meadow and woodland as you want, together with spring of water, at fair prices, and that you have already purchased forty-five acres of meadow land. I can only say that so far as my observation extends there is not a more beautiful spot of earth than that which you have secured in Vermont for the insane.* The location of the publick institutions at Charlestown [McLean Asylum], Worcester, Hartford, Bloomingdale, bear no comparison with it in my mind's eye. I beg of you to perfect your work as to location, by securing as much of the meadow, woodland, and pasture as you will ever want, before you have to pay the exorbitant prices which this selfish world will charge such an institution, as soon as it is understood that the land must be had. They have actually been obliged to purchase several acres at Charlestown this spring, for the use of the asylum, at $1000 per acre. We shall be obliged to lay down the principles in our Report of the present year, which will make it manifest that your institution must have more of that land, and when this is done it would not be strange if the price of the land should rise one-half or one-third at once. If you cannot now purchase, can you not get the refusal, or a bond for a deed of so much as you require. I want you should have at least one hundred acres of meadow land, and fifty of woodland and pasture.

"One word as to the enlargement of your buildings : do not do it without being certain of doing it right. If you secure Dr. Rockwell, and let the correspondence between him and those who have experience be full and free before you decide, I think you will not err. Dr. Lee's plan I admire. I think I sent you a rough draught. It is much approved by Dr. Woodward, I understand. I have nothing

---

* Lest this description of the chosen site be suspected to be overdrawn or too high colored, I note the view of Dr. D. Hack Tuke, the celebrated English alienist, who visited the United States in 1884—a half century later, to wit :

" I may say in conclusion, that it is difficult to convey an adequate idea of the beauty of the grounds and surrounding hills of the Vermont Asylum. English medical superintendents should supply the defects of my description by a personal visit."— *The Insane in the United States and Canada. Page 106.*

further to communicate concerning Dr. Rockwell, than was contained in the copy of Dr. Lee's letter, which according to my minutes, I sent you, and which I supposed decided the case in favor of Dr. Rockwell. You, or any one whom I had heard mention, never intended to compare the young gentleman under Dr. Lee, in his present stage of education and experience, with Dr. Rockwell; and Dr. Lee never mentioned him as a person being *now* qualified to take charge of an institution, but only as one who had most valuable foundation to build on for future usefulness in this department of labor. So far as my knowledge extends, I think you would do very well to secure Dr. Rockwell, and to do it at once, for the reasons mentioned in your letter. * * * * * * * *

* * * I shall write to Mr. McVean, one of the commissioners for locating the New York asylum, that they ought not to locate without sending one of their number to Brattleborough, that he may see what advantages of nature and art can be secured in the location of an asylum, if proper care and pains are taken. I congratulate you, and the gentlemen associated with you, on your most excellent location. I hope it may be an example to many of good sense, and wisdom, and humanity in the location of such institutions."

The site having been secured, the next step of the Trustees was the election of a medical superintendent. As foreshadowed in the foregoing letter, Dr. Rockwell was the choice of the Board, as appears by the following record:

At a meeting of the Trustees held June 28th, *Voted*, "To appoint Dr. W. H. Rockwell of Hartford, superintendent of the Asylum for one year, to commence in September ensuing, or as soon as the premises can be prepared for the reception of patients. Salary, one thousand dollars—himself, wife and two children to be boarded by the institution, and to reside in the building free of rent; he to furnish the parlor and his own chamber,—it being understood that himself and wife also discharge the duties of steward and matron." Also, *Voted*, "To build an addition to the present building sufficient to accommodate twelve to sixteen patients, as soon as possible; Mr. J. C. Holbrook to make arrangements for the same being done."

Dr. Rockwell having agreed to the terms, it was concluded to commence operations with the Institution as soon as arrangements could be made.

It is a matter of record also, that Dr. Rockwell surrendered voluntarily four-hundred dollars of his salary the first year, a fact showing how strongly he felt himself personally identified with the success of the enterprise at its very beginning.

On the 7th of October the Trustees met and adopted the following

REPORT.

To the Honorable General Assembly of the State of Vermont, now in Session.

The undersigned, Trustees of the Vermont Asylum for the Insane, respectfully submit their Second Annual Report. During the past year the attention of the Trustees has been directed to the selection of a suitable site for the Institution, and the preparation of the necessary buildings. After mature consideration and consultation with several gentlemen in different parts of New England, best qualified to give advice on the subject, a situation was selected and purchased, which it is believed combines as many advantages as that of any other similar institution. The premises consist of a large dwelling-house, surrounded with grounds tastefully laid out, and ornamented with rare and valuable shrubbery and fruit trees, and about four acres of highly cultivated land additional [six acres in all], sufficiently retired, and yet in the immediate vicinity of the village of Brattleboro. Gardening and agricultural occupations being found among the most successful remedial means in the treatment of insanity, it was deemed highly important to attach a small farm to the Institution. Accordingly about forty-five acres of meadow adjoining the first-named premises were purchased, and in this respect the institution will have a decided advantage over any other similar one now in operation in this country. An addition has been made to the dwelling-house, consisting of a wing containing eight rooms, the whole affording accommodations for about twenty patients. The cost of the original purchase was $6,200, including the meadow land. That of the additions when completed, together with the furniture, will increase the expenditure to about $9,000, absorbing nearly all the funds now on hand. It is expected the arrangements will be so far completed as to admit of the reception of patients early in the ensuing month.

For the office of superintendent the Trustees believe they have been exceedingly fortunate in securing the services of Dr. William H. Rockwell, lately assistant superintendent of the Connecticut Retreat for the insane. That institution, it is well known, stood in the first rank under the care of the late Dr. Todd. Dr. Rockwell had the advantage of being for some time connected with it during the life of Dr. Todd, and for a year after his death the whole superintendence of it devolved on himself, and during a portion of the time the stewardship also.

While the Trustees, in the expenditures which they have made, have of necessity confined themselves within the narrow limits of the pecuniary means at their command, yet they have constantly borne in mind that probably the plan of the Institution would eventually be extended so far as to meet the wants of the large class of persons in the State for whose benefit it is designed. They have therefore endeavored so to order their arrangements that in an enlargement of their plan, with more liberal means, their present expenditures should not in any considerable degree be lost. The present arrangements, however, are considered in a great degree temporary. The Trustees, although aware that they had not the means to establish such an institution as it is evident the State requires, yet feel very desirous of extending the benefits of such a one as it was in their power to erect as far as possible and as soon as practicable to their fellow citizens, and thus carry into effect the benevolent designs of its founder.

They have therefore proceeded as far as their limited means would admit, and they now respectfully submit it to your Honorable Body to decide whether the advantages to be derived from such an institution shall be extended through your enlightened charity to all the citizens of the State who require them, or be confined to the comparatively few whom it will be practicable to accommodate on the present limited plan.

A select committee of the last Assembly reported that there were · upwards of three hundred insane persons in this State. It is at once evident that the present plan of the Institution is far, very far, from offering them relief, and yet it is extended to the utmost limit of the funds at command. To accommodate one-quarter part of this number in a proper manner, would require a building which should cost at least $15,000 or $20,000. The Trustees believe the enlightened benevolence of the people of this State would sanction any measures which you might adopt for the establishment of an institution which should be commensurate with the wants of the State. While they would acknowledge the charity of the Assembly in the appropriation which they made toward this object, yet they respectfully represent that it by no means meets the necessities of the case. Besides the inadequacy of the amount to accomplish the object designed, it furnishes no certain fund, either present or prospective, on which the Trustees would be authorized to act, inasmuch as the appropriation is liable to be discontinued at any moment. Nothing of consequence could be safely commenced under that act towards the erection of an extensive establishment until the expiration of

five years. The State would thus be deprived of the benefits of the
Institution for a considerable time. The Trustees would therefore
respectfully pray your Honorable Body, either to appropriate such a
sum as may seem to be sufficient to accomplish the object, or so to
alter the act of the last session appropriating money to this object
as to increase the annual sum to five thousand dollars, and by
repealing the provisos at the end. This done, the Trustees would
immediately proceed upon the strength of the act, to erect suitable
buildings for the accommodation of a large number of patients, borrowing the funds to be repaid annually in part from the appropriations of the act. The citizens of the State would then be
enabled to avail themselves of the benefit of the Institution with
little delay.

A leading object in all such charities at present should be to
bring the advantages of the Institution within the reach of all classes
of society. It is those of moderate means especially, forming the
largest proportion of insanity among us, who most require to be
benefited. The rich are enabled of themselves to give their unfortunate friends the advantages of the best means of relief. Such an
institution as the present should ever therefore have sufficient funds
to enable the managers to offer its advantages at the very lowest
possible expense, that the poorest may share the advantages with
their more wealthy fellow citizens. In the present case, even
were the building sufficiently extensive to accommodate all who
need its advantages, yet having no funds for the support of the
superintendent and his assistants, the terms of admission must
be proportionately higher than they otherwise would be.

The Trustees have not thought it advisable to appeal directly
to the citizens of the State for aid in establishing the Institution, for
the reason that being calculated for the benefit of all classes it is an
object peculiarly worthy of legislative aid. The conviction of this is
strengthened by the fact that many of the neighboring States have
viewed similar institutions in this light, and by liberal appropriations
have manifested that their establishment was deemed an object
of high importance. The Legislature of New York at its last session appropriated. the sum of sixty thousand dollars for a similar
object. In Massachusetts no sum has been refused which was shown
to be needed for the hospital in that State. Maine, Connecticut and
Ohio have also each made liberal appropriations for similar institutions.

The Trustees therefore submit the subject for consideration,
in the hope that some measures will be taken to enable them to

go forward in the establishment of such an institution, as, while it shall do honor to our benevolence, shall extend its blessings to a most interesting and numerous class of our fellow citizens, a class in which no man, however talented, rich, or prosperous, has any security that he shall not ere long be numbered.

All of which is respectfully submitted.

SAM'L CLARK,
JOHN HOLBROOK,
E. SEYMOUR,
JOHN C. HOLBROOK.
} Trustees.

October, 1836.

The response to the foregoing report was the following:

"AN ACT making an appropriation for the Vermont Asylum for the Insane, to wit:

"It is hereby enacted by the General Assembly of the State of Vermont, that the Treasurer of this State be directed to pay to the Trustees of the Vermont Asylum for the Insane, the sum of two thousand dollars, out of any moneys in the Treasury, not otherwise appropriated."

" Approved Nov. 15, 1836."

As usually happens in the beginning of all enterprises, the opening was delayed by the tardy working of the mechanics. The end of Autumn had come before the building was ready for occupancy, but on the 30th of November the Trustees ventured upon the adoption of the following Circular and Terms of Admission for Patients, to be published in the newspapers, to wit:

THE VERMONT ASYLUM FOR THE INSANE

OPEN.

The Trustees of the Vermont Asylum for the Insane would announce that this Institution is now ready for the reception of patients. The building is finished in a manner adapted to the classification and convenience of its inmates. The two wings are so constructed as to afford pleasant and commodious rooms, and that the sexes may be entirely separated. Rooms are prepared for the sick, removed from all annoyance, where the immediate relatives and friends of the patients can, if they desire, bestow their kind attentions and sympathy. Experienced nurses and attendants are procured, and none will be retained except those who are kind and faithful to their trust. No harsh treatment will ever be for a moment allowed. Several rooms are prepared in the center building for those who require additional accommodations of attendants and luxuries, which will be furnished according to the desire of friends, and the compensation to the Institution. For this class of patients superior accommodations are offered. They will be received into the immediate family of the physician, and not only be under his constant care and watchfulness, but partake of all the enjoyments of social life. Arrangements are also made for the reception and accommodation of persons, who, though not insane, are afflicted with nervous diseases, requiring medical treatment. Pleasant and well furnished rooms, and good board in the family of the physician will be afforded ; and from his experience and study he will be enabled to adopt a course of treatment more likely to be successful than that of ordinary physicians who have not made such diseases their peculiar study. Due provision has been made for the exercise, amusement and employment of the patients. Connected with the Asylum is a farm of nearly fifty acres, in which the patients will be employed in gardening and farming, in such a degree as shall be conducive to their health. Such employments are now admitted to be among the most important and successful means of restoration, and in this respect this Institution has a decided advantage over any other in this country. Battle-door, chess, draughts and the like amusements will be afforded. The females will be employed in knitting, needlework, painting, etc. Carriages will be provided for the daily riding of the patients in suitable weather, and they will also take their daily walks with nurses and attendants. A small and select library, the newspapers of the day, and several periodicals, will be furnished for the purpose.

The situation of the Asylum is healthful and delightful. It has the appearance of a cheerful country residence, and every resemblance to a place of confinement has been carefully avoided. Immediately in front of the Institution is presented a landscape of a rich and cultivated meadow, extending in the distance into picturesque and romantic scenery, so well adapted to arrest and remove the morbid fancies which enslave the minds of the insane. The view is also enlivened by the passing and repassing of carriages and travellers on two large thoroughfares in front of the Institution. Though retired, it is yet in the immediate vicinity of the village, and the grounds about the establishment are tastefully laid out in beautiful walks, and ornamented with many rare and valuable trees, shrubs and plants, all of which conspire to make the abode of its inmates at once pleasant and cheerful.

The whole will be under the charge of Wm. H. Rockwell, M. D., who for the last several years has been connected with the well known Retreat for the Insane at Hartford, Connecticut.   From his experience under Dr. Todd, and his success and devotedness to this branch of his profession, the Trustees are confident in the belief, that all that kind, assiduous and skilful treatment can contribute towards the restoration of reason, will, with the blessing of God, be accomplished at this Asylum.

TERMS OF ADMISSION.

For convenient accommodations in the wings, *Three Dollars* per week.

Those who require a room in the center building and those laboring under nervous diseases, will be received at reasonable prices, according to accommodations required.

[In consideration of the assistance rendered to the Institution by the State, and from a desire to extend its advantages to all classes* of the community, the Trustees have determined to receive indigent patients at an extremely low rate, *less than they can be maintained properly elsewhere.*]

Indigent patients *in this State* whose disease is not of more than *three months'* standing, *Two Dollars* per week, provided that a certificate is lodged with one of the Trustees signed by a majority of the selectmen where the patient resides, stating that they are of the opinion that said patient or his or her parents, or husband (as the case may be) does not possess property to the amount of one hundred dollars.   No patient, however, shall remain in the Institution upon the said terms over six months, as that term will generally suffice to determine whether the case is probably curable or not.

No patient will be received for a less term than three months, and payment for that term will be required in advance.   If the patient shall recover before the expiration of that term, the pay for the unexpired time will be refunded.   If the patient remain longer than three months, the subsequent payments will not be required in advance, but only for the time the patient remains.

N. B.   *It should be borne in mind that in the first three months of insanity, the chances of recovery by proper treatment are vastly greater than at any subsequent period.*   Insane persons should therefore on the *first appearance* of the disease, be placed under curative treatment.

Application for the admission of patients may be made by letter or otherwise to Dr. Wm. H. Rockwell, or either of the Trustees.

On the 12th day of December following, the first patient was received, and on the 16th of the same month the second was admitted.

Thus was the institution launched upon its mission.   It will be seen by the foregoing opening announcement that it was the evident intent of the Trustees from the beginning, that the citizens of the State in which the Asylum had been located should especially enjoy its privileges; and the terms were thus made correspondingly favorable.   The cost of reconstructing and enlarging the building for the reception of patients was $3,560.65.

RECORD OF 1837.

THE opening year of the Institution was an auspicious one. The Superintendent entered upon the work with zeal and discretion and his sanguine spirit was infused into both managers and helpers. Every feature belonging to the family system was endorsed without modification in the daily life of the household. It was essentially the same as was nearly a half-century afterwards instituted in an appendage to the Asylum, by the establishment of a Summer Retreat, which will be noticed in due chronological sequence. The story of the first nine months is embodied in the Report of the Trustees and Superintendent for this year, and is here entered *verbatim et literatim*, barring some tabular statistics which have little value, inasmuch as they stand alone, not being carried into subsequent reports.

The following is this document:

TO THE GENERAL ASSEMBLY OF THE STATE OF VERMONT:

The undersigned, Trustees of the Vermont Asylum for the Insane, in compliance with the statute which makes it their duty to present annually to the General Assembly a particular statement of the condition of the Asylum, respectfully submit the following as their first annual

REPORT.

That the Asylum was opened for the reception of patients on the 12th of December, 1836. Great care had been taken by the Trustees so to construct and arrange the building that it should be adapted to the convenience, classification, and safety of its patients, and at the same time to remove, as much as possible, every appearance of a prison, or a place of confinement. So well have they succeeded in this respect that it has the appearance of a spacious country residence.

From the commencement an excellent farm of about fifty acres was procured, as a necessary appendage to the Institution. We have determined to have a fair trial made of employing the patients on the same, and have the effects strictly noticed.   Here we add our own, to the universal testimony of others on the subject, that useful labor for convalescents and all chronic cases is the best moral means that can be made use of in the treatment of insanity.   It is difficult to divert patients from cherishing their hallucinations, unless some interesting employment is furnished for them.   The patients thus employed are generally cheerful and happy during the day, and sleep quietly at night.   The exercise gives them an appetite for food, and the whole physical system, as well as the mind, seems to be invigorated.   It recalls to mind their former employments and pursuits, rouses into action those faculties of the mind which had before lain dormant, and gives rest to those who have been unduly excited.   As the number of our male patients has been small, not only the quiet, but also those who were more excited, have been taken on the farm, and in every case regular employment has been found to be highly beneficial.   No patient has been restricted in the use of tools, either at the wood-yard, in the garden, or on the farm, and yet not the slightest accident whatever has happened.   The patients consider themselves as enjoying the confidence of the officers, and make every effort that it should not be misplaced.   '

Notwithstanding the embarrassments that must necessarily attend the commencement of every operation, enough has already been accomplished to prove that employing the patients on the farm is not only highly conducive to their recovery, but will lessen their expenses at the Asylum by increasing its income.   Besides, the inhabitants of this State are chiefly agricultural people, and most of the male patients may be profitably employed on the farm, while a much less number could be employed in a shop to any advantage.   Our farm possesses a rich soil, and is easy of cultivation.   Many improvements are needed upon it, which will afford much pleasant and useful labor for the patients.

That an institution of this kind was needed may be learned from the fact that within seven months from the commencement of its operations it was filled with inmates, and that thirteen have already been rejected for want of room to accommodate them.   Since the opening of the Asylum, forty-eight have been admitted, and fourteen discharged, leaving thirty-four, which now remain.

☞ When the Asylum was first opened, in order to assist in defraying its expenses, a class of nervous patients who were not insane were received.   But so soon was the Institution filled with those who were insane, that only three were admitted, and none of these remained after the last of May.   These, of course, were not included in the number of those who were admitted and discharged as before mentioned.*

In regard to the number of cures, justice to the Superintendent requires us to say, that but a small proportion of them have had an adequate time of trial. It is but nine months and a half since the Asylum was first opened, and during the first six months all, with the exception of four, were old cases. According to the annals of all similar institutions, those cases where the disease was of so long continuance required a proportional length of time for their restoration; and we are unable to find among them a single instance in which many of these chronic cases have been restored. Notwithstanding the forlorn appearance of many of these cases, we are gratified to learn that several have been already restored, and others are regularly convalescing. It is no less a subject of congratulation that those whose disease had become incurable have been greatly benefited at the Asylum. Several who had been caged and shut out, not only from the society of their fellow-men, but also from the light of Heaven, and deprived of the pure air we breathe, have become quiet and peaceable inmates, mingle in society with the rest, and partake of the exercises and amusements and pastimes of the Institution.

From the history of all similar institutions, we learn that the proportion of old cases that were admitted at the commencement of their operations, has always been great. From the opening of this Institution to the 1st of July twenty-five out of twenty-nine cases were of this description. The friends of these patients, actuated by a generous humanity, were ready to make use of means, however ineffectual they might prove, of which they had heretofore been destitute. The gratification of those who may be permitted to see their friends restored is inexpressible, and even those who fail of this are comforted by witnessing their improved condition, and by the grateful reflection of having done their duty. Several who were obliged to be confined, and were wild and ferocious in their conduct before admission, have now not only become quiet, but partake also of many of the comforts and pleasures of life.

The grand system of moral treatment as pursued in this Institution is kind treatment, useful employment, and wholesome discipline. When a patient enters the Asylum [however violent and distrustful he may formerly have been] he soon perceives that the principles of kindness pervade every regulation of the Institution. By experiencing

*It may here be stated, that none of that class of nervous cases bordering upon insanity but not strictly insane, admitted in subsequent years, have ever been included in the published admissions and discharges.

constant proof of the parental kindness and regard of the Superintendent, he soon cherishes for him the sentiments of friendship and esteem, and cheerfully confides in the plan adopted for his restoration. By continual employment, his former associations and habits are awakened and cherished, and his mind and body become invigorated. From the well-regulated discipline which everywhere prevails in the Institution, and which is adapted to the welfare of his little community, he finds that his own rights are regarded and protected. In this manner the violence of the disease is diminished, and his mind gradually becomes divested of its hallucinations, and is finally restored to its natural healthy state. It is generally understood that there are few chances for the recovery of the insane so long as the patient remains amidst those objects and scenes which originated and continually operate to aggravate his disorder, while of those who are placed at a well-regulated Asylum on the first approach of this disease, as great a proportion are restored as of any acute physical disorder in which the symptoms are equally violent. At no other place can an insane person be made equally comfortable. Here he will quietly acquiesce in the discipline of the Asylum, notwithstanding his impetuosity and violence at home. He is now removed from every cause which excited and exasperated his disorder, and enjoys that liberty in which he could not be indulged in any other place. Here, also, he is furnished with wholesome and nutritious food, his person is kept clean and neat, and he is protected from every exposure. And last but not least, his friends are relieved from an insupportable weight of care and anxiety, knowing that he here enjoys every comfort and convenience of which his case will admit.

The Trustees regret that they are unable at the present time to furnish a precise statement of the financial condition of the Institution. E. Seymour, Esq., the treasurer, is unexpectedly and unavoidably absent from the State, and will not return in season to present his report. However, the expenditures for the farm, and for erecting and furnishing the buildings, about balance the receipts. Whether the expenditures are greater or less than the receipts, we are unable precisely to say, but are fully of the opinion that there can be but little difference. The current expenses of the Institution are kept by the Superintendent, and are as follows:

The whole amount of expenditures up to Sept. 1st,
inclusive, is $3,484,71

[This sum includes the cost of a large quantity of fuel, provisions, etc., for the present season.]

The amount actually received for board of patients,
    etc., to the same time is $1,866.73
Amount of same not received is 863.56

    Total, · $2,730.29

It should not be forgotten that in addition to many expenses which are peculiar to the commencement of every similar institution, the price of almost every article of consumption and supplies has been unusually high during the past year, and of course has greatly increased the amount of expenditures.

In consideration of the funds granted by the State, the Trustees have received all the indigent insane of this State that have been offered, whose insanity was not of more than three months' standing, at the low rate of two dollars per week. Several other indigent patients of this State, whose disease was of much longer duration, have been received below the ordinary price of three dollars. The Trustees did not think it just to receive all the indigent old cases at two dollars per week until another building was erected; for in that case the Institution would soon be filled with incurables, to the exclusion of those who may be restored to reason and usefulness. Before this Institution was established, persons possessing somewhat less than an average of property could not, according to the commonly received notions of ability to bear expense, afford to send the insane members of their families to those institutions at which the wealthy could receive the benefit. And we wish to be distinctly understood, that whatever funds the Legislature may grant for the use of this Institution, will be directly applied for the benefit of the less wealthy portion of the community. We trust the Legislature will not fail to make all necessary provision for that portion of our population, who, without any fault or offence of their own, suffer the greatest calamity to which human nature is liable, and are deprived of the means of procuring relief.

While it is a subject of congratulation to the Trustees, that the present building was so soon filled with inmates, it is also a subject of deep regret that they are unable to receive all who apply for admission. No less than thirteen applications have already been rejected. The Trustees would therefore most respectfully solicit of the Legislature that pecuniary aid which would enable them to erect another suitable building, which shall be sufficient for the wants of the State. In that case, this Asylum would possess advantages superior in some respects to any similar institution in our country. The present building would then be occupied by the convalescents, and also the quiet and neat class of patients, who would otherwise be likely to suffer from the noise and confusion of the wilder patients; while the new building would furnish accommodations for all other cases. By erecting the proposed building, a greater number of patients would be received, and there would consequently be a greater annual income, without a corresponding increase of the expenditures, as the same officers would attend to all. This arrangement would not only allow of a more complete classification, but would present a strong inducement to every patient to exercise that self-control which would allow of his being placed among the most orderly class, and could not fail to produce an effect highly conducive to his recovery.

It is most respectfully suggested to the consideration of the Legislature, whether it is not consonant with the views of a sound policy, and of strict and just economy, to make provision for the recovery of our insane population. If the present insane of this State had received the benefits of a well-regulated asylum, within six months from their attack, at least three-fourths of them would probably have been restored to reason and usefulness, but are now a burden to their friends and community. Of all the plans devised by a generous and enlightened philanthropy for lessening the misery of the unfortunate, no one, we are bold to say, in proportion to the extent of its means and the range of its operations, has added more to the stock of public happiness or subtracted more from the mighty mass of human misery, than institutions of this character. Is it not our duty as Christians, and as men, to endeavor to relieve the distressed; and what portion of the community has equal claims upon our sympathy and regard? Can there be an object which better deserves the aid of a humane and enlightened government, than that which endeavors to restore a deranged intellect to its former soundness and vigor, and thus release the victims of madness and despair from the greatest of human afflictions? Surely, "The blessings of many that are ready to perish" will fall upon all those who aid this benevolent enterprise.

The remarks of the Superintendent are appended to this report, and will be eagerly read by those who take an interest in this afflicted portion of the community; and the Trustees cannot conclude their report without expressing their entire confidence in his ability and skill, and their firm belief that the unexpected success is chiefly attributable to his untiring zeal, and judicious treatment of those committed to his care.   SAMUEL CLARK,
JOHN HOLBROOK,
EPAPHRO'SEYMOUR,
Brattleboro, October 16th, 1837.   JOHN C. HOLBROOK.

SUPERINTENDENT'S REPORT.

SUMMARY.

Whole number of patients admitted from the opening
of the Asylum to September 30th, 1837 :

Males,	.	.	.	.	20
Females,	.	.	.	.	28 —— 48
Whole number discharged,	.	.	.	13	
Died,	.	.	.	1 —— 14	
Whole number remaining,					
Males,	.	.	.	13	
Females,	.	.	.	.	21 —— 34
Recent cases of less than six months' duration,				14	
Old cases of more than six months' duration,			34 —— 48		

A reference to the table will show that a large proportion of old
and incurable cases have been admitted into the Asylum. This
is the usual consequence with all similar institutions in the commencement, unless situated in the immediate vicinity of others which
have been longer established. There having been heretofore no institution of sufficient proximity, these old cases have accumulated
in private families, and as soon as the Asylum was opened for their
relief, their friends wished to discharge their whole duty by making
this last attempt for their restoration. The friends of some, however, being conscious of the hopelessness of their state, have placed
them here from motives of benevolence and humanity, being
well aware that their condition would be made far more comfortable
than in their private families, besides relieving themselves of
much anxiety and solicitude for their protection and care.

The importance of placing the insane, on the first approach
of their disease, at a proper asylum, cannot be too forcibly urged
upon public attention. No time should be lost in placing them upon
a course calculated to restore them to the duties and enjoyments of
life. The probability of their restoration is in an inverse ratio to
the duration of the disease. Besides, the length of time necessary to
restore the old cases is proportionally longer than for those which
are recent, and consequently the expenses will be much greater, so
that a regard to strict economy, as well as a prospect of cure,
requires that the patient should be placed early in the disease
at a proper asylum. It is impossible to fix upon any precise time
when all cases cease to be recent and assume the chronic form,
as some cases run their course in a shorter time and pass into
the chronic state, than others. I have in this report considered all
those cases as recent, where the disease has not been of more

than six months' duration; and all those chronic which have exceeded that time.

I wish not to be understood as endeavoring to discourage the friends of those patients, whose disease has been of long standing, from making an attempt at their restoration. It should be remembered that "While there is life, there is hope," and we should not despair or relax in our efforts to remove this afflictive malady, although they are not immediately crowned with success. An old case is not necessarily incurable, nor should the case be given over as desperate, until every proper remedy has been judiciously applied. There are instances where cures have been performed under the most discouraging circumstances; and when a cure has not been effected, the patient has been restored to a very comfortable state. My former experience has been abundantly confirmed, that there are very few cases, however wretched and violent, that may not be greatly ameliorated by judicious treatment. All that I wish to urge is the prompt removal of the patients from the scenes and persons associated with their hallucinations, and the great comparative advantage of placing them in an asylum in an early stage of the disease.

This Institution has not been in operation a sufficient length of time to ascertain what will be its success in recoveries. It is little more than nine months since it was first opened. The average time of the residence of the patients in the Asylum has been short. We have, notwithstanding, the cheering fact that eleven have been restored.

It is generally known that chronic diseases of the body require the judicious application of means for a considerable length of time, even when the course is successful; how much more so is it necessary in chronic cases of insanity, which depend on physical disease? —for in these cases the disease is to be removed, and former associations and habits are to be awakened and restored. One of the greatest trials of the physician of 'a lunatic asylum is the premature removal of patients. I will mention one instance which recently occurred at this Institution. A young man was brought here when disease had been making insidious but gradual progress for more than a year, and at the end of three months was removed by his friends. Although he appeared to be regularly convalescing, I was grieved to see him thus prematurely taken away, to continue insane perhaps for life, when the residence of a few months, and perhaps only a few weeks longer, would have been sufficient for his recovery. I make not these remarks because I think we have more trials of this kind than occur at other institutions, but to show that old cases generally require longer time for restoration. There are frequently cases which do not appear to improve in three months, which at the end of six or twelve months entirely recover.

No one at the present time, I believe, who is acquainted with the ministrations of a lunatic asylum, questions the importance of useful labor in restoring to reason the minds of the insane. Having been connected with an institution of this kind for nearly ten years, I have invariably found that for a large majority of male patients exercise in the open air was far preferable to that which was taken within doors. The accustomed employment of most men is in the open air, and when they are confined within doors, their health and reason are soon affected. Females are also benefited by exercise in the open air, as in riding, walking, etc.; but as their former employment has been so much within doors it is much less indispensable for them than for men. Useful labor whether within or without doors is most desirable as a means of restoration for curable patients, and is perhaps no less so to promote the happiness of those for whom all we can do is to make them as comfortable as their condition will admit. With the exception of those cases where the mind is unduly excited, few things can be much worse for the insane than inactivity of body and mind. Even the sane mind, when suffered to remain in continued inaction, loses much of its vigor and energy, soon begins to languish, and often ends in a state of torpitude. So the insane, when their minds are suffered to remain in inaction sink into a state of brutish indifference. Sometimes when the mind ceases to employ itself on things without, it soon begins to prey upon itself. The pleasures and comforts which it had proposed to take from this incorrectly termed state of rest, are never realized. The idler is frequently at a loss how to occupy his vacant hours because weary of himself and all things about him, and finally complains of his wretched existence. And too frequently has his internal misery so oppressed him, that in a dark moment of despair he has deprived himself of that life which he considered as intolerable. In the same manner, when the insane are confined and shut up from any employment they become fretful and irritable, tear their clothes, become violent and filthy, and hasten to an incurable state. But give the inmates of a lunatic asylum some useful employment, they will then be quiet and cheerful through the day, and sleep well at night. Their former habits and associations will be awakened, the mind and body will be invigorated, and reason will often be restored.

It has been a great object with those who have had charge of this Institution, that as many of the patients as were in a proper condition should be regularly engaged in some useful employment in the open air. We have employed our males by working in the garden and on the farm, and also by walking, riding, reading, and various amusements. The principal exercise of the females in the open air has been by riding, walking, gathering flowers, and the like. They have also been occupied in various kinds of needle work, knitting, reading, and amusements within doors.

From the opening of the Asylum we have introduced religious worship among our patients. Our family worship, in which all quiet patients are allowed to partake, consists in reading daily, after tea, a portion of the Scriptures, singing a hymn, and a prayer. On the Sabbath, in addition to the above, a short sermon is read. The effect of these exercises on the patients has been highly salutary, and has shown that they are no less a means of cure than gratification to them. At these seasons they are very quiet and attentive, and several have begun to exercise that self-control which has resulted in their restoration. The monotonous routine of daily life is hereby interrupted, and they are led to the recollection of former and happier days on which their minds delight to dwell, and they confidently look forward to the time when they shall again be restored to their friends and society. Here, also, the despondent forgets for a time his cares and sorrows, and experiences the consoling and soothing effects of religious worship. He is comforted and sustained by the reflection that there is a Friend, who, while on earth, was "touched with a sense of human infirmity," and is able ever to relieve the afflicted and heavy laden. They perceive that they are united with, and are remembered by their fellow-men, and thereby place a greater confidence in those to whose care they are committed. Were it not for our religious exercises on the Sabbath, Sunday would be the most tedious day of the week. As all labor, exercise, and amusements are suspended on that day, if the patients are deprived of the privilege of uniting in religious worship, they consider themselves as shut out from the society of their fellow-men, and are induced to cherish an irritable and misanthropic disposition, which only aggravates the disease. Those that are in a suitable condition attend church on the Sabbath.

It is a source of much gratification to the physician, that we are favored with such an abundance of pure water, salubrious air, and cheerful scenery at the Asylum. The patients have been remarkably healthy during the past year, and only one death has occurred. This was one of the old cases, where the physical system had been much impaired, and being violently attacked with an acute disorder, the powers of life were too nearly exhausted to withstand the disease. Considering that insanity is owing to a disorder of the physical system, and also considering the impaired health of many of our patients when they are admitted, we cannot but rejoice in the healthiness of our situation, and the salutary system of our regulations.

The discipline of this Asylum is truly parental. As soon as the patients are in a proper condition, they eat at our table, are received into our parlor, join with us in our family worship, go with us to church,—in a word are members of our family. The convalescent and orderly class of patients take their meals regularly with the family in the central part of the building; which operates as a powerful motive to exercise that self-control, without which they cannot obtain what they consider a great privilege. The food, however, is precisely alike throughout the Institution, except in those cases where the diet is prescribed by the physician.

Notwithstanding several attendants have been employed who were at first wholly unacquainted with their duties, no serious accident whatever has happened to any person (patient or otherwise) at the Asylum. The patients have quietly acquiesced in the discipline of the Institution, and generally become so orderly and inoffensive after a few days' residence, as to require but little constraint. The impartial and well regulated discipline of a lunatic asylum does not irritate them, nor diminish their confidence in those under whose care they are placed; on the contrary, they regard it with a loyal feeling, and consider it necessary to their comfort, and welfare. We have never provided, much less used, chains or strait-jackets in this Institution.

The building as now prepared is well adapted for the number it accommodates. But until another building is erected, so urgent are the applications for admission, that hereafter it will probably be crowded. We humbly trust that an Institution so humane and philanthropic in its character, so beneficent in its operations, and reflecting so much credit upon the munificence of the Legislature, will receive that pecuniary aid which will enable it to extend its usefulness to the wants of the State. When another building shall be completed, the present one will be a very desirable retreat for patients so soon as they emerge from the thick cloud which envelopes their minds. Having thus propitiously begun, we trust that public expectation is satisfied. May we not hope that the time is not far distant, when this Asylum will take no humble rank among the distinguished charities of our country

WILLIAM H. ROCKWELL, Superintendent.

Brattleboro, Sept. 30, 1837.

Upon the adoption of the foregoing report in October of this year, Samuel Clark was authorized and requested to proceed to Montpelier, and make application to the Legislature (then in session) for further pecuniary aid in the erection of an additional building, the need of which had been fully set forth in this report.

The following was the result:

"AN ACT Concerning the Vermont Asylum for the Insane.

"It is hereby enacted by the General Assembly of the State of Vermont, that the Treasurer of this State is directed to pay the Trustees of the Vermont Asylum for the Insane, the sum of Four Thousand Dollars, out of any moneys in the Treasury not otherwise appropriated, for the purpose of erecting another building for the Asylum, payable on the first day of April next. Provided, in future admissions to the benefits of said Asylum, a preference shall be given to resident citizens of this State.

"Approved Nov. 1, 1837."

Upon the passage of the foregoing Act, the Trustees held a meeting at the Asylum to consult about the erection of a new building, and without coming to any conclusion adjourned to meet at the Bank, December 15th following.

At this meeting they received various proposals for furnishing materials, and *Voted,* "That John Holbrook be requested to make estimates of the cost of a building," after which they adjourned to meet again on the 23d of the month.

At this date the Trustees directed the Treasurer to credit and settle the accounts of the Superintendent for the past year, and *Voted,* with the concurrence of Dr. Rockwell, "That the same arrangement with him for the superintendence of the Asylum, which was made the past year, be continued another year.

"After fully examining the state of the funds of the Institution, and the plans and estimates of a new building submitted to the Trustees, *Voted,* That immediate measures be taken to erect a new building the coming season according to a general plan submitted by Dr. Rockwell, with such alterations and amendments as may seem to be proper hereafter.

"The general plan as follows: A center building fifty feet wide, forty feet from front to rear, three stories high from basement, with two wings thirty-six feet wide, by about sixty-two feet long, containing twenty-eight rooms in each story, eight by ten feet, and a hall twelve feet wide. The wings two stories above the basement. The materials to be brick, except the basement, which is to be stone."

This plan was essentially after the old Worcester Hospital, at that time one of the most recently built institutions in this country, and regarded as one of the best.

Correspondence has been preserved showing that Dr. Woodward was conferred with at this time, particularly in respect to securing a master-builder. A letter from him to Mr. John C. Holbrook, under date of 25th of December, reads thus: "I received your letter of the 23d inst. and hasten to reply. Elias Carter, Esq., is the man of all others that I would recommend to you as suitable to superintend the erection of your buildings, and the fitting up of your hospital. He removed from Worcester the present season and now resides in Springfield, I believe in Chicopee village, but am not quite certain. He is responsible and competent, and I may add experienced. Capt. Merchant Toby of this town is another man who assisted Mr. Carter in building this hospital, and is an excellent mechanic and truly worthy man. I will see Capt. Toby myself, and send him your letter. I shall be happy to lend you any aid in my power at any time. May I be permitted to say, that I believe you will always be sorry that you build two stories instead of three. Walls cost little compared with roof and foundation. Our third story is much the pleasantest in the house, quite the warmest, and quite the most retired. You can build the walls and furnish at a future time, if not needed now; but I forbear."

The principal interest attached to this letter is the gratuitous advice touching the plan, which is directly opposed to that given by Dr. Julius, the German specialist (see page 10.)

As a result of the preceding inquiry Capt. ·Merchant Toby of Worcester next appears upon the scene, bearing the following letter of recommendation from Dr. Woodward to Trustee John C. Holbrook, under date of December 26th:

"I take pleasure in introducing to you Capt. Merchant Toby, the master-builder of the Hospital which I superintend, under the supervision of Mr. Carter, whose partner he has since been. Capt. Toby is one of our most estimable citizens, a man of respectability of character, a Christian, and in every respect worthy of your confidence.

"As a mechanic, he stands in the first rank, and is undoubtedly competent to go forward and erect your Hospital without any assistance from others. I have never seen a man who managed a gang of workmen so ably as Capt. Toby. For some months after I came into this Hospital he was at work with ten or fifteen journeymen, who were proverbially civil and attentive to business. I can say in conclusion that if I had a building to erect of any magnitude, I would employ him sooner than any other man."

On the 28th of December it is recorded, "The Trustees met to confer with Capt. Merchant Toby of Worcester, Mass., with reference to contracting with him to erect the new building for the Asylum. Gave him the outlines of the plan determined on, and agreed with him to prepare full and accurate drawings, plans and elevation suitable to predicate estimates upon, and to build by, and to make proposals for doing the building at a specified time by contract, or for superintending the work,—all to be presented a week or two hence. He not to be paid for his plans if we contract with him, but if we do not, he is to be paid."

This closed the work of this year.

Among the cases admitted in the opening year were some of much interest, among whom is that of a clergyman, which I transcribe from the Case Book:

" Mr. H. is a native of Connecticut, and a resident of B——, Vt. He had been a preacher of the Congregational denomination for about fifteen years, and about three years since he became a Baptist. He has a wife and six children in indigent circumstances. When he changed sentiments he lost the support of one denomination, and as he was for open communion, the Baptists withheld their support. He became perplexed and distressed in his pecuniary circumstances, and also in his religious relations. He became nervous, and has been partially insane." · Such is the original entry to which is appended the following letter from a friend, of which the patient was himself the messenger:

" The bearer, the Rev. Mr. H., has resided for a part of the time . for two years in this town, and is considered by all who have the most intimate acquaintance with him, partially deranged and a proper subject for your Institution. He is perfectly poor, and unable to perform any common manual labor from bodily debility and mental derangement. The family, consisting of a sick wife and six children, are mainly subsisted from the charities of the neighbors except what little they can earn. A few individuals have made up a small sum to enable him to reach your place, and we hope enough to support him a few weeks, hoping that such medical aid and treatment as you are in the habit of allowing to others, may render him in a short time capable of earning a living. Could he not be with you, and be employed in some of your factories or book-binderies so as to earn his living while he stays? I think I have never been acquainted with a more wretched man than he now is. I think if any man is a worthy object of your charities, he is the man deserving it. I have no interest in his case any more than the community in general have. I hope you will thoroughly try your best in his case, for I am confident he is a proper subject.   J. C."

The first entry after his admission shows him to have been greatly depressed, and incapable of directing his attention to anything continuously, and disturbed in his sleep by distressing dreams. He was placed under medical treatment and before the expiration of a week, one "comparatively cheerful" day is noted.

On the second Sunday after his admission he took some part in the religious service. After this a transient eruption appeared upon his skin, followed by a dejected state of mind again. Again, however, with the return of the Sabbath he assisted. Three weeks after admission, while laboring under a melancholy in which the fact of a sister having been similarly afflicted, also his brother (who died insane), seemed to prey upon his mind and add hopelessness to his own case, he wrote the following expressive lines, which are made part of his record:

"'T was phrenzy's hand that sadly marred
    A sister's fairest form ;
  My *only* brother's boat went down
    In just so wild a storm.
  And such, I fear, will be my fate,
    On life's dark raging sea ;
  But I must trust in Providence
    Wherever I may be.

Yes, I must trust in Thee O *God*,
    Tho' the mind is marred and broken,
  I feel thy just and dreadful rod—
    The hand of disease is the token,
  And what thou doest *I know not now*,
    But shall *know* at the judgment morning ;
  To thy dark designs, I must humbly bow
    And wait for the *light* of its *dawning*.

Before the expiration of a month he became a boarder in the Doctor's family, and was given unrestricted parole. Thenceforward it is noted that he steadily improved, and regularly officiated at the Sunday Asylum service ; and he was discharged recovered at the expiration of six weeks from his admission.

RECORD OF 1838.

A CTIVE building operations were entered upon with the opening of this year. It is recorded January 24th that the "Trustees met, and after considering fully the plans and estimates of a new building for the Asylum, submitted by Capt. Toby, and the state of the funds of the Institution, *Voted*, To proceed immediately and build the walls of brick of a center building and one wing, on the plan of Capt. Toby ; except the wing to be only five windows long instead of seven,—and to purchase materials for finishing one, and to finish one or both as far as our funds will admit. Also *Voted*, To employ Capt. Merchant Toby of Worcester to superintend the erection of the buildings, make contracts for work and materials, etc., and that he be directed to proceed forth-with with the work. Agreed with Capt. Toby to pay him three dollars per day while actually employed in this business, and to pay his stage fare to and from Worcester. He to board himself."

On the 16th of May the "Trustees met again, and in consequence of the advice and recommendations of Capt. Toby and Dr. Rockwell, and from consideration of the ultimate wants of the State and the economy of the measure, *Voted*, To direct Capt. Toby to extend the wing of the Asylum now being erected, to seven windows,—the length originally proposed by Capt. Toby in his plan."

June 18th another meeting is recorded: "Trustees met and elected Asa Keyes of Brattleboro a Trustee of the Vermont Asylum for the Insane to fill the vacancy occasioned by the death of John Holbrook, which occurred on the 6th of April, 1838."

On the 16th of October the "Trustees met, all present, and adopted their Report to the General Assembly of the State. Also received the annual Report of Dr. Rockwell the Superintendent, and accepted it, also the Report of the Treasurer, and forwarded the whole to the Legislature. *Voted*, To apply to the Legislature to authorize the Treasurer of the State to accept the drafts of the Trustees for the remainder of the annual payments appropriated by the Act of October, 1835, payable at the times when they would be due according to the terms of the Act, to enable the Trustees to anticipate their payments, and thereby to complete the building now begun.

"Asa Keyes appointed committee to attend to the procuring of an Act.

" *Voted*, To authorize John C. Holbrook and Capt. M. Toby to purchase two springs of water for the use of the Institution, of H. Pike, on the best terms possible."

The latter negotiation was accomplished at a cost of $150. (Oct. 20th, 1838.)

The State Treasurer was also authorized to accept the drafts of the Trustees, as requested ; and the Trustees were thus enabled to go on with safety in the prosecution of their work of erecting permanent buildings.

The first Report upon the operations of the Asylum (Oct. 1837) has been given in full in the record for the last year, for the reason that it nowhere exists in any State Document, although five hundred copies were ordered to be printed for distribution.

The two preliminary Reports have also been given in full, as they were never printed for circulation. The first (Oct. 1835) was published in epitome, in Journal of the Assembly, pages 144-145. The second (Oct. 1836) is found in Journal of the House, pages 18, 19, 20, in full.

The second regular Report (Oct. 1838) exists in permanent connection with the House Journal of this year. See Appendix to same, p. vii, and as all the subsequent Reports are permanently preserved in State Documents, only their salient points will hereafter be noticed in connection with these Annals.

The Trustees in their Report for this year indulge the pleasing anticipation of speedily occupying the new buildings with their added advantages for the care of the insane, and especially manifest a lively interest in the methods of treatment employed, and results already attained. In the construction of the buildings durability has been first considered, but not to the exclusion of other considerations. The *moral effect* of appliances for security seems to have been borne equally in mind. "Each room," they say, "is to be furnished with a bed, and a permanent seat in the angle of the walls. In addition to this, the rooms of those patients who are in a suitable condition, will also be furnished with a chair, a work-table and a small mirror. Each of these rooms is lighted by a large window, in which is an upper and lower cast iron sash firmly fastened to the window frame. The upper sash is glazed, the lower one is not ; but corresponding to the lower one in size and appearance is a glazed wooden sash which can be raised and lowered at pleasure.   The whole sash is painted white, and has the appearance of a common window.   This removes the prison-like appearance of iron bars, and at the same time prevents escape and injury."   This quotation is made especially to illustrate the correspondence of ideas then, with those now gaining ground.   After a generation prolific in devices for window guards of ornamental pattern, the conclusion is being reached that it all results in making the means of security principally conspicuous ; and that a plain iron sash corresponding exactly to the window panes in shape, when painted in the same color as the wood sash, is least noticeable and objectionable.   The conviction of Dr. Rockwell that occupation and especially out-door labor, should be urged and instituted as a remedial measure, was heartily endorsed by the Trustees, who appear to have especially observed its working and thus note its results.   " The anticipations of the benefits resulting from constant exercise in the open air while laboring on the farm, have been more than realized.   As a moral remedy in the curative treatment of the insane it is second to no other.   One of the patients, a respectable farmer who had been insane about three years, fancying among other things, that he was a great personage and consequently above labor, resided six months at the Asylum without perceptible benefit. During this time he was so much opposed to labor that it was not enforced.   Perceiving that there was no prospect of improvement in the course that had been pursued, sufficient motives were presented to induce him to labor and in three months he was entirely restored. It is now ten months since he left the Institution, and we are happy to learn that he continues well.   Another man, who had been insane several years, was brought here in chains.   A proposal was immediately made to him, that if he would do no injury and would labor upon the farm, his chains should be removed.   He immediately complied, and the next day he was taken into the field and labored well.   Other cases might be mentioned where the benefits resulting from labor were equally apparent."

Their Report concludes with the following: " There is one subject on which the Trustees would not fail to remark.   The Asylum is entirely a public institution, and whatever funds may arise, from the board of patients and other sources, are applied exclusively to promote the objects of this charity.   The Trustees serve gratuitously, and in no respect is the Institution a source of profit pecuniarily to any individual.   The terms are fixed as low as consistent with the support of the establishment."

The Superintendent's Report shows that forty-seven cases were admitted during the year ending October 1, 1838, and forty-five were discharged during the same period, leaving at the date just mentioned thirty-six.

Of those admitted twenty-seven were reckoned as old or chronic cases, and twenty were recent cases of not more than six months' duration. Of the latter eighty-eight per cent. are reported to have recovered. Of those called old cases a percentage of twenty-six and a half is also reported recovered.

This latter result very nearly represents the ratio of recoveries in all cases at the present time. Now, however, cases of twice six months would be regarded as recent; hence the percentage in the above would have been considerably lowered had those whose insanity ranged from six to twelve months' duration been included, as would also that of the old cases.

A point is made, however, in showing the importance of early treatment, which fifty years of subsequent experience has confirmed.

These results also tally with those of contemporary reports, but the more careful study of the Curability of Insanity, as pursued by Dr. Earle of the Northampton Lunatic Hospital, 1876-1886, has shown that in these early years no distinction was made between cases and persons, and that many of the cases upon which statistics were based, were recurrent attacks in the same person. When these are discriminated, the percentage of recovery is materially lowered. In the management of the patients the principles of treatment are indicated in the importance given to labor and open-air exercise, religious exercise, and promotion in respect to classification, as a motive to effort at self-control, responsibility being recognized as far as possible.

The views of Dr. Rockwell respecting the nature of insanity are here fully outlined.

"The cruel treatment of the insane among the ancients arose in a great measure from their notions of the pathology of the disorder. They considered the mind as an immaterial and independent principle, and not affected by the corporeal system in health or disease.

*　*　*　*　*　*　*　*　*　*　*

"Bacon was the first to explode this theory. He taught that the absolute source of insanity, if ever fully developed, will be found to exist in corporeal changes, or the effects of external agents acting on the the gross machine, and not primarily on the immaterial principle, as has, unfortunately for the subjects of disease, been too commonly apprehended." *　*　*　*　* . "In the pathology adopted in this Asylum, it is an axiom which has a commanding influence on its practice, that insanity is in all cases a corporeal disease, existing essentially in that class of material instruments or organs of the brain which are immediately and exclusively subservient to the functions of the mind, upon which it acts, and by which it is acted upon, without pretending to understand the nature of that mysterious tie which connects the immortal and immaterial essence to the material organs. The connection is evident, and it is only through the intervention of these organs that the mind can here be manifested. These organs of the mind being therefore considered as the seat of the disease, and the morbid mental phenomena the symptoms only, it would seem to be rational to employ all the agents, moral and physical, which are capable of effecting favorable changes in the state of the corporeal organs. He, therefore, who in the treatment of insanity, confines himself to the employment of one class of agents, whether moral or medical, to the exclusion of the other, must often fail of success, from the want of that efficiency which is found in the combined action of both. Insanity is frequently caused by a diseased state of the body operating through sympathy on the brain, and in almost every case when it is not caused by bodily diseases it is greatly aggravated by them. Medicine, therefore, is frequently essential in the successful treatment of insanity. When we restore health to the body, we have gained an important step towards restoration to reason, and frequently the manifestations of the mind become immediately sane. In the treatment also of diseases of the body, moral management is a useful auxiliary, and sometimes will of itself effect a cure. I make these remarks to show the importance of both moral and physical remedies in the curative treatment of the insane, and of the difficulty of applying both these remedies except in institutions prepared for the purpose."

The current financial exhibit for this year, shows:

Income from board of patients, etc.,	$5,045.46
General expenditures for the year,	4,970.10
Leaving balance on hand,	$75.36

Before the close of the first year's operations, the official organization included Chauncy Booth, Jr., as assistant and apothecary, and Mrs. Ann F. Wilkinson as matron. These officials are still in service at the date of this report.

The cost of the center building and first wing west, principally erected during this year, was $12,399.67.

RECORD OF 1839.

ON THE 16th of February the "Trustees met, and examined the new building erected under the superintendence of Capt. Toby.

"Appointed S. Clark a committee to examine Capt. Toby's account.

"*Voted*, That the Board of Visitors be respectfully requested to visit the Institution the coming week, and examine its condition agreeably to the Act of Incorporation.

"*Voted*, That the Treasurer be authorized to pay the expenses of the Board of Visitors from Newfane to this place, and while here on the above business."

In the Spring of this year another vacancy in the Board occurred by the resignation of its junior member, John C. Holbrook.

On the 4th of June, "Trustees met, and chose Asa Keyes their Secretary until another is chosen, and after examining the condition of the patients, adjourned."

July 2d, "At a meeting of the Trustees at the Asylum, present Samuel Clark, Epaphro' Seymour and Asa Keyes, upon due consideration, Nathan B. Williston of Brattleboro was duly elected and appointed a Trustee of the Vermont Asylum, to fill the vacancy occasioned by the removal from the State of John C. Holbrook; and upon due notice thereof the said Williston accepted said appointment, and is such Trustee."

On the 1st of October, the "Trustees met at the Asylum and heard and adopted the Report of the Superintendent, and prepared their annual Report.

"*Voted*, That said Reports be transmitted to the General Assembly at its approaching session."   •

These Reports may be found in full in Appendix to House Journal page 39.

The Trustees congratulate themselves upon the completion of the center, and west contiguous wing of the permanent buildings. "So urgent were the applications for admission," they say, "that as soon as any part was finished, it was immediately occupied by

•

patients. The superintendent and family, the matron and a few female patients now reside in the center building. The new wing is appropriated exclusively for the accommodation of female patients. All the females therefore are kept in the new building. The assistant physician and all the male patients reside in the former building thereby effecting a complete separation of the sexes."

The Trustees refer especially to the continuance of the system of out-door occupation, and say "there is no moral means which has proved so successful in restoring our curable patients, and in improving the habits of the incurable, as useful labor.   *   *   *   *   "The female patients have also been furnished with employment, according to their former habits and the state of their minds. All of the bedding of the establishment since the opening of the Institution, the making of much of the clothing, except what is furnished by the friends, and the mending of the same, is performed by the female patients, under the direction of the matron and nurses. For this part of our curative treatment much credit is due to the matron, whose whole time and exertions are devoted to the welfare of the patients with a zeal worthy of success."

It is gratifying to note the interest manifested by the Trustees in individual cases, as well as in the general welfare of the whole, as may be seen in the following quotations:

"This Institution has received many a wretched maniac, whose presence seemed to blight every prospect of happiness while he remained with his family; it has removed from the hands and feet of the insane many a manacle and chain; it has furnished for them a pleasant retreat, where they have enjoyed all the liberty and comfort of which their condition would admit; and last but not least, it has restored back to reason, to friends, to society and usefulness, many who would otherwise have dragged out a miserable existence in an incurable insanity.

"One patient was brought to this Institution, who had been confined during the warm season in a stable, but on the approach of cold weather was removed to the Asylum, and in due time recovered. He had been very violent, and no place in his house was supposed to be strong enough to secure him. After the family and physician supposed they had made use of the best means in their power without any benefit, he was removed to the Asylum, accompanied by a letter from the family physician to the superintendent, giving an account of his case and treatment, and concluding by observing, what is best for him I hope some one knows better than

——— ———, M. D.

"Another was brought to this Asylum who was very violent, and in a former paroxysm had been chained, so that the chain had worn in upon the bone of one of his legs.   When he arrived at this Institution all articles of restraint were removed from him, and in three months he was restored to his family entirely recovered.

"Another was the case of a young man whose parents were in very moderate circumstances.   He remained in their family until he became so violent that he was taken to the almshouse, and placed under its keeper.   But his violence was so increased and he was so mischievous, noisy, and dangerous, that he was taken to Windsor (an adjoining town) and placed in the State Prison, as the only place where he could be controlled.   Here, finding himself among criminals and felons, his disease was aggravated, and so great was his disturbance that he was finally brought to this establishment.   He was then mischievous, offering violence to every one who came in his way, and endeavoring to disturb the comfort of all around him. After a residence of three months at this Institution he was restored to reason, and has become a quiet, peaceable young man.   We might mention others who have been brought to this place, who had been caged in out-buildings until their extremities had been frozen ; not to mention many other scenes from which humanity revolts."

These cases are interesting as illustrative of the kind at this time claiming admission, and as witnesses to methods of treatment resorted to before asylums were instituted;—but in the light of a subsequent half century one can hardly attribute recovery in these to asylum treatment alone, when it is known that cases of acute violent mania, whether primary or recurrent in form, recover in an average of three to six months usually, under ordinary hygienic conditions, and often despite some injudicious management and environment.

The Report of the Superintendent shows that seventy-one cases have been received and thirty-eight have been discharged in the last twelve months, leaving sixty-nine in the Asylum at this date. The rate of recoveries is fully as great as in the last year, being eighty-nine per cent. on cases under six months' duration, and twenty-eight per cent. on those of longer standing.

The principles of treatment pursued are indicated in the following quotation: "As soon as a patient manifests any return of reason his liberties are increased, and he is encouraged to exercise his judgment and self-control by joining in the employments and amusements of the convalescents, by associating with them and the officers, and having, so far as is practicable, the privileges of an ordinary boarder at a public boarding house.   To retain this confidence, the patient endeavors to control his disordered feelings and frequently succeeds in regaining the lost balance of his mind. Those who have sufficiently improved walk about unaccompanied by any one, visit the different places in the village, and in a word are their own keepers. They rarely abuse the confidence thus placed in them ; and frequently assist the farmer and attendants in watching those who require it."

Some observations upon the excitants to insanity deserve noting. "Insanity increases with civilization and refinement. The farther we depart from the simple habits and customs of our ancestors the more shall we prepare for the introduction of this disorder. When we take a view of our country and witness its advancement in wealth, civilization and refinement, the many powerful temptations to embark in hazardous enterprises, the sudden accumulation and loss of property which frequently happens, the freedom of our institutions by which the humblest citizen may aspire to the highest office in the gift of the people, the fierce and persevering strifes which are everywhere carried on, both in the accumulation of wealth and in obtaining political distinction, and the many trials of disappointment and mortification to which all are liable, who can doubt the many active and operating causes to increase this disease in our country ? Persons of all classes and stations in life are liable to this affliction. Those who are now rejoicing in the blessings of health and reason may soon be afflicted with this severe calamity."

The influence of religious exercises upon the insane is dwelt upon at some length. The chapel room in the new center building, for Sunday gatherings, is hailed with satisfaction, while the separation of the male patients from the females, in the now detached building, is deplored, inasmuch as their attendance upon family devotions during the week is precluded.

" Much of the good effect of religious worship," says Dr. Rockwell, "depends on the prudence and discretion with which it is managed. We consider the judicious employment of religious exercises an important part of our moral treatment. They serve to promote order, revive their former grateful habits and associations, and recall into exercise that self-control which tends to their recovery. That religion which breathes 'peace on earth and good will to men,' and whose cheering influences extend beyond the grave, affords solace and consolation to the insane, as well as comfort to the rational mind.

" No one who has witnessed the influence of the Christian religion on the human mind can for a moment doubt its efficacy in producing serenity under all the trials of life, and in preventing shipwreck of reason which would otherwise inevitably follow. I have always noticed that the humble believer in Christianity recovered more readily from insanity than one who was not.   As soon as the former has one ray of returning reason he has something to which he clings and which soothes and sustains him under all his troubles. From the effect of proper religious exersises upon the minds of the insane, we have no doubt but the time will soon come when they will be considered as important moral means in the management of every well regulated asylum."

The financial statement for this year shows :

Income from board of patients, etc.,	$7,926.54
General current expenditures,	7,612.68
Leaving balance on hand,	$313.86

No change in the resident officers has taken place the past year.

THE Reports of this year of the Trustees and Superintendent were printed in Appendix to House Journal in full, see page 132. That of the Trustees appeals especially in behalf of the poor insane, as follows:

"As it is the acknowledged duty of governments to provide for the poor and destitute, have not the insane poor of this State paramount claims to those of any other class of our fellow men? The necessity of providing for the deaf, dumb, and blind, is universally acknowledged. But there is not an argument in favor of providing for that unfortunate class, but will apply with tenfold greater force in favor of the insane. While the Legislature has made such ample provision for them, we trust they will not forget a still more afflicted class of our fellow citizens. There are more than twenty insane persons, to one who is deaf and dumb, or blind. A deaf and dumb, or blind person, is not necessarily unhappy, or a burden to his friends. Most of them can amply support themselves. But with the insane, their disease shuts them out from all enjoyment. The families with which they are connected experience the most poignant sensations of grief and anxiety, and frequently are exposed to the greatest dangers. Whatever funds the Legislature may appropriate for the benefit of the insane, remain permanent in our own State (referring manifestly to funds appropriated for the extension of accommodation), the benefits of which those of future generations can partake, as well as those of the present time."

The Legislature is also asked to exempt the attendants of the Asylum from militia duty.

"We ask no exemption for any," say they, "except those whose exclusive duty it is to attend upon the patients. If we could supply their places by temporary substitutes, we would not make the request. Their situation is one which a person unacquainted with its duties, can but poorly perform."

This request was complied with.

The Superintendent reports that seventy-three new cases have been admitted in the year past, and sixty-one have been discharged, leaving, Oct. 1st, eighty-one. The percentages vary scarcely at all from preceding years, eighty-eight of recent cases, and twenty-eight of chronic cases having recovered. Chronicity, on admission, is deplored. One perplexity which is still constantly experienced, that of injudicious removals, is thus commented upon :

"Another mistake in regard to the insane is the premature removal of the patient from the Asylum. It frequently happens that when a patient is placed at a lunatic asylum, his wild and violent conduct soon gives way to that of calmness and comparative quietude, although he may be far from being restored. In the meantime he is visited by some of his friends and acquaintances, who, finding him orderly in his behavior, sadly misjudge that he might as well be at home as at the Asylum. This opinion is frequently communicated to the patient, and his desire to return then becomes so great that there is about as great danger in retaining him—dissatisfied as he will be—as letting him return home and hazarding a relapse. Sometimes the friends of the patient anticipate a recovery before an adequate trial has been made. This more frequently happens in old cases. The friends frequently think six months or a year is an abundant time of trial, for even an old case. We have had several patients recover who had made no improvement the first year.

"One patient was brought to the Asylum in June, 1838. He had been insane two years, and during the last several months was so violent as to be caged and chained. As soon as he was placed in the Asylum he was put under a regular course of treatment, but no radical change occurred during the first two years of his residence at this place. In June 1840, he was apparently in much the same state as he was at the time of his admission, although his habits had improved. Soon after he began to improve, and in September he was discharged entirely well. Had he been removed at the end of six months as is usually the case, and been returned to his former cage, he would undoubtedly have remained insane through life. This, and other facts, prove that old cases are not necessarily incurable, and that some recover under the most discouraging circumstances ; therefore a reasonable trial should be made with them. But the greatest chances of success are with the recent cases, most of which recover when placed under proper curative treatment at a lunatic asylum.

"To show that chronic cases are not necessarily incurable I will mention one or two that have been restored to health and reason.

In October, 1839, a lady who was a widow of superior education and former usefulness, was admitted into the Asylum. She had been insane about six years. When she was brought to this place she was very wild, violent and mischievous. Her friends did not expect she would be restored, but supposed she would be made more comfort-able at an asylum than at any other place. She was put under a regular course of treatment, and after the first six weeks began to improve. Her improvement was slow, but gradual, and at the end of six months she appeared to be perfectly restored. She remained with us until June when she returned in her right mind to her children, to afford them that instruction which they can receive only from a mother.

"Another case was admitted in February, 1840. He was a respectable farmer, and forty-six years of age. He had been insane about five years, and during the last several months previous to his admission, was loaded with irons and chained to the floor in the county jail, where he resided. His hands and feet were chained when he was admitted. His chains were of course immediately removed. He was put under a mild discipline and regular medica-tion, the result of which was that he returned home well in June, and is attending to his farm comfortable and happy."

A detail of individual cases, of exceptional course, is always interesting and instructive ; and the foregoing affords basis for a hopeful prognosis even after the stamp of chronicity is upon them.

The current accounts of this year were as follows:

The income from board of patients,	$9,926.86
The general expenditures,	9,473.67
Leaving balance on hand of,	$453.19

On the 6th of October the "Trustees met, and adopted their Annual Report to the Legislature, also read and accepted the Annual Report of the Superintendent, and directed said Report [the fore-going], to be transmitted to the Legislature at its approaching session.

"And whereas the Asylum is already filled with patients, *Voted*, To memorialize the Legislature to furnish means for the erection of the other wing of the new buildings, and Dr. Rockwell, the Superin-tendent, was authorized to appear before the Legislature, to exhibit and explain to them the pressing wants of this Institution."

The following was the result of this showing :·

"AN ACT making an Appropriation to the Vermont Asylum for the Insane.

"Sec. 1. The Treasurer of this State is directed to pay to the Trustees of the Vermont Asylum for the Insane, four thousand dollars, in two annual instalments, the first instalment to be paid on the 20th day of October, in the year 1841, to enable said Trustees to erect an additional wing to the building of that Institution, and the said Treasurer may accept drafts for the several instalments payable as above mentioned.

"Sec 2. This grant is made on the condition that the amount heretofore granted by the Legislature, shall be exclusively appropriated to the purpose for which the Institution was established, and if the said Institution should at any time cease to exist, the real estate of said corporation shall be held as security to this State for the amount so granted, and may be sold under the direction of this Legislature for the purpose of raising such amount, and the said real estate shall at no time be sold by said Trustees, without the consent of this Legislature.

"Approved October 29th, 1840."

On the 30th of November, "The Trustees met at the Asylum, all being present, and after taking into consideration the liberal grant by the Legislature of four thousand dollars, at their present session, for the purpose, *Voted*, unanimously, That we will as early as practicable the ensuing summer, erect the east wing of the new building, upon the same plan as the west wing, and with similar materials as far as practicable. *Voted*, also, That N. B. Williston be authorized to make contracts for workmen and building materials."

No change in the resident corps of officers the past year.

THE first meeting of the Trustees this year was held at the Bank, January 25th, all being present.

"Epaphro' Seymour resigned the office of Treasurer, which resignation was accepted; and N. B. Williston was unanimously appointed.

"*Voted*, To meet at the Asylum the first Tuesday of every month the present year, at 2 o'clock P. M., the month of February excepted.

"The Superintendent appearing before the Board, and representing that the number of patients was constantly increasing, insomuch that the proposed new wing when completed would be inadequate to accommodate all the patients, and the Trustees being satisfied that it would be economy to enlarge their former plans—

"*Voted*, therefore, That we will build the new wing ninety feet long (10 windows) instead of the length voted at our meeting of the 30th of November last."

At the October meeting the "Trustees adopted their Annual Report to the Legislature, also that of the superintendent, and directed said Reports to be transmitted to the Legislature at their approaching session."

The Trustees refer especially to the appropriation made by the last Legislature, by which they are enabled to erect the east wing, which is expected to be completed during the present year.

"So numerous had been the applications for admission," they say, "it was found the wings of the new building should be of greater length than was originally contemplated. The wing erected the present season is twenty-seven feet longer than the other, which will also be lengthened as soon as the funds of the Asylum will admit, that the symmetrical proportions may be preserved, and greater accommodations furnished." This foreshadows a policy of further extension in obedience to the constantly increasing pressure which from that day to this has never ceased to be felt.

The Superintendent bears testimony to the salubrity of the location, now five years tested : "The mountain air is very favorable to the health of our inmates. Our male patients have been employed in agricultural pursuits and other employments in the open air, more than those of any other similar institution in the country. We also amuse them by walking, riding, playing ball, quoits, and other various out-door amusements. Our female patients are taken out for riding, walking, visiting the garden and culling its flowers, of which we have a great variety. We endeavor to have all our female patients, who are sufficiently quiet, ride every fair day. Those who are wild are frequently taken out to walk about the premises."

The proper association of patients is likewise discussed.

"A proper classification of the patients of a lunatic asylum is of great importance in their moral treatment. The continued efforts at self-control and self-respect, which they make to retain their places or to be promoted, contribute much to their improvement and restoration. The desire of the good opinion of others is so universal a principle of our nature, that whatever calls it into proper exercise has a favorable effect in counteracting those morbid propensities with which the insane are so often afflicted. All our attendants and assistants have it repeatedly impressed on their minds as a fundamental principle of our treatment, that they are at all times to treat every patient with due respect, and that to neglect this rule is to neglect one of the principal means of recovery."

The movement of the population this year shows eighty-four admissions, and seventy discharges; ninety-five remaining at the date of this Report. A singular uniformity in the results as compared with preceding years is maintained; eighty-eight per cent. of recent and twenty-eight of chronic cases having recovered.

Since the date of the preceding Report a change has been made in the assistant medical officer, Dr. Chauncy Booth, Jr., having been succeeded by Dr. Samuel B. Low.

The foregoing Reports in full, may be found in Appendix to House Journal, page 80.

A purchase was this year made (April 7) of an undivided sixth part of the reservoir of water standing west of the residence of the late Dea. John Holbrook, for $112, of one James Minott. Cost of carrying pipe $138 additional.

The current expenses of the year show:

Income from board of patients, etc.,	$11,830.26
General expenditures,	$11,549.13
Leaving balance of	$290.13

The cost of the first wing east, erected this year, was $7,769.87.

RECORD OF 1842.

T HE Annual Reports for this year were adopted and duly transmitted to the Legislature in October. See Appendix to
House Journal, page 132.

At this meeting it was *Voted*, "That the salary of Dr. Rockwell,
the Superintendent, shall be, from and after November 1st next,
twelve hundred dollars per annum."

"Since the last Annual Report, say the Trustees, the new wing
has been completed, which has furnished additional accommodations
and has increased our facilities for a better classification of the
patients. Large and well ventilated halls, neat and pleasant sleeping
rooms, plenty of pure water, and kind and faithful attendants are
furnished the establishment, and everything is supplied to promote
the comfort of the unfortunate inmates. The Trustees confidently
believe that this Institution now possesses all the facilities for restoration, which can be found at any similar institution in our
country."

The Superintendent shows, with the Trustees, the feeling of satisfaction at the enlarged capacity of the establishment, and in turn
reports increased curative results. During the preceding year one
hundred and one were admitted, and eighty-three discharged, leaving
one hundred and thirteen under care. Of those discharged near
ninety per cent of the recent cases are reported as having recovered,
and near thirty-two per cent. of the chronic class.

Testimony to the value of systematic labor is here repeated, and
leaves no doubt of the Doctor's sincere convictions upon this matter
which, inaugurated at the opening of the Asylum, could now be
affirmed with the strength of each year's added experience.

"In our endeavors to restore the insane," says he, "our chief
object is to make use of such means as shall tend to promote the
health of the patient, and keep his mind agreeably occupied. One
of the best means we have found for this purpose is exercise in
the open air. For those of our male patients who are able, and
whose former pursuits have been agricultural, employment by useful

labor in the garden and on the farm has proved very beneficial.   It operates morally by occupying the attention, and diverting the mind from its morbid fancies, and physically by improving the health of the patient.   We are constantly making improvement on the farm, which in a few years will be in a high and profitable state of cultivation.   More land is needed to furnish sufficient employment for our patients."

A change in the resident corps of officers this year occurred in the resignation of Mrs. Ann F. Wilkinson as matron, and the appointment of Mrs. Deborah K. Baker as her successor.

The current accounts of this year are as follows:

Income from board of patients, $12,935.36
General expenditures,   12,615.54
                                                                                          ————
Leaving balance on hand of, $319.82

Additional water supply was also purchased this year from the same source as last year, of Asa Green, at a cost of $150. (Sept. 17, '42.)

The Report of this year was reviewed by Rev. Louis Dwight, in the Report of the Prison Discipline Society of the following year, in a very commendatory strain, as follows: "The terms of admission are, for indigent patients of Vermont $2.00 per week or $100 per year; for all others $2.50 per week for the first six months; after that time $2.00.   No charge is made for damages in any case.   The means of cure in this Institution are abundant, and well adapted to the end.   Its whole history is one of success, with as little variation as can be found in almost anything human."

RECORD OF 1843.

THE Reports of this year may be found in full in Appendix to House Journal, page 60.

The Trustees set forth, "That the present building is fast filling with patients. The right wing, which was built too small (7 rooms in length) needs enlarging, as well for the accommodation and comfort of the inmates, as to preserve the just and proper proportions and symmetry of the building (the left wing being 10 rooms long). It is sincerely hoped that the Legislature will not fail to grant that assistance for this object, which is so urgently needed. We trust that the same fostering care and generous support which they have hitherto extended, will be continued to this Institution, and that 'The blessings of many who are ready to perish' will attend all who assist in relieving this greatest of human afflictions."

This was the last appeal ever made by the Trustees for State aid in providing Asylum accommodations.

The Superintendent notes in his Report of this year a new and novel enterprise, as follows:

"During the past year we have published a small newspaper, called the 'Asylum Journal,' which has exerted a beneficial influence on the comfort and recovery of the patients. We have had more than two hundred exchange papers, besides many other periodicals, to the editors and publishers of which we would tender our most grateful acknowledgments. We have been able to furnish every patient with a newspaper of his own political views, and every sectarian with a religious periodical of his own peculiar sentiments.

"Our obligations to the publishers of our exchange papers, and the gratification with which they have been read, has been well discussed in a former number of the Asylum Journal: 'To our exchange papers we make our humble acknowledgments. We have now upon our list upwards of two hundred, besides quite a number of daily papers, and many of the best periodicals in the country. We have not the presumption to suppose that our little Journal is at all equivalent to the many mammoth sheets it brings in exchange, nor is it wonderful that it should not be so, removed as we are from the mart of news, and swayed by 'crazy minds.' But could they know the infinite satisfaction they give to many of us they would be amply repaid. It is like a wanderer in a distant clime, stumbling suddenly upon a pile of newspapers printed in his own neighborhood, who for months and years, perhaps, has not heard from his native land. With what eagerness he seizes them, retires to his own apartment, runs them over and over—hastily at first, and more leisurely and minutely afterwards, lest some important item be overlooked—gathering from them more than could be embodied in twenty voluminous epistles. And as he skips from advertisement to advertisement, it seems as if he were in reality once more in his native village, wandering from shop to shop, reviewing the long rows of well-filled shelves, and clasping joyously by the hand those with whose names he is so familiar. Like the first rays of the morning sun to him who has been all night grovelling in the dark, they do much towards dispelling the heavy cloud that hangs over us, and shed the first dawn of reason upon our shattered minds.

"But our Journal will soon pass into other hands, and we shall pass into the bustling world without, again to contend with wayward fortune. Think you we shall ever forget the time we have passed within these walls? Never! Our minds will oft recur to the varied scenes our bewildered fancies have conjured up, whose impress, like some thrilling tales stamped upon the susceptible brain of childhood, neither time nor circumstances can ever erase.'"

Exactly whose conception this enterprise was does not fully appear; but it was regarded by Dr. Rockwell certainly as a legitimate extension of the field of occupation, to which he was fully committed.

"A small portion only," he further says, "are capable of writing for it, but many are employed in making selections, and this employment diverts the mind from its own delusions, and aids, with other means, in restoring its just balance. Those of our patients who have been students, we employ to write and select for the Journal, and those who have been merchants and business men we employ to fold and direct the papers. Some who do not compose assist by making selections, and by copying extracts from books or papers. We find the employment of our patients in writing, either by way of copying or of composition, to be very beneficial, as it diverts their attention from their delusions and presents new objects of thought for contemplation. We always furnish them with stationery, and the employing of themselves in writing has apparently been a powerful means

in their restoration.   They are allowed to write on all subjects
except those of their hallucinations."

The appeal to the Legislature for aid in the further extension of
Asylum capacity resulted in the following:

" AN ACT Making an Appropriation to the Vermont Asylum for
the Insane.

" SEC. 1.   It is hereby enacted by the General Assembly
of the State of Vermont as follows: The Treasurer of this
State is directed to pay to the Trustees of the Vermont Asylum for
the Insane, three thousand dollars, to be paid on the first day of
October, 1844, to enable the Trustees to extend one of the wings of
the building, and to make repairs for the purpose of further accom-
dating the patients of said Institution; and the said Treasurer may
accept a draft for the payment, as above mentioned.

" SEC. 2.   This grant is made on the condition that the amount
together with the amount heretofore granted by this Legislature,
shall be exclusively appropriated to the purpose for which the Institution was established; and if the said Institution shall at
any time cease to exist, the real estate of said corporation
shall be held as surety to this State for the amount so granted, and
may be sold under the direction of this Legislature, for the purpose
of raising such amount, and the said real estate shall at no time be
sold by said Trustees, without the consent of this Legislature.

"Approved Nov. 1, 1843."

At a meeting of the Trustees of the Vermont Asylum, on the
8th day of December, 1843.   Present all the Trustees,—

" *Voted*, That we will build the west wing of the Asylum and
extend it the same length as the east wing.

" *Voted*, also, That the west wing be extended north forty-five
feet, and thirty feet wide.

" *Voted*, That Dr. Rockwell and N. B. Williston be a committee
to superintend the erection of the building."

The current expense account for this year stands thus:

Income from board of patients, etc., $13,498.61
General expenditures,   13,050.15
_____
Balance on hand,   . $448.46

No changes in the resident officers occurred this year.

Number of patients admitted, one hundred and eleven; discharged, eighty-eight; remaining, one hundred and thirty-six.

THE Reports of this year were published in full in Appendix to Senate Journal. The extension of the west wing of the main building, according to the plan decided upon by the Trustees at their meeting December 8th ult., was this year made. Into this was put the final appropriation of the State toward the providing of Asylum accommodations. The Trustees say, "We are now able to receive two hundred patients. Our accommodations are now adequate to the wants of the State." This conclusion, so natural to be expressed at this time, did not long hold good, as subsequently to be seen. There is something in a living force that bursts the limits set by solid walls. We see in the development of an aneurismal tumor the bony structures gradually yielding to the constant pulsations of the vital fluid, and so when the walls of an Asylum begin to feel the knocks of internal increasing pressure, they are made to expand and include more room. This result will however be noted in due course of time.

The Trustees in this year's Report cite some interesting cases as follows:

"While we rejoice over those which recover, it is also a source of much congratulation that the old cases can be so much improved, and be made so comfortable at the Asylum. One was brought to us four and a half years ago, a man who had been insane more than twelve years. During the four years previous to his admission, he had not worn any article of clothing, and had been caged up in a cellar, without feeling the influence of any fire. A nest of straw was his only bed and covering. He was so violent that his keepers thought it necessary, and applied an iron ring around his neck which was riveted on, so that they could hold him when they changed his bed of straw. In this miserable condition he was taken from the cellar, and dressed and brought to the Vermont Asylum. The ring was immediately removed from his neck. He has worn clothing, has been furnished with a comfortable bed, and has come to the table and used a knife and fork ever since he was first admitted. He has not destroyed three dollars' worth of clothing, bed and bedding since he came to the Asylum. He has been most of the time pleasantly and usefully employed about the Institution.

"The second case is a man who had been twenty-four years insane, and for the last six years had worn no clothing, and had been furnished with no bed excepting loose straw. He had become very filthy, regardless of everything which is neat or decent. Here was a case which required more skill and exertion than to restore a recent case to sanity. He was brought here a year and a half ago, and in less than three months from his admission he so improved that he has ever since worn his clothing ; has been supplied with a comfortable bed which he has kept neat, has gone to the table with the rest, and used a knife and fork ; and has not injured clothing, bedding, or any other property to the amount of two dollars. This last summer he has worked regularly on the farm, and is peaceable, quiet and happy.

"The third case is a man who has been insane more than thirty years, was sold to the lowest bidder for many years, was caged up, had his feet frozen so that he lost his toes, and endured suffering which no person in his natural state could have endured. He was brought to the Asylum about five months since, and has worn his clothing, has been furnished with a comfortable bed, has gone to the table with the rest, and has destroyed neither clothing, nor any other property. He is a printer by trade, and is now pleasantly and cheerfully employed in setting type for our little newspaper.

"From many, we will relate but one case of a female patient, who is now sixty-one years of age. From the statement made by one of her relatives we copy the following :

"'She has been deranged more or less since a child, and God Almighty only knows the cause of it. She was confined for several years in a half subterranean cage,' etc. This 'subterranean cage' was nothing more or less than a cave, dug into the side of a hill near the house, and straw thrown in for a bed, and no warmth admitted except what was received from the sun. We forbear to mention other particulars. She has been with us more than three years, and since the first three months has constantly assisted the nurse in the performance of her duty. Since the first week she has been at large in the halls, has been furnished with a comfortable bed, and has taken her food at the table with the rest. She is now regularly employed in assisting the nurse, and in mending the clothing of other patients."

I quote these individual histories with peculiar pleasure, illustrating as they do common phases of chronic insanity, and confirming
what may be done to improve even hopelessly insane persons, by
judicious system, changed environment, and the substitution of a
vicarious will power for that lost to the individual beyond recall.

In concluding, the Trustees again say: "We rejoice that the
buildings are so nearly finished, that we shall never have occasion
hereafter to ask the Legislature for funds for their completion; and
that our accommodations are sufficiently extensive for all the insane
of this State who may apply for admission. And while the insane
poor of this State suffer such an immense amount of unmitigated,
undiluted misery, will not the Legislature make suitable provision for
their care?" This last appeal, to make practicable the provision
for them already made, was responded to as will be shortly seen.

The Report of the Superintendent shows that ninety-six cases
were received, and seventy-four discharged since last Report, leaving
in the Asylum one-hundred and fifty-eight.

The highest curative results were reached this year in the whole
history of the Asylum. Upward of eighty-nine per cent. of the
recent cases, and upward of thirty-four per cent. of the chronic
cases recovered.

The following comments deserve note: "It is less than eight
years since the Asylum was opened for the reception of patients, and
less than ten years since Mrs. Marsh's donation was received to
found this Institution. The friends of the Asylum owe her a debt
of gratitude, both for the funds she so cheerfully granted, and also
for commencing an interest in the subject, which otherwise might not
have been awakened for years. Could she have anticipated the
comfort and relief which has resulted to the unfortunate from her
benefaction, her spirit would have rejoiced in the contemplation of
the happiness she was about to bestow. Of her it may be truly said,
'The blessings of many who are ready to perish,' will forever rest on
her memory.

"None but those who have learned by sad experience are aware
of the difficulties of managing the insane in a private family. The
insane conceive that they have claims upon their friends, and if they
are not aided by them in their wild and unreasonable plans, they look
upon them with suspicion and frequently with hatred. Hence
the dislike and complete enmity, which they frequently cherish
towards those whom they had most loved. And all the watchful
solicitude and kind assiduities that the friends can afterwards bestow
upon them, are suspected and misconstrued. But when placed in a

public Asylum they cheerfully submit to the regulations which
govern their little community, and frequently become sincerely
attached to those from whom they have received kindness and
attention. We have in the Asylum an incurable case of a young
man about thirty years of age, who has been insane about ten years.
He had been under the care of different persons, who had made him
as comfortable as could be expected out of a public Asylum. The
last year his mother took him home and had him chained to the
floor, being the only situation in which it was safe for her to take
care of him ; and manifested for him all that sympathy, which none
but a mother feels, and bestowed upon him all that kind assiduity,
which none but a mother could perform. But all her kindness,
attention and sympathy was misconstrued by her unhappy son,
and his condition was made more miserable than when taken care of
by strangers. After remaining in this situation one year he was
unchained and brought to this Asylum about four months ago.
From the time of his admission he has worn no article of restraint,
has destroyed no property, has been at large on our halls, has
assisted on the farm, has associated with the rest, and is now comfortable and happy."

The income this year from patients was, $14,673.19
General expenditures,   14,092.05

Leaving balance on hand of $581.14

During this year Dr. Samuel B. Low resigned as Assistant Physician and was succeeded by Dr. Henry M. Harlow.

Time of making up Report changed this year from October 1
to September 1.

The Legislature of this year, in conformity to the suggestions of
the Trustees of the Asylum passed—

"AN ACT for the Relief of the Insane Poor," of which the following is a copy :

" It is hereby enacted by the General Assembly of the State of
Vermont, as follows :

"SEC 1. A sum not exceeding three thousand dollars may be
drawn from the Treasury of the State, in the month of August
annually, by the Trustees of the Vermont Asylum for the Insane,
and they shall apply the same to the payment of the expenses of the
insane poor of the several towns in the State at the Asylum.

"SEC. 2. Each town shall share in the appropriation made in
Section 1 in proportion to the number of the insane poor in the
Asylum, the expense of transporting them at the rate of eight cents

per mile on the nearest practicable route from their respective residences to the Asylum, and the length of time they have been there, at the rate of one dollar and fifty cents per week during the year next preceding the first day of August annually.

"SEC. 3. The Trustees shall annually on or before the tenth day of September report in detail their doings under the provisions of this Act to the Auditor of Accounts, who shall incorporate the same in his Annual Report.

"SEC. 4. If in any year the expense of supporting the insane poor of the State at said Asylum, at the rate per week above stated, including the expense of transportation as aforesaid, shall be less than three thousand dollars, the Trustees shall not for such year be entitled to a greater share than the aggregate amount of such expense.

"SEC. 5. The several towns and other corporations in the State chargeable with the support of the poor, may at their annual March meetings, make and alter such regulations as they may deem expedient for the purpose of securing the benefit of the provisions of this Act, which regulations may embrace not only town paupers, but other persons destitute of property, and entirely dependent upon relatives not bound by law to support them.

"SEC. 6. An Act for the Relief of the Insane Poor approved Nov. 3, 1841, and an Act in addition thereto, approved Nov. 1, 1842, are repealed.

"Approved October 30, 1844."

Trustees met Dec. 2nd, 1844, and adopted the following regulations relating to the admission of beneficiaries to the Asylum under the foregoing Act.

1. "That each town pauper upon his admission into the Asylum as a State beneficiary shall be accompanied with the certificate of a majority of the selectmen, certifying that such insane person is insane and a pauper of said town.

2. "And the insane poor, not chargeable to the town, having no relatives to support them, shall be accompanied with a certificate of some Judge of a Court in this State, in office, certifying that such persons are destitute of property and entirely dependent upon relatives not bound by law to support them, with surety also that the balance of their quarterly bills shall be paid, in case the State appropriation shall prove to be insufficient.

"*Voted*, also, that Asa Keyes be auditor to audit the accounts of the former and present treasurers [E. Seymour and N. B. Williston] and of the superintendent [Dr. Rockwell] and also take an inventory of the goods, chattels and estate of the corporation, and its liabilities."

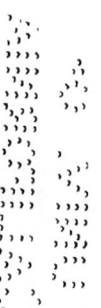

THE VERMONT ASYLUM—1844.

It will be seen by the foregoing Act for the Relief of the Insane Poor, and the Regulations of the Trustees conforming to its provisions, that a practical contract was reached in respect to the care of the insane poor, between the State and the Institution, explicit terms being now for the first time agreed upon for their support. Hitherto these classes had been received by virtue of State grants in enlarging the Asylum, but without the definiteness now reached in respect to provision for their maintenance.

The Report of the Auditor required under vote of Dec. 2nd, 1844, shows the value of the Asylum property in detail as follows:

GENERAL STATEMENT.

Cost of farm,	$2,705.40
Cost of building land,	3,504.98
Cost of springs and aqueducts,	550.00
Repairs of old building,	3,560.65
Cost of center building and west wing,	12,399.67
Cost of east wing,	7,769.87
Cost of west wing extension,	4,654.82
Cost of personal estate,	6,567.50
	$41,712.89

Funds received :—

Marsh Legacy,	$10,000	
State grants,	23,000	$33,000.00

Balance paid from current receipts, $8,712.89

The above summarizes the financial record of the Institution up to the close of the year 1844. It should be noted that an estate of fifty-one acres of land, with buildings affording a possible capacity for two hundred patients, including the use of the basement and attic stories for this purpose, had at this time been created and furnished out of the original legacy, the State appropriations, and the surplus derived from the management, combined.

Some important queries relative to the rights and privileges of the State in the subsequent extensions of capacity, here suggest themselves, but have never yet been raised.

Does the preferred right to admissions, gained by the State on account of the aid rendered for extensions of accommodations, apply to capacity afterward added from other sources? and does the security given to the State upon the real estate of the Asylum for the amounts appropriated by the Commonwealth in event of its ceasing to exist, hold upon lands subsequently acquired, unaided either directly or indirectly by the State? These are unsolved problems.

The editor of the American Journal of Insanity in a review of the Report of this year makes the following comments upon the terms at which patients will be received, viz.: "Two dollars per week, or eighty dollars per year, if the patient remain so long in the Asylum."

"Dr. Rockwell," says he, "has had much experience in the care of the insane, as he was for a considerable time assistant physician at the Retreat at Hartford, Ct., and we understand the Institution which he now superintends has been well managed. But we cannot forbear expressing our fears that the low prices at which this Asylum has recently advertised to receive patients will prove injurious to the best interests of the insane. That such persons can be supported at a low price everyone knows; they are so now in the various poor-houses of the country, but we hope not to see institutions bearing the high name of asylums and hospitals for the insane, and erected expressly for their comfort and care, degenerate into mere receptacles for this unfortunate class of persons. To this, however, they must assuredly come if the price is reduced to what it costs to support sane persons, as they will be obliged to dispense with that care, attendance, etc., requisite for their welfare as *sick persons*, and which in all asylums ought to form a large item of expense, in addition to the cost of board."

We acknowledge the force of this criticism, but we believe the critic did not know or fully understand the Doctor's principles of management. In fact, we know in these respects he was misunderstood by his co-workers in the specialty. The Doctor was true always to his convictions, and so strong in his individuality that he would pursue his own course if it was clear to his own mind, regardless of either criticism or censure.

As already remarked Dr. Rockwell had some years' experience in the care of the insane before he was called to superintend the Vermont Asylum.

This experience taught him that a very large percentage of the insane requiring asylum care, are chronic cases not demanding medical treatment, and he was likewise firmly impressed, as the preceding record shows, with the value of occupation as a means of treatment, and with a belief that by judicious pains the labor of this large class could be turned to some practical advantage, by way of reducing to some extent the actual expenses of their care.

Add to these practical convictions, the necessity in those early days of low rates as an inducement to friends to give the insane member at least *a trial* of asylum treatment, in a State in which every dollar was a hard-earned one, it is not difficult to comprehend the motives, if we fail to appreciate the wisdom, of the course he adopted in this respect, and which was at variance with the more liberal policy indicated in the comments quoted, which was adopted in some other States. This much may certainly with justice be conceded.

The cost of the extension made to the west wing this year was $4,654.82, as per summary, page 71.

THIS year may be said to begin a new epoch in the history of the Asylum. Hitherto it has been conducted after the manner of a proprietary establishment. Henceforth it takes on the character of a public institution.

Its relation to the State is now clearly defined, its obligation to receive the resident insane poor is recognized, and definite rates for their support are agreed upon. By-laws and regulations for the government of its employes are now adopted, and henceforth become the internal organic law.

The pioneer stage in its development has now been passed. ' Its management continues vested in its Board of Trustees, as provided in the will of Mrs. Marsh ; but the State enjoys the preferred right to its benefits.

It seems now to have been determined to ask no further assistance from the Legislature. The experience of the preceding eight years has demonstrated the possibility of making the Institution self-sustaining, and by careful management, self-creative in the future.

A confidence in the success of the enterprise at this time is manifested in the first act of the Board at the beginning of this year, as here chronicled :—

"January 8th, 1845.

" Trustees met, all but Mr. Seymour present.

" *Voted*, That we will enlarge the building the ensuing season, by extending the east wing north forty-five feet and thirty feet wide, thus making it symmetrical with the west wing, and also to build from said wing east seventy-two feet, and thirty-two feet wide.

" *Voted*, That N. B. Williston and Dr. Rockwell be a committee to superintend said building."

On the 1st of August, "Trustees met at the Bank agreeably to notice, Mr. Williston absent. '

" *Voted*, That Asa Keyes and Samuel Clark be a committee to draught and report a Code of By-Laws for the government of the Asylum."

August 15, " Trustees met at Bank, and the committee appointed at the last meeting reported a Code of By-Laws, and after reading and discussing the same at length, they were referred to the Superintendent, and the further consideration thereof continued till the first Monday in September."

September 1st, " Trustees met at the Asylum, and after discussing the By-Laws reported—

" *Voted*, (Mr. Seymour being absent) That the further consideration thereof be postponed till the first Monday in October.

"The Trustees then visited the patients in the several wards of the Institution, and found all things in good order."

Trustees met again on September 23rd.

"Adopted their Annual Report to the Legislature and their Report to the Auditor on the insane poor ; also read and approved the Superintendent's Report, and transmitted said Reports to the Auditor of Accounts at Woodstock, according to the Statute provided in this case."

The Reports of this year cover but eleven months, being made up to August 1st, in conformity with the Act of October 30, 1844, requiring these in future to be incorporated in the State Auditor's Report.

The Trustees report great pressure of applicants the past year, as a result of the Act for the Relief of the Insane Poor of the previous year, one hundred and thirty-seven beneficiaries having shared in the appropriation, which, however, covered but about three-fifths of their expense the past year.

To meet this influx of new applicants, which was foreseen by the managers, was the occasion of their early action toward the further enlargement of the buildings, already recorded.

The policy determined upon at this epoch was the result of careful consideration, as appears in this Report.

"It was desirable that sufficient accommodations should be pro-provided for as large a number as could well be taken care of, in order that the expenses for each patient might be diminished and brought within the means of his friends ; on the other hand, caution was necessary lest the number of patients should be so large that each one should not receive his proper share of attention. After full deliberation it was decided that the accommodations should be increased, and preparations were immediately made for the erection of new buildings containing about eighty additional rooms."

The Superintendent's Report states that two hundred and four cases were admitted since date of last Report, and ninety-nine were discharged, leaving, at date of this Report, two hundred and sixty-three.

"During the past year," says he, "three patients were brought to this Asylum on a bed, two of whom were suffering from inflammation of the brain, and the other from a delirium accompanying typhus fever; two of the three died. When brought to the Asylum they were in a condition not to be returned, and we considered it our duty to receive them and make them as comfortable as possible. We do hope that none hereafter may be offered who are unable to sit up and ride to the Asylum, and that the lives of the patients may not be hazarded by the exposure and fatigue of the journey."

This experience of forty years ago has hardly yet ceased to be occasionally repeated, although errors of diagnosis are now less likely to be made, under the present very explicit medical certificates required.

The following extracts from the Superintendent's Report are noteworthy:—

"Our great means for recovery are medical and moral treatment. Our moral treatment consists in allowing every patient all the liberty consistent with his own good and that of others; in endeavoring to conciliate them by kindness and attention; to excite the sentiments of self-respect, and a regard for the good opinions of others; to awaken their natural and social affections; to exercise their judgment in useful employments, and to divert them from their hallucinations by directing their attention to other subjects. Our medical treatment consists in endeavoring to restore every part of the human system to its healthy functions.

"Many of the inmates of a Lunatic Asylum are affected with diseases of the physical system. Such as are feeble are not only exempt from all employment, but have the most kind and assiduous care during the whole of their indisposition. Most of the inmates, however, are in such state of health that useful employment promotes their mental and physical welfare."

Mention is made in this Report of a shoe shop in addition to other means of occupation previously detailed, and the benefits each year derived from the publication of the little newspaper are again enlarged upon, with the following historical paragraph.

"*The Asylum Journal is the first regular newspaper ever printed in, and issued from, a Lunatic Asylum.* [In 1837 one of the patients of the Connecticut Retreat, who had been a printer, and also an editor, repaired to one of the printing offices in the city of Hartford, and with the assistance of the printers in that office, issued two odd numbers only, of a little sheet called the Retreat Gazette. He continued at the Retreat many months after these were printed, and was finally discharged without being restored."

The financial exhibits henceforward will be understood as including all expenditures, whether for current expenses, improvements, or enlargement of buildings or estate.

That for this year shows,

Income from board of patients, etc.,	$17,341.29
General expenditure,	16,721.45

Leaving balance on hand of, $619.84

Included in the income of each year hereafter, will be any temporarily borrowed funds, and in the expenditures the repayment of any such sums with interest. The Institution in fact has almost always carried a debt, it being the policy of the Trustees and Superintendent to enter upon plans for the development of the Institution as fast as they could see clearly the possibility of working out in reasonable time any temporary involvements on this score.

The Trustees this year secured by purchase of Eben Wells (Oct. 10, 1845) one of the present chief sources of water, at a cost of $200.

"Monday, October 6th, 1845.

"Trustees met (Mr. Seymour being absent). The By-Laws heretofore reported were adopted, and ordered to be recorded. They are as follows, to wit:

" BY-LAWS OF THE VERMONT ASYLUM FOR THE INSANE.

"ART. 1. The Trustees shall hold a meeting at the Asylum on the first Monday of every month at two o'clock P. M., to examine into the state of the Institution, the condition and situation of the patients, the accounts of the officers, and to transact any and all other business deemed expedient when met.

"ART. 2. The Chairman may at any time, and shall on the request of either Trustee or the Superintendent, call special meetings, giving each Trustee personal notice, or notice by letter.

"ART. 3. No vote shall be passed at any meeting unless there be three Trustees voting in the affirmative. Provided, at a subsequent monthly meeting to which any matter may be adjourned, the same may be passed by a majority of those present.

"ART. 4. At the monthly meeting in August which shall be
the annual meeting, the following officers shall be chosen and
appointed, to wit: A Chairman, Treasurer, Secretary and Auditor
of Accounts. A Superintendent, also a Farmer, Matron, Assistant
Physician and Apothecary, to be nominated annually by the Superintendent and appointed by the Trustees. Provided, however, in case of
vacancy or in case said officers shall not be chosen at the annual
meeting such vacancy may be filled or such officers chosen at
any subsequent monthly meeting, and the salaries of all officers shall
be from time to time fixed by the Trustees.

"ART. 5. The Superintendent shall have the general superintendence of the Asylum and grounds, the charge of the patients
and the direction and control of all persons therein, subject to
the regulations of the Board of Trustees. He shall visit the patients
daily, or when he may deem it injurious he shall learn their condition
daily or as much oftener as may be necessary, and shall direct such
medical, moral and physical treatment as may be best adapted to
their relief, giving the fairest trial to kind and moral management.
He shall from time to time give to all persons employed at the
Asylum such instructions as he shall judge best adapted to carry
into operation all the rules and regulations of the same, and shall
cause such rules and regulations to be strictly and faithfully executed,
taking care that the Farmer, Matron, Assistant Physician and Apothecary and all others employed about the Asylum perform particularly all the duties required of them.

"ART. 6. Under the Superintendent's direction the Farmer
shall take charge of the farm and shall purchase furniture, fuel,
stores and other necessary articles, and shall present the bills to the
Superintendent for the payment thereof. By the same direction
he shall hire attendants and domestics and agree with them for their
wages, and shall perform such other duties in relation to the business
in and about the Asylum as shall be required of him by the Superintendent.

"ART. 7. It shall be the duty of the Matron to look carefully
to the female patients, to be with them as much as possible, to direct
the nurses in their duty, to see that the inmates are kindly treated,
that their food is properly served and distributed, and that the female
attendants in all respects do their duty. It shall be the duty of the
Matron also to superintend the kitchen, the cooking, the washing
and ironing, and take care of the clothes and bedding and see that
they are always clean and in good order.

"ART. 8. It shall be the duty of the Assistant Physician to

ascertain and record the history of each case and keep a diary of the same so long as the patient shall remain in the Asylum. He shall see all the patients at least once a day and such of the males as are under medical treatment oftener if necessary, and report the results of his observations to the Superintendent. He shall look to the warmth, cleanliness and ventilation of the halls, to the exercise and amusements of the patients, and see that the patients are properly treated, and do any other duty connected with the medical department of the Asylum required by the Superintendent. He shall wait upon company, give them all suitable information, and show such part of the building and grounds as are open to their examination.

"ART. 9. It shall be the duty of the Apothecary to take care of the office, prepare and put up all medicine, see that all prescriptions be properly administered, and ascertain as far as may be, the effect of the same. He shall perform the duties of librarian and take care of the books belonging to the library. He shall see to the bathing and shower baths, shall keep the record of the clothing of the male patients as they come and leave the Asylum, and do any other duty required by the Superintendent.

"ART. 10. It shall be the duty of the Auditor in the month of July annually to audit all the accounts of the officers of the Institution, take an inventory of all the property of the corporation, also take an account of all the claims in favor of and against the Institution, so as to show its true standing on the first day of August annually. For which services he shall be paid a reasonable compensation to be fixed by the Trustees.

"ART. 11. That the Trustees shall from time to time fix the price of board of the patients, and no patient shall at any time be admitted for a less price than that prefixed by the Trustees, or by their direction, and upon the admission of patients to the Asylum good security shall in all cases be required.

"ART. 12. No moneys shall be expended or debts contracted, except for the ordinary expenses of the establishment, unless directed by the Trustees.

ART. 13. Every officer receiving and paying out the moneys of the Institution shall keep a regular cash account of all moneys received and from whom received, and all moneys paid out and to whom paid and for what purpose paid, which amount shall be laid before the Trustees at their meeting for their examination.

"ART. 14. The Superintendent shall lay before the Trustees at each monthly meeting a statement of the number of patients received, discharged or deceased during the month previous, stating the name and place of residence of each patient, the time of their admission with the security taken therefor, the time of their discharge or decease, and if discharged, whether cured or improved or not."

"After adopting the foregoing By-Laws and examining into the concerns of the Institution, and condition of the patients, made choice of the following officers until the next annual meeting, to wit :

OFFICERS OF THE BOARD.

Samuel Clark, Chairman.
N. B. Williston, Treasurer.
Asa Keyes, Secretary.
Asa Keyes, Auditor.

RESIDENT OFFICERS.

Wm. H. Rockwell, Superintendent.
——— Farmer.
Deborah K. Baker, Matron,
David T. Brown, Assistant Physician.
Henry M. Booth, Apothecary.*

" *Voted*, To send a special agent to the Legislature the approaching session, to attend to the interests of the Asylum before the Legislature, and to procure an increase of the appropriation for the insane poor, and Asa Keyes was chosen such special agent."

The Legislature of this year passed the following Act, which was approved October 27th, 1845, and remained without alteration for near thirty years. It is introduced as showing that the annual sum drawn from the State during this period, was for the care of the insane poor and no other purpose ; many seeming to entertain the impression that it was devoted to providing additional room at the Asylum, as the grants previously referred to, except the last, were.

"An Act in addition to an Act for the Relief of the Insane Poor, approved Oct. 30, 1844.

"It is hereby enacted by the General Assembly of the State of Vermont, as follows,—

"Sec. 1. Instead of the sum mentioned in the first section of An Act for the Relief of the Insane Poor, approved October 30, 1844, the Trustees of the Vermont Asylum for the Insane may

---

*The salary of the farmer, at this date was fixed at $300 per annum ; that of the matron at $208 ; of the assistant physician at $300 ; that of the apothecary, board and tuition.

annually in the month of August draw from the Treasury of this State the sum of Five Thousand Dollars, for the purposes expressed in and subject to the provisions of said Act.

"SEC. 2. There shall be annually appointed by the Legislature a Commissioner of the Insane, whose duty it shall be, monthly, or oftener if need be, to visit said Asylum, with the Trustees or alone, to examine into the condition of the Institution, the receipts and expenditures, the management of the patients, and the general welfare of the Asylum, and to make report thereon annually to the Legislature."

This last section was suggested by Dr. Rockwell. While it did not clothe this official with any authority in the management, which from the beginning was vested solely in the Board of Trustees, it gave the State an agent with free visitorial power, to observe and report to the Legislature each year, whether or not the wards or beneficiaries of the State were properly cared for, and whether the money appropriated toward their support at the Institution was or was not applied in the manner provided and designed.

This office of Commissioner of the Insane was continued for thirty-three years, when it was abolished and a Board of Supervisors of the Insane created, with some additional powers.

The cost of the extension of the east wing effected this year was $6,325.66.

THE Trustees' Report of this year contains the following opening paragraph :

"At the time of making our last Report we were suffering for want of sufficient accommodations for our patients. The buildings, which were then in course of erection, have since been completed, and we rejoice to state that we have accommodations for three hundred patients; as large a number as we think can be properly taken care of in one Asylum."

The superintendent reports one hundred and ninety-seven admissions, and one hundred and sixty-nine discharges; two hundred and ninety-one remaining.

Some remarks upon ill-advised visits to patients deserve notice, and are as true now as then :

"Next to premature removals are the injudicious visits of friends and acquaintances. These visits serve to awaken former associations, which greatly disturb the minds of the patients and create a desire to return to their friends. Not unfrequently has the recovery of a patient been retarded weeks and even months, by an injudicious visit. These remarks do not apply with so much force to those cases which are incurable. But frequent visits of friends or acquaintances may make them dissatisfied with their situation, and less comfortable inmates of an institution.

"While on this subject we wish to be distinctly understood. We have *never refused* the immediate *relatives* of the patients from having an interview, and have always allowed them to do so when they have wished it. In some few cases we consider it advisable for the relatives to see the patient, but in most cases we consider it injurious. We always state our opinion candidly to the relatives, of the probable effects of an interview, and then leave it entirely to their own decision. It is left to the discretion of the superintendent whether it is expedient for any but the relatives to have an interview with any particular patient. The relatives often make a special request that the patient shall not be exhibited to his acquaintances, so long as he remains insane."

The following shows the financial result of the year:

Income, $23,758.46
Expenditure,   23,168.05
                                                 _____
Balance on hand August 1,   · $590.41

A purchase was this year effected of forty-nine square rods of land, contiguous to the first purchased estate, for use as a cemetery. This was bought of Mr. Addison Brown, for the sum of $92, and has since been preserved to that use. Cost of construction thereon of a receiving tomb $58.

The following officers were chosen at the annual meeting of this year:

OFFICERS OF THE BOARD.

Samuel Clark, Chairman.
N. B. Williston, Treasurer.
Asa Keyes, Secretary.
Epaphro' Seymour, Auditor.

RESIDENT OFFICERS.

William H. Rockwell, Superintendent.
James M. Shearer, Farmer.
Deborah K. Baker, Matron.
Francis A. Holman, Assistant Physician.
Henry M. Booth, Apothecary.

RECORD OF 1847.

THE continued expansion of the Institution and increase of patients had demonstrated the necessity for more land in connection with it, but the greater necessity of providing buildings and water supply had hitherto precluded additions to the estate.

This year, however, enlargement of the farm came under consideration, and at a special meeting of the Trustees, in April, it was—

Voted, "To purchase of John L. Dickerman the wood lot and pasture owned by him westerly of the Holbrook meadow, of about thirty acres, at his price, being one thousand dollars."

This piece of land was located a mile away from the Asylum in a north-westerly direction, upon the old road to Newfane, and was purchased principally for the fuel growing thereon, of which the Asylum had great need. The right to lay an aqueduct from the Wells spring, through the farm of Newman Allen, was also this year secured. Consideration $40, and the cost of laying the same with logs was $300.

The Trustees in their Report of this year refer especially to the purchase of the wood-lot, as opening a new field for labor. "Since that time," they say, "the patients have been engaged in cutting the wood and timber and clearing the land. We have already ascertained that the wood and timber, with the labor of the patients, will pay for the whole." "Improvements," they add, "have constantly been made on the farm, which furnishes much produce for consumption in the establishment."

This quotation indicates a full realization on the part of the managers, that now and in the future the success of the establishment must rest upon the basis of self-support, and the practical management must be financially that of economy and sagacious foresight. Yet they were not unmindful of the real objects for which the Institution was founded, as the following paragraph shows.

"In our regular visits to the Asylum we have been gratified to notice the neatness and comfort which prevaded every apartment, and the kindness and sympathy manifested for the unfortunates. At the same time there also appeared a systematic regularity and order, evincing a judicious guidance, which was worthy of all praise."

During the year past one hundred and thirty-five were received, and one hundred and twenty-two were discharged ; remaining, three hundred and four.

The Superintendent notes "That the printing of the Asylum Journal has been discontinued in consequence of the recovery of the printers, who have left the Asylum."

This enterprise deserves to be enlarged upon. Begun in November, 1842, it ended with the year 1846. Its history is intimately connected with that of one of the inmates of this early day :

On the 15th of July, 1842, there was admitted to the Asylum a young man from the northernmost county of the State of New Hampshire, 17 years of age, by trade a printer, four weeks deranged, and laboring under maniacal excitement characterized by exaggerated personal ideas of greatness, dominant in which was the delusion that he was to be a second Franklin.

This morbid exaltation of mind continued, together with other deranged manifestations, according to the record for two months, when symptoms of improvement began to be evident. On the 21st of October following his admission, he had so far improved that he was allowed to go to the Phœnix office to work at his trade, though he was still in a vacillating state of mind.

On the 25th of the same month he is reported as "setting up type for a newspaper," and on the 29th he brought home the proof sheet of the Asylum Journal, the first number of a series, which was continued as a weekly production for two years, and as a monthly publication for two years more, as already stated.

For three months this little sheet was regularly issued from the Phœnix Office, when its success became so well assured a printing press was purchased, and afterward the office of the Journal was at the "White House," the original Asylum building, on the present site of the "Marsh Building." For a year this young man was both editor aud publisher. November 1, 1843, just one year after the date of the first issue, it is recorded "That he went home entirely well,—that he printed it with great ability for one of his age, and wrote some able articles for its columns, and that he had been highly complimented for its mechanical execution, and its good appearance."

November 26, 1844, appears a subsequent entry, " That the Journal has been continued another year, and printed by the same party," who appears to have been employed, at least for this service, by the Asylum. Exactly how it was conducted the last two years, does not fully appear ; but the further history of the young man does not cease here. He was for a time foreman in the Phœnix office, at the time that paper was owned and managed by William E. Ryther.   From Brattleboro he went to North Adams, Mass., to take charge of a newspaper, and thence to Michigan, where he was identified with the Detroit Tribune and subsequently became editor and proprietor of the Lansing Republican, the State paper of Michigan, and was the head of the State Printing Firm at the time of his decease in 1881.

At the monthly meeting in August of this year the annual choice of officers was made, as follows :

OFFICERS OF THE BOARD.

Samuel Clark, Chairman.

N. B. Williston, Treasurer.

Asa Keyes, Secretary.

Election of auditor postponed.

RESIEENT OFFICERS.

Wm. H. Rockwell, Superintendent.

James M. Shearer, Farmer.

Deborah K. Baker, Matron.

Francis A. Holman, Assistant Physician.

Henry M. Booth, Apothecary.

At the September meeting, Mr. Seymour having resigned, Jonathan Dorr Bradley was chosen Trustee in his stead.

On the 16th of November, a special meeting was called, when it was *Voted*, "That the Trustees will the next season extend the center building twenty-five feet in front,* and will raise the roof of the same at some convenient height, say, six, eight or ten feet in the discretion of the committee.

" *Voted,* also, To extend the return wing of the east wing extension eighteen feet.

" *Voted,* That Wm. H. Rockwell and N. B. Williston be a committee to erect said buildings."

At the December meeting this year J. D. Bradley was chosen Auditor.

The financial statement shows:—

Income,	$26,720.09
Expenditure,	26,445.80
Balance on hand,	$274.29

*NOTE. The extension of the center building was made thirty-three feet, instead of twenty-five as per foregoing vote.

A T the monthly meeting in March of this year, the Trustees *Voted*, "To buy the west part of the Stephen Bennett farm, of about fifty acres, for pasture and wood lot." (Situated on the old Newfane road.) This was effected on the 16th of the same month, at a cost of $800.

The enlargement of the center building, and extension of the east wing in its northern section, were under way at the time of making up the Annual Report for this year, and were practically completed before the close of the year.

The Superintendent in his Report for this year enlarges upon the labor question, in a manner that evinces the steadfast convictions of his mind, and conveys to the reader no uncertain ring. The following extracts illustrate his views.

"All out-door employment in which the insane can be interested, has a salutary effect.

"At every Lunatic Asylum there will be much mechanical labor to be performed, such as repairing buildings and fences, making and mending both furniture and utensils, clothing, and many other kinds of work necessary for the use and comfort of the establishment. They give every mechanic, and those who have a mechanical genius, an opportunity to engage in that kind of labor in which he takes the most interest and delight.

' "From all these varieties of manual labor there will be some pecuniary profit. The great benefit resulting from manual labor connected with a lunatic asylum however, cannot be reckoned in dollars and cents. Its advantages can only be estimated as one of the most efficient means for the restoration of the curable, and for the cheerfulness, enjoyment and comfort of the incurable.

"Where one patient can be interested to take charge of another, the effect will be highly salutary to both. The ways in which this can be accomplished are numerous. A patient with sufficient tact and ingenuity, when encouraged by the officers, can engage many patients in this manner. This is one of the most beneficial employments in which a patient can be occupied."

The writer is well aware that the latter assertion is open to criticism, nevertheless it was a rule of action with Dr. Rockwell; and one method in which it was practised was in the matter of giving a parole for purposes of exercise, to two or three, charging each with looking after the others, thus creating a joint responsibility which was felt by all individually.

At the August meeting the annual election of officers was postponed, the full Board not being present, but at the November meeting the following officers were appointed:

OFFICERS OF THE BOARD.

Samuel Clark, Chairman,
Nathan B. Williston, Treasurer,
Asa Keyes, Secretary,
J. D. Bradley, Auditor,

RESIDENT OFFICERS.

Wm. H. Rockwell, Superintendent,
James M. Shearer, Farmer,
Deborah K. Baker, Matron,
Francis A. Holman, Assistant Physician.
———— ————, Apothecary.

Voted, "To ratify the purchase of a piece of land and water right, purchased of Charles Chapin, Nov. 2nd, 1848, for $150."

This included about one acre of land on the west side of the Newfane road, and just beyond the house of Houghton Pike, subsequently owned by David Miller, and sold by him to the Asylum.

The movement of population as shown by the Superintendent's Report, was one hundred and fifty-six admitted, and one hundred and forty-eight discharged, three hundred and twelve remaining.

The income was,	$31,295.34
The expenditure,	30,975.93
Balance on hand,	$319.41

The cost of making the enlargements to center building and north section of east wing this year was $6,485.99.

RECORD OF 1849.

THE Institution this year rejoices over the extensions of capacity, and increased facilities for performing the domestic work, which were effected and introduced last year.

These are referred to in the Report of the Superintendent in detail, as follows:

"Our new buildings were completed soon after submitting our last Report. The increased size and improved arrangement of the chapel is a very good improvement, and furnishes ample room for all of the patients who wish to attend the religious exercises on the Sabbath. The enlargement of the cooking and washing departments, and the introduction of new apparatus for both, have greatly added to the facilities and comforts of those employed in them.

"The addition to the north female wing was greatly needed, both on account of the additional room thereby afforded, and also for the more perfect classification of the patients.

"Two cisterns have been constructed for the purpose of affording a sufficient quantity of water in case of fire. Each cistern contains between eighty and ninety hogsheads of water, and both are constantly kept full. There is one on each side of the center building, and if a fire should happen a good supply of water would be ready for use."

One hundred and thirty-six patients were admitted during the year, and one hundred and thirty were discharged; leaving, August 1st, three hundred and eighteen under treatment.

The income received was,	$35,825.09
The expenditure,	35,110.23
Leaving balance on hand of,	$714.86

The following officers were elected at the annual meeting in August, for the year ensuing:—

OFFICERS OF THE BOARD.

Samuel Clark, Chairman,
N. B. Williston, Treasurer,
Asa Keyes, Secretary,
J. D. Bradley, Auditor,

" And the said Deborah K. Baker having declined accepting said appointment as matron, on account of other engagements heretofore made, Abigail Rockwell of South Windsor, Conn., was chosen matron," to succeed her.

One of the most important additions ever made to the Asylum estate, was this year realized by the purchase of John R. Blake, Sept. 22nd 1849, of the tract of land lying between the main buildings and the village common, and extending easterly to the Putney road, comprising an area of sixteen acres, since devoted to pleasure grounds and culinary garden.

It will be remembered that the original purchase of Nathan Woodcock included the "White House" upon the west side of the road surrounded by a couple of acres of land, and four acres of the terrace in front upon the east side of the road, which together with that now secured of Mr. Blake, embraced the plateau of twenty acres.

On these four acres were commenced the permanent buildings and already the surrounding area was inconveniently cramped, and the outlook from the buildings unsightly by reason of the unimproved lot lying in front.   The price paid for this important tract was $3,500.

Forthwith was effected a vast change in the attractiveness of the surroundings.   The post and rail fence separating the immediate Asylum premises from this field, stretching along the whole frontage and within a half dozen rods of the building the whole way was at once removed, and much done by clearing away all undesirable objects preparatory to opening walks and laying out a garden, the following year.

About one acre of meadow land contiguous to that already owned by the Asylum was also this year secured of Newman Allen (Oct. 15, 1849) at $180.   Also a tract of land of Samuel Thomas, situated upon Chesterfield mountain (25 acres) valuable only for fuel, at a cost of $250.   Deed dated September 15, 1849.

RECORD OF 1850.

I N May of this year the Asylum premises were further enlarged by one-half acre of land upon the west side of the Putney road, bought of Nelson Crosby, for $100.

Much was accomplished this year toward changing the immediate environment of the establishment.

An entrance walk through the newly acquired field in front was made from the street at the foot of the hill, and_it was in June of this year that the hemlock hedge, bordering it on both sides, was set out, which has ever since constituted one of the most perfect and noticeable artificial features of the grounds.

The kitchen garden was also located at the east end of the plateau, where it has ever since been continued.

One hundred and fifty patients were this year admitted, and one hundred and forty discharged ; leaving three hundred and twenty-eight at date of the annual Report.

Concerning the general course of treatment pursued the Superintendent remarks as follows:—

"The same regard to exercise and employment in the open air for our patients; the same care for exercise and amusements in the establishment; the same endeavors to employ everyone in a manner best adapted to his taste, and calculated to divert his mind from its delusions; the same provision of plenty of wholesome and nourishing food; the same attention to the proper temperature and ventilation of all the apartments of the building, and the same desire to furnish the patients with all the nameless variety of comforts, adapted to each individual case, has been pursued and been attended with the same gratifying results that have crowned our former exertions."

At the annual meeting the following officers were chosen:

OFFICERS OF THE BOARD.

Samuel Clark, Chairman.
N. B. Williston, Treasurer.
Asa Keyes, Secretary.
J. D. Bradley, Auditor.

William H. Rockwell, Superintendent,
Warren E. Eason, Farmer,
Abigail Rockwell, Matron,
Oliver S. Lovejoy, Assistant Physician.
——— ———, Apothecary.

The income for the year was,   34,240.12
The expenditure,   33,868.93

Leaving balance of,   371.19

In the autumn of this year (Sept. 12, 1850) a little more than three acres of meadow land was purchased of Newman Allen, contiguous to that bought last year, for which $482 was paid.

At the December meeting this year it was *Voted* "To have an alarm bell to use in case of fire, and J. D. Bradley and Dr. Rockwell were appointed a committee to procure and hang said bell; and it was also *Voted*, That said committee be instructed to examine every part of the Asylum thoroughly, and make all necessary improvements to protect the buildings against fire."

This action was undoubtedly suggested by the melancholy and disastrous fire by which great loss of life and property was occasioned, at the Maine Insane Hospital the same month.

A farm barn, one hundred feet in length by forty in width, was this year built upon the edge of the meadow, and a horse shed also erected. The cost of both was $1100.

A T a meeting of the Trustees, held July 23rd. this year, it was *Voted* "To bring the water from the Wells Spring in an iron pipe of three inch bore, and William H. Rockwell is appointed a committee to procure this pipe, and lay it down. Also " *Voted*, To build eighteen feet in addition to the east wing extension; and Dr. William H. Rockwell is appointed a committee to erect said building."

This work was at once commenced, as appears by the Trustees' Report of this year, from the following quotations:—

"We have commenced enlarging one of the wings occupied by the female patients, not for the purpose of receiving a larger number, but for the better classification and accommodation of the number we now have."

"The logs, which were laid a few years ago for our aqueduct, [1847] do not bring sufficient water; besides becoming defective they require frequent repairs. It is thought to be the best economy to lay an iron aqueduct in their place. We have accordingly contracted with William A. Wheeler, Esq., of Worcester, Mass., to furnish us with 5000 feet of iron pipe, three inches in diameter, which will supply us with an abundance of that indispensable article to a lunatic asylum, plenty of pure spring water."

The result of the action of the Board at the close of the preceding year, in reference to increasing the safeguards against fire, is thus given in this Report:—

"After the awful calamity which occurred at the insane hospital in Maine the last winter, the Trustees lost no time in investigating the condition of the Vermont Asylum, and its means of preventing and escaping the dangers of fire. The Asylum is located at such a distance from other buildings that little danger is to be apprehended from fire, unless it originates upon its own premises. The cooking ranges in the kitchen are so constructed and managed that they cannot be considered dangerous, and while in use are in charge of careful attendants. The furnaces for warming the buildings are so constructed as to prevent any danger. The furnace chambers, and the smoke and warm air flues are built entirely of brick, and plastered on both sides. There is no wood-work of any description which is connected with them. The partitions of all the rooms occupied by the patients are entirely of brick, on which the plastering is done, and no wooden framing or lathing is used. If, however, a fire should be discovered in any part of the establishment, it is believed it would be extinguished with very little delay. We have two cisterns, one oh each side of the center building, which always contains more than 10,000 gallons of water. We have also a reservoir supplied by springs, elevated nearly one hundred feet above the site of the Asylum, which constantly supplies three cisterns, each of which contains nearly 500 gallons, which are placed in different parts of the attic story. From these cisterns, water is conveyed in pipes to every part of the building, and is delivered by faucets in every hall, so that immediate access can be had to it all times. Fire proof iron doors are placed at every avenue between the center building and the wings, to prevent fire extending from one to the other. A bell of sufficient size has been placed upon one of the buildings to give the alarm, and is never to be rung except in the event of fire. We are sufficiently removed from the village to be out of danger by fire from its buildings, still we are near enough to receive at the shortest notice, the services of a well organized and efficient fire department, and the active cooperation of a public spirited people. With all these resources at hand, the Trustees are of the opinion that the Asylum is so secured against fire as to remove any reasonable doubt. The buildings are so constructed that in event of fire there would be no difficulty in removing the patients."

The Superintendent's Report shows that one hundred and thirty-seven patients were admitted, and one hundred and thirty were discharged; three hundred and thirty-five being inmates, at this date.

An epidemic of dysentery this year is chronicled which prevailed during the months of August and September, 1850:

"Ninety-three patients were attacked by this disease, of whom sixteen died. Of these nearly all were old and incurable cases, and many of them had previously suffered from exhausting bodily infirmity. Besides these nearly all of our attendants and assistants were attacked by the same disease, all of whom recovered. The fidelity, kindness and devotion with which they performed their duties during the prevalence of this epidemic, are worthy of all praise."

The following remarks relative to committals are made by Dr. Rockwell, and have noteworthy merit:—

"There is one class of cases especially which are frequently sent too early to a lunatic asylum. I mean that of puerperal cases. We have repeatedly had women brought to the asylum in less than two weeks from their accouchment. Some of them have recovered very soon, but would probably have recovered as well had they remained at home. Others have died, apparently from exhaustion, who might have recovered had it not been for the exposure and fatigue of the journey."

The election of officers at the annual meeting was postponed to the following month.

The following were then chosen:—

OFFICERS OF THE BOARD.

Samuel Clark, Chairman.
N. B. Williston, Treasurer.
Asa Keyes, Secretary.
    J. D. Bradley, Auditor.

RESIDENT OFFICERS.

William H. Rockwell, Superintendent.
Warren E. Eason, Farmer.
Abigail Rockwell, Matron.
Oliver S. Lovejoy, Assistant Physician.
———— ————, Apothecary.

The income this year was,	$35,423.54
The expenditure,	34,349.66
Balance at date of Report,	$1,073.88

The cost of the iron aqueduct pipe was $1,436.04. The addition to the east wing extension was $2,000.

Obligations are this year accredited to E. Weston, Esq., of Boston for "some elegant castings for a fountain," which were put into use the following year.

RECORD OF 1852.

A T the January meeeting of this year, "Samuel Clark, [the first of the original Trustees] appeared and resigned the said trust, on account of his age and ill health, and thereupon the other three Trustees proceeded to the choice of a chairman, when Asa Keyes was duly elected. And the Board then proceeded to elect a Trustee to fill the vacancy occasioned by the resignation of Samuel Clark, and the ballots being taken and counted, Frederick Holbrook of said Brattleboro was unanimously elected, and being notified and called in, accepted the trust."

At the February meeting the Board passed the following vote: "That we build a building the coming season, for a laundry and wash room, and Dr. Wm. H. Rockwell is appointed a committee to superintend the erection thereof."

Of this, the Trustees say in their Report, "This season we have corrected one mistake in the original construction of the main building. The wash-room was originally situated in the basement, and the steam from that room was diffused throughout the establishment. The consequences of this state of things may be easily imagined. To prevent these evils a separate building has just been erected for a wash-house, drying-room and laundry, and is now occupied for that purpose. We have erected an adjoining building for the boiler for generating steam for the wash-room."

This building was erected in the rear of the east wing, having a corner connection with the north section of the east wing extension, was thirty-six feet long, by thirty-two wide, parallel with, and fifty feet back of the east wing, a court being enclosed thereby on three sides, in the rear of the main line of the buildings east of the center. The cost of this with machinery and fixtures was $4000; and was one of the much needed provisions, as may be inferred by the comments of the Trustees quoted.

The Superintendent reports the reception of one hundred and sixty-one patients, the discharge of one hundred and forty-five, and consequent retention of three hundred and fifty-one, since the last official showing.

The Institution has been over fifteen years in successful operation, but now begins to be foreshadowed some of the perplexities incident to multiplied years, and peculiar to the management of such establishments. Since the opening near two thousand cases. have been treated here, and it could hardly be expected that some individual grievances should not have arisen. Dr. Rockwell very truthfully observes :

" Most of our patients who recover, cherish the kindest feelings towards those who have assisted in their recovery. Many of those who do not recover indulge the same hard feelings towards those that take care of them here, which they entertained towards their best friends before they left home."

The officers chosen this year were:—

OFFICERS OF THE BOARD.

Asa Keyes, Chairman.
N. B. Williston, Treasurer.
J. D. Bradley, Secretary
Frederick Holbrook, Auditor.

RESIDENT OFFICERS.

William H. Rockwell, Superintendent.
Warren Eason, Farmer.
Abigail Rockwell, Matron.
Oliver S. Lovejoy, Assistant Physician.
——— ———, Apothecary.

The income this year was,	$38,290.88
The expenditure,	39,673.96
Leaving an indebtedness of,	$1,383.08

This latter occurred mainly from the purchase of land of Houghton Pike, David W. Miller, Addison Brown and Charles Chapin, all in immediate contiguity to the originally purchased estate, at an aggregate cost of $1255.

At the close of this year (Dec. 15th) about three hundred acres of mountain woodland lying over the Connecticut River, opposite the village of Brattleboro, in the towns of Chesterfield and Hinsdale, N. H., previously secured by Dr. Rockwell, were turned over to the Asylum at a cost of $4,800.

At the Legislative session of this year, the disaffection intimated in the Superintendent's Report, culminated in the appointment of a Committee of Investigation.

The following is the Report of this Committee in full:—

"TO THE SENATE AND HOUSE OF REPRESENTATIVES NOW IN SESSION.

" Your Committee, to whom was referred the memorial of Still-man Morgan, and the petition of Samuel James and eighteen others praying for an investigation of the management of the Vermont Asylum for the Insane, beg leave to report, That they have attended to the duties assigned them; that the Committee' of the Senate and House joined in the investigation, and now beg leave to join in submitting the result of their labors. A great mass of testimony was presented by the petitioners and also on the part of the Asylum.

The principal portion of this testimony on the part of the peti-tioners was that of persons who have heretofore been inmates of the Asylum as patients, and now testify to what they say took place when they were thus inmates of the Asylum. If this testimony were to be received without allowance, and fully relied upon, the Insti-tution would doubtless be open to the censure of the Legislature, and unworthy the patronage of the public. But it will at once be perceived that all testimony of this character must be weighed with great caution, and with a wise and careful discrimination. For such witnesses testify to what they believe took place while they were insane, and while their minds were exercised with bitter hostility towards those they regarded in the light of enemies—and as persons unjustly depriving them of liberty—and seeking to do them the greatest of injuries. Indeed, in some of the cases which came under the observation of the Committee, it was perfectly clear that the wit-ness was narrating not facts which had occurred, but the mere delusions of his own disease. How far these impressions thus vividly impressed on their minds while laboring under aberrations of intellect are truthful, it must of course be very difficult to deter-mine. Testimony of this character considered with that of witnesses who had never been insane, led a part of your committee to believe that some instances had occurred in which the attendants had failed to exercise proper discretion in controlling patients when excited and violent; or in other words, that more force was used than was necessary under the circumstances. Your committee think it would be strange if it were otherwise. In the management of such an Institution for sixteen years, with so great a number of patients and attendants, it would be very remarkable if no such instances had occurred.

Your committee all concur, however, in the opinion that the patients must be held under control, or the usefulness of the

Institution would be wholly lost.   But it is indeed difficult to define the precise degree of force which is necessary to accomplish that object.

Your committee did not differ in opinion so much as to make it necessary to offer more than one report of the result of their investigation, for all concur in the opinion that the Asylum has been well managed; that its management should be rather the subject of commendation than of censure; that untiring pains have been taken to employ respectable and intelligent nurses and attendants; that they have been taken from the families of our highly respectable farmers; that the sanitary rules of the Asylum have been well cared for, and great pains taken in regard to the health of every patient.

Your committee beg leave in conclusion to say, that in their opinion the Asylum in all its departments is as well managed as could be reasonably expected; that its usefulness under the present worthy and skillful superintendent, Doctor Rockwell, and the able Trustees, is increasing from year to year with their increase of means; that it is now highly useful and honorable to the State, and well entitled to the patronage of the public.

Your committee, therefore, respectfully recommend that said petitioners and memorialist have leave to withdraw, all of which is submitted by   JOHN F. DEANE, Chairman.

THIS year opened with plans for still further enlarging the Asylum.

At the February meeting of the Trustees they

Voted, " That Dr. Rockwell be hereby authorized to build the new wing, and enlarge the existing return wing, on the male side of the Asylum, on the plan proposed by him."

This work was immediately taken in hand, and with so much vigor that the Trustees in their Report August 1st say,

" We have erected the west extension wing this season, and also enlarged the west return wing [the north section] by which about seventy rooms have been added to the Asylum.

" These additions were necessary to complete the proper proportions of the building, and, what was of much greater importance, to increase the accommodations for room, and the proper classification of the patients."

The Superintendent in his report of this year, shows one hundred and fifty-nine admitted, and one hundred and thirty-eight discharged, three hundred and seventy-two remaining. An epidemic of an unusual kind is this year noted, and stands singly in the catalogue of annual occurrences.

" During the month of March the small-pox made its appearance in the gallery occupied by the better class of female patients. In what manner this alarming disease was introduced among us remains in some measure a mystery. A short time before the first case occurred a patient was admitted from a section of country where this disease prevailed, although neither herself nor any of her family had been exposed or suffered by it. We know of no other way in which it could have been introduced.

" The first case was very mild in its character [varioloid] and attracted no particular attention. About two weeks afterwards, eight or ten other patients were affected with this disease, three of which were of the confluent form, and were very severe. These were immediately placed in a gallery by themselves [an attic dormitory] attended by nurses who had previously been affected with

the same disease, and were familiar with the proper kind of attention and care which they required. All communication with other
parts of the Asylum, was as far as possible prevented, and every
person connected with the establishment was vaccinated. As soon
as any new case occurred it was immediately removed to the same
gallery.

"The disease continued with us about ten weeks. One of our
nurses, and twenty-seven female patients were attacked by it, and
only one, a female seventy-two years of age, died. None of our
male patients were affected with this disease.

" I should do injustice to my own feelings did I not make honorable mention of all who were in any way employed at this time
in the Asylum. Not one abandoned her post of duty but all appeared
to be actuated by the principle, that 'Whatsoever ye would that
others should do to you, do ye even so to them.' May they have
their reward."

Great credit is due Dr. Rockwell for his wise foresight and
judicious management on this occasion, as well as for his own personal devotion to those who fell victims to the infection.

At the outbreak of the malady a panic occurred among employes
and their friends, who on the impulse of the moment were prompted
and tempted to forsake their positions.

Dr. Rockwell calmly reminded them that they had already
been exposed before the danger was recognized, but that every pre-
caution had now been taken; if attacked they would be cared for;
while to leave and go to their several homes would be to incur
the risk of spreading the disease broadcast, and especially among
their own families. This sober second thought prevailed, and the
result attested the wisdom of their decision.

During the whole epidemic. Dr. Rockwell alone performed the
medical service, leaving to his assistant the professional charge
of the non-infected portion of the household.

The following officers were elected at the annual meeting:—

OFFICERS OF THE BOARD.

Asa Keyes, Chairman.
N. B. Williston, Treasurer.
J. D. Bradley, Secretary.
Frederick Holbrook, Auditor.

RESIDENT OFFICERS.

Wm. H. Rockwell, Superintendent.
Warren E. Eason, Farmer.
Abigail Rockwell, Matron.
B. W. Chase, Assistant Physician.
——— ———, Apothecary.

Income this year received, $40,305.73
Expenditure,   41,877.18
                                                              _____
Leaving an indebtedness of, $1,571.45

A piggery was this year built; cost $500. The cost of the west wing addition and extension this year, was $8000. One half acre of land, at the corner of Chase and Asylum streets, was this year purchased of W. E. Eason for $300, and thirty-six acres of the Eben Wells farm for $3700.

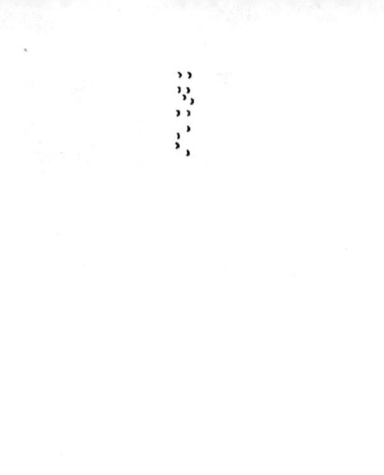

THE VERMONT ASYLUM 1854

THE work of this year commenced with the removal of a line of wooden buildings situated in the rear of the west wing of the main buildings, preparatory to the construction of more permanent ones.

The Trustees in their Report of this year say, "They have erected a new brick building, eighty feet in length, and forty in breadth, with a cellar under the whole, the same being divided into various apartments, which makes it a very convenient and commodious store-house." The cost of this building was $4000.

"Great and permanent improvements," say the Trustees, "have been constantly made on the farm, and especially for the last two years. The products have greatly increased, and those of this year have far exceeded those of any former one.

"It was found there was not sufficient cultivated land belonging to the Asylum to furnish adequate employment for the male patients in the open air. We also needed a large increase of pasture land for the purpose of keeping a sufficient number of cows on our own land. The patients are generally fond of milk, and the excellent fresh article which is furnished from the farm affords a healthy diet.

"We have accordingly purchased most of the farm belonging to the late Eben Wells, Esq., containing, originally, over two hundred acres. We shall now be enabled to keep a large number of cows, besides having some excellent land for tillage. The additional employment furnished our male patients by this means greatly increases the facilities for their restoration."

The Superintendent likewise refers this year to the great improvements made upon the farm and garden by which greatly increased productiveness has been realized, and says, "For these improvements we are under the greatest obligations to Hon. F. Holbrook for the interest, advice and personal attention which he has so generously bestowed upon them." This interest, it may here be remarked, has never waned; and through all the subsequent years the development of the resources of the farm has been his special study and particular labor of love.   Under his direction the meadow has been drained and made to yield under cultivation almost all crops, and land too wet for ploughing has been brought into English bearing grass, while the run out pasture lands have likewise been tilled and restored.

One hundred and sixty-three patients were this year received, and one hundred and forty-six discharged.   Three hundred and eighty-nine were in the Asylum at date of the Report.

A balance against the Institution is this year shown of $701.87. The income being, $44,492.33
The expenditure,   45,194.20
The officers elected at the annual meeting were:—

OFFICERS OF THE BOARD.

Asa Keyes, Chairman.
N. B. Williston, Treasurer.
Wm. H. Rockwell, Secretary.
Frederick Holbrook, Auditor.

RESIDENT OFFICERS.

Wm. H. Rockwell, Superintendent.
Warren E. Eason, Farmer.
Abigail Rockwell, Matron.
Henry M. Booth, Assistant Physician.

The bulk of the Eben Wells farm, this year purchased, cost $5,185.   A small piece of land was also bought of Nelson Crosby for $90, which included a slate ledge, yielding suitable stone for the foundation walls of buildings.

It is gratifying here to note that while the Trustees were greatly engrossed in the development of the Institution according to will of the founder, they did not lose sight of their obligations toward those who were committed to its care, and for whose benefit it was created.

At their May meeting this year, at the suggestion of Mr. J. D. Bradley, it was *Voted*, "That the several wards be numbered, and blank interrogatories be printed [as per form furnished] and that each attendant answer them each month."

The following are the questions:—

1.   In which ward or department have you rendered services during the past month? and in what capacity?

2.   Has any violence or constraint been used towards any patient in your ward, other than that ordinarily incident to mere detention?

3. If so, towards what patient?

4. By whom was it ordered?

5. For what cause?

6. To what extent or degree?

7. Who were present?

8. What were the circumstances?

9. Has any patient, during the past month, used any violence against any attendant or other patient, or against himself?

10. If so, state the circumstances.

11. Whether you were present? and from whom your information was derived, and who were present?

12. Have you known in this Institution during the past month, of any misconduct on the part of any attendant toward any patient?

13. Or of any neglect of duty on the part of any attendant?

14. Or of any act of any attendant showing a temper unfit for the care of insane patients, or showing a want of the special patience and forbearance which such a trust requires? If so, state particulars.

15. Has any patient in your ward attempted any escape during the past month?

16. If so, state the circumstances, and how far the attempt succeeded.

17. Do you assume the duty, so long as you shall be connected with this Asylum, of giving each month candid answers to the foregoing questions?

This requirement, thus instituted, continued in force for some ten years, when it fell into disuse.

RECORD OF 1855.

A T the first meeting of the Trustees this year it was *Voted*, "To engage Jacob Catlin as apothecary to the Institution, with an annual salary of two hundred dollars."
This office, although created by the Trustees, it will be noticed had never been regularly filled, and was often left vacant at the annual elections. But the continued increase of numbers now made it necessary to fill it, and add to it a suitable salary, as seen above.

At the February meeting of the Board it was *Voted*, "That W. H. Rockwell be hereby directed to build an infirmary for the male department of the Institution, and that said building be made of brick, and be constructed with the greatest practicable safety against fire ; and also one for females."

This work was immediately entered upon and practically completed during this year. The site for the building, in connection with the male department, was secured by removing the rear wing of the "White House," and was constructed sixty feet long by thirty-six feet wide, and two stories in height. That for the female department was connected with the new laundry building, of the same width and height as the latter, and extended westward fifty feet, in the rear of the center building.

The erection of these two wings seems to have been suggested by the epidemic experiences of the immediately preceding years.

The Trustees in their Report of this year say, "Our accommodations for the sick, heretofore, have been as good probably as those in other similar establishments, but in all institutions of this kind there should be a hospital department, where the sick can be removed from all annoyance, and where the immediate friends can, if they desire, bestow their kind attention and sympathy."

In addition to the work of building, it became necessary this year to take measures for the protection of the bank in the rear of the buildings, lest the foundations of the latter be weakened from the washings of heavy rains, the descent from the building plateau to the meadow below being some sixty feet in the perpendicular height. To secure this, a foot-wall two hundred and sixty-four feet in length, eight feet in height, and six feet in thickness was constructed, which still remains.

The Superintendent reports that one hundred and sixty-four patients were received since the last Report, and one hundred and fifty-nine were discharged during the same period, three hundred and ninety-four remaining.

Immediately after the date of the last Report, another epidemic of dysentery seized upon the household, and continued with unabated severity through the hot season of 1854.

Of this Dr. Rockwell says, "When a disorder of this kind obtains a foothold in a building where there is a large assemblage of persons, there is sufficient effluvia arising from the sick, to vitiate to a greater or less degree the surrounding atmosphere, and unquestionably many persons are attacked who otherwise might have escaped.

"To be in readiness for emergencies of this kind in future, we have commenced the erection of two infirmaries, one for males and the other for females. By isolating the sick in this manner the physician can visit them frequently during the day and night, without disturbing others or exciting their fears ; and at the same time the rest of the household are free from the exposure which must otherwise exist."

In this case the provision thus planned proved analagous to putting a lock upon the stable door after the horse had been stolen. No epidemic of any kind has since then gained a foothold, and the buildings created for this emergency have been devoted to ordinary occupancy.

It may be remarked that all the three epidemics now noted were in reality endemics. They did not prevail in the surrounding population. Beyond a doubt the dysenteries were of local origin. The causes for this are at this distance of time necessarily more or less speculative, but in all probability they were external to the buildings, else each year would have developed more or less of the malady. At that time malarial influences were less understood than now, but looking at certain facts existing at that period, in the light of to-day, it does not seem difficult to arrive at the probable secret of these special outbreaks.

The sewers from the beginning of the establishment opened out upon the slope in the rear of the buildings, and the sewage was conducted in spouts to the meadow level, where was situated a compost bed which took up at first the liquid discharges, but after this they were absorbed by the meadow bottom.

At the time of the first epidemic the meadow had not been drained, and it is remembered that the season was unusually dry. The unusual evaporation from this stagnant deposit undoubtedly gave rise to the development of the germs of disease which were wafted by the prevailing winds to the contiguous buildings, thus in all probability, giving rise to the disorder therein developed.

At the time of the present epidemic the conditions were similar as to drought, but the drainage had been effected. Advantage had, however, been taken of the dry time to grade to some extent the meadow surface, and in doing this the ground saturated for many years with sewage deposits, had been broken and turned over to a large extent, hence setting free again the germs to be borne by the same wind currents toward the buildings, to be followed by like unsanitary effects. Howbeit, no subsequent like experiences have resulted, since the sewage was thus provided with a direct channel to the river, and the meadow ceased to absorb and retain it.

The income this year was, $49,805.11
The expenditure,   50,924.42
                                                 _____
Balance against the Asylum, $1,119.31

At the annual meeting this year it was *Voted*, "To appoint annually two assistant physicians to the Vermont Asylum."

Made choice of the following officers:—

OFFICERS OF THE BOARD.

Asa Keyes, Chairman.
N. B. Williston, Treasurer.
W. H. Rockwell, Secretary.
F. Holbrook, Auditor.

RESIDENT OFFICERS.

W. H. Rockwell, Superintendent.
W. E. Eason, Farmer.
Abigail Rockwell, Matron.
E. R. Chapin, ⎱ Assistant Physicians·
H. M. Booth, ⎰
Jacob Catlin, Apothecary.

At this meeting it was *Voted*, To purchase certain lands upon the mountain side for purposes of fuel, which was done at a cost of $450, by deed dated December 28th.

This purchase was made of Dr. Rockwell, who had previously secured the same, and was contiguous to that likewise secured by him in 1852. Fifty acres adjoining this was also purchased of John L. Sargent, December 28th for $210.

A wood-house was this year built at the Marsh Building cost, $400. The cost of the two infirmaries was $5,000 each. Total, $10,000.

It is a matter of record that Mr. Keyes was this year deputed to procure an Act of the Legislature providing for the appointment of a medical examiner, whose duty it should be to certify to the insanity of applicants for admission to the Asylum; no statute heretofore existing relative to this requirement.

THIS year opened with no new plans for enlargement. It will be seen that more than ordinary expenditures and liabilities were incurred the preceding year, both in new erections and in securing additional land. This year therefore it was necessary to suspend fresh outlays.

At the February meeting it was *Voted*, "That the Superintendent furnish, as soon as may be, sufficient ladders for all the buildings of the Asylum," and it seems to have been a year devoted mainly to the current work of the Asylum, professionally and otherwise.

One hundred and seventy-two patients are reported as having been received during the preceding year, and one hundred and fifty-nine discharged; four hundred and seven remaining August 1st.

The Report of the Superintendent is largely given to the discussion of insanity, and the practical bearings of its treatment. The following quotations show its drift:

"However mysterious and incomprehensible the operations of the human mind in the natural state, the brain, the organ by which the mind is manifested, must be in a sound and healthy condition.

"Insanity is frequently the result of an impression made upon the brain by some sudden and powerful emotion, or prolonged and inordinate action of the mind. The brain in such instances is usually prepared or rendered liable to the influence of such impressions, either from development of a constitutional predisposition or from disease in itself, or from sympathy with some other diseased organ, or from debility in common with the general powers of the whole system.

"But in whatever manner insanity occurs, a continual exposure to the exciting cause that gave rise to it would evidently have a strong tendency to increase the difficulty. Therefore it becomes the imperative duty of the responsible friends of a deranged person

to remove him at once from the associations by which he is surrounded at the time of the attack, and to place him in a hospital for
the insane, where alone such diseases can be treated with much
chance of success.

"Although it is very desirable that cases of insanity should
be placed in some proper Asylum in the early stages of the disease,
still, we would caution those who are interested not to bring their
friends who are afflicted with other diseases, or before their insanity
is fully developed. It is no uncommon circumstance to have sent
us a case in the early stage of delirium, and while suffering from
acute bodily disease. When they reach us they frequently are
too feeble to be returned to their homes. These cases frequently
prove fatal, and death in many instances is hastened by the exposure and fatigue of the journey.

"The removal of patients before they have had a fair trial is fortunately becoming less common than in former years. From this
Asylum they are seldom prematurely removed, save occasionally
under circumstances which the following case will illustrate.

"A young married lady had been a few weeks in the Asylum, and
was rapidly convalescing. When she came she was in a highly
excited state, and her mind was filled with the strangest delusions.
She had now become more calm. The delusions had nearly all
faded away, and she began to be conscious of her situation. But
her mind was still in a very weak state, liable to a relapse at any
moment, and the greatest caution was necessary to keep from her all
extraneous excitement. At this critical period her husband came to
see her. He was charged with a common idea that there might
be something in his presence that would have a happy influence
upon the mind of his wife. We endeavored to dissuade him from
seeing her, but his mind was fully made up to take the risk. He
found her much better than he expected, and she seemed better the
longer he talked with her. She asked after every member of
the family, and said she was glad he had come for her. His mind
was not made up to take her away just at present, but she talked so
well, and had so clear a recognition of her past situation, that
he could not resist the eloquence of her arguments and appeals, and
they went home together. The result was anticipated by us. Her
mind soon gave way under the rush of old associations and new excitements, and she was brought back again in a worse condition than
at first. It will be a long time before she will be so near well again,
and it will be fortunate indeed if she is not a confirmed lunatic."

At the annual meeting this year the Trustees made choice of the following officers:—

OFFICERS OF THE BOARD.

Asa Keyes, Chairman.
N. B. Williston, Treasurer.
W. H. Rockwell, Secretary.
Frederick Holbrook, Auditor.

RESIDENT OFFICERS.

W. H. Rockwell, Superintendent and Physician.
Warren E. Eason, Farmer.
Abigail Rockwell, Matron.
E. R. Chapin, } Assistant Physicians.
J. P. Clement, }
W. H. Rockwell, Jr., Clerk.

The office of apothecary here ceases.

The income this year was,	$53,609.03
The expenditure,	53,161.59
Balance in treasury,	$447.44

At the September meeting the Trustees *Voted*, "That W. H. Rockwell be authorized to remove the building called the 'White House,' and to erect on the same site another building made of brick, and to be constructed with the greatest practicable safety against fire.

"Also, *Voted*, To give a site for the school-house on the common and move it on the same, provided the school district would consent to have it done."

The school district, on the 10th of this same month, acceded to this proposition, "On condition that the Asylum furnish a site and build a new building, of one school room, to the acceptance of a committee appointed for that purpose; the material of the old house to be used as far as practicable."

The work of the removal and re-location of the school house was entered upon without delay, and effected during the autumn and winter succeeding.

THE MARSH BUILDING: 1857

E ARLY this year a wood lot of fifteen acres, upon the West River road in Brattleboro, but disconnected from the Asylum estate proper, was purchased of P. B. Francis at a cost of $300.

On the 30th of March the Trustees formally turned over the reconstructed school-house, and gave to the school district a deed of the new site at the corner of Chase and Asylum streets, where it still stands. By this was accomplished the desired object of freeing the village common of all obstructions to the view from the Asylum in front.

The Congregational church, which also formerly stood upon that ground, was removed to its present site on Main street in 1842. The grounds of the Asylum and those of the village common, being both laid out in walks and planted with trees, and separated from each other only by a low hedge of buck thorn and Osage orange, along the brow of the hill, now gave to the stranger the appearance of an extended and continuous park; an effect alike advantageous to the Asylum and the village.

Land, small in area, was also this spring purchased in contiguity with the Chase street school-house, of the Misses Crosby, for $600.

At the April meeting it was *Voted*, by the Trustees, "That Frederick Holbrook and W. H. Rockwell be authorized to build an addition to the center building, for the purpose of protecting the records of the Institution against any destruction by fire."

It was determined by the committee that fire proof safes in the offices would meet best the requirement, and such were accordingly procured.

"In noticing the events of the past year," say the Trustees, "steady and regular improvements have been made for promoting the comfort and restoration of the patients.

"Last fall we removed the old wooden building with which we first commenced operations. On the same site we are now erecting a larger building of brick, and better adapted for the purposes of the Institution. It is one hundred feet in length, thirty-seven feet in breadth, and three stories in height. When completed it will greatly increase our facilities for the classification and treatment of its inmates.

"During the past year great improvements have been made on the common in front of the Asylum. The school-house and buildings connected with it have been removed. Much labor and cost has been expended in improving the grounds, laying out walks, transplanting trees, and otherwise beautifying the grounds, all of which has contributed to make the view from the Asylum pleasant and delightful."

The Superintendent's Report shows one hundred and forty-seven admitted, one hundred and forty-one discharged, four hundred and thirteen remaining.

Dr. Rockwell refers in this particularly to the burdens felt by the relatives of the insane, in the following graphic manner:

"The families of insane persons have often an amount of trials and perplexities to endure, and difficulties to overcome, before they make up their minds to remove their afflicted friends to an asylum for the insane, that few individuals, besides those in charge of such institutions, have any adequate conception of.

"In the course of our inquiries into the circumstances that may have had weight in giving rise to a disorder of the mind, we are often made acquainted with many sad experiences on the part of the distracted family, that are scarcely to be equalled in intensity, in any other of the numerous misfortunes of life. None but they can know how terrible a shock to them is the discovery that one of their number has become insane. The disease sometimes comes on suddenly, following severe illness, or some overwhelming misfortune; but oftener its approach is by slow degrees, frequently giving rise to no suspicion of its presence, until some overt act forces the sudden conviction that the past vagaries of the mind are all evidences of insanity. The long growing eccentricities and irregularities of conduct, that had caused much sorrow and bitterness of feeling, and perhaps estrangements between individual members of a family are thus accounted for, and their hearts are filled with sorrow as they reflect upon the unjust and unholy thoughts they have so long harbored against an innocent relative.

"Perhaps the trial is as hard to be borne when the fond mother becomes the unhappy victim to this dread disorder. She, upon whom they had leaned in the hour of sickness and trial, the center of all their affections, has become changed by this mysterious malady into a being strange and all unlike herself. The integrity of the family circle is broken by this sad calamity, and like the affliction of death it seems to bind the remaining members more closely together. They naturally resolve to spare no efforts to soothe their mother's excited or perverted spirit, and win it back to reason again. They · strive to anticipate every wish, and oppose her will in nothing. Above all they endeavor to avoid anything that may irritate a sensitive mind. Thus weeks and months roll on, and though their efforts are redoubled with the increasing extravagancies of their insane parent it is usually of no avail, and the disease goes on increasing in intensity, and unknown to them perhaps the very sacrifices and efforts they are making to allay the malady only tend to increase its force. At length to her everything appears changed. The strongest attachments become objects of suspicion, distrust and enmity. Her husband appears cold, indifferent and careless of her comfort. She fancies the hearts of her children are turned against their mother. In vain with kindness and caresses all try to dispel these painful illusions, with strongest arguments and appeals to her better judgment. At this stage of her disorder it is evidently the true interest of all parties to remove the afflicted person to a hospital especially adapted and designed for the treatment of disorders of the mind. But one who has no experience in such matters would be surprised to learn the obstacles, real and imaginary, that lay in the way of such an apparently simple act of duty and interest. Often by the difference of opinion among the immediate relatives, friends and acquaintances of the patient, through indecision, false pride and other motives, she remains at home until her case has become incurable. · After it is too late the friends vainly regret that they had not in due season used the proper means for her recovery."

The Report shows the income to have been, $55,745.43

The expenditure,   56,238.12

Leaving balance against Asylum of, $492.69

The Trustees at their annual meeting made choice of the following :—

At the October meeting the Trustees *Voted*, " To purchase the Prouty lot," so called, which was negotiated for and secured of Nathaniel Samson and Charles S. Prouty, together, for the aggregate sum of $2010. Cost of Marsh building $10,000.

Thus far the year had been one of unequaled financial prosperity, but it was not destined to close without a reverse. The large farm barn, erected in 1850, was, with all its contents, in the last month of this year totally destroyed by fire. The Trustees lost no time in taking steps toward replacing the same, as appears by the . following record on the second Monday of December :

" *Voted*, That the Superintendent make the necessary preparations for the erection of a new barn early in the spring."

The village newspaper [The Phœnix] of December 12th, gives the following detail of this occurrence :

"ANOTHER FIRE IN BRATTLEBORO—MORE INCENDIARISM.

" Just three months from the great fire in September the torch of the incendiary was lighted in our village. About half past eight o'clock on Saturday evening the large barn connected with the Vermont Asylum for the Insane was discovered to be completely on fire. Upon immediate inspection the doors at the north end, which had been closed for the night, were found sufficiently open to admit the passage of a man. As that was the windward as well as the rear end of the barn, the incendiary had selected it for his ingress and egress. The barn was so thoroughly on fire, the flames being facilitated by the cellar below and ventilator above, that it was found impossible to release the cattle from their stalls, or in any way arrest the progress of the devouring element. Consequently the barn, which was 100 feet long by 40 wide, with about 100 tons of hay, eighteen selected cows, six oxen and five calves were destroyed. The cattle were probably all dead when the fire was discovered, as they were not heard to make any noise. The fire was prevented from communicating to the large piggery on the south, containing about one hundred swine, and to a shed and corn barn on the north, in which was stored about one thousand bushels of corn, by the efficient efforts of all branches of the fire department. The loss is estimated at $4,000,—$1,500 each on the barn and stock and $1000 on the hay. There was $1,450 insurance on the property, $850 on the barn and $600 on the produce, all in the Vermont Mutual.

"The next morning tracks were discovered in the snow, leading from the north end of the barn up the banks, over fences, across roads, through wood lots, and into the street where they were lost. There can be no doubt that the fire was the work of an incendiary or incendiaries. What their motive could be in causing such wanton destruction of property no one can tell. We trust our citizens will see the necessity of instituting a rigid examination into the origin of the fire, and if possible discover the perpetrators of such a villainous deed."

The guilty party was ultimately found to have been the author of other incendiary acts, the motive for which was believed to have been morbid in its nature.

The Journal of Insanity, Utica, N. Y., in a review of this year's report makes the following comments:

" In the annual reports of his institution Dr. Rockwell confines himself very uniformly to the general statistics of the year, the various architectural or other improvements which may have been made, suggestions in relation to the admission and removal of patients, and brief remarks on the cause and treatment of the disease, designed more particularly for popular instruction. Very few gentlemen in our specialty have a larger experience in the care and treatment of the insane, or in the management of institutions for their reception. A professional connection of several years with the Retreat at Hartford, and twenty-two years of service in the institution at Brattleboro have given him the possession of no ordinary amount of practical knowledge. Although he has· not deemed it expedient to occupy the pages of his annual reports with the discussion of subjects strictly medical, .we sincerely trust that the profession will receive the benefit of his ripened experience in some other and perhaps better way."

It is for the reason that we have no other written exposition of his views upon any subject connected with psychological medicine, that we have gleaned so closely as we have from his reports, which contain the only published evidence of his views upon the specialty to which he devoted his entire life.

At the second meeting of the American Association of Superintendents of which he was a member, he was appointed to report

upon " The comparative value of the different kinds of manual labor for patients, and the best means of employment in winter," which he did in a written paper at the third meeting of the Association in New York in 1848.

In 1850 he prepared and presented to the Association at its fifth meeting, in Boston, an article on "The diet and dietetic regulations for the insane," and in 1858 at·the meeting in Quebec, a paper upon "The general characters of epilepsy connected with insanity," which elicited a strong discussion.

These we believe to have been the only occasions in which his views upon subjects of professional interest were elaborated upon paper, and these with all his other manuscript writings were lost in 1862, by the fire which then destroyed so large a portion of the Asylum buildings and their contents.

If we mistake not greatly, the points we have thus dilligently extracted from ˙the foregoing annual reports, will show him well abreast with the specialists of his time in his general views and principles of management of the insane, and in some points standing signally alone, as in respect to the question of parole, more fully noticed in the history of the year 1848.

In the great practical result of Dr. Rockwell's labor in developing the Institution, the annalist feels that the Doctor's professional reputation became to a notable extent overshadowed by his superior administrative accomplishment.   It has been therefore his endeavor to bring into the record each year, so far as possible, those proofs of sound professional theories and skilful medical practice, of which there are ample evidences, and which the writer personally knows he possessed in no ordinary degree.   This point certainly calls for recognition, all the more from the fact that it was never made prominent by himself.

I N February of this year, a small purchase of land was made of Shepard Rice, [thirty square rods], giving a connection between the " Prouty lot," last year purchased, and lands previously owned by the Asylum. Price paid, $20.00. In March, the farm of Newman Allen was negotiated for, containing one hundred and seventy-five acres more or less, and being the bulk of the so called " Kingsley farm," originally offered to the Trustees as a site for the Asylum [see 1836]. The cost of this extensive purchase was $10,500, which was paid for in annual instalments of $1,000 ; the same being secured by a mortgage upon the property. This constitutes the principal portion of the meadow and cultivated part of the farm, to-day.

This month was also secured additional woodland upon the mountain, of John Heywood and others, at a cost of $840.

While the Trustees were thus with wise foresight enlarging the domains of the Asylum, they were not unmindful of the needs of the household in detáil, and the sanitary welfare of the inmates of the Institution.

The evils incident to a crowded house were now sensiby felt, and along with this, measures for overcoming practical inconveniences were suggested. At the April meeting of the Board, it was *Voted*, " That J. D. Bradley and F. Holbrook, together with the Superintendent, be a committee to devise the best mode of ventilation." The method of heating the Institution being by hot air furnaces, a forced system of changing the air was impracticable. It was, therefore, determined to increase the exit flues, which was done by constructing additional chimneys in each wing, with registers opening into them from each floor.

The report of the Trustees gives the following authentic statement of the burning of the farm barn at the close of the preceding year.

" On the fifth of December, the larger barn belonging to the Institution was entirely destroyed by fire. It contained about ninety tons of hay, twenty-nine cattle, and a considerable amount of grain.

"The fire was discovered about 8 o'clock in the evening, and was evidently the work of an incendiary.   It spread with such rapidity that the whole building and its contents were in flames before it was discovered.   But so prompt, vigorous and efficient were the fire companies of this village, that the fire was confined to the large barn, and the three large contiguous buildings were saved.   Too much praise cannot be bestowed on the fire companies especially, and also on the citizens of this village generally, for their efficient and successful efforts in stopping the progress of the fire.   A new barn has since been built of larger dimensions and in an improved manner." The cost of the latter was $2,000.00, toward this an insurance was received of $1,448.63.

The Trustees also refer as follows to the recent enlargement of the estate :

"We have purchased the farm lately owned by Mr. Newman Allen, and which lay in the midst of land belonging to this Institution.   This farm is easy to cultivate, and the soil is rich and productive, and will afford much useful and pleasant employment to the patients.   With the exception of one or two small pieces of land, which are nearly surrounded by that belonging to the Institution, we shall not need any further addition to the farm."

The Superintendent reports admissions, one hundred and fifty-seven ; discharges, one hundred and fifty-five ; remaining August 1st, four hundred and fifteen.

He refers to the building erected the preceding year, on the site of the original "White House," and which at its opening was designated the " Marsh Building," in remembrance and honor of the founder of the Asylum, and says, "it has added greatly to the facilities for the classification and treatment of the patients.

" It greatly relieves us " [he further adds] " from the crowded state of the Institution, from which we suffered before it was completed. In the front part of the building, we have a number of suits of rooms, where a limited number of quiet patients can be accommodated. They can take their meals with the Superintendent, and be entirely separated from the rest of the patients."

This arrangement for a limited number of patients as boarders, cases of dipsomania, or nervous disorder short of pronounced insanity, in persons of superior social position, was continued as shown above, for many years.   It is further noted, that "great improvements have been made the past year for warming and ventilating all the buildings throughout the establishment, which are occupied by the patients."

The income for the year was, $58,663.44
The expenditure,   58,890.58
                                                 _____
Balance against the Asylum, $227.14
   The following officers were chosen for the year ensuing:

OFFICERS OF THE BOARD.

Asa Keyes, Chairman.
N. B. Williston, Treasurer.
W. H. Rockwell, Secretary.
F. Holbrook, Auditor.

RESIDENT OFFICERS.

W. H. Rockwell, Superintendent and Physician.
Alanson Weatherhead, Farmer.
Abigail Rockwell, Matron.
F. C. Weeks, } Assistant Physicians.
G. M. Buffum, }
W. H. Rockwell, Jr., Clerk.

A T the first meeting of the Board this year, the Trustees *Voted*, "That Frederick Holbrook and W. H. Rockwell be a committee to erect a brick horse-barn, in a substantial and improved manner."

This it was determined to locate contiguously to the brick storehouse at its eastern extremity, and in the line of buildings at the rear of the west wing of the main buildings. The wooden building heretofore serving as stable, was removed still further to the rear, and fitted up as a shop for mechanical work. Other changes were likewise made in the rear line of wooden structures between the new stable and female infirmary, particularly in providing a store-house for fuel in the rear of the center building. The cost of these improvements was $2,500.00.

In June of this year a half acre of land near the Asylum was purchased for the sum of $30.00 of Mary A. Knowlton.

One hundred and fifty-six patients are reported as received, and one hundred and forty discharged; leaving August 1st, four hundred and thirty-one. The Superintendent refers below with especial satisfaction to the improved means of illumination, in connection with the village enterprise this year established.

"Arrangements have been made with the Brattleboro Gas Company, by which the Asylum is now brilliantly lighted in this manner. The air of cheerfulness, which now pervades the Institution, is in striking contrast with its former condition."

He also discourses as follows upon the importance of, and difficulties in securing proper persons as attendants. " Few things are more important in an Asylum for the Insane than a proper selection of suitable persons for attendants. Unless they possess a good share of common sense, together with kindness, industry, and tact in entering into the views of the patients, and making their situations agreeable, and are themselves governed by the golden rule ' Whatsoever ye would that others should do to you, do ye even so to them,' they should never engage in this important calling. They

should ever bear in mind that the patient is insane, that his outbreaks are the result of his disease, and that he is not responsible
for acts over which he has no control. Unless such persons are
employed for this purpose the endeavors and labors of the Superintendent will, in a great measure be frustrated."

.   The finances of the year show,

Income, $59,433.70
Expenditure,   60,408,76
                                                     _____
Balance short, $975.06

At the annual meeting the following officers were chosen :—

OFFICERS OF THE BOARD.

Asa Keyes, Chairman.
N. B. Williston, Treasurer.
W. H. Rockwell, Secretary.
F. Holbrook, Auditor.

RESIDENT OFFICERS.

W. H. Rockwell, Superintendent and Physician.
Alanson Weatherhead, Farmer.
Abigail Rockwell, Matron.
F. C. Weeks,)
G. M. Buffum, } Assistant Physicians,
W. H. Rockwell, Jr., Clerk.

Additional land upon the mountain was also this year secured by
Dr. Rockwell, and turned over to the Asylum by him December 17th
at a cost of $100.

I N March of this year eighteen acres of cultivated land were added to the Asylum estate, by purchase of Keith White, for the sum of $1700. This is the open lot upon the western side of Cedar street, opposite the Asylum Park.

In June three meetings were held by the Trustees, to discuss the question of raising all the roofs of the main line of wings, thus adding another story for occupancy by patients.

At the third meeting it was *Voted*, "That J. D. Bradley, Esq., invite Mr. Silloway, architect, of Boston, to visit Brattleboro and ascertain the practicability of raising the buildings," and also, *Voted*, "If considered practicable, that the said buildings be raised one story next year."

The report of the architect showed the project to be feasible, and preparations were accordingly begun without delay.

This was a year devoted to the current routine of Asylum work. "Since the opening of the Institution," say the Trustees, "an almost uninterrupted success has attended its operations. We are ready to admit that some would have recovered at home, but many others would have passed into an incurable state, and prolonged a wretched existence deprived of the comforts and enjoyments of life, and a source of constant anxiety and affliction to friends.

"Improvements are constantly being made for the comfort and welfare of the patients, and the facilities are increased for their restoration.

"The Trustees, in their visits to the Asylum have noticed the comfort and good order which everywhere prevailed, and believe the designs of the Institution are carried out in a faithful and judicious manner."

The Superintendent's Report shows constantly increasing numbers treated. One hundred and forty-three were received, and one hundred and thirty-eight discharged, leaving four hundred and thirty-six in the Asylum August 1st.

His report is devoted largely to the consideration of mental disease, from which the following extracts are made :

"Insanity is evidently on the increase in this country. There are various causes for producing this result. The rigid discipline of our ancestors in the education of their children, has given place to another extreme which is far more injurious to the healthy action of the mental faculties. By permitting the passions to riot without control, a character is forming which will prove unfavorable for preserving a well balanced mind.

"Overtasking the young mind is another fruitful source of insanity. In childhood the brain is too tender an organ to be excited by any over exertion of intellectual labor, without hazarding serious and permanent injury. Parents are too frequently desirous of hastening the mental attainments of their children, and at the same time are almost entirely neglectful of their physical welfare.

"The exciting and hazardous speculations in which the people of this country frequently embark, and which so often result in disastrous failure, and consequent mortified pride and disappointment, are frequent causes of insanity. Besides these and various other causes, anything which tends to disturb the health and nervous system, predisposes to insanity. In attempting the restoration of the insane one of the first indications for their recovery is to remove them from all the influences that operated to produce the disease, and place them in situations that shall awaken new associations, and divert the mind from all those painful impressions with which it has been afflicted.

"In the classification of our patients we have always endeavored to associate those together who shall be a mutual benefit to each other, or at least shall not be injurious. Regard is always had to their former condition, education and habits of life. The sensibilities of the insane are frequently rendered more acute by their disease, and require the greatest caution that they are not annoyed by those whose habits are disagreeable and unpleasant."

The resources for the year ending August 1st were, $59,270.28

Expenditures,   57,809.68

Balance on hand, $1,460.60

The following officers were elected at the annual meeting :—

OFFICERS OF THE BOARD.

Asa Keyes, Chairman.
N. B. Williston, Treasurer.
W. H. Rockwell, Secretary.
F. Holbrook, Auditor.

RESIDENT OFFICERS.

W. H. Rockwell, Superintendent and Physician.
Alanson Weatherhead, Farmer.
Abigail Rockwell, Matron.
F. C. Weeks,
Joseph Draper, } Assistant Physicians.
W. H. Rockwell, Jr., Clerk.

RECORD OF 1861.

THIS year was devoted to the work planned in the preceding, and was otherwise uneventful.

The Trustees in their report say, "During this season we have raised the roofs of the wings of the main building, and are adding another story, thereby furnishing nearly one hundred additional rooms. Our means of classification and facilities for restoration will be greatly improved. This last story is in progress of completion, and we hope will soon be finished for the accommodation of patients."

One hundred and forty were this year admitted, one hundred and thirty-eight discharged, leaving August 1st, four hundred and thirty-eight in the Asylum.

The Superintendent refers to the chief work of improvement in the following terms:—.

"For several years the buildings have been so crowded that we have experienced the want of additional room to furnish all the accommodations necessary for the comfort and restoration of the inmates.

"From the inconveniences and annoyances attending the alteration and enlargement of the buildings, the care and duties of all in charge of the patients were greatly increased and rendered difficult and laborious. I have the pleasure and satisfaction of being able to state that all these duties were performed with a cheerfulness and alacrity which was worthy of all praise."

The following professional observations command notice.

"I would recur to the oft repeated fact, the great importance of placing the patients at a proper asylum in the first stages of their disease. If the patient be suddenly attacked with a violent form of mania, or because dangerous, and the friends have not the means of restraining him, he will be generally taken to an asylum where the usual facilities and appliances for his recovery can be available, and he will usually be restored to his friends and usefulness in a short time. But when the incipient stage of insanity comes on insidiously and almost inperceptibly, is slow in its progress, and the patient is harmless and passive in his conduct, the friends cherish the hope that the disease will soon wear away, and they will be saved the painful necessity of parting with their dear relative, and committing him to the care of strangers. Notwithstanding they act from the very best of motives and kindest intentions, this course has been the means of depriving many of a radical and permanent cure, consigning them to a hopeless, incurable state.

"Among the causes which tend to produce this afflicting malady, intemperance has long been known to be one of the most prolific. Its effects are not confined to that form of insanity familiarly known as delirium tremens. In noticing the causes of insanity many causes are attributed to 'loss of property,' 'ill health,' 'domestic affliction,' and similar causes, all of which are frequently produced by intemperance. Insanity and death are both more liable to be produced at the present time by intemperance than formerly. The recent developments of the poisonous adulteration of alcoholic stimulants should be sufficient to deter everyone from the use of all, excepting as unavoidable medicines, and then the purest liquors only should be used."

Income this year, $59,704.75
Expenditure,   61,797.24

Balance short, $2,092.49

At the annual meeting the following officers were chosen for the year ensuing :—

OFFICERS OF THE BOARD.

Asa Keyes, Chairman.
N. B. Williston, Treasurer.
W. H. Rockwell, Secretary.
Frederick Holbrook, Auditor.

RESIDENT OFFICERS.

W. H. Rockwell, Superintendent and Physician.
Alanson Weatherhead, Farmer.
Abigail Rockwell, Matron.
F. C. Weeks, } Assistant Physicians.
Joseph Draper, }
W. H. Rockwell, Jr., Clerk.

The expenditure involved in the raising of the roofs of the wings and building another story under them, was $12,000.

A FTER another story had been superimposed upon the wings, some difficulty and inadequacy of heating the same from the existing furnaces, was experienced. The subject early came under discussion by the Board of Trustees, and the matter reached the following action at their July meeting :

Voted, "That W. H. Rockwell be authorized to procure the materials for a new building, for the purpose of warming the main building by steam, and for other purposes."

The report of the Trustees, August 1st, notes the completion of the work of the previous year, and adds, "We are now realizing all the benefits we anticipated by the addition of a whole tier [flat] of excellent rooms, the opportunities for greater classification, and the increased facilities for the restoration of the inmates.

"Improvements have also been made on the farm, in the mode of its cultivation, and in the increased products which have resulted from it. The farm, although its pecuniary consideration is of secondary importance, is still of great value, by its furnishing healthy employment for the male patients, and by its contributing to their comfort and recovery."

In the financial affairs of the Asylum the Trustees say, they "have carefully watched the expenses and income and fixed the terms as low as practicable, consistently with the best interests of the Institution. While they have studied economy, they have also endeavored to withhold no reasonable expense in the curative treatment of the patients."

The Superintendent reports four hundred and sixty-three patients in the Asylum, August 1st. One hundred and forty-six having been admitted, and one hundred and twenty-one discharged, in the preceding twelvemonth.

Dr. Rockwell says, "There has been little of novelty in our mode of treatment the past year. Whenever we find physical disease we endeavor to remove it by the usual means, and restore the general health of the patient. In our moral treatment we endeavor to furnish pleasant and useful employment for all we can engage in that manner, not neglecting the usual amusements and entertainments afforded at the Institution.

"Provision is made for reading, walking, riding, various games, and other amusements, which serve to divert the mind from its delusions. We encourage especially all amusements which require exercise of the body as well as diversion of the mind, · such as ten-pins, billiards, quoits, and the like.

"When the patients can be induced to take an interest in some useful employment requiring active physical exercise, the result is more lasting and beneficial. The grounds in front of the Asylum, the flower and culinary garden and the extensive farm furnish abundant occupation in the summer season for all our male patients who will assist in their cultivation and improvement. The pleasant reflection of having done something for the benefit of others, affords them much satisfaction.

"In our mechanical shops we have furnished useful and pleasant employment to many who have derived pleasure in contributing their share in benefitting the Institution. We have endeavored to employ each one in his own particular department, and much by way of repairing and improvement has been accomplished by this means.

"The female patients are employed in making and repairing their own dresses, and those of other patients. Much is also done by them in making and repairing bedding, and other work for the Asylum. Some are employed in embroidery, painting, drawing, playing on the piano, and like occupations.

"One great source of novelty and entertainment to the patients is the various manifestations of ideas by other patients. Those whose minds are not too imbecile or demented easily perceive the insane notions of the other inmates. By this means their minds are diverted from their own delusions, and they begin to distrust their own wild fancies, and a commencement is made towards their recovery. It is supposed by some that the wild notions of the insane in a lunatic asylum would retard rather than accelerate the recovery of the rest. This is not the case when the inmates are judiciously classified.

"Many of the patients have received benefit by administering to the wants and comforts of their fellow inmates. We always encourage these acts of benevolence, as beneficial to both the giver and receiver."

This last paragraph is particularly significant, and illustrates again a principle firmly believed in by the Doctor, of recognizing and encouraging mutual dependence, and the mutual sharing of responsibilities.

The following is the result of this year's annual election:—

OFFICERS OF THE BOARD.

Asa Keyes, Chairman.
N. B. Williston, Treasurer.
W. H. Rockwell, Secretary.
Frederick Holbrook, Auditor.

RESIDENT OFFICERS.

W. H. Rockwell, Superintendent and Physician.
Ira X. Haywood, Farmer.
Abigail Rockwell, Matron.
Joseph Draper, ⎱ Assistant Physicians.
W. H. Rockwell, Jr. ⎰

The financial statement shows,

Income,	$60,381.02
Expenditure,	59,653.59
Balance on hand,	$727.43

In November twenty-five acres of mountain woodland were purchased of Farnsworth & Colburn for $200, and in December another tract of forty-four acres of Colburn & Cobleigh for $400.

The Superintendent closed his report August 1st, in the following words:—

"Encouraged by our increased facilities and the success which has attended our past labors, we would again commend this Institution to the same protecting Providence which has thus far sustained it, humbly trusting that the means here used for the benefit of the unfortunate will promote their comfort and restoration."

But events totally unforeseen were destined to occur before the close of the current year.

In September Hon. J. D. Bradley, a member of the Board of Trustees for the fifteen years past, was removed by death.

At the December meeting of the Board on the second Monday of the month, the Trustees remaining, proceeded to elect a successor.

"The ballots being taken and counted, Hon. Daniel Kellogg was unanimously elected, and being notified of his election, accepted the trust."

Immediately following this date, on the 21st of the month, occurred the most disastrous fire that has ever befallen the Institution.

The following account of this event is taken from the Vermont Phœnix of December 25th.

THE FIRE AT THE ASYLUM.

"A fire broke out in the Asylum in this village on Sunday morning last about 2 o'clock, and before it could be arrested the center and the wings west of it were consumed. The night was bitter cold, and the wind was strong, but fortunately blew in a direction favorable for saving the buildings in the rear, on the north side. The engines were there as promptly as the distance [half a mile] would allow, and did good service. The first thing was to take the patients to a place of safety. They were removed as soon as possible to the building on the west side of the road, and to the Center church in the village. A part of the furniture, stores, clothing, bedding, etc., was removed from the entire building, and every exertion was made to stop the progress of the flames. It was hoped at one time that the center might be saved, and strong efforts were made to that effect, but without success. In consequence of the brick wall and the iron doors leading from the center to the wings on the east, and by judiciously playing with the engines, the fire was held at bay in the center, and the east wings were saved with but slight damage. It was a difficult thing to convey the patients to safe places, as many of them were so bereft of reason, and were so much excited by the fire, that they were as likely to run to, as from the flames. Considering their number, and the circumstances of the case, we should naturally expect that a large number would have perished in the flames, but it has not been ascertained with certainty that more than one perished. The loss of property is great, but is covered, we understand, to the amount of something more than twenty-eight thousand dollars. None of the propety lost was insured in this State, but in several insurance companies in Massachusetts and Connecticut. Arrangements will very soon be made so that the patients will again have comfortable quarters, and as soon as the weather will permit we presume the buildings destroyed will be rebuilt. Several of the patients wandered away or ran away during the fire, but most of them have been recovered.

"Much credit is due to the fire companies for their prompt and efficient services, and to our citizens generally who turned out on that inclement night to save life and property. Many men and many women exposed themselves that dreadful night to render what assistance they could. We have heard several persons speak of the self-possessed, cool manner in which young Rockwell, son of the superintendent, gave information of the situation of things, and instructions as to what should be done, and how his directions might be carried out. How the fire caught is not positively known. It commenced in the basement near one of the furnaces, but whether from some defect in the furnace or the chimney connected with it, or from some other cause we are unable to say. It is a great calamity, public and private, and Doctor Rockwell and his family, and patients have the deep sympathy of many friends in this sad misfortune.

The people of the village freely sent supplies of food to the patients, until arrangements were made otherwise to furnish them, and on Sunday forenoon some of the churches in the village omitted public religious services for the performance of a pressing religious duty to the suffering.

P. S. We learn since writing the above that of the patients missing after the fire all but five have returned, and two of those five have been heard from; also, that it is not quite certain that even one perished in the flames."

An authoritative communication to the American Journal of Insanity, in the January number following, states that, "During the removal of the patients from one building to another at the time of the fire a considerable number escaped. All have been returned but four, and two of these have been heard from. It is not known that any one has been destroyed by the fire."

It may here be stated that no certain knowledge of the missing four, referred to in the latter account, has ever been obtained; and it is possible they may have fallen victims to this casualty.

PROMPTLY, at the first regular meeting of the Board this year, the Trustees *Voted*, "To rebuild that portion of the establishment which was destroyed by fire, as soon as possible."

In their report of this year we have an official statement of this occurrence:—

"Since submitting the last annual report the center building and adjoining male wings were destroyed by fire. . At two o'clock in the morning of the 21st of December last, the fire was discovered in the room directly over the furnace in the male wing, immediately adjoining the center building. The stairway which led from one story to another, and made of combustible materials, was directly over the furnace, and served as a means of communicating the fire to the upper parts of the wing. In consequence of a high wind, the flames extended rapidly to the center building, which with the male wings were entirely destroyed, excepting the outer walls of the wings. The walls of the center building were rendered entirely useless. The fire companies were immediately on the spot, and prevented the fire from extending to the female department. By the extraordinary exertions and well-directed management of those who had the care of the patients, they were removed to a place of safety, while nearly all of the furniture and other property in the consumed buildings were destroyed.

By appropriating the large Marsh Building, which previously was only partially occupied, and the female infirmary for the accommodation of the male patients, they were made quite comfortable, and especially so as soon as a portion of them could be removed by their friends."

The decease of Mr. Bradley is thus commented upon by the Trustees:

"During the past year the Institution has lost one of its early and devoted friends, in the removal by death of the Hon. J. D. Bradley, one of the Trustees. He always manifested a strong sympathy for the unfortunate, and was always ready to cooperate in any proper way for the amelioration of théir condition. His labors for the interest of this Institution, and the welfare of its unfortunate subjects, will be held in grateful remembrance."

In the report of the Superintendent, Dr. Rockwell observes:—

"I should do injustice to my own feelings if I failed to pay a passing tribute to the memory of the late Hon. J. D. Bradley, one of the Trustees. He was a member of this Board more than fifteen years. He was not merely a nominal officer of the Institution, but during the whole of this time he manifested a deep interest in its welfare, and was always ready and willing to contribute his time and influence to its best interests. He was always kind, affable and courteous in his intercourse with all, and the patients looked on him as their particular friend."

In consequence of the destruction of so large a part of the buildings, the number of admissions this year falls much below that of the immediately preceding ones. Ninety-eight were received, and one hundred and nineteen discharged; leaving August 1st, four hundred and forty-two under care.

It will be remembered that at this time too, our country was in the midst of that great struggle for national life, which during its continuance vitally affected the population of every state, and might be supposed to figure more or less as an element in developing the insanity of the time. Upon this point Dr. Rockwell thus writes:

" In noticing the causes of insanity we have failed to see as many cases produced by the progress and results of the war as might be anticipated.   The fears, the anxieties and suspense of those who have had some dear relative in their country's service; the grief and affliction of those whose affectionate objects have died on the battlefield or in the hospital, not to mention the fears of those who suffered intensely lest they should be drafted to sustain and defend their · country and its liberties, all have had their influence, if not in producing, at least in giving a form to the insanity of the time.

"On the other hand, the general, if not universal desire to lessen the hardships of a soldier's life, and to promote his comfort and welfare while in his country's service, has called forth that generous labor, and awakened that disinterested benevolence, and diverted the mind from its personal trials and afflictions, the tendency of which is favorable to the preservation of mental soundness."

The income this year was,	$60,488.51
The expenditure, ·	63,151.81
Balance short,	$2,663.30

The cost of rebuilding the burned portion of the establishment was $41,000.

This is not included in the current receipts and disbursements, but was expended in the building account, and if included, should be offset by the addition of this amount to the item of improvements and repairs.

Toward this an insurance was received of $25,300.

The following additions of land were this year made:

One lot of ten acres upon the meadow, of Gov. Frederick Holbrook, for $1,700. This gave to the Asylum complete possession of the whole tract between the Newfane road and West River. About seventy acres of woodland of John F. Stearns, Sally Nurse and others of Dummerston, for the price of $1,752.

The following was the result of the annual election in August:

OFFICERS OF THE BOARD.

Asa Keyes, Chairman.
N. B. Williston, Treasurer.
W. H. Rockwell, Secretary.
F. Holbrook, Auditor.

RESIDENT OFFICERS.

·W. H. Rockwell, Superintendent and Physician.
Ira X. Haywood, Farmer.
Abigail Rockwell, Matron.
Joseph Draper,
W. H. Rockwell, Jr., } Assistant Physicians.

THE record of this year shows but a single unusual event. The Trustees in their report make note of a bequest, which though small, is the only one of which the Institution has been the recipient since that of Widow Anna Marsh, the founder.

"We are glad to be able to state [say the Trustees] that the late Amherst Willoughby, Esq., of Berkshire, Vt., in his will bequeathed the interest of one thousand dollars annually to the Vermont Asylum, to be expended for the benefit of the insane poor of this state. We hope the example may be followed by others; and we are sure that more deserving objects of charity cannot be found, than within the walls of this Institution."

At the annual meeting the following choice of officers was made:

OFFICERS OF THE BOARD.

Asa Keyes, Chairman.
N. B. Williston, Treasurer.
J. D. Bradley, Secretary.
Frederick Holbrook, Auditor.

RESIDENT OFFICERS.

W. H. Rockwell, Superintendent and Physician.
Ira X. Haywood, Farmer.
Abigail Rockwell, Matron.
Joseph Draper, } Assistant Physicians.
W. H. Rockwell, Jr. }

The Superintendent reports one hundred and twenty-eight admissions, and one hundred and twelve discharges; leaving August 1st, four hundred and fifty-eight in the Asylum.

Dr. Rockwell writes, "We have of late discovered no important new principles in the treatment of the insane. We watch the progress of improvement in this great cause of humanity, both in this country and in Europe, and endeavor to keep pace with every advancement that may be made. The medical and moral treatment of each patient is varied by the particular indications of each case.

" There are always more or less patients in a lunatic asylum who are disposed to be usefully occupied when opportunity presents.   If these persons are confined in the halls they frequently become irritable, discontented and unhappy. ·But if they are allowed to engage in some useful occupation, they become cheerful and pleasant, and use the direct means for improving their physical and mental condition.   We have always noticed that those patients who have been suitably employed have been the soonest to recover.

"We encourage amusements as well as useful occupation for the benefit of the patients.   Almost any kind that will occupy the attention, and divert the mind from its delusions, will promote their recovery.

"One of the most important objects in the treatment of the insane is to create in them the feelings of self-respect, and the most effectual way of accomplishing this is to treat them with all kindness, respect and attention.   By so doing they will exercise all the self-control of which they are capable, and endeavor to deserve all the confidence they receive.   In order to accomplish this system of management, it is very desirable that the attendants possess the necessary intelligence, kindness and tact for their situation.   With few exceptions we have been very fortunate in obtaining this class of assistants."

An abstract of the state of the finances shows:

Income,	$61,744.27
Expenditure,	64,335.14
Balance short,	$2,590.87

At the close of this year forty-six acres of woodland were purchased in Vernon, of Mr. Wells Goodhue for the sum of $1800.

The following biographical facts, relative to the before mentioned donor of the fund to the Asylum, have been obtained largely from Judge Myron W. Bailey of St. Albans, and persons of whom he made inquiries.

Judge C. R. Brewer of Enosburgh, Vt., thus writes: "I have made some inquiries about Amherst Willoughby, of his old neighbors in East Berkshire (Vt.) and give you what little I could learn. I was unable to learn for certain when he was born, nothing appears on his monument.   *   *   *   The old neighbors think he was born in Connecticut; could not learn where he took his degree in medicine.   I learn that he married Miss Hannah Bingham of Tinmouth, Vt., and first kept house in Russia, N. Y.; practiced

medicine there.   From there he came to Richford, Vt.   How much
he followed his profession there I could not learn.   '*   *   *
From there he moved to East Berkshire and was in trade awhile;
formed a partnership with Solomon Bingham and William Barber.
I cannot learn that he ever had any particular love for his profession, or practiced very long.   I could learn nothing definite as
to what prompted him to make the bequest for the poor insane."

Another says, "Both he and his wife were people of great
refinement and culture, moved in the highest circles, were capable of
adorning any position, and had but few intimate friends."

As to what induced him to make the bequest to the Asylum,
Judge Bailey says, "I have heard Judge Barber, the executor of his
will, state that a few years before he died, a poor clergyman, who
had charge of the parish where he lived was taken insane [and
I think taken to the Asylum] and Judge Barber thought that
this event caused him to make the bequest."

Dr. Willoughby was a devout Episcopalian, and during his life
time built the little church opposite his dwelling in East Berkshire, which he made residuary legatee, after the Vermont Asylum
bequest and the legacy to the Vermont Episcopal Institute. He
died July 27, 1855, at East Berkshire.

The vagueness and broadness of this legacy to the Asylum,
in respect to its application, has prevented its benefits from being
fully appreciated by any one in particular, and is a suggestion that
to be of most real advantage, such bequests should be applied to
meet the want of a specific class of individuals. If this was
suggested by the needs of a poor insane clergyman, as above hinted,
and had been bequeathed specially to such cases, its benefits would
have been more pronounced.

M—— W——, one of the patients of note, died this year, after a
residence of more than twenty years in the Asylum. He was
admitted first in 1841. A blacksmith by trade and of gigantic
stature [six feet four inches in height], he became insane in consequence of a blow upon the head, while at work near Lowell, Mass.
He was not maniacal, but on the contrary labored under a constant
apprehension of being injured; and for the first two or three months
after admission would cry in the most puerile manner, at the most
trivial causes, such behavior being almost ludicrous when observed
in connection with his giant size. He then became actively suicidal
for a time. A year after admission he became violently maniacal
and destructive to property and clothing, and this phase lasted
nearly through the second year.

About the beginning of his third year he began to improve, and conceived the idea of making a wooden man, and being naturally ingenious and accustomed to the use of tools, he was indulged in his fancy. The making of this image occupied him many weeks. "A queer thing it is, too," says the record; and it is much to be regretted that it has not been preserved. Soon after, he became wild and troublesome again, then comparatively docile, but still unsettled. At this stage he was removed; and for a year and a half was kept closely confined in a room, by the authorities of the town where he belonged. He was then returned to the Asylum where he remained until his decease. Seven months after his return it is recorded that he was allowed about the premises on parole, and was employed in the care of the dairy. From this time on he was never again obliged to be closely confined, and henceforth Moses became a marked character. He was childish in many things and delighted in fantastic ornaments, and display of watch chain with odd appendages; but ingenious, industrious, and always good natured and obliging. He had also natural executive ability, and nothing so much pleased him as the managing of two or three fellow inmates, willing workers, but passive, in the accomplishment of some piece of work for which he felt himself responsible, and in which he could lead and direct. His quaint expressions were always to the point, showing at bottom strong common sense and keen comprehension. When the capped granite posts at the foot of the front door steps were erected, on the rebuilding of the center building after the fire in 1862, Moses surveyed them for a few minutes in silence, then broke into a laugh and walked away, wagging his head and saying "Well now, everybody that comes 'll think the Doctor is dead," which in his view would be a huge joke. His parole grew unlimited and in the last ten years extended to menageries, circuses, and attendance upon the county fairs. When dressed in his Sunday and holiday suit, with tall hat, he was certainly a marked personage. He died of pulmonary consumption, but resisted the progress of the malady with the most invincible courage, unwilling even to admit he was ill until compelled from sheer inability longer to keep about, and being confined to the bed in reality but a few days. His affection for the Asylum was great, and he would have felt at home nowhere else. His case shows that chronic insanity even is not without some mitigations, and that it is not, as is sometimes affirmed, always a "living death." Not only was a fair measure of enjoyment his, but the little world in which he moved, at least, was the better for his having lived in it.

RECORD OF 1865.

THE first action of the Board in relation to the work of this year, was taken at their February meeting, when it was *Voted*, "To authorize the superintendent to erect a suitable barn at the Newman Allen place, in a proper location."

At a special meeting on the fourth Tuesday in May the salary of the superintendent was taken into consideration, and it was *Voted* "To pay him fifteen hundred dollars a year for his services, to date from August 1st, 1864.

It may here be remarked that no change had been made in the salary of this official since November 1st, 1842, when it was fixed at twelve hundred dollars. Prior to that it was one thousand dollars.

The changed values of all comodities as well as labor, by reason of the disturbed state of the country at this time, very much deranged all ordinary calculations, and occasioned difficulties of management that were felt by the Trustees with unusual anxiety.

"Much skill," say they in their Report, "has been required to manage the financial affairs of the establishment so that the patients would have all of their usual comforts and facilities for recovery, and at the same time to confine the expenditures to the income which we derive from the various sources. The superintendent deserves much credit for the success with which he has managed this difficult part of his labors. The large farm has been of great service in sustaining the Institution, as well as in affording the means of cure for many of the male patients.

"In an institution of this kind there must necessarily be a large outlay for repairs and improvements.

"One of the old barns had become so decayed as to render it unsafe for occupation any longer. It was therefore wholly removed to make room for a large, new, and substantial one, which has been erected this season, containing many improvements upon the old building."

The cost of the new one was $2,500. The resident number of inmates August 1st this year had reached four hundred and eighty. One hundred and forty-four were received, and one hundred and twenty-two were discharged, during the year immediately preceding.

The Superintendent, in his report, discourses as follows upon the subject of insanity:

"The great increase of nervous diseases in this country, which to say the least, predispose to insanity, makes it necessary to allude to some of their causes in order to prevent their occurrence.

"The want of proper or suitable mental and physical education, frequently lays the foundation, and prepares the way for insanity. Physical education is all important for mental as well as physical labor. For any great mental exertion it is desirable that a person should have a sound mind in a sound body; whatever promotes the general health also promotes the strength and energy of the mind. Without health it is nearly as difficult to perform mental labor for any considerable time as to perform physical labor without it. A proper exercise of the mental or physical system imparts strength, energy and power to each; and each system is weakened by the excessive use, or by the neglect of exercise of either.

"The youthful brain should not be over taxed with studies which require too much mental labor. On the other hand a judicious mental exercise is necessary for healtny mental exertion. Avoiding physical exercise will never strengthen the physical system, so the unemploying of the mind will never qualify it for healthy exercise.

"One predisposing cause of insanity is the excessive mental labor in the process of education. It is rare that insanity is induced in childhood, but over exertion produces that morbid condition of the brain and nervous system, that sooner or later will result in insanity by apparently slight and insufficient causes. It is a fortunate circumstance that most children have not sufficient fondness for study to have their minds or brain receive any injury. But there are cases in which excessive mental labor proves injurious if not fatal.

"Uncontrolled desires, and unrestrained indulgence of temper, will often prepare the young for that disordered state of the brain which strongly predisposes to insanity.

"One great preventive of insanity is the forming of correct habits. A person of a peevish, fretful habit, and inclined to look on the dark side of things, is far more liable to become insane than one of a cheerful and hopeful disposition, who makes the best of every condition of life.

"Another preventive of diseases of the nervous system and insanity, is a temperate and regular mode of life. Regular sleep, regular meals, plain nutritious food, and plenty of exercise in the open air are necessary, and whatever tends to promote the general physical health also directly tends to prevent nervous diseases and insanity. The great desire of many to embark in some active and even hazardous speculation, is a fruitful source of insanity. To engage in some regular and legitimate business, which will ultimately result in success, is too slow a process for their ideas of acquiring a fortune. They must engage in something which will cause so much hope, fear, anxiety and difficulty, as to result in sleepless nights, and frequently to complete failure of the enterprise. Disap- pointment and mortified pride follow in the train, and the mind is strongly predisposed to mental disorder.

"Among the agents which produce insanity, that of intemper- ance has a prominent place. Opium and tobacco also have their victims. Intemperance is one of those sins which are vital upon the children of succeeding generations. It frequently produces insanity in the next generation, when the parent escapes it. The children of intemperate parents who escape insanity are frequently afflicted with epilepsy, idiocy or some mental obliquity or vicious propensity.

"Persons predisposed to insanity should avoid everything that has a tendency to impair the general health, such as want of physical exercise in the open air, passing too much time in warm rooms, sleeping on feathers, engaging in employment that will not allow of sufficient sleep at proper hours, and allowing themselves to be too much disturbed by the unpleasant trials of life.

"The patient after recovering from insanity, should carefully avoid the causes which produced his disorder. But there is a class of unfortunate cases, who, after having recovered and returned home, find the same causes operating which produced their disorder. The pecuniary embarrassments, the loss of dear relatives, the enfeebled health, the domestic afflictions of various kinds which surround them, continue to operate, and unless they are fortified against these trials their minds will be apt to succumb to the outward pressure which produced their former insanity."

Income,	$66,164.93
Expenditure,	67,358.37
Balance short, August 1st,	$1,193.44

The following officers were, at the annual meeting, chosen for the year ensuing:—

OFFICERS OF THE BOARD.

Asa Keyes, Chairman.
N. B. Williston, Treasurer.
W. H. Rockwell, Secretary.
F. Holbrook, Auditor.

RESIDENT OFFICERS.

W. H. Rockwell, Superintendent and Physician.
I. X. Haywood, Farmer.
Abigail Rockwell, Matron.
W. H. Rockwell, Jr., } Assistant Physicians.
N. D. Rumsey,

RECORD OF 1866.

A T the February meeting of the Board the question of providing shelter on a large scale for the storage and working up
of fuel, was considered, and it was *Voted*, "That the superintendent erect a suitable wood-house on the west side of the road."
There was accordingly this season erected a building 100 feet long
by 40 feet broad, open upon one side, and capable of containing
a whole year's supply of wood.

The cost of this was $1,500, and it was situated south of the
Marsh building.

At the meeting in June the water question again came under
consideration and it was *Voted*, "To lay a lead pipe from a spring
on the south side of the Allen lot [farm] to the Asylum."

In their report of this year the Trustees say, "Few things contribute more to the health and comfort of the insane than an abundance of pure spring water. We had a good supply, but the bursting
or rather breaking of the iron pipe last winter, which conveys the
water from the [Wells] spring to the Asylum, during a spell of
severe cold weather, caused such an inconvenience for a short time
that we concluded to lay another pipe from another source, which
yields a large quantity of excellent water. It would be singular
if both sources should fail at the same time."

By the constant increase of inmates, the requisitions for water
and air become always the most pressing necessities. We have
already referred to the demand for additional ventilation, and now
the added water supply claims attention; and also the experience of
the last winter demonstrates the undesirability of a dependence upon
a single source. Two points are therefore this year made—the
securing of an added and an independent supply.

Four hundred and ninety-three patients are reported in the
Asylum August 1st. The movement of population shows one hundred and sixty-one admitted, and one hundred and forty-eight discharged in the twelve months last past.

Dr. Rockwell in his report observes, "The farther we depart from the simple customs and habits of our ancestors the more we shall prepare for the introduction of this disorder. When we take a view of our country, and witness its advancement in wealth, civilization and refinement, the many powerful temptations to embark in some hazardous enterprise; the sudden accumulation and loss of property which frequently happens, the freedom of our institutions, by which the humblest citizen may aspire to the highest office in the gift of the people; the fierce and persevering strifes which are everywhere carried on, both in the accumulation of wealth and obtaining political distinction, and the many trials of disappointment and mortification to which all are liable; who can doubt the many active and operating causes to increase this disease in our country? Persons of all classes and stations in life are liable to this affliction. Those who are now rejoicing in the blessings of health and reason may soon be afflicted with this severe calamity."

Income for the year,	$76,289.19
Expenditure,	76,904.17
Balance short,	$614.98

The following officers were chosen this year:—

OFFICERS OF THE BOARD.

Asa Keyes, Chairman.
N. B. Williston, Treasurer.
Wm. H. Rockwell, Secretary.
Frederick Holbrook, Auditor.

RESIDENT OFFICERS.

W. H. Rockwell, Superintendent and Physician.
Ira X. Haywood, Farmer.
Abigail Rockwell, Matron.
W. H. Rockwell, Jr., } Assistant Physicians.
E. B. Nims, }

About one hundred square rods of land was this year purchased of Henry F. Smith, in immediate contiguity to the Asylum cemetery, at a cost of $250.

RECORD OF 1867.

THE experiences of the last year in respect to the water supply, though temporarily bridged over, seem to have resulted in a conviction that the source hitherto depended upon, even when supplemented by the smaller spring upon the farm, as detailed in last Report, was inadequate. This year therefore the Asylum secured of James H. Capen a second supply, equal in volume and quality of water to that purchased of Eben Wells in 1845, which since that time has been principally depended upon. These two, the Wells and the Capen springs, the latter some half a mile beyond the former, in the same direction from the Asylum, constitute at present the dependence of the Institution for this most essential element; and it is safe to assert that so far as abundance of pure water and air go, no asylum in this country is better off.

The reports of the officers of this year show five hundred and eleven patients in the Asylum August 1st; one hundred and forty-three having been received, and one hundred and twenty-five having been discharged since the previous report.

The Superintendent states, "It is gratifying to know that we have accommodations for all of the insane of this state that require hospital treatment. With the exception of one year, when part of the buildings were destroyed by fire, we have not refused to receive any patient of this state, whatever might have been the condition of the patient."

The income this year was, $78,938.29
The expenditure,   78,450.11

Leaving on hand August 1st, $488.18

The following officers were chosen at the annual meeting:

OFFICERS OF THE BOARD.

Asa Keyes, Chairman.
N. B. Williston, Treasurer.
W. H. Rockwell, Secretary.
Frederick Holbrook, Auditor.

W. H. Rockwell, Superintendent and Physician.

Ira X. Haywood, Farmer.

Frances M. Palmer Matron.

W. H. Rockwell, Jr., ⎫
E. B. Nims,   ⎬ Assistant Physicians.
                       ⎭

"During the past year," writes the superintendent, "the former matron, Miss Abbie Rockwell, who had so ably and faithfully labored to promote the comfort and welfare of the patients and the best interests of the Institution, died of pneumonia. Miss Frances M. Palmer has been appointed in her place, and has thus far filled it in a manner to gain the approbation and confidence of the officers and friends of the Institution."

RECORD OF 1868.

E XTENDING along the main road to Newfane upon its western side and to the north of the Marsh building, stood a row of houses owned and occupied by old residents from the opening of the Asylum until now. They were four in number, and all, together with their gardens attached, occupied an area of but small extent, not exceeding three acres, with some six hundred feet of frontage. The whole settlement together was known as "Pikeville," from the name of the oldest inhabitant, Houghton Pike.

Three of these small proprietary free-holds were this year purchased [those nearest to the Asylum buildings] of Willard Edwards, Francis T. Green, Mary A. and William Knowlton respectively, for the aggregate sum of $5,400.

Apart from the purchase of these additions to the real estate, no extra outlays were this year incurred, for the very good reason that the Trustees had no funds to appropriate in any direction outside of current expenses, as appears from their report, in the following quotation:

"The high price of labor and of most of the necessaries of life, has continued through the year; but by skilful management, with the aid of a large farm, we have been able to furnish the necessaries and comforts of life, and the means of restoration of the patients, with the regular income of the Institution."

The report of the Superintendent shows five hundred and fifteen inmates in the Asylum August 1st, one hundred and thirty-five having been received and one hundred and thirty-one having been discharged since the date of the preceding report.

The income received was, $79,554.28
The expenditure,   78,943.72
                                                             ‾‾‾‾‾‾‾‾‾‾
Leaving balance, August 1st, $610.56

Choice was made of the following officers at the annual meeting this year:

OFFICERS OF THE BOARD.

Asa Keyes, Chairman.
N. B. Williston, Treasurer.
W. H. Rockwell, Secretary.
F. Holbrook, Auditor.

RESIDENT OFFICERS.

W. H. Rockwell, Superintendent and Physician.
I. X. Haywood, Farmer.
Frances M. Palmer, Matron.
W. H. Rockwell, Jr. }
E. B. Nims,   } Assistant Physicians.

RECORD OF 1869.

THE constantly increasing number of residents, since the rebuilding of the Asylum after the fire of 1862, has been noticed. The pressure for additional room becoming more and more felt each year led to new plans for enlargement. The laundry built in 1852, which was thirty-two by thirty six feet in dimensions, and two stories in height, had become insufficient for the wants of the constantly increasing household, but being connected with wings occupied by patients, at both ends, could be made most serviceable in that connection, by subdividing its interior into apartments for patients and by extending the central hall of the female infirmary through this, wards eighty-six feet long could thus be obtained, which were very desirable.

To effect this it was determined to erect a building to the westward of the female infirmary, its front on line with the rear wall of the last mentioned building, and its rear line forty feet to the north. The length of this building was seventy feet, and it occupied the place of the wood store-house for fuel and other uses, mentioned as fitted up for this purpose in 1859. This was constructed of brick, two stories in height, and has served to the present time for laundry, sewing rooms, and steward's department.

The cost of its erection and fitting up, and washing machinery with new boiler and engine, and that of reconstructing the old laundry into wards and rooms for patients, was $12,000.00

By these changes, rooms were provided for about thirty additional patients.

The following officers were chosen at the annual meeting, for the year ensuing:

OFFICERS OF THE BOARD.

Asa Keyes, Chairman.
N. B. Williston, Treasurer.
W. H. Rockwell, Secretary.
Frederick Holbrook, Auditor.

The income this year was, $81,472.07
The expenditure,   80,028.63
                                                   _____
Balance on hand, $1,443.44

The reports of the Trustees and Superintendent show a year devoted to the every-day duties of asylum life, without any notable incidents.

The state commissioner this year reports his observations as follows:—

"I have in every instance found the Superintendent at his post, constantly watching and guarding his trust. His assistant physicians are gentlemen of kind and benevolent natures, well-fitted for the place. The matron and all the help, so far as I am able to discover, are kind, patient and industrious, doing all in their power for the comfort and benefit of those under their care. I have never been able to discover any deficiency in the quantity or quality of their food. There was always as much variety as could reasonably be expected or required for the health of the patients."

At the annual meeting this year it was *Voted*, "That Daniel Kellogg be employed to investigate the legality of using the water of a spring on our own land."

This was a question arising in connection with the purchase of the Capen spring in 1867, it being claimed that its use by the Asylum would be to the detriment of a water privilege depended upon by parties below, to which it doubtless contributed.

There were admitted this year one hundred and twenty-four, discharged one hundred and twenty eight; five hundred and eleven being the resident number at date of the annual report.

I N March of this year the Trustees *Voted,* " To remove the wood-
house [erected in 1866] from its present site [south of Marsh
building] to the lot purchased of Mary A. Knowlton in
1868.

" Also, *Voted,* To build a new house for the farmer of the Institution, on the same site as where the old one now stands."

This constituted the principal work of improvement this year.

On the 29th day of July, 1869, Mr. A. H. Bull, a resident of
Brattleboro, died, leaving an estate of $130,000, which, by will dated
June 25th, 1867, made the Vermont Asylum residuary legatee of the
bulk of this property, after the Hartford Retreat, in event of the
latter declining or forfeiting the same. The conditions of the will
were such that neither institution could afford to accept the bequest,
and moreover the validity of the will was contested by the heirs, and
the widow's provision waived by her. At this juncture the Trustees
took the following action thereupon, under date of July 7th, 1870.

"*Resolved,* that whereas, A. H. Bull, late of Brattleboro. deceased,
in and by his last will and testament made the Trustees of the Insane
Retreat at Hartford, Ct., residuary legatee, in trust for certain
purposes therein named, and in case of the non-acceptance by said
Insane Retreat made the Vermont Asylum for the Insane residuary
legatee subject to the same trusts, which said will has been allowed
in the probate court, and is now pending in the county court by
appeal of the heirs at law. Now therefore—

" 1. *Resolved,* That we will do nothing toward the establishment
of said will, and will pay no part of the expenses thereof.

" 2. That if said will be established, and said trust shall fall upon
the Vermont Asylum by the non-acceptance of the Insane Retreat
at Hartford, we will not accept the same, under the burdens and
duties therein imposed by said will."

The provisions by which the legacy was encumbered were in
brief, that the income should be annually devoted to "Such indigent
clergymen of the Orthodox Congregational or Presbyterian faith,

professing the Calvinistic doctrines, as have labored faithfully in
the cause of Christ, and have become so far advanced and infirm as
to be unable to support themselves by further labor in said cause,
and have become insane; and also the support at said Retreat [or
Asylum] of the wives of such clergymen, always giving preference
to such as have labored in the missionary cause, provided that
not more than five dollars per week shall ever be expended for
the support of one such person at said Retreat [or Asylum], provided, also, that no distinction shall be made between clergymen
of different States."

The Trustees say in their annual report that " At no time since
the Institution was first opened, has it been in a more prosperous
condition, or had so great facilities for the benefit of its inmates.

" The improvement of the older buildings and the erection of
new ones have increased the expenditures the past year.

The whole income has been, $85,281.72
The whole expenditures have been,   83,163.49

Leaving a balance in favor of the Asylum of, $2,118.23

" Many improvements are yet to be made, most of which must
be postponed to the next year."

The number of patients in the Asylum August 1st of this year
reaches its maximum in the whole history of the Institution, standing at five hundred and eighteen.   One hundred and twenty were
received and one hundred and thirteen discharged, during the fiscal
year.

The Superintendent, in his report, dwells somewhat upon the
great principles of treatment, and emphasizes particularly the value
of occupation, as follows:

" By proper employment the maniac expends his excitement to
some useful purpose, rather than in noise, violence, and mischief,
and annoying his fellow inmates.   The attention necessary for the
melancholic to perform any kind of labor withdraws his mind from
his gloomy forebodings, and serves to awaken more rational views
of life.   The monomaniac forgets his delusions in the occupation of
his mind on more rational subjects, and will eventually find his
vagaries supplanted by more correct ideas."

While the foregoing observations must be recognized as true, the
reader must not suppose that the practical application of these principles can be demonstrated in all cases.   Extreme cases of excitement, depression, or delusion constitute exceptions to the rule, for
reasons that are obvious on reflection.   And while this qualification

must be interpolated it is but just to say, particularly as we are now quoting from the last report made in full by Dr. Rockwell, Sr.. that to him, more than to any other superintendent during his lengthened period of practical work, is due, beyond question, the credit of instituting and developing the labor question, both in its curative and its economic aspects and results.   He fully believed in it, and carried it out with the courage of his full convictions, to the end of his official connection with the Asylum.

At the annual meeting the officers of the last year were re-elected for the year ensuing.

.   OFFICERS OF THE BOARD.

Asa Keyes, Chairman.

N. B. Williston, Treasurer.

W. H. Rockwell, Secretary.

Frederick Holbrook, Auditor.

RESIDENT OFFICERS.

Wm. H. Rockwell, Superintendent and Physician.

Ira X. Haywood, Farmer.

Frances M. Palmer, Matron.

W. H. Rockwell, Jr., }
D. H. Lovejoy,   } Assistant Physicians.

At the November meeting the Trustees *Voted*, "To purchase Henry H. Rice's farm at a reasonable price."

This was situated in contiguity with land already belonging to the Asylum estate, and added especially to the pasturage.   It contained seventy acres and cost $3,500.   The cost of the farm-house erected this year was $2,500.

BY AN ACT of the General Assembly of the state of Vermont, approved November 1st, 1870, it was made the duty of the Trustees and Superintendent of the Vermont Asylum for the Insane, to make their reports thereafter biennially, in conformity with the change in the State from the annual to the biennial system, and such reports were henceforth to be addressed to the Governor, and published in the volume of State Officers' Reports, instead of with that of the Auditor of Accounts, as since 1844.

In chronicling the future annals of the Asylum therefore, it will be most convenient, as well as most satisfactory, to consider the results of each brace of years together, as the statistics are thus summed up in association in each biennial report.

A current record of the doings of the Trustees, and of the operations of the Asylum each year, will however be continued as heretofore, as the change in the State system only affects the Institution in respect to the requirement noted.

In March, 1871, the purchase of David Miller of the Pike homestead for $2,600 gave final possession to the Asylum of all the properties referred to in 1868, and jointly known as "Pikeville."

At the annual meeting in August the following officers were duly elected:—

OFFICERS OF THE BOARD.

Asa Keyes, Chairman.
N. B. Williston, Treasurer.
W. H. Rockwell, Secretary.
F. Holbrook, Auditor.

RESIDENT OFFICERS.

W. H. Rockwell, Superintendent and Physician.
Ira X. Haywood, Farmer.
Frances M. Palmer, Matron.
W. H. Rockwell, Jr.,
C. H. Tenney, } Assistant Physicians.

. It was *Voted*, "That W. H. Rockwell be authorized to negotiate with Calvin Weld and Isaac Taft, on the best terms for the Asylum, in supplying an additional amount of water."

This action was supplementary to the vote of August, 1869, making Daniel Kellogg the agent of the Board to determine certain legal points in reference to the use of the Capen spring.

A practical result was promptly reached after the present action by the purchase [September 5th, 1871] of Calvin J. Weld, of all his right, title and interest in said spring, for a cash consideration of $500; and [September 11th, 1871] of Isaac B. Taft, his right, title and interest, for a money consideration of $250, and a reservation of "the right to take from said water sufficient to fill a half inch pipe, and carry the same to his house or elsewhere."

The like reservation was also made to James H Capen, when the spring was purchased of him in 1867, the cash consideration being nominal, and supplemented at this date [September 11th, 1871] by a deed conveying right of way through his land for the aqueduct, also at a nominal consideration.

The like right of water-way through land of James A. Capen was also negotiated for, and purchased from his executors, for the sum of $50; and thus was secured the way for laying the three-inch iron pipe from this spring to the Asylum, which latter was immediately procured of B. S. Benson & Sons of New York, at a cost of $3,375.44.

Following these important negotiations, the estate of the late James A. Chase, lying in contiguity to the Wells farm purchased in 1853-4, embracing some twenty acres, was purchased November 3rd, 1871, of the executors and heirs, at a cost of $3,075.

The year 1872 affords an unusual record. It is memorable especially for unlooked for changes. Other events that were to some extent anticipated, also reached their culminating point this year. It is seldom that the administration of the internal affairs of an institution, continues so long without a change in the chief executive. For near thirty-six years had Dr. Rockwell conducted the affairs of the Asylum, both professional and financial, with signal ability, and with great success, as the preceding annals show. Nevertheless his labors were about to close, in a manner as unexpected as painful. On the 10th of May of this year he was overturned and thrown from his carriage as he was leaving the Asylum for a drive, and sustained a fracture of the neck of the thigh bone, together with a severe concussion of the system, which was succeeded by prostration from which he never fully rallied, and for the remaining eighteen months of his life he was wholly confined to his bed, in a gradual decline.

By this unlooked-for occurrence the charge of the Asylum at once devolved upon his son, then senior assistant, who conducted as acting superintendent the affairs of the Institution for the remainder of the current year.

At the annual meeting in August Dr. Rockwell, Sr., tendered his resignation as superintendent, by reason of the disability detailed. It was accepted as inevitable;* and the following expression of the feeling of the Board on this occasion, prepared by Ex-Gov. Holbrook, chairman, was submitted and ordered to be recorded.

" *Whereas*, Dr. Wm. H. Rockwell, having tendered his resignation of the office of superintendent of the Vermont Asylum, on account of advanced years, and particularly of the injuries occasioned by the severe accident which happened to him a few months since, and which he fears may result in permanent infirmities,

" It is therefore *Resolved* by the Trustees of said Asylum, this day in full Board assembled, that while they reluctantly accept Dr. Rockwell's resignation, they hereby express their full approbation of his past services as superintendent of said Asylum, and their high estimate of his unwearied labors in building up the Asylum from its infancy, and carrying forward its interests and its benevolent mission to the present time.

"And it is further *Resolved*, in appreciation of the long and eminent services of Dr. and Mrs. Rockwell in behalf of this Institution, and of their benevolent and self-sacrificing labors, for the comfort and care of the many unfortunate insane persons who have found asylum here, that the Board of Trustees do hereby tender to them a home at said Institution during the remainder of their lives, and during the life of the survivor.

" *Resolved*, that the secretary is directed to furnish a copy of these resolutions to Dr. and Mrs. Rockwell."

The Trustees then proceeded to the election of officers, and the following were unanimously chosen:

*W. H. Rockwell, Jr., Superintendent and Physician.
Ira X. Haywood, Farmer.
Frances M. Palmer, Matron.
C. H. Tenney,
———— ————, } Assistant Physicians.

Dr. John M. Clarke was selected to fill the place of second assistant physician, and entered upon duty October 1st of this year.
The income for the two years preceding

August 1, 1872, was, $160,708.51
The expenditure,   155,771,73

Leaving balance on hand of, $4,936.78
The number of patients in the Asylum August 1st, 1872, was four hundred and ninety-five; two hundred and forty-one having been admitted and two hundred and sixty-four having been discharged, in the two years preceding that date.

As the time of the legislative session of this year approached, it became evident that some movement was contemplated looking to an investigation into the management of the Asylum. Twenty years had elapsed since the first inquiry, which has been detailed in the record of 1852. Nothing is truer than that complaints are cumulative, and are gradually magnified by repeated telling, as is the snowball by every turn, until at last an irresistible avalanche is created. It is also true that every institution which in the mission it performs cannot be with propriety freely open to the public, is naturally looked upon with some degree of distrust, predisposing it to the suspicions of the public.

But perhaps it is most likely to suffer from the misapprehensions or perversions of fact, imbibed by those under care, whose malady instead of terminating in recovery, becomes only so far modified in respect to its violent manifestations as to permit a release from custody. In such cases the morbid impressions are circulated wherever the individual goes, and being erroneous conceptions, or at least exaggerations of fact, are nevertheless believed more or less fully, by those who knew the statements of the individual formerly to be reliable. In many cases the person is sincere in his convictions, but his premises have been misapprehended; and those who know him are themselves ignoront of the real basis of delusion, hence all parties may be honestly misled.

*The salary of the superintendent was at this date fixed at $2,000 per annum; that of the farmer at $450; that of the matron at $300; that of the first assistant physician at $1,000; and that of the second assistant at $600.

In other cases insanity more especially affects the moral character, the intellectual faculties being little disturbed apparently. In such, perversion of facts becomes often a mania, especial delight is taken in creating false impressions, and the integrity of the intellectual processes lends to the most perverted statements an element of plausibility that is irresistible to credulous minds.

However this may be, the investigation of this year grew largely out of the statements made by two individuals, who had been inmates of the Asylum.

It is not my purpose to criticise the judicial decisions in these cases; they stand to be judged of from the individual standpoint of each one who may give them attention. But in all such cases there is an inside history, which in these in question I feel bound to give, as they especially figure in the official investigation which follows.

In 1869 [July 24th] there was committed to the Asylum a patient from Pennsylvania, one Joseph A. Stockton, who had been adjudged a lunatic under the laws of that state, and been placed under the guardianship of a "Trustee of person and property," and who had been in three different asylums in Pennsylvania, viz., that at West Philadelphia under charge of Dr. Kirkbride, that at Harrisburg under Dr. Curwen, and that at Dixmont under Dr. Reed, for a period averaging two years in each, before he was committed to this. He was transferred directly from the Dixmont asylum to Brattleboro. Back of his asylum history he had a war record and ranked as colonel. There were irregularities in this period which could only be excused on the ground of mental disorder. His insanity was due to long continued habits of intemperance, and partook largely of a disposition to exaggerate and misrepresent, while his irrepressible conceit and love of notoriety amounted to a monomania for distinction of any kind, in which he might play the hero. While in asylums he was ever restless, and always charging illegality in the proceedings. Facts upon which opinions were based respecting his sanity, if pointed out to him, his ever fluent and plausible tongue assigned reasons for, either specious or untrue. He was a disturbing element everywhere. Outside of asylums always getting into personal trouble; inside, a promoter of disaffection. Opinionated, he became by reason of his conceited and dogmatic utterances, the oracle of those naturally of much better talents than himself, but whose disordered minds were overshadowed by the clouds of progressive dementia, as well as the leader of those of similar derangements to his own. He made bold to assert that many of the inmates were not insane, and never failed to charge upon the officers of asylums mercenary motives.   He had a penchant for writing, and while at Dixmont asylum wrote a book of verses, which in his own estimation ranked with the poets of classic authority.   Clandestine acts were much more to his liking than straightforward ones, and there was an unscrupulous disregard of truth characteristic of that state of degeneracy and demoralization which is consequent upon prolonged dissipations and irregular life.   If it be questioned whether an asylum for the insane is the best place for such a person, that guardianship and restraint are needful cannot be doubted; nor will it be disputed by alienists that such a case is one of mental derangement, affecting especially those attributes upon which moral integrity depends.

In the Asylum at the time of the admission of Stockton was one Peter H. Shaw, an inmate of the Asylum for the second time (since March 15, 1869), whose somewhat erratic history may be briefly stated as follows: He was a clergyman of the Presbyterian faith, 71 years of age, and by the account of a near relative always possessed of some peculiar traits, "a man of very strong feelings, and prejudices equally strong.   If he once formed a dislike for any person or thing, he could never overcome or subdue that feeling; no matter how the circumstances might change he would remain perfectly invulnerable." He lacked, however, steadiness of purpose, had little real efficiency, and was exceedingly egotistical and overbearing.   At the age of 23 he was licensed and settled over his first charge, and also married.   In this year he also sustained a pecuniary disappointment by the failure of an expected legacy, which seemed permanently to have affected his mind.   After being settled over his first charge six years, his health somewhat failed him; he was troubled with dyspepsia, and always suffered more or less from it.   Being advised at that time by physicians to use as little meat as possible, he then espoused the theory of vegetarianism, which he subsequently carried out and perfected in his own way.   Upon this subject and pecuniary questions, he all his life entertained, to say the least, "cranky" views.

For several years after resigning his first charge he was without a settlement, though supplying some of the time a pulpit.   Then he secured a second pastorate which he held for about eight years, subsequently taking charge of a parish for one year, and at the age of 40 virtually retiring from the ministry, never subsequently bringing any support to his family, always declaring that "he could find no society adapted to himself, and that people did not appreciate

him; always possessing himself of the feeling that he was something superior to any one else, a feeling which he always carried out
even to his own family."

Soon after resigning his last charge he was brought very low
with typhus fever; for two weeks lying with constant hiccough, and
for three months confined to bed. All his natural traits seemed
afterwards intensified, and a "morbid inertia" took possession of
him, so far as the ability to apply himself to steady labor was
involved. His hair at that time changed, and his whole appearance
became altered. In his family he was irritable and arbitrary, always
asserting his own rights, no one's opinion or judgment having any
weight with him. This animus gradually cut him off from the sympathy of friends and relatives. His wife died and he became to
some extent a recluse in his habits, not mingling with the family
with whom he lived except at meals, and, except when out taking
exercise, remaining in the seclusion of his own room. At the time
of his wife's death, he had forbidden all her relatives the house.

Another disappointment of a cherished plan was the dissipated
course of a son whom he designed should enter the ministry; and
henceforth is to be traced the unfortunate influence of this son upon
the subsequent life of the parent, which continued up to the time
of his commitment to the Asylum.

Though supported by the voluntary charity of relatives for many
years, he was continually chafed by the manner in which it was done.
He could not understand why the means necessary for that purpose
should not be placed in his hands, to be expended by himself in his
own way. The demands of the son referred to were never resisted
by the father, but given without discretion to the fullest extent of his
ability. Doubtless the exactions of this kind, which were never
ceasing, induced to some extent a course of action on the part of
the father, which for three or four years preceding his confinement,
he was especially addicted to, that of borrowing on false pretences
and promises sums of money from any and all friends, relatives, and
benevolently disposed persons, indiscriminately. This became his
chief occupation, and so notorious did he become, that even his
brother clergymen declared him "the most accomplished beggar they
ever saw, and that he was certainly laboring under a monomania,
and a fit subject for a lunatic asylum."

His daily habit and uniform practice for some time preceding his
commitment to the Asylum, was to take his hat on rising from the
breakfast table, and start out on these begging excursions (living
then with a member of his family in Brooklyn), and his usual state-

ments were to the effect that he was starving, without a home, and without friends, refusing to give his address if asked, but always promising to return the moneys at a specified time, and never doing so in an isolated instance.   Under these circumstances his friends instituted his examination, and by men familiar with his personal history, by competent medical authority, he was declared a lunatic "so disordered in his senses as to endanger his own person, and the persons and property of others, and that it is dangerous to permit such lunatic to go at large."

With this history, and this decision as to his mental unsoundness, he was received into the Asylum on the 22d of June, 1868, from Brooklyn, N. Y., but was removed by his son on the 4th of July following.   Eight months after he was recommitted, this time by the authorities of his native town of Barnet, Vt.

In the history of these two men some points of resemblance may be noted.   It will be observed that both broke down mentally soon after middle life, though from the operation of different causes. The moral sense in each suffered more than the intellect, and in fact became in both quite lost.   Both were possessed of excessive self esteem, which not only survived the moral faculties but seemed to flourish over their decay until its overgrowth amounted to a species of monomania, both entertaining the most overweening consciousness of their superiority over their fellow men.

It is curious to trace the phenomena of the fraternization of these two inmates, in which, however, · the controlling influence of the younger is apparent.   By artfully affecting a pious turn of mind, he succeeded in completely duping the man of God into the belief of his sincerity, as the following testimonial in the hand-writing of the latter indicates; though whether a solicited or voluntary tribute does not appear:

"It has been my privilege to form an acquaintance with Col. J. Addison Stockton of Pittsburgh, Penn   Have had more or less of intercourse with him daily for some weeks.   Am happy to say I find him a Christian gentleman of much more than ordinary literary acquirement.   This has been shown by prose and poetical compositions, submitted to my inspection.   His religious poetical talent is quite above what is common.

"Col. Stockton is desirous of being useful in a Christian sphere. My own opinion is that with some preparation he might be quite useful in the Christian ministry.   His Biblical acquirement is already considerable.   P. H. SHAW.

"Member of the Presbytery of New York, September 6th, 1869."

This early sympathy established between the two, and continuing for some three years, predisposed them to act together when the hour struck their time; and as might be expected the leader lost little time in bringing to his aid his devoted dupe, relying not a little upon his clerical standing and affiliation for countenance and presumed veracity.

The ball was set in motion by the elopement of Stockton, May 30th, 1872. He soon after appeared in Burlington in this State, and the authorities of the Asylum being notified that he was there held, sent for him, but before he could be returned from there, he was brought before Judge Pierpoint of the Supreme court of Vermont upon a writ of *habeas corpus*. At the hearing in the case, July 10th, Judge Pierpoint, learning the fact that he was under guardianship by reason of insanity, and was therefore legally held at the Asylum, recommitted him thereto. Before, however, he could be returned to the Asylum, another writ was issued bringing him before Judge Smalley of the United States court, upon the ground that Judge Pierpoint had no jurisdiction in the case, as Stockton was a resident of another State, the hearing being set for the following day. At this, Judge Smalley decided the case to come within his jurisdiction, and fixed upon the 2d of August for a full investigation into its merits, and meanwhile remanded Stockton to the charge of the proper officer, with directions "to restrain him no more than might be necessary to have him present at such hearing." From this time forth therefore, he had the liberty of the city, and with the aid of lawyers and sympathizers inaugurated a line of inquiry having for its object the investigation of the Asylum by the Legislature, which was to convene in October following.

It is interesting to note the intense enjoyment of the situation by the patient, at this turn in his affairs, by which his mania for notoriety gained free scope. In a letter dated at the " Jail," July 2d, to an attendant at the Asylum, he writes, "My friends are going to make it a very *interesting trial*. I secured three good attorneys here, two more have *volunteered*, and there *will be others*. Gov. Stewart will be invited to be present, so he can understand the *workings of and at the Asylum*. Of course Lovejoy [Dr.] will be here, so Dr. Tenney and I will have a good *week's work*. I have to thank him for being made a *lion* of. I have quite *distinguished visitors* hourly, but, think of it, *bouquets of flowers*, almost equal to those on J—— F——'s grave!"

At the hearing before Judge Smalley on the 2nd of August, at which testimony was presented upon both sides, Stockton was adjudged sane and unconditionally discharged.

The next step in the progress of the scheme was, as may be anticipated, the institution of legal proceedings in the case of Shaw. He too was brought before Judge Smalley on a writ of *habeas corpus* and discharged as sane on the 5th of the following month.

In the foregoing sketch of these two cases the writer, having no personal acquaintance with either, has drawn entirely upon documents in the possession of the Asylum, and as may be inferred by preceding quotations, principally in the handwriting of the parties, and covering the whole period of their stay in the Institution. The animus pervading them all is such as would hardly fail to convince any expert of the mental unsoundness of the writers, which is most manifest in two directions, to wit: in a demoralization, and a certain puerility and garrulousness belonging only to a state of mental degeneracy, consequent upon cerebral disease or senility, or both combined.

The subsequent history of these men throws no new light upon their cases. Inquiry of the relatives of both concerning after facts, shows that both died within a couple of years after their release from this Institution. Col. Stockton after his return to Pennsylvania, "was carefully examined" writes one of his family, "by two of our best physicians, and pronounced unmistakably insane. As a result he was placed in a private institution near Philadelphia, where he died about two years after."

Information concerning the subsequent history of Mr. Shaw, derived from similar inquiry, elicits the following facts:

After Mr. Shaw was taken from the care of the Asylum in 1872, he was for several months at Northfield, Mass., then went to Brooklyn, N. Y., where he remained through the following winter with his daughter. In the spring of 1873, at the instance of his son, he went to New York to board at a hotel, where he died in September of that year.

A friend of his and of his family thus writes, "I had known Mr. Shaw since the year 1845, and more intimately from the year 1857, continuously until he was taken to your Institution. I considered his mind as gradually failing from the year 1850 until then; and from my subsequent knowledge of his case up to the time of his death am satisfied that he was hopelessly insane. I had every opportunity of knowing the above to be true."

After the judicial decisions in these cases, active work was entered upon under the guidance of these two discharged inmates, and in the month intervening before the General Assembly convened, other disaffected and unrecovered ex-patients were sought out, and made ready for a sensational *denouement* at the proper time.

The Legislature convened on the 2nd of October. On the 4th a Joint Resolution was passed, "That a committee of two senators and three members of the house of representatives be appointed to visit, investigate, and make report upon the condition of the persons confined in the Vermont Insane Asylum as insane persons, and whether any persons are now or have been confined there during the last two years as insane persons who are not or were not insane, with full power to send for persons and papers."

On the 1st day of November following a second Joint Resolution was also passed in concurrence, "That the special committee already appointed to visit and inspect the Insane Asylum at Brattleboro, Vermont, be authorized and instructed to visit the Insane Asylum at Concord, New Hampshire, for the purpose of comparing the condition and treatment of the patients in the two asylums, and the State Lunatic Hospital at Northampton, Massachusetts," and they were further authorized, if necessary, "to pursue their investigations after adjournment of the Legislature, and make report to the Governor on or before July 1st, the following year."

The minutes in full of this investigation were not printed, but the conclusions of the committee were embodied in a report to the Governor, under the instructions noted, and will be given in due chronological sequence. It may here be remarked, however, that in this inquiry, as well as in that of 1852, the committee found it necessary to exclude the testimony of former inmates, principally, for the same reason as then, that their statements were so colored by their morbid feelings and disordered impressions, that they could only be taken at great discount and with many allowances.

The election of Dr. Rockwell, Jr., to the superintendency, at the annual meeting of this year, was accepted by him reluctantly and with the understanding that he should be early relieved, as it was not his desire to continue in the specialty; although in view of the critical condition of health of Dr. Rockwell, Sr., he recognized it as an expedient duty for him to perform for the time.

At the December meeting of the Trustees (on the 11th of the month), he tendered to the Board his resignation of the office. "After due consideration it was *Voted*, To offer the position to Dr. Joseph Draper, at present First Assistant Physician of the Asylum at Trenton, N. J., and the secretary was instructed to write him to that effect."

At another meeting of the Board held on the following day, plans for the future were more fully discussed, and with a view to putting in steam-heating apparatus and increasing the facilities for ventilation, it was *Voted*, "To build two additional wings, as it would be necessary to use the basements [hitherto occupied by patients] for putting in the fixtures for heating by steam; and F. Holbrook and W. H. Rockwell, Jr., were appointed a committee, to make estimates and contracts for the same." *

The superintendent elect duly received the official communication of the secretary, and on the 14th of the month signified to the Trustees his acceptance of the charge and his willingness to enter upon its responsibilities at the earliest practicable moment.

It will be noted that this is the second action of the Trustees looking toward the introduction of steam heating. The first was in 1862, as already recorded, but the great fire immediately following, prevented the immediate carrying of it out, and the constant pressure of other plans subsequently, delayed it to the present time.

D R. DRAPER assumed the medical charge of the Asylum on the 16th of February.

The superintendence of the constructive work, determined upon at the close of the preceding year, devolved upon Dr. Rockwell, Jr., and the general charge of the finances remained in his hands until May of the following year.

At the regular meeting of the Trustees in May, 1873, it was *Voted* "That Dr. Rockwell, Jr., be authorized to procure a portrait of his father, for the use of, and at the expense of the Asylum," which was duly accomplished as desired.

On the 30th of June the joint committee of the General Assembly of the preceding year made report of their findings to the Governor, which was published in the newspapers of the State.

At the meeting of the Trustees in July following, this Report was discussed by the Board, and while in many respects it seemed unjust, and upon many points requiring explanatory comments, they did not deem it best to respond to it in any official way in the public prints.

This Report commences with the somewhat remarkable confession that, "It was a matter of surprise to some members of your committee to learn at the inception of their investigation that the Asylum was not the property of the State." Then followed an epitome of the history of its original endowment and subsequent development, including the nature and amount of aid it had received from the State, concluding with the perhaps unintentional but somewhat unfortunate statement that "The property is *owned* by a private corporation, the Trustees of which are Asa Keyes, N. B. Williston, Frederick Holbrook, and Daniel Kellogg."

The objection to this phraseology is that it tended to perpetuate a quite prevalent supposition, that it was a joint stock corporation for money-making purposes, instead of a property in trust for a specific object, out of which, under the provisions of its charter, it would be impossible for its managers to appropriate anything to themselves, personally.

"The Trustees," they then proceed to say, "While refusing to recognize any authority in your committee, yet afforded them free access to all parts of the buildings and grounds, and inspection of. the records and other papers of the Institution, and treated us with uniform courtesy."

The primary complaint entered against the Institution was in reference to the number of its inmates, and against the use of the basement story for patients, as follows:—

"At the time of our first visit, we found the number of patients at the Asylum to be four hundred and eighty-five, a number, as the committee believe, and as the officers of the Institution admit in their testimony, far too large for the capacity of the buildings comfortably to provide; in this view your committee is sustained by the testimony of Commissioner Bullard, who fixes three hundred patients as the maximum number which the Asylum could accommodate.

"About seventy-five of the patients were at the time of our visit confined in underground apartments, which are damp, unwholesome, and entirely unfit for occupation by human beings. The sleeping apartments in this underground portion were small, illy ventilated, warmed and lighted. The sleeping apartments of the males being altogether too small, while some in the female ward were only nine feet in depth by four feet in width and eight in height, opening into a narrow hall, and ventilated only by eight two inch auger holes through the door. About midway of the length of one of these lower wards, and at the end of another ward, and at the side, are sinks which receive the urine and slops from the wards above, and at all seasons of the year must impart unwholesome odors. On the occasion of our first visit, although disinfectants had been freely used, your committee found the odors extremely unpleasant. The officers of the Institution offer as an excuse for confining patients in this unwholesome manner, that at the time the Asylum was built it was common to use underground apartments for confinement of patients; and Dr. Bancroft of the New Hampshire asylum informed us that a portion of that asylum was so built, but had not been used for any such purpose for many years past. We believe the confinement of any person, sane or insane, in these underground apartments to be cruel, and that the officers and employes of the Institution should be prohibited under heavy penalties from hereafter placing any insane person in these apartments."

That the number of inmates was, and had been for several years much beyond the actual capacity of the Institution, could not be disputed; and to this cause, more than to all others combined, the writer is disposed to charge all the complications at this time involved. The average number in the seven years immediately preceding this year, had been in excess of five hundred. Just in proportion as an institution becomes crowded, are discomforts increased, frictions engendered and classifications subverted, while individuality is over-looked if not lost. Then it is that restless spirits riot in their oppor-tunity, and chaos rather than order prevails. Universal experience would doubtless show that harmony and effective work go hand in hand with comfort and judicious association, and that perplexi-ties and results short of satisfactory follow in proportion as depar-tures from these conditions are forced upon such a household. Even if the number of attendants is proportionately increased, the evil is largely irremediable. Collisions are necessarily more frequent, and coercive measures become more frequently unavoidable. That such at least had been the experience realized at this Institution, seems evident.

Again the constantly crowded state of the Asylum had rendered almost impracticable many changes in the accommodations of the Institution that were desirable, and deferred the introduction of increased facilities for care and treatment of the inmates, which were recognized by the management as needed. The committee especially dwell upon the evils connected with the basement story of the building, and from their description of the same, quite a false impression of these accommodations went abroad. They were spoken of as "underground apartments," while full half this story was above the ground level. In fact the arrangement of this floor exactly coincided in its construction with those above. There was the same long central corridor with rooms on either hand, and the brick partition walls dividing the apartments above rested upon foundations upon the basement level, and enclosed here the same spaces. In the matter of light, too, each room had its window three feet in height and of the same width as those above, in the upper half of the room and resting upon the foundation belt of stone above which the brick walls were superimposed, and entirely above the ground level. The only exception to this arrangement was one which was adopted from the pressure of circumstances which neces-sitated more rooms for the separate isolation of violent cases, and which consisted in dividing upon the rear side of the building some rooms into two, giving the dimensions quoted in the foregoing extract from the Committee's Report, and the doors to these apart-ments being made of a double thickness of boards, had circular openings in their upper portion for the purpose of observing the occupant without always opening the door. These narrow apartments had each a window of half the width and equal height with those given as the the general size; yet the impression given in this Report was that of unlighted and unventilated cells, save by these apertures in their doors. In fact the idea conveyed of this whole story was that of a cellar, instead of a basement floor. Again, the sanitary arrangements for these basement wards were specially complained of, but differed in no respect from the arrangements in the upper wards. Faulty, it may be conceded; but essentially unsanitary they were not, else epidemics of disease would surely have co-existed. In thus critically reviewing these comments upon constructive faults, we do not attempt to extenuate them; but we submit that such wholesale condemnation of an institution by a Legislative committee, seems to some extent unwarranted, when it is remembered how little this State had done toward making provision for its wards, in comparison with those of the neighboring States, whose asylums this committee were instructed to visit and compare with this, unless some conclusions were likewise to be drawn, based upon the relative expenditures of the several States in creating asylum accommodations.

In the second place we read, " Your committee find the fact that the whole of said Asylum was at the time of their first visit, inadequately warmed and ventilated; we also noticed at this and subsequent visits, the almost entire absence of anything to relieve the harshness of restraint; very few pictures broke the hard outlines of the hall walls; while at Northampton and Concord, we found the walls embellished with pictures, not costly, but pleasant to the eye and sense, and which we believe must tend to draw these unfortunates from contemplation of themselves, and form a means toward their cure. At Northampton we found a large yard decorated with shrubs and yet securely enclosed, where the more dangerous class of patients might exercise; and in the center of this yard an artificial mound had been made enabling these unfortunates to enjoy the beautiful landscape. At Brattleboro we found nothing of this kind except some small yards enclosed with high and close board fences, without tree, shrub or even grass to relieve their untidiness. We were told, it is true, that other classes of patients had exercise in labor upon the farm, or in walks taken under the direction of their keepers, but for this class no effort looking toward opportunity for out door exercise or amusement seems to have been made. The cost of such yards as the one at Northampton can be but trifling, and we recommend that suitable yards be built. We also find that

at Northampton nearly every evening the patients, or at least as
many of them as are able, are collected together in the chapel of the
asylum and some of the officers of the institution read, or cause to
be read to them poetry or prose, and entertain them with music or a
lecture; and that patients' minds are thus for the time turned from
themselves or the particular subject of their mania into other channels, and in the language of Dr. Earle, the superintendent, 'are
relieved much more rapidly, and their minds regulated and much
sooner restored than they would be without this diversion.'   No
such exercises are practised at the Vermont Asylum, though we learn
incidentally that Dr. Draper, the new superintendent, has introduced
them to some extent."

In respect to the inadequacy of warming and ventilation, it may
be said that under the old method of heating by furnaces, the
Asylum was unequally warmed as compared with the subsequent
method by steam, but that this was inadequate in amount could
hardly be affirmed with truth.   As to ventilation it was doubtless
open to criticism, by reason chiefly, as already affirmed, of the number
of inmates in excess of its proper capacity.

Portions of the building were also, as stated, devoid of ornamental
furnishings, but not the wards devoted to the better grade of patients.
Particular and undue stress, as it seems to us, was also laid upon the
small court yards devoted to the limited number of the most excited
and most demented classes, while the full and free use by the female
patients generally, of the front grounds and garden walks, which had
always been the rule, escaped the notice or recollection of the committee entirely.   Religious and other exercises commented upon
favorably in the other institutions visited, suggest some additional
facts in this connection.   The careful reader of these annals will
have observed the inauguration of family worship in the early years,
and subsequently the institution of a Sunday service, in which a
sermon was read by the superintendent, with the usual devotional
program, singing, etc.   This was continued through the whole term
of service of the elder Rockwell.   But in addition to this, provision
was early secured for the attendance in the churches of the village
of any and all of the inmates of the Asylum whose condition would
allow of this privilege.   Pews in the several churches in the village
were early purchased for this purpose, and deeds of twelve slips
in five of these churches are now held as vouchers for this fact in the
archives of the Asylum; and these were used by virtue of these
deeds of ownership, or by the payment of rentals, during the whole
period of the charge of Dr. Rockwell, Sr.

When the superintendency devolved upon Dr. Rockwell, Jr., the practice of procuring the services of the clergymen in town to offic- iate on Sundays at the Asylum was instituted, and has since then been continued. It may also be added that when the present Super- intendent entered upon service, a series of dramatic exhibitions had been inaugurated, preceded by a dance on Christmas evening, 1872.

The committee further say, "We find punishments are sometimes inflicted at the Vermont Asylum." Upon exactly what testimony this conclusion was reached, the present writer has no data; but cer- tainly every rule and regulation governing officers and employes in the care of the insane, was directly opposed to any such principle of management, and it is totally at variance with every sentiment drawn from the published utterances of the veteran superintendent, as quoted in these annals for the period of an entire generation. More- over the authorization of any such practice was distinctly denied by the resident officers at the time. Such facts, therefore, if proven to the committee, must be relegated along with other departures already deprecated, from the domain of responsible control to the realm of incidental irregularities, principally resulting, as before stated, in the opinion of the writer, from the overcrowded state of the Asylum, in which year by year individuality in the matter of treatment became more and more overlooked or lost.

Again the committee say, "We are satisfied persons have been admitted to said Asylum who were not insane," but as this statement was deduced, as expressly stated, from the cases already fully dwelt upon, comment upon this point further is uncalled for. Some redeeming features were conceded in concluding, as follows:—

"Your committee find that the supplies of food at the Institution are sufficient in quantity and quality, and we are unanimous in the opinion that the food is well cooked and properly served."

Again, "Your committee find that, notwithstanding the draw- backs surrounding the Institution, the death rate among its patients has been for ten years past less than at any other institution of the kind in New England, except the New Hampshire at Concord, and but a small per cent above that."

The following article by an anonymous writer in defense of the management, appeared in the Boston Daily Advertiser in the issue of July 29th, 1873, and is here introduced as the candid and just expression of the views of the citizens of Bratttleboro who had best opportunity to judge of the life-long character and work of Dr. Rockwell and his son, in the charge and development of the Institution, now subjected to critical investigation.

"We have read with astonishment and indignation the Report of the investigating committee of the Vermont Asylum for the Insane. Dr. Rockwell has long been known among us as an upright and honorable man, who has given his best endeavors for many years to benefit the Asylum committed to his charge.   He took the Institution in its infancy,. and with a meagre endowment of $10,000 and $23,000 given by the State, has raised its pecuniary value to $500,-000 through his able management and great financial ability.   At present confined to a bed of lingering sickness, disabled from answering the charges brought against him, it is but right that his friends should defend his character when it is so bitterly attacked. In many instances the Report is so worded as to entirely mislead the mind of the reader.   When in the account of some of the so called 'dungeons,' rooms that in reality are not sunk nearly so low beneath the level of the ground as the basement kitchens common in cities, it is said 'these are only ventilated by eight two inch augur holes bored through the door,' omitting all mention of the windows with which all the rooms are provided, and which certainly contribute to the ventilation.

"Again the Report, after speaking with commendation of the enclosed yards at Northampton, adds, 'At Brattleboro we found nothing of the kind except some small yards enclosed with high board fences, without trees, shrubs, or even grass to relieve their untidiness.'   No mention is made of the large and beautiful grounds belonging to the Asylum to which all patients, with the exception of a few of the very worst and most dangerous, have access, and while an impression is given that no amusements of any kind are afforded, to our knowledge theatricals and dances have often been got up for the entertainment of the patients, and the female patients are frequently taken to drive.   Every Sunday afternoon regular service is held in the chapel, conducted by one or other of the different clergymen of the village, or by strangers who may happen to be visiting the town.

"When the committee were so careful to mention all the faults, real and imaginary, that they could find in the Institution, it is a matter of regret that they did not enlarge a little on some of its merits, as they briefly mention that there is very much in the conduct of the Asylum that they can commend.

"Dr. Rockwell is not responsible for the laws of the State of Vermont touching the insane.   He has neither made, nor has he broken them.   Doubtless they could be much improved, and none would hail the improvement more gladly than himself.   The most serious

charge made by the committee is that 'they are satisfied .that persons have been admitted to said Asylum who are not insane.'   Why
are they so satisfied?   The only case mentioned is that of Joseph A.
Stockton, who was discharged as 'sane' in the face of testimony
proving that he had already been confined in three asylums in
Pennsylvania, had made frequent attempts on his own life, and that
while in the army, when sentenced to the penitentiary for a year,
and to pay a heavy fine on account of misdemeanors committed, his
friends, and among them the late Secretary Stanton, procured his
release on the ground of his insanity.   The decision under these
circumstances that he was to be considered a sane man, is certainly
a strange one.   Stronger proof than this should be given before such
heavy charges are made.

" The case of the Rev. Peter Shaw, frequently commented on in
the newspapers, is a somewhat analogous one.   This poor old man
was the victim of monomania, and on the Superintendent's testifying
that he was harmless, was discharged by the judge, who advanced
the doctrine that none but dangerous lunatics should be considered
insane enough to be confined in asylums.

" At the investigation this old gentleman testified that two patients
from Canada, were, upon their arrival at the Asylum set upon by the
attendants, *stamped to pieces*, killed, and the remains boxed up
and sent to their friends.   He could not give the names of these
victims, nor did he assign any motive for the useless murder.
He also testified that he saw another patient cruelly beaten by
an attendant whose name he gave.   When minute distinct charges
are made they are easily refuted.   It was at once proved that the
attendant in question had left the Asylum a year before the time
stated in the accusation, and that Mr. Shaw, being in another hall
from the much abused patient, could not have witnessed the beating
even if it had been inflicted.   The officers of the Institution distinctly deny the charge that punishments, *as such*, are ever used
by them, and it is from testimony like the above, the creation of disordered minds, that sensational stories, which have been going
the rounds of the papers, of a system of torture worthy of the dark
ages, have sprung.

" The committee admit that the quantity and quality of the food
are all that could be desired, and the significant statement made by
them that the death rate at the Vermont Asylum is less than at any
other asylum in New England, with the exception of that at Concord,
N. H., coupled with the kindred fact that the number of those
discharged as cured is larger than at most of the similar asylums,

would of themselves prove the absurdity of the stories of neglect,
· insufficient care, inadequate warmth and ventilation, ill treatment,
etc.; such results do not follow such causes.

" The final representation made in the report is that the present
changes and improvements have been in progress since the appointment of Dr. Draper, the present Superintendent of the Asylum.
This is true, but it is also true that these improvements were planned
and commenced by the former Superintendent, and are now going
on under the charge of Dr. Wm. H. Rockwell, Jr., in whom the
Trustees have high and deserved confidence.   This young man was
for a few months, in consequence of his father's illness, placed by
the Trustees at the head of the establishment, but with the express
stipulation, made by himself, that he should resign as soon as a successor could be found.   He was neither turned out for extravagance,
—as the Springfield Republican asserts—nor did he resign on account
of intended investigation, as the Rutland Herald states.   He left of
his own free will, and in opposition to the urgent request of the
Trustees, that he would still continue at his post.

" We ask you, in the name of justice, to publish these few and
simple statements of facts.   What seems to us a cruelly unjust story
is being spread far and wide through the land.   We claim at least
the privilege, given us by long acquaintance and high esteem, of
speaking in defense of the accused."

At the annual meeting the following officers were chosen:—

At the October meeting a Code of Rules for the government of
the attendants and employes of the Vermont Asylum for the insane,
prepared by the Superintendent, was approved by the Trustees and
ordered to be printed.

On the 30th of November of this year Dr. Rockwell, Sr., died at
the Asylum.   More than thirty-seven years before he had entered

upon the work of building up the establishment, with what result the preceding annals show. Save by reason of sickness he had never ceased to labor, and virtually he died, as it had been his oft expressed wish that he might, in harness.

For the year and a half preceding his death he was confined to his bed, suffering much from his fractured limb, gradually wearing away and sinking to his final rest; and then it was that the strong points of his character shone out with the most striking brilliancy. Realizing that his work was done, and that he had done it faithfully, he expressed his willingness to be judged by it. Undisturbed by the shafts of malice and indiscriminate censure, he calmly observed, "that his work would be better appreciated and his motives be better understood after he had gone." And so he passed away; dying as he had lived, strong in the faith of his life-long convictions, and relying with unshaken confidence upon the Divine justice, which metes out to every man the full measure of his deserts.

At the May meeting of the Board, 1874, Judge Kellogg offered his resignation as Trustee, which was duly accepted, and the remaining members then proceeded to the election of his successor.

Voted, and chose Dr. Wm. H. Rockwell. Judge Keyes then tendered the following communication, likewise resigning his office:

"To THE TRUSTEES OF THE VERMONT ASYLUM FOR THE INSANE:

" Having served as one of the Trustees for about thirty years, and having arrived at the age of eighty-seven years this month, I deem it my duty as well as privilege to decline further continuing in said trust. I do therefore resign.

ASA KEYES."

James M. Tyler was then nominated and elected to fill the vacancy.

At this time also the charge of the finances, which had hitherto remained in the hands of Dr. Rockwell, was placed in those of the Superintendent.

The following officers were chosen at the annual meeting:—

OFFICERS OF THE BOARD.

F. Holbrook, Chairman.

N. B. Williston, Treasurer.

J. Draper, Secretary.

W. H. Rockwell, Auditor.

Joseph Draper, Superintendent and Physician.
·Asa Gilkey, Farmer.
Frances M. Palmer, Matron.
J. M. Clark, ⎫
H. T. Whitney, ⎭ Assistant Physicians.

Since the last election Mr. Haywood had resigned the position of
farmer, and Mr. Gilkey had been selected to fill his place.

Dr. Clark had performed the duties of first assistant since the
death of Dr. Tenney, [April 27th, '74,] and Dr. Whitney had been
secured for the vacancy of second assistant, and entered upon
the work.

The Report of the Trustees to the Governor of the State of Vermont is here given in full:—

"The Trustees of the Vermont Asylum for the Insane respectfully present this, their biennial report for the preceding two years.

"The Superintendent's Report shows that 699 patients have been
inmates of the Asylum during the past two years.   There were 495
August 1st, 1872, since which 204 have been admitted, 228 have
been discharged, and 471 now remain.

"The past two years have been the most eventful of any since
the Asylum was founded; as during this time we have suffered the
irreparable loss by death of Dr. W. H. Rockwell, who for so many
years filled the responsible position of Superintendent, and by whose
forethought, fostering care, and remarkable executive ability, the
Institution has attained the position it now maintains; also by
the resignation of two of the most honored and best known mem-
·bers of the Board, Judges Asa Keyes and Daniel Kellogg, who have
been identified with the best interests of the Asylum since its
infancy, and who by their counsel and aid have done so much
for its welfare, and for that of the unfortunate class committed to its
care.   .

"In 1872 Dr. W. H. Rockwell, Jr., was appointed Superintendent
and accepted the position temporarily, as he had long expressed
a desire to retire from the Asylum, having then been in active
service there for more than fifteen years; and on his resignation
in 1873, we appointed Dr. Joseph Draper, who brought with him
a long experience in the care and treatment of the insane, to fill
the vacancy.

"During the past year we have completed two additional wings
to the Asylum, and also a boiler house for the steam heating appa-

ratus, in which we have placed four large boilers and a steam engine, but have been unable to complete our plans, owing to lack of funds. We, however, hope before another winter to have them in full working order.

"Owing to the outlay for new buildings, steam works and other improvements, the expenses have exceeded the receipts by $45,000, which we have had to borrow from banks and individuals; and there are still other bills that have not been settled, which will swell the amount to a larger sum.

"We would respectfully request the Legislature for an increase of the rate we are now allowed to charge for those receiving State aid, as the present amount is not sufficient for their support, being less than the average cost of each one, and less than that allowed to other institutions in this State, and much less than is paid to any other asylum in the New England States. The number of patients steadily increases each year, thereby debarring us from receiving as many from elsewhere—for we are continually importuned so to do— and consequently materially lessening our income, as they pay a larger amount than those from Vermont.

"We have frequently visited the Asylum during the past two years, together and individually, and have endeavored to watch over the welfare of those under its care, and from our personal observation believe the designs of the Institution are faithfully carried out. We would cordially commend it to all, as well worthy of the confidence and esteem it so long has held."

The Superintendent's Report elaborates as far as possible the statistics of the two hundred and four cases anmitted, and the two hundred and twenty-eight discharged, and dwells largely upon the general history, objects, and practical working of the Institution; the late Legislative inquiry having shown that many misapprehensions concerning it were prevalent, even among persons of general information and intelligence.

In doing this, The Policy of the Institution in Relation to Admissions and Discharges, The Organization of the Institution, and General Principles of Treatment, The Ownership of the Asylum, Legacies, Public Supervision, Capacity of the Buildings, Heating and Ventilating, Embellishments, Religious Services, Amusements, Policy of the Institution in Relation to Labor, Correspondence, Medical Certificates, Appropription of State Aid, and Legislation of the State in Reference to the Insane, were separately discussed and commented upon.

The following quotation, supplementing the detailed statement of the work of the past two years contained in the Trustees' Report, is added to make the record more complete.

" Between the 24th of January last and the 13th of April following, the new wings were opened, and the entire basement story vacated by patients, seventy-five inmates being then transferred to better constructed wards. They were for the most part cases of chronic dementia, long habitues of the place, who little minded the change apparently, and some even moved reluctantly, and manifestly failed to find in their new quarters that degree of contentment which they had grown to feel in their old tenements. Still we rejoice in the change as a step in the advance, and in accordance with the ideas of the times. And the vacated story subserves an equally necessary and important purpose in locating new heating pipes and radiators for warming the building by steam, and for the purposes of storage.

" In addition to the construction of the buildings, a good deal has been done in the way of furnishing; movable settees in the halls have been replaced by an approved pattern of permanent wall seat, and one hundred iron bedsteads have been introduced in furnishing the new wings.

" The libraries [of which there are three] have been increased, and additional framed pictures have been hung in the recesses of the halls.

" So far as our income has allowed we have endeavored constantly to add to the conveniences and arrangements of the household, without losing sight of means less practically useful, but scarcely less essential in a moral point of view to the welfare of the patients; with larger resources we would gladly do more."

The Report closes with brief obituaries of Dr. Rockwell and Dr. Tenney, and acknowledgements due for gifts, and individual services.

The financial exhibit for the two years shows, $213,810.66 received and $213,929.11 expended, leaving a deficit of $118.45, August 1, 1874.

The debt of $45,000 incurred in 1873 principally, seemed to forbid the introduction this year of the works in detail, and hot air furnaces were therefore placed for temporary use under the new wings.

The cost of the east and west extensions of the wings, constructed in 1873-74, was $43,214.18, of the boiler house, chimney stack, tunnels, boilers and engine, $13,000.00.

The cultured taste shown in the embellishment of the grounds of the Asylum, it is proper to say in this connection, was the result of the personal oversight and direction of Mrs. Rockwell, Sr., whose interest in it was unflagging, and whose enjoyment in it was so genuine as to make this a pastime rather than a labor.

In the care of the flower garden, shrubbery, etc., she had a useful assistant in one William Moss, an inmate of the Asylum some seventeen years, and who deserves an honorable mention in this connection. This patient was an Englishman by birth, and bred a gardener in the old country. His dominant delusion when admitted, and which in fact continued up to his removal a few months since by a daughter who had married and settled in the West, was, "that he was about to be arrested or murdered, or in some way injured or kidnapped." At first he was very wretched, afraid to sleep in his bed, spending his nights in watching at his door, and holding conversations or remonstrating with imaginary persons whom he believed he heard plotting against him. After a few weeks passed in this unhappy manner, he was induced to go into the garden to work. Here Mrs. Rockwell interested herself in him, and became his friend, and by her he was taught to read. Thus was the intensity of his mental derangement relieved and his condition improved by the occupation of his hands, and the new resource afforded by the acquirement of the art of reading. Like Moses, whose case has been before detailed, Moss became an individual of consequence and note in the Asylum community. His parole was limited to the premises, but an extension of it would have been useless, as he felt safe nowhere outside, nor scarcely within. Once only was he known to leave the boundaries of the grounds, and this was on the occasion of the great fire of '62, and then great fears were entertained when he was found missing, lest he had perished in the flames; and there was great rejoicing when after twenty-four hours he was returned from an adjoining town with only a frost-bitten toe. His tormenting hallucinations on this occasion drove him away, as he was safely out of the building and standing beside the garden fence, when he thought he heard some one say, "There he goes, sieze him! sieze him!" He then fled from his imaginary pursuers. On a subsequent occasion he was missed and no trace of him could be found for two or three days, when he reappeared, having taken refuge from· his haunting fears under the summer house in the grounds, from which retreat he had heard his absence noted and discussed by various members of the household during the whole time, but made no sign.

This case illustrates the possibility of usefulness, even without lucid intervals, and while constantly laboring under the most harrassing suspicions and fears.   Had it not been for the continued efforts of his special patroness, however, aided by the co-operation of others generally, it is more than probable that his delusions would have come to wholly possess his mind, possibly impelling him to have terminated his wretchedness by his own hand, from very intensity of apprehension and irresistible fears.

A T a meeting on the 11th of May, 1875, the Trustees *Voted*, " To complete the introduction of the steam heating apparatus the present year, and that Dr. W. H. Rockwell be the authorized agent of the Board for carrying out the work to its completion."

At the July meeting, the full Board being present, Mr. Williston resigned the office of Trustee, which he had held for thirty-six years. His resignation was accepted, and Mr. Richards Bradley was then elected his successor by a unanimous vote.

At the annual meeting in August the following officers were chosen for the ensuing year:—

OFFICERS OF THE BOARD.

F. Holbrook, Chairman.
W. H. Rockwell, Treasurer.
J. Draper, Secretary.
James M. Tyler, Auditor.

RESIDENT OFFICERS.

Joseph Draper, Superintendent and Physician.
Asa Gilkey, Farmer.
Frances M. Palmer, Matron.
J. M. Clark, } Assistant Physicians.
H. T. Whitney, }

The introduction of the steam heating apparatus, in accordance with the vote in May, was completed in the wings of the main building this season. It was tested on the 10th of November and found to work most satisfactorily. At this point further work in this direction was suspended until the opening of another year.

At the annual election, 1876, the following officers were duly chosen:—

OFFICERS OF THE BOARD.

Frederick Holbrook, Chairman.
W. H. Rockwell, Treasurer.
J. Draper, Secretary.
J. M. Tyler, Auditor.

The office of Matron, vacated by the resignation of Miss Palmer, was not filled at this election.

The Report of the Trustees dwelt at some length upon the steady increase of the dependent classes, seeking admission and gaining the preponderance in the Institution over those self-supporting, and in view of this fact the necessity for an increase in the rate allowed for their support, in order that the receipts necessary for maintaining the establishment, might be sufficient for the creditable accomplishment of this purpose. From their report I make the following supplementary extract:

"The Board would especially press upon the attention of the Legislature the fact that upwards of seventy thousand dollars have been expended by them in the past four years in thoroughly modernizing the establishment. The increased comforts and advantages resulting from the changes effected have been most largely shared by the insane of the State, who constitute two-thirds of the resident number at the present time, and the proportion of whom is steadily increasing. For the benefits of these added appliances, we have received no corresponding compensation.

"We believe the Institution to be on a par with those of the neighboring States in all essential appointments, and in return ask that the State allow for the care and treatment of its wards, a sum more nearly approximating to that deemed just and adequate for their proper care and support in the other New England commonwealths.

"We have carefully observed the operations of the Asylum and find it compares favorably in its results with kindred institutions. In directing the management of its affairs we have been constantly mindful of the rights and interests of the State, and have made it in all practical points meet its requirements by receiving at all times applicants of whatever class, if residents of Vermont, although this policy it will be seen, has been adverse to the pecuniary interests of the Institution.

"In the discharge of our trust it has been our constant endeavor to perfect the establishment in its appointments and increase year

by year its benefits.   We are satisfied that under its present organization its objects are being carried out with faithfulness, and a good
degree of success.

  "We are at the present time engaged in completing the introduction of the steam heating apparatus.   It was so far accomplished
last year that all the wards in the main building were heated by
this means during the winter past.   There still remains to be connected with it arrangements for supplying the establishment with
hot water, and for cooking facilities, which will involve an expenditure of several thousand dollars additional, and which are indispen-
sably necessary."

  The connection of steam radiation was fully completed in the
center building and at the Marsh building this year, so that all
the furnaces heretofore depended upon for heating, were henceforth
abandoned in every part of the Asylum.

  The Superintendent's Report shows four hundred and eighty-nine
inmates; two hundred and twenty-two having been received, and
two hundred and four having been discharged, since the last biennial
report.

  The Organization of the Institution, etc., The Plan, Accommodations and Appointments of the Institution, Occupation, Diversions,
Correspondence of the Inmates, Religious Privileges, State Aid
and Provision for the Insane Poor, Legislation, The Modern View
of Insanity and its Treatment, Morbid Sympathy, and The Lessons
of the Past Two Years, were successively made the topics of discussion and comment.   The following remarks upon The Modern View
of Insanity and its Treatment, are quoted as illustrating the theory
and practice of the Asylum at this period.

  "The recognition of the dependence of mental disorder upon
diseased brain action, marked an important era in the progress
of human biology.   It was a grand stride which embraced mental
functions within physiological laws.   It opened wide the door to all
the humanizing influences of social life.

  "To the extent that all physical maladies are amenable to medical
treatment, mental disorders are amenable in the same manner as all
pathological or diseased physiological conditions are susceptible
of modification and change by the use of medicinal agents; and
so have mental disorders become but the evidences of cerebral
disease, and the term insanity almost a misnomer.

  "But the recognition of the brain as the seat of morbid action
in mental derangement, and of that diseased center as the one
toward which medical treatment may be properly and successfully

directed, is not a terminal point. It is a basis for treatment upon medical principles, but medical treatment is not applicable to mental disorders further than to other physical diseases in general. It is not absolute in curative power. To institute medication in ignorance of the pathogenetic causes, will accomplish little or nothing; disappointment will be the ordinary result.

" In the treatment of mental disorders, however, we are sometimes compelled to labor under such difficulties, at least for a time. We recognize the seat of the malady, but are unable to fathom the underlying and perpetuating causes, or the same may be so complicated and intricate that only a partial benefit is secured. The mischief is kept up by the disturbing causes, which treatment only paliates and does not remove; but in this view are embodied principles which are as yet but in the infancy of their development.

"Looking backward, the maxim has been 'no cure but by medicine.' Looking forward with unshaken faith in the steady progress of the future, and to the gradual development of clearer knowledge concerning the laws of life, it will become more and more the province of the physician to point out the way to health, and less and less to counteract and combat morbid states by means of drugs.

"A knowledge of physiological laws lies at the very basis of all medical knowledge. It is a first principle that every physical organ shall respond to its appropriate stimulus, and a healthful activity results from due stimulation. But only within certain limits does healthful action follow even its legitimate stimulus. It is but a step from pleasure to pain, and undue excitement is attended and succeeded by evil consequences. We have often to look for the causes of physical disorders in excesses of natural functions rather than to the operation of extraneous irritants. Apply this principle to mental derangement, and a broad field is opened to view. The mental functions respond to moral stimuli, hence we have in this direction multiplied agencies of great power which may be turned to curative ends."

The receipts of the biennial term (August 1st, '74 to

August 1st, '76) were,	$180,818.55
The expenditures,	180,584.06
Leaving on hand,	$234.49

The amount expended in the work of permanent improvements, chiefly in constructing steam heating and ventilating flues and extending the heating apparatus, in this period, was $17,313.54.

The foregoing report and record of the last two years is one of steady progress, and unqualified success. In many respects it must be regarded as a period of advancement in respect to new methods. Yet the Asylum again suffered an assault, which after the lapse of ten years the writer cannot but characterize as causeless and unwarranted.

The Legislature of 1874 elected to the office of Commissioner of the Insane a medical gentleman who two years before had himself been an inmate of the Asylum for a number of months, and who left it before convalescence had been established. It will doubtless be conceded that one who had sustained such relation to the Institution, could hardly be unbiassed in his judgment respecting it. The outcome of it, as might have been anticipated, was the arraignment of the Institution from its beginning to the present time, by the Commissioner in his report to the Legislature. This Report the officers of the Asylum felt compelled in self defence to review, and the following quotations will show the points raised and combated.

Under the several heads of the History of the Asylum, the Financial Relation to the State, the Vital Relation to the State, Well Established Truths and Principles, Does this Asylum Apply these Well Established Truths and Principles in the Care and Treatment of the Patients? and Does it Meet the Requirements of a Well Regulated Institution for the Cure of the Insane? Explanation of the Failure of this Asylum as a Hospital for the Insane, and Recommendations, the Commissioner presents his points. Concerning the History of the Asylum nothing need here be repeated.

The Financial Relation to the State shows the value of the Asylum property and gives the whole cost of the establishment prior to 1873 as $234,870.00 which is substantially correct. Since that time there has been expended in the erection of two additional wings, boiler-house, etc., as shown by Report of 1874, $56,214.18, and subsequently as shown by Report of the present year, [1876], for the introduction of steam heating apparatus $17,313.54, or the sum of $83,527.72, in the past four years, making the total cost of the Asylum to the present time $308,397.72; but in making these recent improvements, the Trustees have incurred a debt of $45,000 which at the present time remains unliquidated. The constructions of 1873 are spoken of in the Commissioners Report as "large additions," implying at least a corresponding increase in capacity, hence liable to mislead the public. By reference to the Report of the Asylum 1874, it will be seen that these enlargements of the buildings, were not in fact so much extensions of receiving capacity, as the creation of improved accommodations, for simultaneously with the occupancy of these new wings, that of the entire basement story which had previously been occupied by patients was discontinued and devoted to other uses; and the twenty-six additional rooms gained for use of patients by the erection of said wings, have subsequently been offset and practically lost, by the substitution of tiers of rooms in the old wings for other necessary uses, so that in reality there has been no extension of the capacity of the Institution for the past fifteen years.

"If from the cost of the Institution [$308.387.72] the original bequest of the founder [$10,000], and the appropriations made by the State [$23,000] be taken, there remains $275,397.72 as the result of the financial management of the Institution to the present time, 'more than two-thirds' of which, the Commissioner states, 'should in equity belong to the State, and be divided among the different towns that have sent patients to the Asylum,' etc., etc.

"We cannot imagine more specious logic than this : Nothing in the charter, nor in statutes subsequent thereto, provides for or contemplates any such distribution of ownership. We herewith submit the financial history of the Institution, showing from what sources surplus receipts have been derived, and which of the two—the Institution or the State, has in reality been the gainer, by what the Commissioner styles 'a partnership' of near forty years duration.

"The financial relation of the State with this Institution will be best understood by the statement hereto appended.*

"With more of truth and reason, than of error or injustice, might the assertion of the Commissioner that "the Corporation have all the profits and the State a dearly bought experience," be reversed in its application.

"The Commissioner enters into an 'analysis of the additions' to the buildings from time to time, and of the numbers, and relative proportions of each class of patients at different times, with the view of showing that the additions were made for the accommodation of patients from other States, and were unnecessary for the wants of this State alone, and states that, as long ago as the year 1841, eighty-two, or one-half the resident number were from out of the State, and the number of this class has been increasing year by year, so that the present year it is one hundred and sixty-two.'

"The exact number of patients from out of the State, at the dates mentioned is correct; but if the statement is designed to indicate

*See Table of Construction in Appendix.

that the proportionate number of those from other States, to those of
this, has been steadily increasing, the exact reverse of this is the
truth. For thirty years past, we have exact data showing the number of each class each year, and for fifteen years past [since the
capacity of the Institution has been practically the same as at
present] the relative proportions of State and outside patients have
gradually changed, until at the present time two-thirds of the resident number are from Vermont, and the actual number of the class
of private patients, was the lowest on the first of August last, that it
had been at any time since the year 1856.

"Again the Commissioner complains that 'the Trustees having
the sole superintendence and direction of the Asylum' have planned
these additions and executed their plans without previously consul-
ting the Legislature of the State, and have almost invariably afterwards as each one was made, in their own reports or through those
of the Commissioners of the Insane, requested the Legislature to
contribute towards paying for them by increasing the price of
board, etc.

"It must be evident when the actual independent status of the
Asylum is considered, that consultation with the Legislature in matters which the Trustees were specially responsible for in the discharge
of their trusts, would be at least anomalous ; and we are not a little
astonished at the succeeding statements relative to applications for
increase of pay after each addition made to the Asylum accommodations. That this statement was somewhat inconsiderately made
appears evident from the contradictory facts given before and after,
to wit: 1st. That three of the seven additions enumerated as having
been made to the Institution, [after, in the opinion of the Commissioner, it had attained its proper capacity] were made before any
increase was made in the rate charged for State beneficiaries. And
all the additions previous to the last were made while the State price
did not exceed $1.75 per week. 2nd. That until the year 1855 the
State paid but $1.50 per week. $1.75 from that date to 1864, $2.25
from 1864 to 1869, and $3.00 subsequently. Showing that in the
whole forty years there had been but three changes of rate by the
Legislature, and these changes when made, did not *immediately*
follow upon the erection of buildings, as appears by the date of the
additions, two or more years having intervened in each case between
the last erections and the change of rate, and this being necessitated
more by the times, than by reason of enlargement as charged. If it
be still affirmed that the statement applied to 'requests' not actual
changes, this too is squarely contradicted by the assertion that ' the

State has with confiding generosity granted their requests, with only one exception we believe, and that the last one made.'

"The Commissioner refers to statements made by the Officers of the Asylum in their Report of 1874, [and which are also repeated in that of the present year] concerning the cost of the support of the pauper insane in the Asylums of New England, which averages more than $4.00 per week, and says that the chronic insane in the Asylum at Cranston, R. I., and Tewksbury, Mass., were not included in the average.   This was not as he charitably presumes 'an unintentional error.' It was not the design of the Officers of the Asylum to compare the cost of the support of the insane in the State Asylums, with that of their support in Institutions not exclusively devoted to their care.   The Institutions at Cranston and Tewksbury are State Almshouses, and hence under a different system of economy from that of the Asylums for the Insane, and ought no more to be included in comparisons of cost, than the Almshouses of the towns in this State, Comparisons are useless, unless confined to institutions of the same class.

"The Vital Relation to the State, as shown by tabular statistics in the Report of the Commissioner, give results totally at variance with facts.

"The Commissioner has not followed statistical law, in arriving at his percentages, which is that the per cent. of recoveries should be based upon the admissions, and that of deaths upon the average resident number of each year, or period of years.

"His results are, therefore, inaccurate, except as to the per cent. of recoveries in the first years, which could not be otherwise, as at the opening of the establishment there were none to be taken into account with those who were subsequently received.   In every other period, however, there was a previously accumulated burden to be considered, adverse to recoveries, but bearing constantly upon the death rate.   The premises being erroneous, it follows, of course, that all the conclusions from them are calculated to mislead the reader.

"The first table compares the per cent. of recoveries in the first two with those of the last two years.   It is correctly stated at 32.62 for the first period, but not for the last, the percentage being 25.22 per cent., instead of 8.08, a very vital difference.

"The per cent. of deaths is incorrectly made both in regard to the first and last periods being cast upon the whole number under treatment in each instance, instead of the average resident number, which latter basis gives for the first two years 5.55 per cent., and 5.66 per cent. for the last two, a scarcely material difference.

"The same table shows in the second place the percentage of recoveries for the two years ending the first decade of the Institution, and in the third place the same for the two years just ended ; and here we find widely varying results.   The first period shows 38.15 per cent. of recoveries and 9.24 per cent. of deaths ; while the latter period gives 25.22 per cent. of the former to 5.66 per cent. of the latter.

"The second table gives the comparative results of the first and the last ten years.

"The per cent. of recoveries for the first period is correctly stated by the Commissioner at 42.05, but for the second period is about 10 per cent. higher than there given, viz., 32.04.

"The percentage of deaths is 7.42 for the first period and 7.02 for the last, there being a fractional difference in favor of the last ten years.

"The third table compares the first seven years with the year 1854 alone, and is the most fallacious of all.   The latter year, as the Commissioner states, was selected because the whole number under treatment, (that is those in the Asylum at the beginning of the year, and those admitted during that year, taken together) *coincided* with the number admitted during the first named period; obviously no such comparison could have been made, had statistical laws been followed, unless for the purpose of supporting a preconceived theory; however, the legitimate results of the comparison show a larger per cent. of both recoveries and deaths, than during the first seven years, hence so far as the percentage of recoveries goes is in favor of the single years' results.

"We do not propose, however, in refutation of garbled statistics, to resort to the like method; but rather to rest upon the whole history of the establishment, for its statistical results, and then, as far as possible, compare them with the results of the other New England Asylums.

"The large number of chronic cases carried by the Institution, necessarily limits the admissions, hence we find in most of the New England Institutions a more rapid movement of the population than in this,—and as the recoveries come from the current admissions almost wholly, we should expect to find a larger percentage in those where the movement is greatest.

"The statistics of the Vermont Asylum for the whole forty years are as follows: Percentage of recoveries, 42.09; of deaths, 8.35. For the last ten years they are as follows: Percentage of recoveries, 32.04; of deaths, 7.02.

"The mean average of recoveries and deaths in the State Hospitals of New England: Maine, New Hampshire, Worcester, Taunton and Northampton, Mass.; Butler Hospital, R. I., and Connecticut, for the ten years past, is as follows: Percentage of recoveries, 32.14; of deaths, 10.25.*

"The Commissioner justly anticipates the explanation that may be given of a lessened number of recoveries in the latter years, but as the corrected statistics show so much less difference in the actual results, it is scarcely necessary to refer to them. A careful and somewhat extended analysis of Asylum statistics by Dr. Jarvis some years ago, amounted to the conclusion, that of every one hundred patients treated, forty-two would recover, eight die, and the remaining fifty continue in a state of mental invalidism. In the whole history of the Vermont Asylum the results do not materially vary from this. It *is* true that the Institution has retained these chronic cases, where other asylums have discharged them. The point is not waived by the statement that 'they are only transferred into other institutions' so far as the statistics of the Asylums from which they are thus transferred are concerned, for they are counted as discharged there, whether they go to other institutions or elsewhere, and in view of the fact just stated regarding the curability of insanity, the charge that the chronic insane cared for in the Vermont Asylum are 'of its own making,' falls to the ground of its own weight, and could hardly have been made by any careful, candid and unprejudiced mind.

"Accepting as 'Well Established Truths and Principles' that ' insanity is a disease of the brain,' and that it 'is a disease amenable to proper treatment in a large proportion of cases for its cure, and in many other cases for its amelioration,' and that 'institutions of proper size, and under good management, and with all the necessary appliances and appurtenances have an advantage in the treatment of insane patients over those treated at their own homes, both in economy and success in the way of cure,' the three points made by the Commissioner, we pass to the inquiry, 'Does this Asylum apply these well-established Truths and Principles in the care and treatment of its patients, and does it meet the requirements of a well regulated institution for the care of the insane?'

* In Connecticut the eight years existence of the State Hospital at Middletown, and the two previous years of the Hartford Retreat (which, until the opening of Middletown Institution, served the purposes of the State), are included to make up the period.

"In the 'opinion' of the Commissioner 'it does not now, and has not since the first ten years.' Here we take issue. The capacity of the Institution is complained of, as being 'far beyond the size capable of the best success in the cure of insanity.'

"This is a point that has been much discussed by those engaged in the management of such establishments, and the Association of Superintendents of the insane asylums of the United States, has twice placed itself on record in this matter. Formerly the curability of insanity was regarded as much greater than at present, and acting upon this belief, it was the expression of that body that 'two hundred and fifty was the highest desirable number to be treated in one institution.' This was twenty-five years ago. Fifteen years elapsed and during that time the pressure upon all the asylums in the country greatly increased. New institutions were not created as rapidly as they were demanded. This led to the adoption of the policy quite universally of discharging the chronic to make room for the acute cases. This filled the almshouses with incurables and entailed manifold evils. Then arose the question of separate provision for the two classes. Institutions exclusively for the incurables were opposed by the association, on the ground that where curative agencies were not deemed indispensable, the character of asylums would tend to degenerate into that of almshouses—the question of dollars and cents being uppermost, and the policy of providing for all in a uniform manner, whatever might be their prospect for recovery, was favored, as having on its side the best interests of the insane.

"In 1868, therefore, the same body expressed the opinion that institutions 'embracing the usual proportions of curable and incurable insane, in a particular community, may be properly carried to the extent of accommodating six hundred patients,' and such is the capacity of many of the asylums since erected, or in process of erection at the present time, and others in existence previously have since been enlarged to correspond with the later conclusions. It will be seen therefore, that the Trustees of the Vermont Asylum have not pursued a policy contradictory to the views which have shaped State policy throughout this country.

"Again, the Commissioner urges that this Institution 'has put upon its superintendents such a burden and so much labor, that they have little time to use, and improve those high qualifications of medical skill and experience, for which they were mainly selected,' and further, that 'they are reduced by this pressure upon their time and energies to mere superintendents comparatively, and anything like individual treatment of patients is impossible.'

"It is true that the responsibilities, attaching to such positions are onerous enough. The Commissioner, however, fully agrees that in the organization of an establishment of this kind, its practical working 'must be under the control of one man, to act both as superintendent and physician,' hence it follows that the efficiency of all such establishments must depend upon the systematic carrying out of the working plan in its practical details. It is not expected that the physician in chief of a hospital will perform all the medical and surgical duties incident to his charge personally, although the responsibility is his; but that he will be the counsellor of his medical assistants, and the director of the working corps, in every department.

"In respect to the number of assistants and subordinates necessary for the efficient administration of its internal economy he is expected to be the judge; and if the superintendents of the Vermont Asylum have had any cause to complain of inability to exercise in the most efficient manner their prerogatives, it has not been from any limitation on the part of those having the oversight.and direction of its affairs, but solely from the lack of means; and certainly no person practically acquainted with the management of asylums, would consider the professional duties incident to the care of a household of the proportions of recent and chronic cases which at present compose the numbers under treatment, more difficult than would be the care of half the number composed largely of acute cases.

"Again the Commissioner asserts that 'the Institution has not increased its appliances and facilities for cure, as the size increased.' In a word, the reader is led to infer that the Institution saw its best days before it had existed ten years, and has been gradually declining for the last thirty years, until it has now reached its lowest ebb.

"We note with special astonishment the remarks of the Commissioner relative to religious exercises, and amusements. Although the history of the Institution as embodied in its annual reports, seems to have been thoroughly reviewed, he seems not to have taken into account its small beginning and gradual enlargement, and that many things which were practicable in its early years, became impracticable after the establishment outgrew the family organization. Without enumerating the list of amusements specified, and lugubriously reflected upon by the Commissioner, suffice it to say, that at no period in the history of the Institution has greater attention been paid to the subject of diversions, and to the securing of adequate religious privileges, than during the Commissioner's term of office. So important have these influences seemed to us, that we have each year marked out and carried out a regular course of entertainments, consisting of social parties, dramatic exhibitions, exhibitions of magic lantern views with descriptive readings, concerts, lectures, etc., all of which have been enumerated with their dates, in the Report of the Officers of the Asylum for the period just past—and I find by reference to memoranda made at the time that the Commissioner himself was present on no less than four occasions at these entertainments, yet no mention whatever is made of anything of the kind.

" It has been the effort of the officers of the Asylum to secure to its inmates as far as possible, all those privileges and diversions from which they are, by isolation from society, deprived; and if in any one direction our efforts have been especially successful, we think they have been in this; and in our arrangement for Sunday services, we secure every possible advantage to our household by rotation in our clerical supply, thus affording to those of all denominations the valued privilege of hearing in turn their own.

" The officers of the Institution do not regard the general plan of the Asylum as specially defective. When founded more than a generation ago, it was in accordance with the most approved architecture of the time, and though built by successive additions of wings, and carried ultimately somewhat beyond the original design, the extensions have nevertheless followed the arrangement of institutions planned for the like capacity of this at their beginning, and which have been found to embody the greatest practical advantages.

" Minor defects have been mainly remedied, and the recent improvements made, will be found more fully detailed in the report of the operations of the Asylum for the biennial period just passed, to which we would refer in detail, and respectfully request its examination in connection with that of the Commissioner.

" To the complaints that the Institution has locked doors and guarded windows, and that mechanical restraints are employed, we have only to reply, that we have in use no safe-guards, nor restraints not deemed essential to the proper management of every similar institution throughout our land.

" The complaint against the enclosed airing courts for the use of patients who cannot with propriety be taken out upon the open grounds for exercise, ignores the fact that such persons ought rather to be protected from, than exposed to public observation, and that such provision is of the most vital importance in securing to this class, who otherwise could rarely be taken out, the constant hygienic advantages of open air and sunshine, in common with the larger class, who from the wards in general, enjoy their daily exercise in the eighteen acres of unenclosed grounds in front of the Asylum, or in longer walks along the roadside or in the fields.

"The Commissioner's 'Explanation of the failure of this Asylum as a Hospital for the Insane,' calls for little final comment. The points have been all met in the preceding pages of this review. The 'melancholy results, as shown by the vital statistics,' have been corrected, and will be seen to be favorable to its 'management' rather than otherwise, and creditable in comparison with the other State institutions of New England.

"Its 'policy' in respect to extension, has been shown to be consonant with the general State policy; and the assertion that 'all its obligations were to this State' rests upon no shadow of foundation. The Commissioner conveys the impression that the interests of the insane in this State have been greatly prejudiced by the admission of those from other states, and the inference is drawn that because the Institution was patronized by the State, it should have devoted itself *solely* to its interests.

"That no such exclusiveness, however, was contemplated, or entered into originally, is sufficiently evident by the proviso of 1837, giving residents a first or preferred right; hence such an assumption at the present time is unwarranted, as is that relative to the building up of an establishment beyond the capacity required for the number belonging to this State, and the consequent reception of a limited number from other States, as having been detrimental to those from Vermont. It is from these that the surplus receipts of the Institu- have been largely derived, and out of which have been afforded many of the advantages all have enjoyed.

"Its 'enormous expense to the State,' pecuniarily, and 'of the lives and welfare of citizens committed to its care,' will be best understood by the statistical facts, carefully prepared, and herewith submitted.*

"To the 'Recommendation' of the Commissioner, that 'the Legislature dissolve the unnatural relationship of the State to the Vermont Asylum for the Insane,' and erect as soon as may be a Hospital for the Insane, which shall be under its own control and management,' the Trustees have only to say that this is a question for that body to decide; perhaps such a step would relieve the Vermont Asylum of some of the gross misrepresentations to which it is now subjected. The Trustees have kept scrupulous faith with the State

*See Tables of General Results in Appendix.

in respect to the relations existing between it and the Asylum, and believe the interests of the former have been better served thereby, than have those of the latter. They would, however, respectfully urge the insufficiency of the allowance made by the Legislature for the support of the State insane, and feel that it is unfair at least to institute critical comparisons between this Asylum and those of the neighboring States, without taking likewise into account what Vermont has done towards securing adequate provision and proper care of its insane, in proportion to the other States.

"The officers of the Vermont Asylum feel that it is quite time that the relations of the State to the Institution should be fully comprehended; and that if these relations are to be continued, there should be an end of all antagonism, and that henceforth a more liberal policy, and a more charitable feeling should be exercised toward the Institution. These chronic complaints and expressions of distrust, are alike injurious to the public and the Institution, and ought for the common good to be silenced.

                                    J. DRAPER,
            Secretary of Board of Trustees and Superintendent.
Vermont Asylum for the Insane, Brattleboro, Oct. 25, 1876."

The Legislature of this year (1876) amended its standing Rules, by creating a joint committee consisting of five members of the House with three of the Senate, to take into consideration all matters relating to the insane, and to be denominated the "Committee on the Insane." This Committee visited the Asylum and made the following Report:

To the Honorable Senate and House of Representatives
  - now in Session:

"Your Committees, to whom was referred that part of the Governor's message relating to the insane, beg leave to state that although they were appointed by each House as separate standing committees, yet they have acted jointly in their investigations, and, therefore, take the liberty of submitting their conclusions in a joint report.

"Before entering upon a statement of our finding of facts and the conclusions deducible therefrom, it may be pertinent to give a brief resumé of the oft-repeated history and relation of the Asylum for the insane at Brattleboro to the State.

"The Institution had its origin in a bequest by Mrs. Anna Marsh, of Hinsdale, New Hampshire, of ten thousand dollars, and was incorporated by the Legislature in November, 1834. From the years 1835 to 1843 the State donated, in a series of installments, the sum of twenty-three thousand dollars for the benefit of the Institution, and by the terms of the acts of appropriation passed in 1840 and 1843 (that of 1843 being the last appropriation to aid in building) the State reserved a lien upon the real estate of the corporation, to be enforced whenever the Institution should cease to exist for the purposes contemplated in its charter. Shortly after our appointment, we requested the Commissioner for the Insane, Dr. Atwater of Burlington, and the Superintendent of the Asylum, Dr. Draper of Brattleboro, to meet us at Montpelier, which they did ; and such information upon the questions at issue was at that meeting obtained as was practicable. Afterwards on the last day of October and first of November, we visited the Asylums at Brattleboro and Northampton, Massachusetts, making as careful an examination and comparison of the two Institutions and their methods of operation as we were able in the time expended. Subsequently, we again met the Commissioner and Superintendent at Montpelier, concluding our investigations at that hearing.

"Is the treatment of the insane at the Brattleboro Asylum successful? This question we deem to be the one of paramount importance and upon its solution practically depends the whole issue.

"Has the Institution the means and appliances which, if brought into proper use, would secure the result desired? This leads us to the consideration of the location and construction of the Asylum buildings, their capacity and adaptation for the purposes used.

"The buildings are located about one mile from the depot at the beautiful village of Brattleboro, having in their immediate vicinity grounds and surroundings affording a most satisfactory opportunity for pleasant outside exercise. The main or principal structure stands upon the east side of the road leading from Brattleboro northerly, and the so-called Marsh Building upon the west side of the road, opposite the main buildings. Their external appearance is not that of a "huge pile of brick and mortar," but in architectural design and construction is such as would rank fairly with other buildings of like character in the country. The internal arrangement of the rooms in the principal buildings, as to size, light, cleanliness, ventilation and means of controlling temperature, was a matter which attracted our special attention and most careful examination, and upon the whole we were inclined to the opinion that it was in neither respects mentioned substantially defective or objectionable, although some of us thought a few of the sleeping rooms hardly sufficient in size. We

did not find the internal construction of the Marsh Building as satisfactory as that of the others in all respects, although not very materially exposed to criticism, but we were assured by the Trustees that
it was their present purpose to overhaul and thoroughly renovate
this building, as soon as found practicable, considering their means
for so doing.

"We discovered no want of furniture, bedding, etc., either in
quantity or quality, and thought it sufficient for the comfort of the
patients.

"Although of minor importance, perhaps, in some respects, yet
we think it our duty to suggest that a comparatively inconsiderable
outlay in the direction of additional adornment of the walls is desirable, and might at least produce an appreciably beneficial result.

"A few words about the court yards connected with the buildings
may not be out of place. They were provided for the purpose of
securing a more extensive and less expansive admission of a certain
class of patients to air and exercise than they would otherwise have.
The one connected with the main buildings seems not to be faulty,
but that adjacent to the Marsh Building is certainly "not a thing of
beauty," however well it may serve purposes of utility, although in
justice it may be said that this yard was designed and is used for a
class so near a state of dementia as to be apparently hardly capable of
discerning or appreciating beauty. This much will suffice concerning
the location and construction, external and internal, of the building.

"Have the buildings sufficient capacity for the number of patients now there in keeping, and, if so, is it for the best interests of
successful treatment that so large a number should be kept together
in one asylum under one direction and management?

"If the second question should be unconditionally answered in
the affirmative, the first might be relieved of any considerable difficulty, as the buildings are not over-crowded, but upon the second
question hangs the doubt. It is probable that a preponderance of
opinion of the experts upon this subject is in favor of limiting the
number of patients in any institution for the treatment of the insane,
to three hundred, claiming, as reasons for that belief, that each hospital must be under the sole control of one man, to act both as superintendent and physician, who cannot properly discharge his duty
to each patient having a larger number than that under his care for
treatment, and further, that they cannot be as well classified and are
exposed to unreasonable and extraordinary perils of epidemics and
casualties. Upon the other side, it is urged that no detriment results
from the keeping together of a very much larger number, and that

the whole question is one of comparative means and necessities. That while one superintendent may not be able to treat and direct the treatment and care of a number exceeding three hundred patients, yet he may be entirely able to faithfully and efficiently discharge his obligation to an institution having many more than that, among which are a proportion of incurables, sufficiently large to reduce the number of those who could possibly be benefitted by treatment to much less than three hundred. Quite a proportion of the inhabitants of the Asylum at Brattleboro are in a chronic stage of disease, many being hopelessly incurable, and being past the reach of medical treatment do not necessarily engage any considerable attention from the Superintendent as directing physician. The theory of the learned upon this subject seems to favor about three hundred patients as the maximum number allowable, while the practice of the same enlightened class, particularly in public institutions in this country, tolerate a much larger number.

"Next, is the treatment of the inmates at the Vermont Asylum of that approved character as would be expected to produce reasonably beneficial effects? We have heard no complaint about the manner in which they are clothed or fed, and certainly discerned no cause for any. We were not able to determine to our utmost satisfaction as to the efficiency of their open air exercise, although we were assured by the managers that it was fully up to their needs and the requirements of health. Judging from what we saw and were able to learn respecting diversions by way of entertainment and amusements, it would be unjust to find the management markedly faulty in that direction.

"We found a comparatively small number of patients undergoing different kinds or forms of restraint, but in no instance, in our belief, did the cause or method involve cruelty or impropriety. A few were secluded by being locked in separate rooms, but this small number included none whom it was safe to allow in company or association with others. This fact was perfectly patent from the appearance of the patients. In conclusion of this subject we could not find that mechanical restraints, locks, grates or bars, occupy any more prominent position in the ordering or direction of the Vermont Asylum than in the Asylum at Northampton. No evidence has been discernable to us that the active medical treatment of the patient was less or different from that which the best skill would suggest ; and we certainly would not feel justified in indulging in speculative conjectures in the entire absence of proof and against the presence of probabilities.

"The number and apparent standing of the corps of medical attendants we found to be equal to that at Northampton, and the number of subordinate attendants a few more than at the last named hospital, and the number of inmates at the two institutions the same.

"Our statement thus far has been confined to what we conceived to be such facts and conclusions of fact as are true and material and bearing upon what might be expected for results

"We now come to the results as proved by the statistics of the Vermont Asylum in comparison with those of other states. We make comparisons for the last ten years and find the percentage of recoveries for that time at the Vermont Asylum to be 32.04; and of deaths, 7.02. The mean average of percentage of recoveries and deaths for the rest of New England during the same time, we find to be as follows :

" Percentage of recoveries, 32.14 ; of deaths, 10.25. These. comparisons have been made with institutions similar in character with that at Brattleboro, and we believe them a fair test, which, if true, leaves the conclusion inevitable that the treatment of the insane at the Vermont Asylum is at least reasonably successful.

"We could hardly do full justice to the question involved without briefly stating our opinion in regard to the tendency of the Institution at Brattleboro, in the direction of improvement and reform. It is quite clear that it has not reached a state of perfection, but quite as evident that the last few years have witnessed a substantial change in many respects, all of which have materially bettered its condition, and at the present time still further modifications and changes in the direction of reform are in contemplation. We are fully satisfied that the Institution is under the management of humane, competent and conscientious officials, whose single purpose is to do their duty fully and well.

"At this point we may be pardoned for venturing an opinion upon the question of propriety of establishing a State asylum. If one were to be erected, its capacity should undoubtedly be equal to the accommodation of three hundred patients. According to the best authorities the expense for buildings, apparatus and appliances, at the lowest estimate, would be at the rate of one thousand dollars for each patient to be accommodated, making the cost, if authority and the experience of other States are at all reliable, three hundred thousand dollars.

"The cost of the asylums in Massachusetts, with one or two exceptions, have been largely in excess of the above estimate.

" In view of these facts, we do not feel self-sacrificing enough to take upon ourselves the burden of attempting to secure the necessary appropriation for that purpose.

" We have been requested by the Superintendent and Trustees of the Asylum to recommend a bill increasing the pay for keeping the State insane to three dollars and fifty cents per week, and the aid to towns to one dollar per week.

" We are of the opinion that the State should pay the Asylum the actual cost of keeping and supporting its insane, and no more—and are also of the opinion that the cost, upon an average, is three dollars and thirty-three cents per week, for each patient—we therefore recommend the passage of the accompanying bill herewith submitted.

HENRY C. BELDEN,	Committee
C. W. BRIGHAM,	of the
E. P. GEORGE,	Senate.
R. C. ABELL,	
RALPH SHERWOOD,	Committee
E. O. PORTER,	on part of
CHARLES W. CLARK,	the House.
P. R. FOLLANSBY,	

The result of the foregoing Report and Review in the way of Legislative action was the passage of the following Joint Resolution in relation to the insane of the State and the statutes in relation to their confinement and treatment.

" RESOLVED BY THE SENATE AND HOUSE OF REPRESENTATIVES:

" That the governor be directed to appoint three commissioners, whose duty it shall be to inquire into the statutes now in force, in relation to the confinement and treatment of the insane of our State, and see what changes are necessary, if any, in said laws; also, to inquire into the treatment of our insane, and determine what, if any, legislation is necessary, and transmit their report to the next session of the Legislature."

This was approved Nov. 28, 1876.

O N the 13th of February, 1877, the Institution suffered the loss by fire of the boiler house, stable, carriage house, straw house and ice house, with most of their contents, also of the contents of the cellars.   Estimated loss $25,000, insured for $8,000.

The following account in detail is taken from the Vermont Phœnix of the 16th of the same month:

"At twenty minutes past seven on Tuesday morning, in the midst of one of the worst gales of this season, the village was aroused by the sound of the Asylum fire-whistle, and its warning note had hardly reached the ears of the people before a dense volume of blinding smoke came pouring down Main street, giving rise to the gravest apprehensions.   A general alarm was immediately given, followed by a rush of nearly every able-bodied citizen for the scene of the fire.   To those who were first on the ground the situation was indeed an alarming one.   The streets were black with smoke, and so dense and threatening was the cloud that rolled over and enveloped the buildings, that even from the top of the hill near the common they were entirely invisible.   The fire proved to have originated in the stable which stood in the rear of the west wing of the Institution, and by the time the first outside help arrived, both the stable and the carriage house, straw barn and wagon shed which adjoined it on the side next the street, were a mass of thick smoke and flame, which roared and leaped from the doors, windows and roof, and in the terrible northwest gale drove straight toward the main building in a way which seemed to render its immediate destruction inevitable.   Adjoining the stable on the other side, stood the new boiler house, and the upper part of this building was also soon wrapped in raging flames which threatened every moment to spread to the laundry building and thence to the north wing, and so on through the whole Institution.   Altogether the prospect, if not a hopeless one, was such as called for instant and decisive action, and made the stoutest heart grow faint at the thought of the possible consequences.   The citizens as they arrived went promptly to work, and the fire department was soon on hand.   Phœnix Company No. 6 was the first to reach the spot, but not having correctly understood the order how and where to reach the water, Fountain No. 4 took a position at a reservoir on the grounds just west of the main entrance, and got the first stream of water on the fire, it being directed toward subduing the flames at the corner next the west wing and keeping them from spreading to the main building at that point.   The Phœnix was meantime placed in the street, and took water from Hydropath No. 3, which was stationed at the resorvoir on Oak street.   This stream was used to check the fire in the boiler house and to keep it from spreading in that direction.   The rest of the department was actively employed, and Estey's steamer was sent for and did effective service in playing from the reservoir on the common.   The most exposed point, and the one where the most imminent danger existed was at the north end of the west wing, where the heat from the burning barn and shed was intense and overpowering.   By the heroic efforts of the firemen, however, nobly seconded as they were by those of a determined corps of citizens, the fire was kept from getting a lodgment in the main building until the blazing walls and roof fell in or were pulled down.   Equally effective work was also done on the roof of the boiler house, with the fortunate result that in something like an hour from the time when it started the fire was under control and the worst danger was over, although watchful and untiring work was necessary for some time longer.

"The behavior of everybody on this occasion, in doors and out— firemen, citizens, and employes of the Institution—was of the most admirable character.   There was nothing like a panic, and no exhibition of undue excitement.   There is no doubt that the fire caught from the chimney or stove in the stable, the common theory being that the chimney took fire and burned out in the fierce wind.   The flames were first discovered by the engineer, or his wife, and he at once opened the fire-whistle and gave the alarm.   It unfortunately happened that Dr. Draper, the superintendent, had been subpœnaéd to attend the trial of Hayden, the Derby Line murderer, as a witness, and for this reason had been compelled to leave for Irasburgh on the previous day.   In his absence Dr. Clark, first assistant physician, proved himself equal to the emergency by his prompt and cool-headed action.   His first thought was for the patients in the most exposed part of the west wing, and after seeing them removed to a place of comparative safety, he lent his personal efforts to fighting the fire in a way which won him universal praise.   The ladies of the house manifested a most praiseworthy calmness, ready for whatever might come. The first care of the out-door employes was for the horses in the stable, and these were all safely removed. The patients in the various wards, strange to say, manifested but little unusual excitement, so that in no respect was there any such scene of confusion as one might imagine would attend a fire in a place like this. Pails of hot coffee were freely distributed from the kitchen to the firemen and others.

"The newly organized fire police proved their efficiency by promptly taking possession of the laundry wing, and in a rapid but orderly manner clearing it of all movable articles. These men were afterward distributed through the main building to keep out the sparks and cinders which the wind continually drove in under the window sashes, making a source of constant danger.

"The total loss involved cannot as yet be stated with precision. The stable, carriage house, etc., which was of brick, and with the boiler house formed a continuous line of buildings from the street to the laundry wing, is a total loss, although portions of the walls are standing. The lower part of the boiler house is in good condition and the boilers and their connections were happily found to be uninjured, so that early in the afternoon the fires were rekindled and the whole Institution was warmed and made as comfortable as ever. The store house, meat house, cellars, etc., contained upward of two tons of butter, two thousand bushels of potatoes, a large quantity of other vegetables, and stores of various kinds, all of which is a total loss. The wheeled carriages, several of which were very valuable, were burned, with two exceptions. Only one of the sleighs was saved.

"In many respects it seems little less than miraculous that the loss was confined within such bounds as it was. The wind which prevailed in the streets of the town at the time of the fire was as nothing compared with its fury as it swept up from the river and interval and across the corner where the flames raged fiercest, making it at times impossible for one to keep his feet, or make headway against it. That the Institution was saved must be attributed to the fact that the buildings are so nearly fire proof. Had even the cornice of the west wing been of wood, its rescue would have been impossible. It was a notable fact that every individual present worked, and evidently felt as though he had a personal interest in saving the property. The officers of the Asylum fully realize this,

and they have asked us to express to the fire department and citizens, their deep sense of appreciation of their laborious services, and
of the fact that to them alone it is due that the Institution still stands
practically unharmed.''

At a meeting of the Trustees, on the 15th of March following, it
was decided to locate the stable and carriage house farther from the
main buildings, and upon the west side of the road, using for this
purpose the large wood-house built in 1866, and removed to its
present site in 1870, and to rebuild the burned line of buildings
[190 feet x 40], using the seventy-five feet adjoining the laundry
building for boiler room below, engineer's work shop on first story,
with farmer's lodgings above, as before, the central section [40 feet]
for stores, both stories, and the seventy-five feet next the road, the
height of both stories in one, for the purposes of a gymnasium; the
latter the suggestion of Mr. Bradley.

June 5th the full Board convened for the discussion of the plans
for the new buildings, and determined to have the brick work done
by day's work instead of by contract, under the charge of a foreman,
and general oversight of the architect, the whole being under the
supervision of Dr. Rockwell, as the agent of the Board.

The annual election of officers took place at the August meeting,
no changes being made.

OFFICERS OF THE BOARD.

Frederick Holbrook, Chairman.
W. H. Rockwell, Treasurer.
J. Draper, Secretary.
J. M. Tyler, Auditor.

RESIDENT OFFICERS.

Joseph Draper, Superintendent and Physician.
Asa Gilkey, Farmer.
—— ——, Matron.
J. M. Clark,
F. W. Spaulding, } Assistant Physicians.

At the September meeting it was decided to introduce steam
cooking apparatus, which was begun without delay.

In October the small cottage situated near the Cold spring,
together with a half acre of land more or less, was purchased of
Rinaldo N. Hescock for the sum of $775.

· The cost of reconstructing the wood-house into a stable and
carriage house, and rebuilding the burned line of buildings this year
was $23,449.29.

At the November meeting this year the Trustees considered the matter of the revision of the By-Laws, which had been little changed since their adoption in 1845, and directed the secretary to revise those articles defining the duties of the resident officers, and submit the same to the Board for their consideration, at the next meeting.

The revision being submitted as ordered, was carefully considered and adopted, with other articles relating to the duties of the officers of the Board, by the Trustees at their meeting in January following.

BY-LAWS.

ARTICLE I.

SECTION I.   There shall be a meeting of the Trustees at the Asylum on the second Tuesday of every month, at two o'clock, P. M., to examine into the state of the Institution, the condition and situation of the patients, the accounts of the officers, and to transact any and all other business deemed expedient when met.

ARTICLE II.

SEC. I.   No vote shall be passed at any meeting unless there be three Trustees voting in the affirmative ; provided, at a subsequent monthly meeting to which any matter may be adjourned, the same may be passed by a majority of those present.

ARTICLE III.

SEC. I.   At the monthly meeting in August, which shall be the annual meeting, the following officers shall be chosen and appointed, to wit : A chairman, treasurer, secretary, and auditor of accounts ; a superintendent and physician, two assistant physicians, a matron, and a farmer, who shall be resident officers. The assistant physicians, matron and farmer, shall be nominated annually by the Superintendent, and appointed by the Trustees. Provided, however, in case of vacancy, or in case said officers shall not be chosen at the annual meeting, such vacancy may be filled, or such officers chosen at any subsequent monthly meeting, and the salaries of all officers shall be from time to time fixed by the Trustees.

ARTICLE IV.

SEC. I.   The chairman may at any time, and shall on the request of either Trustee or the Superintendent, call special meetings, giving each Trustee personal notice, or notice by secretary, and shall preside at the meetings of the board.

ARTICLE V.

SEC. 1. The treasurer shall have charge of all deeds, and other securities and obligations belonging to the Asylum, and shall receive and hold all bequests, or trust funds of the Asylum for specific purposes, and disburse the same under the direction of the Trustees, and in accordance with their specified objects.

SEC. 2. He shall also hold all policies of insurance, effected by Trustees for the preservation of the property, and shall be the agent of the board in all matters pertaining to said trusts and insurance.

SEC. 3. He shall likewise direct the deposits, and oversee the disbursements of the current funds collected by the Superintendent, and shall make report annually to the board of the condition of the securities and funds in his charge, and of the amount of insurance carried, together with any suggestions relative to the same that may seem to him advisable or necessary.

ARTICLE VI.

SEC. 1. The secretary shall have charge of the records of the Trustees; shall attend the meetings of the board and record their proceedings therein. He shall also have charge of all papers of a historical character, and record, in addition to the proceedings of the board, any other papers or statements that the Trustees may order to be so recorded. He will also, under direction of the chairman of the board notify the members of the meetings to be held.

ARTICLE VII.

SEC. 1. It shall be the duty of the auditor in the month of July, annually, to audit all the accounts of the officers of the Institution; take an inventory of all the property of the corporation, and take an account of all claims in favor of and against the Institution, so as to show its true standing on the first day of August, annually. He shall also audit all bills contracted for building or other purposes outside of the current expenditures, as they fall due, and are referred to him by the superintendent or other agent of the board.

ARTICLE VIII.

SEC. 1. The superintendent, under the direction of the Trustees, shall have the general oversight and superintendence of the Asylum in all its departments, and all the associate resident officers shall be subordinate to his authority.

SEC. 2. In the discharge of his duties his first care shall be for the welfare of the patients committed to the charge of the Institution, and this care must be so far personal that he shall be at all times conversant with the actual condition of each individual case, and he must be responsible for the classification of the inmates, and the general course of treatment pursued.

SEC. 3. He will also be responsible for the current financial management of the Asylum, under the direction of the Trustees ; determining the number of employes in the various departments, establishing for them regulations, and so governing the expenditures of the several departments that a wise economy may be practiced, and as much as possible be accomplished with the resources of the Institution at command.

SEC. 4. He shall make up the accounts of the patients as they accrue, collect the same regularly, and pay all bills as they fall due, keeping a bank account in the name of the Institution, and subject to the direction and oversight of the treasurer, where all his deposits shall be made ; and shall carefully take and preserve vouchers for all monetary transactions, for the inspection of the auditor, and shall refer all bills, except for current expenditures, to the auditor before settlement of them.

SEC. 5. He shall endeavor in every way to promote the efficiency of the staff of resident officers and the corps of employes, and hold each in his place to faithfulness in the performance of his duties ; and on his part carry out the designs of the Institution, and the views and instructions of the Trustees, upon its general management and policy.

SEC. 6. All assistants and employes will be directly responsible to the superintendent, and subject to his regulations.

SEC. 7. Records of all cases admitted and treated, and of all the transactions of the Asylum, shall be kept, or caused to be kept, by the superintendent, and shall be at all times subject to the inspection of the Trustees.

SEC. 8. He shall give his whole time to the interests of the establishment, engaging in no other business whereby the welfare of the Asylum shall be compromised, and in case of his temporary absence shall require both his medical assistants to be on duty, unless by special leave of the Trustees, but in no case shall the Asylum be left without a medical officer.

SEC. 9. He shall lay before the Trustees at each monthly meeting a statement of the number of patients received, discharged, or deceased during the month previous ; stating the name and residence of such patients, the time of their admission and the security taken therefor, the time of their discharge or decease, and if discharged whether cured or improved or not ; together with an account of all moneys received and paid out, from and·to whom, and for what, which account shall be balanced so as to show the exact state of the finances each month, and on the first of August annually, these monthly statements shall be embodied in an annual report to the Trustees, which shall thus embrace the current results of each year's operations.

ARTICLE IX.

SEC. 1. The duties of the assistant physicians shall be to carry out in detail the medical treatment of the inmates, as well as the plans for their exercise and recreation, and the system of amusements that may from time to time be adopted. They shall have charge of the dispensary, and of all medicines, instruments and apparatus belonging to the medical department of the Asylum, and keep the same in good order at all times.

SEC. 2. For the more efficient discharge of their duties, their work and responsibilities shall be divided; one of them (in the discretion·of the superintendent) taking charge of the male, and the other of the female wards. Besides attending to their professional duties as above defined, they shall be required to support the discipline of the corps of employes, and to render to the superintendent such aid in the administrative departments as naturally devolves upon them under the regulations governing the attendants and employes.

SEC. 3. Each shall keep the records in the case books of his department, in as full a manner as may be required by the superintendent, and keep any other records that may be necessary in the prosecution of extended observations, in any line of professional inquiry that may be instituted, requiring the co-operation of the medical officers. Both will be expected at all times and in every way practicable, to labor for the interests of the Institution, and afford to the friends of patients, and to visitors, all proper and requisite information relative to the inmates, and the Institution.

SEC. 4. They will daily, and as much oftener as may be necessary, report to the superintendent upon the cases under treatment, relative to the progress made, and concerning any occurrence of an unusual or unexpected character, and consult with him in reference to any changes in classification or course of treatment, that may be indicated. Any instances of ill treatment of patients, or evidences of unsuitableness for position on the part of attendants or others employed, they will also report, and will uniformly endeavor to instruct them in the discharge of their duties, so that humane and kindly treatment may be secured to the inmates.

SEC. 5.   Both shall not be absent from the Asylum at the same time unless by permission of the superintendent.   In the absence of the superintendent, the senior assistant physician shall act in his place, unless by other special provision of the Trustees.   Their routine of daily duty shall be so far defined by the superintendent as to insure a frequent and vigilant oversight of the patients and their attendants.

ARTICLE X.

SEC. 1.   The matron shall look carefully to the wants of the female patients in reference to their individual needs, visit their wards daily, and bestow special attention upon the sick and feeble generally, (visiting the sick in the male wards, if so desired by the superintendent).   She shall see that suitable bedding is everywhere provided, and that the dining rooms and clothing rooms of the wards are properly cared for, and that the wearing apparel of the female patients especially, is duly registered and preserved, and judiciously worn; that the dietary prescriptions of the medical officers are properly prepared and served; that those having care of the sick perform their duties in a kindly manner, and give such instructions to the attendants in reference to the general care of the wards as may be necessary to secure the proper standard of cleanliness and good order.

SEC. 2.   She shall ascertain the wants in the way of supplies for the sewing departments and female wards, and supervise the drawing, marking and distributing of the same, under the regulations of the superintendent.

SEC. 3.   She shall likewise oversee and direct the work in all the domestic departments, the cooking, washing, ironing and sewing, and see that all are properly done, and that proper order and neatness in these departments prevail.

SEC. 4.   She shall exercise forethought in the making up of clothing and bedding, and see that prudence is observed in the use materials, and that as much as possible be accomplished in each department.

SEC. 5.   In every way possible she will endeavor to promote the efficiency of the emyloyes, and add to the personal comforts of the inmates, and will report to the superintendent any evidences of unfaithfulness to duty, or unkindness to patients, that may come to her knowledge.   She will be expected to render constant service to the Institution, except when allowed leave of absence by the superintendent.

ARTICLE XI.

SEC. 1. The farmer, under the superintendent's direction, shall take charge of the operations of the farm in detail, and have immediate direction of the persons employed for the farm service, and shall be responsible for the timely and seasonable management of the crops, the proper care of the dairy and other stock, and the teams employed in the farm work, together with the team wagons, sleds, and farming utensils of every description.

SEC. 2. He shall be responsible for the good order of the barns, farm yards, and their appendages; the good condition of the fences; the utilization of the sewerage and fertilizing resources of the Institution; the preparation and housing of the supply of fuel and ice, and the slaughtering of the animals which are the products of home fattening.

SEC. 3. He shall also attend to the performance of any other work or improvement upon the farm, garden, or Asylum premises, that may be required of him.

SEC. 4. He shall exercise constant care and watchfulness over the patients placed under his charge for employment, and over those having the immediate care of them; see that work suitable for each is provided; that due discretion is exercised in the use of tools and implements for labor, and above all that they are not imposed upon in any way, but are treated with the consideration and respect properly due persons in their condition of mind, and shall carry out in every way possible the plans of the superintendent for their welfare and treatment.

SEC. 5. All wants in his department involving expenditure shall be referred to the superintendent; and no purchases or sales of stock or produce be made, except by his direction. He will give his time and attention exclusively to his charge, and not absent himself from duty without the knowledge and permission of the superintendent.

ARTICLE XII.

SEC. 1. The Trustees shall from time to time fix the price of board of patients, and no patient shall at any time be admitted for a less price than that prefixed by the Trustees, and upon the admission of patients to the Asylum good security shall in all cases be required.

ARTICLE XIII.

SEC. 1. No moneys shall be expended, or debts contracted, (except for the ordinary expenses of the establishment,) unless directed by the Trustees.

The subject which earliest engrossed the attention of the Trustees in 1878 was the matter of disposal of the sewage which hitherto had been deposited in an artificial basin or settling bed at the foot of the bank on the meadow level, from which it was annually removed, and fresh material for compost thrown in. After much discussion it was decided at the July meeting to abandon the settling bed, and construct a conduit from the bank about thirty-five rods to a stream in the meadow, by which it would be conducted thence to the West River.

At this meeting it was also determined to erect a brick building in rear of the gymnasium for a carpenter's shop in the lower story, and a painter's shop above, and connect with the same a wing, the lower story and cellar to form an ice house, and the upper story a lumber room.

The following officers were elected at the annual meeting, 1878:

OFFICERS OF THE BOARD.

Frederick Holbrook, Chairman.
W. H. Rockwell, Treasurer.
J. Draper, Secretary.
J. M. Tyler, Auditor.

RESIDENT OFFICERS.

Joseph Draper, Superintendent and Physician.
Asa Gilkey, Farmer.
Mary Draper, Matron.
J. M. Clark,   ⎫
O. W. Phelps, ⎬ Assistant Physicians.

The financial exhibit of this biennial period shows
income received, $187,261.96
Expenditures,   •   187,036.16
_____

Balance on hand, $225.80

In their report of 1876, the Trustees urged an increase in the rate allowed for the care of the insane poor, for the reason that the Institution was becoming more and more devoted each year to this class, and also because the rate now allowed was much below that for the like class in the neighboring States.

This is urged in their Report of 1878 still more forcibly, as follows:

"The Trustees desire in this Report to state explicity and in detail, the difficulties under which the Institution is at present laboring, and what they conceive to be their duty in respect to the relations existing between the Asylum and the State. They would first remark that by virtue of their position, as the Trustees of a property designed for a specific and benevolent object, they are charged with a two-fold duty, to wit: the preservation of the property intact, and the maintenance of the Institution in a condition suited to the successful carrying out of its chartered objects.

"It will be remembered that the Asylum had its origin in a private bequest of $10,000, in 1834, and that it was upon this alone that the establishment was put in operation. That subsequently the State co-operated with the Trustees in increasing the capacity of the Asylum, by granting small appropriations amounting in the aggregate to $23,000 between the years 1835 and 1843, since which time the Asylum has received no aid whatever from any source, but has been dependent wholly for its maintenance and subsequent development upon the income derived from the care of its inmates annually. A preference in the matter of admissions to the Asylum, was, by the appropriations made by the State for the purpose of increasing the capacity of the Institution, conceded to applicants from Vermont, and the result has been a gradual, but steadily increasing percentage of inmates belonging to the State from the date of the arrangements thus entered into to the present time. In the year 1846, after the last appropriation had been made and expended, the average number of the insane poor supported in the Asylum was 121. The average number of the same class supported during the past year was 293. Ten years ago the respective numbers of insane poor and self-supporting patients were 207 of the former and 306 of the latter. At the present time there are 295 of the former and 164 of the latter.

"The result of this change it will be seen has very considerably modified the resources of the Asylum, and materially limited the income at the disposal of the Trustees, inasmuch as the rate paid by the State has always been below the average cost as shown by the officers of the Asylum in their review of the report of the State commissioner for 1876, with the single exception of the biennial period of 1871-2 as therein shown. The change in the relative proportions of public and private patients has been very marked in the past six years. During the biennial period of 1871-2 there were supported an average of 233 public and 273 private patients; in 1873-4, 254 public and 219 private; in 1875-6, 277 public and 200 private; in 1877-8, 293 public and 179 private. In the reception of patients from Vermont, we have never discriminated against, nor refused any class, but have received alike the poor, those self supporting and those sent by the courts, who have been adjudged irresponsible for their crimes by reason of insanity, as well as those convicted persons who have become insane while serving the penalty of their crimes.

"In reference to the latter class we desire to say that in our judgment other provision should be made for them. In some States separate institutions have been created for them. This is the case in New York. In Massachusetts provision has been made for them in connection with the new prison at Concord; such provision is a practicable one in any State.

"The statistics already given show plainly that the Asylum has been more and more exclusively devoted to the wants of the State each year, though most decidedly, as will be seen to the pecuniary disadvantage of the Institution. The practical result of the lessening in this way of the annual income of the establishment has been the creation of an indebtedness of $45,000 incurred for the improvement of the accommodations of the Institution, which still remains unliquidated.

"These facts have been clearly shown to the Legislature in 1874 and in 1876, and we have respectfully asked an increase of rate per capita from $3 to $3.50 per week, but no increase has been made, altho' the committee to whom the question was referred has each year reported in favor of additional remuneration.

"By a reference to the abstract of receipts and expenditures for the two years, it will be seen that the average cost per capita has been $3.81 per week. There has been no material difference in the item of wages and medical supplies between the past and the previous biennial period. The cost of stores and provisions has been somewhat less. In this connection it may be proper to state that the produce of the farm contributes very largely toward the support of the household, and the crops have been exceptionally good in the last two years. It does not, however, enter into the estimates of cost in this Report, nor has it ever been considered in the annual statements of receipts and expenditures. The furniture and clothing account has been more than in the preceding two years. The fuel account appears for the first time as an item of expense, the wood having been previously cut upon the Asylum property; but in future it will be an increasing item, as the consumption amounts to some fifteen hundred cords per annum, which will each year have to be more and more largely purchased, as the supply upon the farm is nearly exhausted.

"The expenditures for current repairs and renovations have been for four years past less than their proper average, on account of the expenditure of moneys largely in buildings and permanent improvements. The latter account has been larger in the past two years than usual in consequence of the occurrence of the fire already referred to, but an insurance of eight thousand dollars aided in rebuilding. So long as the indebtedness of the Asylum remains unliquidated the item of interest upon it must become a part of the current expense, as also that for taxes and insurance, which latter we have felt obliged to increase since the late casualty. It will be seen by the facts cited, that the Trustees have been somewhat straightened financially and circumscribed in their plans for improvements, in consequence of the relations of the Asylum to the State, and their scrupulous adherence to the conditions relative to admissions. whereby the annual income of the establishment has, been year by year reduced. But they desire in this connection to state that they do not acknowledge the right of the Legislature alone to determine the rate at which the insane poor of the State shall be supported at the Asylum. They regard this as a question which they have a voice in determining, and while it has been their uniform endeavor to make the cost as low as possible, consistently with the proper care of this class, they cannot continue a policy that for the five years past has been detrimental to both the present and prospective interests of the Institution in their charge. They feel that if the Asylum is to be more and more devoted to the use of the State, they have a right to demand an increased compensation for the care of those who are supported by it. They would call attention to the large amount, expended in the last five years to improve the Institution in its appointments, and to the fact that the amount allowed for the support of the insane poor of Vermont, is considered everywhere else in New England insufficient for the just requirements of the same class, in institutions exclusively devoted to their care and cure.

"We are satisfied with the working organization of the Asylum and believe the objects of its founder are being faithfully regarded and the interests of the State honestly served; but feel that the Legislature in the last four years has done injustice to the Asylum, and fallen short in its provisions for a class of persons who are the special objects of its beneficence by refusing an adequate compensation for their maintainance and care."

We have quoted thus largely from this report for the reason that on no occasion before nor since, have the Trustees so fully defined the relation of the Asylum to the State, and expressed the obligations they felt under in the discharge of their trust.   They close their report in the following words.

"We must again respectfully request that the Legislature shall at least make the increase shown to be absolutely requisite for the wants of the insane poor of this State.   We can no longer continue to care for them at the rate hitherto allowed."

The Legislature responded to this appeal by increasing the rate from $3.00 to $3.50 per week by an Act approved November 26, 1878.

The Report of the Superintendent shows one hundred and sixty-seven admitted, and one hundred and ninety-seven discharged, since August 1, 1876; four hundred and fifty-nine remaining.

The Causes of Insanity, Moral Agencies in the Treatment of the Insane, and the Care and Classification of the Insane, were specially discussed together with the statistics of the cases under care, and the following detail of the work of the past two years, is stated and here quoted, as showing more explicitly the modernizations of the older portions of the Asylum:

"The work of rebuilding the wing burned in the winter of 1877, was necessitated by the accident of fire, and was not embraced in the plan for improvements, with which we commenced the biennial period.   Since the completion of the two extreme wings, in 1873, and the subsequent introduction of steam heating, a renovation of the original wings which have been long in use, and subjected to most wear, has, you are aware, been going constantly on.   This has been necessarily a slow work, as it has had to be done under the disadvantages of constant occupancy, but we have so far accomplished it that the wards have all been painted throughout the Asylum, and many minor alterations made in the original construction to enable us to introduce modern conveniences, many of which have been detailed in the two last published reports.

"Early in the winter of 1877 somewhat important alterations were commenced in the centre building by which the first floor was wholly converted into public use, and additional rooms for visiting secured; and also at the extremity of each wing from the centre, was constructed a staircase opening into each story and terminating in the attic, and having at the bottom, on the first story, a door opening out upon the grounds for the daily use of patients occupying these wings, and serving also as a fire escape in case of necessity.   These alterations were completed during the winter.   Early

in the spring were commenced alterations in the interior of the
Marsh Building, by which the rear halls were united with the main
ones at right angles, and a large ventilating shaft was constructed at
the angle of the two wards, by which very eecellent results were
secured, and later in the season the wooden wing at the rear of this
building, no longer required for storage of fuel, was removed, and
the airing court for patients extended so as to cover its site. These
with the removal of the rear staircase, and the renovation of several
of the rear rooms the present year, have placed this building in
a very satisfactory state of repair.

   "In the kitchen department the work has been very materially
facilitated by the introduction of steam cooking apparatus.   By this
change several separate fires have been rendered unnecessary
and the risks from that cause materially lessened, while over the
great oven has been built a fire proof section of flooring, most effectually shutting off the possibility of danger from that source.

   "At the junction of the laundry with the contiguous wing,
iron safety doors have been set, so that altogether we do not hesitate
to assert that the security of the buildings is now as complete
as is possible, where absolute fire proof arrangements do not exist.

   "Since the date of the last report the steam heating apparatus
has been extended to the Marsh Building, and applied to the cooking
arrangements, so that this department may be regarded as practically
complete, and by the introduction of the fan the present season, the
effectiveness of the ventilation we fully believe will in future be
found adequate.

   "It is with no little rejoicing that we are able to record the
establishment of a gymnasium. This is one of the compensating
considerations resulting from the fire which was a serious pecuniary
loss, and unmitigated save by the advantages secured by improvements in rebuilding. This annexation to the Asylum occupies the
entire section next the road of the rebuilt block, and is abundantly
adequate to the purpose, being about 75x40 feet in dimensions, and
having the height of two stories in one, finished in the roof to the
ridge.   A bowling alley is laid the entire length on one side, and a
gallery formed by a second story twenty-four feet wide across the
western end of the building gives a billiard room, which is furnished
with a fine table, the gift of a life long friend of the Asylum."

   At the September meeting plans for further improvements were
discussed, and the Trustees unanimously approved the suggestion of
extending the rear halls through the north return wings, to the rear

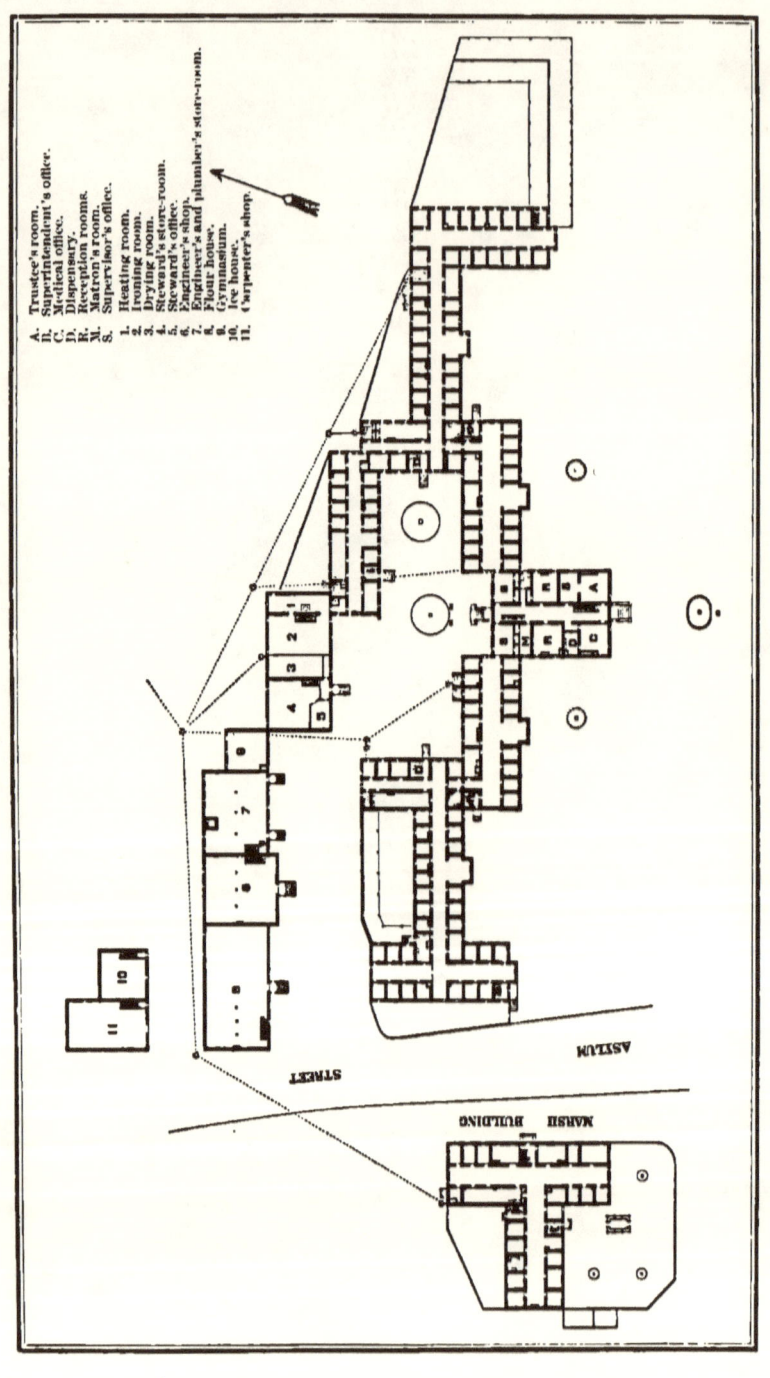

A. Trustee's room.
B. Superintendent's office.
C. Medical office.
D. Dispensary.
R. Reception room.
M. Matron's room.
S. Supervisor's office.

1. Heating room.
2. Ironing room.
3. Drying room.
4. Steward's store-room.
5. Steward's office.
6. Engineer's shop.
7. Engineer's and plumber's store-room.
8. Flour house.
9. Gymnasium.
10. Ice house.
11. Carpenter's shop.

STREET

ASYLUM

MARSH BUILDING

center court, thus improving them in respect to light, ventilation and classification, which work was entered upon about the close of the year.

There was expended in the years 1877-78 in completing the system of steam heating, introducing the ventilating fan, and also steam cooking utensils, tea and coffee boilers, and all their necessary connections, $8,888.21. The cost of work shop and ice house, also erected in the latter part of the year 1878, was $5,000.

The Commission appointed by the governor under the Resolution approved November 28, 1876, made its Report to His Excellency at the session of the Legislature in October of this year. Dr. M. Goldsmith of Rutland, Dr. O. F. Fassett of St. Albans, and W. H. Walker, Esq., of Ludlow, were the commissioners.

In the exercise of their functions they endeavored to make an exhaustive investigation of the Asylum and its management, and in so doing manifestly went beyond the scope of legislative authorization. The chairman of the Commission states at the outset, that, "In the division of labor among ourselves, that which relates to the legal part of our duties was assigned to Mr. Walker. That which relates to the medical or other treatment of the insane, was assigned to Dr. Fassett.

The construction of the Asylum, its fitness for the care of the insane, the air space, ventilation, food, washing, and administration, was committed to Dr. Goldsmith."

It may here be remarked that Dr. Goldsmith had had an extensive experience in army hospitals, hence his ideas in respect to all hospitals bore the military stamp; and those points in the Asylum that did not conform to the military notion, were naturally construed as falling short of the hospital idea; nevertheless, he does full justice to the faithfulness of the Trustees in the discharge of their trust, according to their conception of their duty.

"These Trustees," he writes, "are a body of men in which changes are seldom made except as death makes them, and in most cases the son takes the honored father's place.

"The most searching inquiry has failed to find that a single dollar of the millions which have passed through their hands, has ever been misappropriated or unaccounted for. They have always served without fee or reward, and fidelity to trust seems to be, and to have been, in each and every case the household God, heredity or not."

The following are the "Comments of the Officers of the Asylum upon the Report of the Special Commissioners," in full:

To the Joint Committee on the Insane, and the Insane Asylum, of the Senate and House of Representatives of the General Assembly of Vermont, now in Session :

"Inasmuch as the Report of the Special Commissioners, appointed by His Excellency, Governor Fairbanks, 'To inquire into the Statutes now in force, in relation to the confinement and treatment of the insane of our State, and see what changes were necessary, if any, in said laws ; also to inquire into the treatment of our insane, and determine what, if any, legislation was necessary,' contains some conclusions from which the Officers of the Asylum dissent, and some criticisms which they deem unjust ; they, therefore, respectfully submit the following statement relative to the points of disagreement, and request that the same be submitted by you, with your Report upon that of the said Commissioners, to the General Assembly.

"For the sake of brevity, the officers of the Asylum will confine their remarks solely to those points upon which they entertain different views from the Commissioners.

"The chairman of said Commission, who, in the division of the labor, assigned to himself the investigation of 'The construction of the Asylum, and its fitness for the care of the insane, the air space, ventilation, food, washing and administration,' states that in three things, 'space to live in, pure air to breathe, and sufficient attendance, the great deficiencies of the Asylum consist, and render it unfit for holding so many as it now holds and undertakes to care for.'

"The over-crowding to a definite extent being conceded, that is, so far as necessity has obliged the duplicating of beds in single rooms, still the assertion is made that 'in the rooms provided, even when occupied by the number they were designed for, the space and air supply are not sufficient.'

"The capacity of the Asylum, according to its original design, is for 400 persons, patients and attendants, allowing in associated dormitories the average cubic space for each occupant that each single room contains. While we can see advantages in larger rooms, and would construct them larger if the buildings were to be designed anew, we are fully convinced that the health of the inmates would never be prejudiced if the capacity of the Institution upon the basis originally made were not exceeded. Even with the overcrowding, which in the past has been greater than it is at present, we fail to find evidences of injury to health in consequence.

" The mortality, in comparison with the other Asylums of New England, has been above three per cent. less than the average in the past twelve years. This fact is admitted by Dr. Fassett, who says : ' The ratio of deaths to the average number of inmates is less than in most Asylums in the country, while many show a much larger death rate—even double that of the Vermont Asylum.'

" In explanation of this favorable record, he suggests that fewer ' new case's—many of which are liable to 'be acute and fatal '—are treated than in some asylums ; and that many having ' friends and homes, as the end of life approaches, are taken to their homes to die among friends.'

" Whatever force there may be in the first assigned cause, there is none in the latter ; so rarely is a chronic case removed to die at home, that we cannot recall one at the present time.

" But a stronger argument even than the light mortality, in favor of the good general hygienic condition of the inmates, not only at present but in all the years past, is found in the large number of old residents comprising the present household. By reference to the tabular statements contained in the Commissioners' Report, it will be seen that twenty have been thirty or more years in the Asylum ; sixty-five between twenty and thirty years, and one hundred and eighteen between ten and twenty years. We venture the opinion that this state of facts could not exist had the sanitary condition in which they have lived been decidedly bad in any essential particular.

" In noting the structural arrangements of asylums, reference is made to the openings over the doors of the rooms, and the opinion expressed that ' transoms· only permit the more ready diffusion of gases. They cannot be said to cause or allow ventilation.' Also, ' that in effect the air in asylum corridors is absolutely still in cold weather, or whenever the windows are closed,' unless in them the air may·be moved by artificial means.'

" We are disposed to accord more practical advantages to the transoms as an aid to ventilation than does Dr. Goldsmith. In truth, the air in the corridors upon which the rooms of the patients open, is never absolutely still. There are ventilating flues from these corridors communicating with the chimneys of the buildings—thirty-eight in number, amounting to an area of about ninety square feet, which, if all concentrated in a single shaft, would require one of about nine feet by ten in its diameters—through which foul air is constantly passing out from the building, even without the aid of artificial means. In rooms, therefore, not having special flues, the transom affords the substitute ; and as there is always an escape of foul air going on from the corridors through the flues mentioned, it follows that there is an exhaust force acting to draw the air from these apartments through these transoms or openings above the doors of the rooms, which is supplemented and aided by any inlet of air from the window, which is opposite the door and transom of each room. Even when the window is closed, this amounts to considerable, Dr. Goldsmith granting it, 'to supplement one-fourth of the ventilation required,' but since the introduction of the fan, the movement of air throughout the building has been so greatly facilitated, its working having even exceeded our expectations, that this exhaust force upon the rooms admits of easy demonstration. Dr. Goldsmith gives the cubic contents of the sleeping apartments at 291,134 feet, which, upon the basis of 1,000 feet per person, equals the requirements for 291 individuals, and adds that '502 are made *to live* in what is the minimum space for 291.' This is not strictly true. To arrive at the total space in which the inmates *live*, the cubic contents of the corridors themselves, in which the patients pass fully two-thirds of their time, (assuming they are always indoors), must be added to that in which they *lodge;* but by a singular oversight, as it seems to us, the day space in the buildings is nowhere taken into account. This constant use of the term *live* in, instead of *lodge* or *sleep* in, we think, tends to mislead the reader. Adding to the cubic contents of the sleeping rooms, already given (291,634), the capacity of the corridors (292,464), we have a total space which, on the basis of 400 inmates, gives to each 1,459 cubic feet in which to *live*, and this, with our present means of ventilation, it is possible easily to change once an hour, which Dr. Goldsmith himself regards as a sufficiently rapid movement. In this computation no account is taken of the stairways, bath-rooms, nor dining-rooms, which are used some portions of each day by the inmates, to the relief of the wards; nor is the time reckoned which is spent by the patients out of doors, still further in favor of the more perfect ventilation of the corridors and sleeping rooms. It should also be mentioned that there are many lodging rooms of the class designated unventilated, in which the doors are lattice-work, thus very largely favoring the air supply. This is the case in some of the most crowded of the female halls, where there are two beds in single apartments.

"On the occasion of the Commissioners most thorough inspection, the ventilation seems to be the point most criticised. 'In every room occupied by an inmate who had the door and window closed, the air was foul and fetid,' 'fearfully bad in rooms of filthy patients, etc.,'

"By reference to the testimony it will be seen that we are careful to select, for the use of persons who are obliged to be confined to their rooms both day and night, those specially heated and ventilated, and we are also careful to prevent, as far as possible, the voluntary use of sleeping rooms in the daytime, except with open doors. Practically, the bedrooms are all day undergoing an airing for night use, and the occupancy of rooms that have become foul and fetid is exceptional.

"As regards the wards and rooms of those cases in which the calls of nature are disregarded, and there are quite a percentage in every asylum, we do not think it an evidence of defective ventilating arrangements, if disagreeable odors are perceptible; we have observed it in the most perfectly ventilated buildings we have visited. It is the frequent necessary renovation of such wards and rooms, on account of the filthy and destructive habits of such inmates, that swells the annual account for current repairs, which, to those unfamiliar with the practical care of such institutions, appears disproportionately large.

"In commenting upon the quality of the atmosphere in the different apartments, the remark is made that it was found 'most pure in the double rooms containing only one inmate, commonly an attendant.' The impression conveyed by this is that the attendants are specially favored in this respect. But the use of double rooms by single attendants is not the common arrangement. It is the case, in fact, only at the Marsh Building, and these rooms are also used as visiting rooms by friends of patients, therefore not exclusively for the attendants' use. In all cases the rooms for the attendants are selected by the officers, and wholly with reference to the best convenience, welfare and oversight of the inmates.

"The position of the buildings in relation to the points of the compass are thus commented upon: 'The long axis of the group of buildings. constituting the Asylum, trends east and west, as will be seen on an inspection of the maps. It will also be seen that there are nearly one hundred rooms that have hardly a ray of sunshine entering them. This is always inevitable wherever there are rooms on both sides of a corridor, and the building trends east and west. If asylums could be built as our military hospitals were, every room in them would be flooded with sunshine some time during the day.'

"As Dr. Goldsmith intimates, this is a general fault or fact, applicable to other institutions as well as the one under consideration. But there are some considerations that mitigate it, some even that favor it. The general non-occupancy of the rooms during the day renders it less necessary that all should be 'flooded with sunshine', while in cases of acute maniacal excitement, it is often the case that . sunlight is prejudicial. This principle has in some institutions led to the use of close shutters, making the rooms dark, for the use of patients in this state. We have one case of periodical excitement, now under treatment, in which a congested state of the conjunctival mucous membrane is an invariable accompaniment, and who for this reason would be unable to use a bright sunny room. In another, for the same reason, we have used the blue glass window, with advantage to the eyes if not to the mind.

"It is not thought that the arrangement of double lines of rooms with corridor between, is a disadvantageous one to the general welfare of the inmates of institutions of this kind, as there are always cases who can occupy the rooms *from* the sun, if not with positive advantage, at least without actual detriment. We willingly admit that too much sunlight cannot be let into the corridors and alcoves appropriated to day use. Another fact should be remembered in connection with the use of the rooms upon the side opposite to the sunny exposure, such rooms are subject to frequent changes of occupants. Many patients are subject to paroxysmal excitements and require for a few days or weeks the use of the rooms thus situated, but few have constant occupants. During the hot season these rooms become the preferable ones by reason of their greater comfort, being more exposed to the breezes and less to the solar heat.

"We are inclined to the view that the location of asylums throughout the country, in respect to the points of compass, has been determined by local advantages connected with the geography of the site. We are not aware that a special preference in respect to frontage has been found an essential desideratum. Certainly some of the best asylums have the same general trend of buildings as the Vermont Asylum. The McLean, and the new Worcester, in Massachusetts, the Butler Hospital at Providence, R. I., the Bloomingdale and Utica Asylums, New York, and the Morristown and Trenton, New Jersey, are of like trend.

"Between the temperature of rooms specially heated and those not thus supplied, there is a difference of about 20 degrees as a rule; while the former are kept at 70 degrees, the latter would stand at 50 degrees. This latter temperature Dr. Goldsmith pronounces 'not warm enough.' "

"For a feeble person, 50 degrees might not be sufficient, but for a healthy one it seems to us better than any higher degree. We should regard 70 degrees as enervating to a person in ordinary health. We believe three-quarters of our household better off to sleep in a temperature of 50 degrees than in any higher, and it must be borne in mind that these statements of temperature apply to the sleeping apartments, not to the corridors.

"On the paper which bears the outline of the buildings, sewage, etc., will be seen a sketch of one ward of the asylum at Concord, N. H. The reader is left to the inference that this sketch is typical of the whole of the wards of that excellent institution, but such is not strictly the fact.

"The building from which this plan is made was erected and opened in 1875. It is their latest improvement, and contains rooms for twenty-seven patients. In 1868 the extension, called the Kent Building, designed for thirty-three female patients of the excited class, was erected. These embrace every modern convenience, and the advantage of ample space. The previously built portion, which still constitutes the main portion, was built substantially upon the same scale as the Vermont Asylum as to capacity and size of rooms; both were essentially modelled after the same plan.

"As elsewhere stated, the Vermont Asylum has a total space, in the opinion of Dr. Goldsmith, for only 291 inmates. He, however, states that 'it may be so altered in his judgment as to have space and ventilation ample for 325 or perhaps 350.' At present, however, in his opinion, 'it has ventilation enough for only 149.'

"In the testimony taken last June we stated that the system of ventilation, as designed by us, then lacked the motive power to make it complete and effective. This has been supplied and put to use since the final visit of the Commissioners. We are convinced that the practical working of this fan will be to supply the needed changes of atmosphere for the fullest requirements of the number for which there is space.

"Dr. Fassett, to whom was assigned the investigation of 'That which relates to the medical or other treatment of the insane,' discusses at the outset the questions of seclusion and restraint, and quotes from Dr. Folsom, the able secretary of the Massachusetts Board of Health, 'The Criminal Lunatic Asylum, at Broadmoor, England, which held, in 1875, a daily average number of 503 inmates, of whom 204 had been sent there for murder and 110 for attempt to murder, maim, etc., and yet no form of mechanical restraint was used in any part of the asylum during the year.' And 'with all this, there were no instances of the commission of premeditated acts of violence, no attempt to escape was even partially successful, and there was no accident which could have been prevented by the use of mechanical restraint.'

"In referring to the Reports of the English Commissioners in Lunacy, we find the explanation of this remarkable disuse of mechanical restraint. In Report of 1874, page 299, note the following: 'Mechanical restraint has not been employed, but during the last 13 months 67 men and 12 women have been secluded, on account of violence, dangerous propensities, or for safe custody, the former altogether upon 2,768 occasions, the latter upon 63 occasions.' This was upwards of 15 per cent. of the average resident number (508). 'Besides the above, 54 men and 22 women have been secluded from time to time, owing to maniacal excitement, etc.' This made 15 per cent. additional, or upwards of 30 per cent. that were subjected to more or less seclusion.

"In explanation of this large percentage of seclusion, the Commissioners say it is explained by the medical superintendent 'to be due to the necessity which arose in the early months of the year for taking extra precautions for the safety of patients and attendants, owing to the violence and misconduct of a few of the most troublesome patients of the convict class; but chiefly in the latter months of the year, in consequence of the escape of two patients, necessitating stricter measures generally, in order to insure safe custody.'

"In England seclusion is preferred to mechanical restraint. In this country it is the opinion that the interests of the insane are best served by the avoidance of seclusion, even if restraint must be a condition of its avoidance. There are now some indications of a common practice being ultimately reached. Even the English Commissioners, in their report of 1872, p. 276, thus speak: 'It is our opinion, many times strongly expressed in these reports, that all the bad qualities of such inmates are exaggerated by excessive seclusion.' In the light of the present, therefore, we believe we are best serving the cause in discarding neither, but in reducing both to the minimum as far as practicable.

"Under the head of 'Employment,' Dr. Fassett considers all outdoor privileges, and comments unfavorably upon the airing courts for the disturbed and demented classes, which he considers too small. This, he says, 'seems to us the most inexcusable of any of the faults of the institution.' We do not think the purpose of these airing courts was fully taken into account by the Commissioners.

"They are designed for the use of but a limited number at most. The larger proportion of the inmates enjoy the use of the unenclosed grounds in front of the buildings, and are taken out in groups for exercise and diversion regularly each half day by their attendants, and when the winter closes in, the new gymnasium, with sleigh riding, etc., will afford the like opportunities for healthful recreation. The airing courts are immediately connected with the buildings or wings occupied by the excited or demented classes, and are provided exclusively for these classes, in recognition of the necessity of open air for all, yet recognizing, also, that such are to be protected from public observation and remark, while laboring under demonstrative insanity, or having reached a helpless state of fatuity.

"No feature of an asylum is, in our view, more beneficent in its practical working than this. The size of these courts has been determined by the surroundings. They could not be materially larger without exposing to public view their occupants. This is the point which, it did not seem to us, the Commissioners fully comprehended.

"In considering the sanitary condition of the Asylum, Dr. Fassett states, 'they have estimated the lack of ventilation, not only by their own senses, but by the effect upon the health of the inmates,' and that 'the effect upon the health was painfully evident in the pale, mottled faces, the cold, clammy hands, the feeble circulation, the lack of vitality.'

"With such a state of health, we would naturally expect that the death record would show a large mortality from tuberculosis and acute affections, which would be quickly fatal under such conditions. But the record for the past two years shows but five cases from acute diseases all told, and but three from consumption out of a total of sixty-four, and this latter is a malady that would be specially fostered, as is well known, by living in impure air. We have taken pains to ascertain the death rate in all the State Asylums of New England for the 12 years last past, and find the mean average to be 10.38 per cent. on the average population of each institution each year.

"The mean average of the Vermont Asylum for the same period upon its average population, has been but 6.95 per cent. We have also ascertained the percentage of recoveries in the same institutions for the same period of time upon those admitted, which we find to be 31½ per cent., and in this respect the Vermont Asylum does not fall below the others; there is scarcely a fractional difference.

"With this state of facts, the remarks made by Dr. Fassett relative to the sanitary condition of the inmates, in the last quotation,
seem contradictory. 'The pale mottled faces, the cold clammy
hands, the feeble circulation, the lack of vitality,' are, however,
attributable, we believe, to another cause, and that incident to the
malady under which all the inmates labor. That cause is exhausted
innervation. Such patients are not in a condition of impoverish-
ment 'of blood, but there is a want of tone by reason of deficient
nerve force. In such cases there is always a weak capillary circulation which gives rise to the apparent paleness and lack of vitality.
Yet such cases do not die ; they often live on for years in just the
condition described, and at last drop off from sheer nervous exhaustion, without any acute disease whatever, simply because the nerve
force runs at last to so low an ebb that the vital processes can no
longer be sustained. In contrast to these cases, Dr. Fassett comments upon the 'ruddy faces and more animated manner of the
classes regularly employed,' drawing the inference that this better
grade of cases illustrate simply the difference between indoor and
outdoor advantages. But here again we think he is largely in error.
Those whom it is practicable to employ out of doors in a regular
way, are those who are yet a long way from that condition of
advanced dementia which is coincident with the degree of enerva-
tion, which is characteristic of the class he so graphically describes.
The latter, by outdoor exposure, might indeed lose some of the
paleness incident to indoor life,—become browned by the sun,—but
no amount of sunlight and forced labor, for it could not be other in
cases of advanced dementia, would infuse into them the ruddy glow
of health and the animated manner that belongs to the earlier stages
of mental disorder.

"In reference to the medical treatment of the patients, we think
an erroneous impression was given in the statement that 'each
(medical assistant) testified that he has charge of one side of this
large hospital, with the aid of Dr. Draper, when needing advice.'

"The duties of the Superintendent are much more individual
than would be inferred from the above quotation. Under the
By-Laws the duties of the Superintendent are clearly defined in this
respect, as follows:

"ART. VIII, SEC. 2. 'In the discharge of his duties, his first
care shall be for the welfare of the patients committed to the charge
of the Institution, and this care must be so far personal that he shall
be at all times conversant with the actual condition of each individual case ; and he must be responsible for the classification of the
inmates and the general course of treatment pursued.'

" In the testimony of the Superintendent before the Commissioners appended to their Report, occurs this question, by Dr. Fassett, and
answer :

" *Ques.*—' Do you personally superintend the treatment of every
individual in the Asylum, or do you only see them as you are called
in consultation?'

" *Ans.*—' For the general direction of everything I am responsible, but the carrying of it out in detail is intrusted to my assistants.
My custom is to visit one department of the Institution each day
with the assistant of that department. The assistants are required
to make two regular visitations each day, but each one of us is subject to the nurses' call at any time.'

" The professional duty of the Superintendent, it will be seen by
the above showing, is really something more than that of counselling
physician in cases of special difficulty ; it embraces primarily the
determination of the general course of treatment of the patients
individually ; and the professional responsibility of the assistant
physicians will be best understood by reference to the By-Laws, Art.
IX, Sec. 4, which reads as follows :

" ' They will daily, and as much oftener as may be necessary,
report to the Superintendent upon the cases under treatment, relative
to the progress made, and concerning any occurrence of an unusual
or unexpected character, and consult with him in reference to any
changes in classification or treatment that may be indicated.'

" Of the value of professional experience no one can be more
sensible than ourselves, and in this respect it does not seem to us
that we are open to much criticism. The senior medical assistant
has had full six years' experience in the specialty and entered it after
one years' service in the Hartford City General Hospital. The
second has now had about one year's experience in his present position. We know of no school but this practical one, where the experience desired can be obtained, and neither certainly at present can
be regarded as inexperienced.

" We gladly bear witness to the careful and thorough investigations of the Commissioners, both in reference to the fitness of the
Asylum for its purposes, and in reference to the actual treatment of
the inmates; yet, with all due respect, cannot but believe that a
personal, practical experience of their own in the care of the insane,
would have modified more or less their conclusions and recommendations.

" In the Report of Mr. Walker upon the legal relations of the
Asylum to the State, he remarks that ' The Trustees have always

sought the patronage of the State and been *willing*, so far as the Commissioners have been able to learn, to receive the State benefi-ciaries at the prices fixed by the Legislature.

" How far this statement holds, does not require very extended research to show. This is the third time that the Legislature has respectfully been asked to raise the price of caring for the insane, to a figure that would cover the actual cost, and that the Trustees have publicly and emphatically expressed their *unwillingness* to care for these classes at the expense of others, as the refusal of the request has obliged them partially to do.

" In respect to the admission to, and discharge of patients from the Asylum, the Commissioners are of the opinion that the laws are defective, and ' recommend the enactment of such laws as will tend more effectually to prevent the wrongful detention of persons, claimed to be insane, in any Asylum in the State.'

" The manner in which the insane poor may be wrongfully detained is dwelt upon, and the statement made that ' the Commis-sioners fear there may be one or more such cases now confined at Brattleboro who ought to be discharged.'

" In replying to this, we deem it sufficient to say that, in our judgment, no person of sufficiently sane mind to be safely at large and capable of caring for himself or herself is there detained.

" It is stated that ' the Commissioners have learned that formerly it was the custom of the Superintendent to allow patients to execute deeds of real estate ; but that they have not learned whether this practice is still continued or not.'

" The present Superintendent has no recollection of any occasion for such a transaction during the time he has been in charge, and is not cognizant of any such at any former period.

" On the question of the supervision of the correspondence of the patients, the views of the Superintendent are given in the printed testimony, and need not be here repeated. We would only say that in this matter we have pursued the universal course, which the past experience of those qualified to judge has shown to be for the best interest of the inmates, who, from the nature of the malady they labor under, are irresponsible, and require guardianship and over-sight to shield them from the indiscretions incident to their insanity. As a matter of fact, much of the correspondence of the patients passes unread and even unopened, the supervision being only that of a general knowledge of the channels in which it drifts.

" Though the statement is made in a general way that 'some

insane asylums' adopt the unrestricted course of exercising no oversight of the patients in this respect, it is not supported by citing any
institution in which this practice prevails, and we know of none. In
addition to the reasons given in the testimony of the Superintendent
referred to, there is one which is not there noted, but which seems to
us worthy of mention, as showing it to be an advantage for the physician having charge of the patient to have also the supervision of his
correspondence. It is that the letters or writings of the patient are
the best key to his mental state. In conversation the patient may be
reticent or suspicious of all inquiries made of him, or he may dissem-
ble and endeavor to appear better than he is, in the hope of an early
release from confinement ; but in the absence of an interrogator and
uninfluenced by the presence of any one to check or turn the current
of his thought, by writing he expresses more the genuineness of his
ideas and the delusions that possess him. It is in this way that the
first evidences of convalescence and coherence may often be
detected, and the understanding of individual cases be materially
aided.

"The large proportion of the patients of this State, who are
supported or aided by the State, and the small number who are
supported by private means, is commented upon by Mr. Walker, who
remarks, this fact 'suggests wrong somewhere.'

" In explanation of this, his first inquiry is : 'Do the citizens of
the State, who are able to pay for the support of their insane, send
them out of the State, and avoid the Vermont Asylum because other
States have superior hospitals, where the patients are better cared for
and treated ?'

"On this point we have the testimony of Dr. Fassett in reply.
We were assured by him on the occasion of his last visit at Brattleboro, that in his visits to other asylums he had made investigation
upon this point, but failed to find this to be the case to any extent.
In the Concord Institution, the nearest and most available to Vermont, he found but one. The question is therefore unanswered by
this inquiry. Again he essays a possible solution of the distasteful
fact : 'Can it be possible that the State is being defrauded by individuals and officers of the Asylum combining to have private patients
classed as State beneficiaries?' On the page immediately preceding
this inquiry, Mr. Walker observes, 'Men and corporations are unfortunately greatly influenced and moved by money considerations.
Such influences are potent ; they permeate almost every measure.
Benevolent and philanthropic measures and institutions do not
always escape them.' That the key note were here struck might

indeed be imagined, if by this arrangement the Asylum would receive a higher rate per week ; but the facts are, that while no private patient is received for less than $3.50 per week, besides clothing, beneficiaries are received at $3.00, and the Asylum has the privilege of clothing them at its own expense ! This second query, therefore, fails to give a satisfactory answer, and Mr. Walker propounds no further. The facts, whatever their significance may be, are as follows :

"The whole number of patients belonging to Vermont in the Asylum August 1st, 1878, at date of last Report, was 326, instead of 364 as stated by Mr. Walker, no doubt by error. Of this number 31 were supported wholly by private means, but 21 of these paid but $3.50 per week besides clothing ; 127 were wholly supported by the State at $3 per week inclusive of clothing ; 168 were beneficiaries, *i. e.*, received 75 cents per week from State in aid of their support. Of these 142 were supported by towns, and 26 only were aided by the State, on the certificates of the selectmen of the towns where they reside, that they were proper subjects to receive such aid, under the provisions of the Statutes for the relief of the insane poor. The friends instead of towns, make up the balance of support in the latter cases.

"It is in respect to this latter class that Mr. Walker 'apprehends there may have been some who have received the State aid of 75 cents per week improperly.' This is a matter for which the selectmen of the towns where such patients reside are wholly responsible, and if any are thus improperly aided, it is doubtless due to a misapprehension of the strict meaning of the Statutes, by which indigent though not absolutely destitute and dependent persons, are made beneficiaries. This is not a matter in which the officers of the Asylum can be in any manner an interested party.

"The recommendations of Mr. Walker claim careful consideration. It matters not to the Asylum whether the supervision of the insane be committed to a board, or assigned to a commissioner as under the existing law. The proposition, however, to delegate to a supervisory board the arbitrary power of discharging patients, that have been placed by their friends or the public authorities in the care of the officers of the Asylum, in compliance with every legal requirement, will in our opinion be liable to lead to conflicts of authority, culminating in acts in which the rights of committing parties, and the professional judgment of the medical officers will be set aside. The value of special experience in dealing with and judging of the insane, the Commissioners who make this report particularly dwell upon as essential; and the question naturally presents itself, will the qualifications of such a board as it is proposed to create be likely to be adequate to the responsibility it is proposed to shoulder upon it?

"Inhibatory legislation must be very guarded not to defeat by reaction the real interests of the class of persons whose welfare is at stake, and the officers of the Asylum recognize in the propositions urged a tendency to antagonistic, rather than co-ordinate working, in a cause having but the single ultimate object for all engaged, namely, the welfare of the insane.

".Concerning the correspondence of the inmates, the officers of the Asylum desire that every needed privilege should be secured to them, but are convinced that the recommendations of Mr. Walker go a step farther than is practicable, necessary or wise. After specifying the privileges in this respect in detail which should be inviolable, all the rest of the correspondence, Mr. Walker suggests, ' Should be *sent unread by the officers of the Asylum* to the *guardian or someone of the next of kin*, or other *suitable person, to be disposed of as he deems best for all concerned.*'

" First, this is not practicable, for the reason that but few patients comparatively are under guardianship, and many have no near kin. In the absence of guardians or near kin, Mr. Walker does not indicate who would be a 'suitable person.' But evidently he does not consider the *value* of this surplus correspondence much, as he is willing to leave it to anybody *but the officers of the Asylum*, (to whom it might possibly be a benefit, as affording a clue to some of the obscurities of the patients' mental disorder,) 'to be disposed of as seemed best for all concerned!'

"We regret to feel obliged to criticise with apparent severity these recommendations, but the tendency of them seems to be to create antagonisms of authority, and to place those in charge of Asylums in a false attitude toward the inmates. There is at least an implied reflection upon their honesty.

"We respectfully submit that in all this matter *somebody must be trusted.*

"The penalties suggested for the imaginary infractions of the proposed laws are severe, and we think without precedent; and so long as but one Asylum exists in the State, its officers cannot but understand that in all this proposed stringent legislation, they alone are meant.

"In all the recommendations made we note no suggestion that the insane of the State, not in the Asylum, should be looked after!

although this was a point pressed by Commissioner Calderwood in his report for the two years past, who states that 'there are scattered throughout the State not less than 180, of whom 60 are cared for by towns, either boarded out in families, or kept in poor houses,' which latter places Dr. Fassett states, 'none claim to furnish any proper treatment.'

"The supervision proposed therefore embraces but a moiety of the insane of the State in its provisions, and that portion, too, the one already under a chartered, permanent official oversight. It seems rather the Asylum and its officers, than the insane, for whom legislation is proposed! To those in other States where a broad and comprehensive system of supervising public charities exists, embracing not alone the asylums and the insane, but the prisons and the reformatories, and their inmates, all classes of dependents; such partial and special legislation cannot but be regarded as narrow rather than wise, liberal and broadly philanthropic.

"To the concluding recommendations of the Commissioners, the officers of the Asylum have little to say. The meaning of the clause immediately preceding the recommendation for a new Asylum, viz.: 'Considering the condition in which we found the pauper insane in the Asylum at Brattleboro,' is somewhat vague, but seems rather to reflect upon those having them in charge. If this be so, we would respectfully ask, does the cause for blame lie with the officers of the Asylum, or with the State?

"Mr Walker reluctantly concedes, that the present rate leaves the Asylum in debt, even after throwing out of account all expenditures of a permanent character, and the item of interest on the debt incurred for improving the accommodations for the insane, in the five years past.

"Dr. Fassett affirms that 'There is no similar institution in New England where the cost is not more than that allowed the Vermont Asylum,' and further says, the policy of the State in reference to the care of the insane reminds him of an old history, 'For there shall no straw be given you, yet shall you deliver the tale of bricks.'

"Dr. Goldsmith virtually admits the necessity for more liberal support, by recommending $3.50 per week for the inmates of the embryo Asylum.

"The Vermont Asylum asks it, that it may receive the actual cost of caring for those at present in its keeping.

J. DRAPER,
Secretary of Board of Trustees and Superintendent.
Vermont Asylum for the Insane, Brattleboro, Nov. 11, 1878.

The following is the Report of the Joint Legislative Committee of this year in full :

To the Honorable Senate and House of Representatives now in Session:

"The Standing Committee of the Senate and House of Representatives on the Insane Asylum respectfully state :   That in compliance with a joint resolution in that behalf they have performed their duties, and now present this their Report:

" That on the eleventh day of November, A. D. 1878, they visited the Insane Asylum at Brattleboro, and made as full examination of the same as time would permit ;   and also examined the Trustees and officers of the Asylum as to matters pertaining to the administration of the Institution, as well as the relation of the same to the State.

" In view of the late report made by the Commission created under joint resolution No. 137, of the session of 1876, we did not deem it necessary to carry our examination and investigation as far as we otherwise might.   As we understand the matter, the report of said former Commission states correctly the relation of the State to the Asylum, and we need hardly to say that the relation is not only peculiar, but is of itself an anomaly.

" The State has been for years and now is sending its insane paupers to the care of an Institution over which it has no control—except to regulate abuses, if any there are—and in which it has no recognized interest, upon terms as to compensation of its own making from time to time, and so far as it appears without even the implied assent of the officers of the Asylum ; it is only necessary to state this fact to make apparent the unusual, and, to say the least, not creditable position of the State in the premises.   Your committee are of the opinion that the price paid to the Asylum by the State for the support of its insane is quite sufficient in view of the somewhat limited, if not inadequate, accommodations furnished a portion of the patients ; at the same time it is but just to say that the past and present expense to the State for the support of its insane poor, is undoubtedly much less than it would or could be in a State asylum, especially if regard was had to expense of building and furnishing an asylum; at the same time your committee cannot avoid the conclusion that while the Asylum at Brattleboro gives to the State a fair return in a pecuniary point of view for what the State pays, the care and accommodations furnished to our insane unfortunates, are not such as to meet the approval of the good sense and humanity that pervades a large majority of the people of the State. And in this connection we do not intend or desire to reflect upon the managers or management of the Asylum at Brattleboro, but on the contrary we desire to put upon record our approval of both managers and management. The trouble lies in the fact that the asylum has not sufficient capacity to meet the wants of the State, and at the same time to receive such other patients as the managers naturally prefer ; so that the Institution is crowded to such an extent that as to some of the "wards " or " halls" there is a very apparent want of ventilation and of attendants. To cure these real or supposed ends would require quite a large outlay of money in the erection of new buildings, and in having a larger corps of attendants, an expense which, in the judgment of your committee, we cannot reasonably expect the managers of the Institution to undertake for the benefit of the State. Your committee have carefully considered the report of Dr. Goldsmith and his associates hereinafter referred to, and desire to say that the result of our examination and investigation is such that without scarcely an exception we can and do approve of their comments, strictures and conclusions, and especially do we believe *that it is the first duty of the State to take and carry out the necessary measures to erect, furnish and complete a State asylum for the Insane*, the same to be plain but substantial, and built with reference to the comfort and health of patients, aided by the many modern appliances now in use in similar institutions in our sister States ; and in the opinion of your committee there is no subject with which the State has at present to do, that so earnestly calls and demands the action and persistent efforts of our present Legislature as the one in question. We apprehend that there are many persons in the Asylum at this time who are not State beneficiaries, in fact, but "*town* paupers," who have been improperly saddled on to the State under the selfish and loose (if not reprehensible) practice of town authorities in that behalf. Legislation is needed to cure this abuse.

"Your Committee have given attention to the report of William H. Walker, Esq., hereinbefore referred to, so far as the same suggests legislative aid on enactments in reference to the subject under consideration, and we recommend that his suggestions be followed in the main, and to that end we herewith report certain bills for your consideration and action.

"Your Committee further recommend, that it is the duty of the State to provide for the safe and comfortable care of the insane convicts and criminals of the State, at or in connection with the State prison, rather than by sending them to the Asylum, to be kept with the insane unfortunates not convicts or criminals ; and we respectfully suggest that this matter may be very properly considered in connection with the proposed additions to the State prison.

"Your Committee have received the 'Comments of the Officers of the Vermont Asylum for the Insane, on the report of the Special Commissioners,' but have received the same too late for perusal, and we call your attention to it, believing that it merits your candid consideration.

"All of which is respectfully submitted,

E. J. ORMSBEE, Senate Committee.

W. F. TEMPLETON,
J. L. HARRINGTON, } House Committee.
A. F. HUBBARD,
F. A. DWINELL,

"While I concur with the majority of the Committee in the greater part of their report and recommendations, I must say that I could not discover a "want of proper ventilation" in any part of the Asylum, with the exception of the Marsh Building (so called), and the managers of the Asylum informed us that they were preparing to remedy the same, and shall remove all cause of complaint.

"In my judgment if the State will take measures to remove from the Asylum the insane criminals there confined, and the demented paupers, that the accommodations of the Institution will then be ample to properly supply all the wants of the State.

"I do not approve of all the *comments, strictures* and *conclusions* of the Commissioners referred to in said report, nor do I believe that the State at the present time should erect a State asylum for the Insane.

C. W. WITTERS,
Of Senate Committee.

The Legislature, at its session in 1878, made a complete revision of the lunacy laws. The office of Commissioner of the Insane, instituted in 1845, was this year abolished, and a Board of Supervisors of the Insane created. This Board was to be always composed of two physicians and one lay member, and besides being charged with visitorial power, they were empowered to examine into all complaints and to order the discharge of any persons in their judgment unwarrantably confined in the Asylum. In short, a permanent investigating committee was henceforth established.

A T the Annual Meeting, 1879, the officers chosen were the following :

It was Voted—"To amend Article III of the By-Laws, so as to embrace in the list of resident officers a steward, who shall be annually elected by the Trustees, in the same manner as the assistant physicians, matron and farmer ; " and Porter C. Spencer (who, since May, 1877, had filled the position of business clerk), was elected to the position with the following defined duties :

SEC. 1. The steward shall have the oversight and charge of the stores, and of the disbursement of supplies to the wards and to the various departments, and issue the same under the approval and regulations of the superintendent, keeping books showing receipts and disbursements, and accounts with the different patients and departments as the superintendent may require.

SEC. 2. He shall assist in maintaining the police of the establishment, see that the yards, cellars, basements, sewers, store-houses, shops, farmer's quarters, gymnasium, and all the buildings except those occupied by the patients and the farm buildings proper, are kept clean and orderly at all times by those whose duty it is to care for them in detail, and look carefully to the economy of the stores of the establishment in every way, allowing nothing to be wasted or to run to waste from neglect.

SEC. 3. He shall assist the superintendent in the way of business generally, and ascertain and report the wants of the establishment to him, and make, under his direction, such purchases as he may authorize, rendering accounts to him daily, or at such times as he may require.

SEC. 4. He shall be on duty during the day time, and not absent himself during business hours from the Asylum, unless in the line of duty, or by permission of the superintendent.

Voted also, " That the superintendent be instructed to go on with the work of improving the wards (especially those in the first wing adjoining the centre, on the east), by new ceilings and flooring in the halls, and all other repairs needful to their thorough renovation."

April 2, 1880, the house and lot, with blacksmith's shop thereon, situated upon the west side of the Newfane road, between the David W. Miller place and the Newman Allen farm, was purchased of George and Polly C. Person for the sum of $1800. At the July meeting of the Board, the Trustees signed a petition to the select-men to lay out and open a road from Mechanics', or Forest Square to the Newfane road north of the David W. Miller place, and *Voted*, " To give the land and fencing." This road separated from the farm proper about thirty acres of land west of the main highway, including the wooded hill above the Marsh Building ; and this, upon the sug-gestion of Mr. Tyler, it was determined should be developed into a park for the use of the patients. Thus was this feature established and entered upon.

At the Annual Meeting this year the following elections were made.

OFFICERS OF THE BOARD.

Fred'k Holbrook, Chairman.
W. H. Rockwell, Treasurer.
J. Draper, Secretary.
Fred'k Holbrook, Auditor.

RESIDENT OFFICERS.

Joseph Draper, Superintendent and Physician.
J. M. Clark, 1st Assistant Physician.
O. W. Phelps, 2nd Assistant Physician.
Mary Draper Phelps, Matron.
P. C. Spencer, Steward.
Asa Gilkey, Farmer.

The Report of the Trustees for the biennial term ending July 31, 1880, is brief, and this period is characterized as one of quiet, steady work, and of progress in all the essential objects of the Institution.

The Trustees remark upon the extensive alterations and improvements made in some of the wards, which have reduced somewhat the receiving capacity of the buildings by appropriating to other important uses some space formerly occupied by sleeping rooms. The detail of "Improvements in the two years," is given in the Superintendent's Report, in substance as follows :

"In the beginning of 1879, were commenced the alterations and partial reconstruction of the wards in the rear wings approved by the Trustees at their September meeting, 1878. This work occupied the whole year, as it had to be done under the disadvantages of constant occupancy ; but it is safe to say that no one year's work has more essentially changed for the better the interior of the buildings. There is now no ward of the Asylum that does not open freely to the light and air at each extremity, and that has not likewise an alcove upon the sunny side, in which, as in a sitting-room, the patients may congregate. These alterations involved the construction of six new bath rooms, water closets, and clothing rooms, three upon each side of the house, thereby adding greatly to these most necessary accommodations. Floors had to be relaid and ceilings made entirely new. A new staircase had to be constructed in each wing thus altered, and this was made to include a brick shaft for soiled clothing from each story. Old walls had to be taken down from attic to cellar, and new ones built up ; and in doing this, additional flues for heating and ventilating were introduced. Altogether, the work was a thorough one, and made a radical improvement in the plan of the buildings. Simultaneously with this, very considerable improvements were made in the Marsh Building. A tunnel was constructed from the main buildings beneath the road, through which were carried all steam and water pipes, and by this means this detached building was likewise brought within reach of the fan, and under the system of forced ventilation. Nothing has been more satisfactory in its practical working than this artificial aid to ventilation. Our anticipations from it have been more than realized. The extremity of the air chamber in the rear wing of the Marsh Building was made to terminate at a bench of heating radiators, supplying rooms before indirectly warmed and which were supplemented by flues communicating with an additional ventilating chimney.

The work of renovating the east wing next the center, as directed at the annual meeting, 1879, engaged attention early in the year 1880, and occupied nearly the whole season.

Considerable space is given in the Superintendent's Report to the discussion of the Causes and Phases of Insanity, which is here reproduced :

"The deeper we penetrate into the subject, the more we grow into the conviction that constitutional predispositions operate much more potently in the production of insanity than the multiplied exciting causes, which have come to be regarded as factors. .

"An intelligent understanding of insanity requires a more or less intimate comprehension of the great subject of human development and progress. The history of civilization throws much light upon insanity. In tracing its progress, which in its course has uplifted mankind and steadily developed human possibilities, we find in every age there have been those who have fallen out by the way, or gone into blind paths which lead to silent resting places. The track of civilization is studded with fossil deposits of human kind.

"There is always a process of elimination accompanying the course of civilization, which conduces to the ultimate advancement of the race. There are deteriorating families which, after the lapse of a few generations, cease to play their part and become fossilized, while the living mass moves on. A careful survey of mankind at the present time will afford abundant evidence of this view. Not only will we discover individual families who have dwindled down to a few single representatives, by reason of the vices of ancestors that have become constitutional in their descendants, until their accumulated weaknesses become incompatible with the continuance of a healthy manhood, and terminate in physical infirmities and mental imbecility. That such is the origin, course and character of a certain proportion of the insanity of our time, is certain.

"We may go further still in this view and not go far wrong. Outside the domain of recognized insanity there is much actual mental unsoundness. The humanitarian who directs his attention to the different families of dependents upon public bounty, will find little difficulty in recognizing whole classes who represent the waning phases of mentality. If he visits the almshouses or eleemosynary public institutions, he is struck with the weakness and incapacity prevailing among the inmates, still more strikingly evident in the family histories he investigates, which are a mingled record of thriftlessness, want of moral sense, petty dissipations and vices, all the outcome of chronic constitutional qualities. If he visits the reformatories and prisons he will recognize a somewhat different type of mentality, still a distinctive one, which likewise is connected with a preceding line of erratic ancestry. More intellectual capacity will be found to characterize criminal psychology, but this is associated with such perversions or absence of moral sense as renders the possession of intellectual power all the more dangerous.

"In many respects the lines of pauperism, criminality and insanity run parallel with each other, and are so interwoven with each other as to be often inseparable; certain it is that many of the former class drift helplessly into the latter, and representatives of each are always to be found in asylums. This kind of insanity is very unfavorable for recovery, or permanent improvement. It is too intimately ingrained in the individual. It is not so much a morbid state that has come upon him as a disease, as a development of his natural tendencies, leading through various erratic phases to ultimate dementia. The notable feature of these cases is the exaggeration of natural traits, rather than the more or less complete reversal of normal characteristics, which is observed in insanity from extraneous causes. A naturally weak individual, never endowed with the average amount of cerebral energy, slowly, but almost inevitably, drifts into a state of dementia and becomes a dependent upon public charity. The fault is less that of the individual himself, than of his progenitors. If he lacks the ambitions and thrift common to others, it is rather because he is wanting in that innate power which is the foundation of a healthful activity. It is an error to suppose an imbecile less liable to the supervention of ordinary insanity than those of average capacity.

"It is not unusual in the experience of asylums to see true mania engrafted upon imbecility, and recovery take place from this secondary complication; but exemption from recurrences is less hopeful than in those of average endowments, and the progress of such a case towards dementia is usually more rapid, by reason of less power of resistance.

"In the insanity of the criminal classes we see derangement most largely in the direction of their natural tendencies. They become less changed than exaggerated in their dominant peculiarities. In childhood vicious, in youth artful, immoral and engaged in schemes of dishonesty or villainy, and living without visible means of support, or any recognized calling. This irregular life gradually becomes one of recklessness and settled dissipations, in which all power of self control becomes lost and actual insanity supervenes; in which the dominant passions play their part no longer with method, but in obedience to any impulse or transient incentive that may arise, or to hallucinations of sense that have developed as the outgrowth of their vicious lives.

"Public hospitals for the insane shelter the representatives of both these classes. Those of aimless lives, by reason of constitutional weaknesses, are at last arrested in their vagrant wanderings

and find a home in asylums, which afford them better sanitary
surroundings and hygienic conditions than they have ever before
been able to provide for themselves, or known.   And the same
humanity which recognizes and provides for these weak ones, likewise extends the helping hand to those who have been offenders
of the laws, but upon whom has fallen the heavy affliction of
insanity.   The philanthropy that moves in all these cases is the true
sort, but some questions need to be further considered in respect to
the latter classes.

" If there is reason for separating those of bad lives from their
fellows in health, ought not that separation still to be maintained in
event of the visitation of insanity, provided that the resources of
the healing art be afforded them according to the best light of
the time?   The influence of the general tenor of an individual life
is always to a certain extent felt, despite the mental disorder that
may have have supervened ; and there is a certain manifest injustice
felt by every one who reflects upon the matter, in the forced association of the criminal with the non-criminal insane, and which those
in charge of asylums feel obliged to modify by separate classification
or isolation.

" The representatives of these types of insanity are hardly free
agents from the time they reach a responsible age, till they pass
beyond earthly responsibility.   Their mental organization contains
so many and so fixed crooks, that they are governed by natural
predispositions, rather than influenced by the motives and incentives
surrounding them, and those principles which move the masses
generally.   The mere fact of insanity having existed in some
branches of one's family, or even in one's immediate progenitors,
does not give in all cases a pronounced hereditary character to the
insanity of an indivdual though it is always a fact significant, and
one to be studied in its bearing upon a case.   Sometimes it may
have been the result of an accidental cause, and may have occurred
in the progenitor long after the birth of his children, in which case
it would have little bearing upon the insanity of the latter.   In many
cases it may doubtless be found to amount to little more than a dormant tendency which may render exciting causes somewhat more
potent in the production of insanity.   True heredity, in the practical
sense, applies rather to those cases in which qualities of organization
instead of mere tendencies are stamped upon the individual, and
such are not apparent in all cases in which insane members may be
genealogically traced.   A disease so frequent as insanity, and
increasing rather than diminishing, with an advancing civilization,

well deserves the most careful investigation of its causes. While it may be admitted that its increase may to some extent be more apparent than real, nevertheless its glaring prominence in the face of increasing light in the direction of the laws of life, is a fact not readily harmonized with human progress.

"It must be admitted that the term insanity is a very comprehensive one, and the tendency of modern thought has been to widen its application. In its legal signification it includes every form of mental defect, whether congenital, or of subsequent development. In the earlier ages of civilization, only the most demonstrative forms of insanity were recognized; subsequent light has developed to view more subtle phases, and even very nice shades of mental unsoundness, all of which fall under the general term, and have come to bear upon the social status and the civil condition of the individual. By reason, therefore, of the increasing comprehensiveness of the subject, the remote predisposing causes become more and more questions for study, and no case can be thoroughly well understood without the light that may be thrown upon it from the family history.

"In the analysis of those admitted to the Asylum in the two years past we have not contented ourselves with recording only the single dominant cause, but have allowed all known agencies to count upon the result. This method was adopted two years ago. Twenty-eight causes have been credited with contributing to the insanity of those admitted in the last biennial period.

"Hereditary tendency was traceable in eighty of the one hundred and seventy-seven cases, or fifty-five per cent of all whose histories were ascertained. Self-abuse, intemperance, and excesses of various kinds, contributed to the development of about twenty-five per cent. Diseases or injuries of the nervous centers, complicated about fifteen per cent. Nervous exhaustion, overwork, over-study, general ill health, and diseases common to both sexes were assigned as causes in about twenty-three per cent. Diseases peculiar to females figured in about twenty-eight per cent of the ascertained cases of women.

"Moral causes seem to have been more or less operative in about thirty per cent. of all whose histories were learned, and those of a domestic nature, involving the affections, seem to have been about twice as frequent as those of a business kind, including also excitements of a religious or political character."

There were four hundred and forty-seven patients in the Asylum

August 1st, 1880; one hundred and seventy-seven having been received, and one hundred and eighty-nine discharged, during the biennial term.

The receipts for the two years were,	$168,493.28
The expenditures,	168,352.06

Leaving on hand, $141.22

The cost of the radical changes in the plan of the buildings as detailed in the record of 1879, was $4,853.00.

At the October meeting, the Board took under consideration a proposal to straighten and establish a line at the northeast corner of the meadow, between lands of the Asylum and Dorman B. Eaton, and it was voted to adopt a line as surveyed by Geo. H. Clark (surveyor), and James M. Tyler was appointed by vote of the Board to draft and execute a proper instrument on the part of the corporation for the establishment of said line, which was done under date of October 15th, 1880, and duly recorded in the office of the town clerk.

In the autumn of this year Mr. E. W. Bowditch of Boston, a landscape gardener, was employed to make a careful survey and plan of the proposed new park, and lay out upon the same walks and other desirable features for its new uses, for practical guidance in the work of development. This was very carefully done, and subsequent work has followed it with very few deviations.

The Report of the newly created State Board of Supervisors of the Insane, for the biennial period, was an endorsement of the management of the Asylum.

Concerning that part of their duty by which they were authorized to order the removal of persons who ought to be discharged, they thus speak : ·

"Only four patients have been discharged during the past two years by the advice or direction of the supervisors, three of which were demented and harmless, and one of these only upon sufficient assurance that the patient should be properly cared for. We found but three persons (one since deceased) not insane according to the general acceptance of the term insanity, and these three were demented State paupers, and were committed under the orders of probate courts. We are satisfied there is no place where this class are better cared for than at the Asylum. From quite careful observation we believe there is no disposition on the part of the superintendent to detain patients when he is convinced that it is for their best good to be set at liberty.   We are pleased to report that the Trustees and superintendent are endeavoring to make the Asylum more distinctively a State institution, and to that end are discharging patients from without the State for the purpose of making room for State patients."

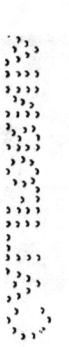

THE SUMMER RETREAT—1881.

RECORD OF 1881-2.

A SPECIAL meeting of the Board was called May 20th, 1881, and the request of the superintendent for three months' leave of absence from the middle of June, to enable him to take a trip to Europe, was granted.

June 4th, Trustees met, full board being present; and visited the wards of the Asylum and domestic departments, discussed plans for work, and decided to build a root cellar at the farm-house barn, and to replace the wooden fence between the two north sections of the west wing, with a brick connecting wall; also discussed arrangements for internal administration during the absence of the superintendent, and directed the securing of some young physician as a third assistant. Dr. Shailer E. Lawton was secured for this position. By reason of the absence of the superintendent the annual election of officers was postponed from August to October, when those of last year were re-elected, without change.

OFFICERS OF THE BOARD.

Frederick Holbrook, Chairman.
W. H. Rockwell, Treasurer.
J. Draper, Secretary.
Frederick Holbrook, Auditor.

RESIDENT OFFICERS.

Joseph Draper, Superintendent and Physician.
J. M. Clark, 1st Assistant Physician.
O. W. Phelps, 2nd Assistant Physician.
Mary Draper Phelps, Matron.
P. C. Spencer, Steward.
Asa Gilkey, Farmer.

At this meeting the superintendent brought before the Board a proposition for the purchase of the Miles school property, an establishment situated about a mile distant from the Asylum, for the purpose of fitting it up as a summer retreat, after the manner of some connected with similar institutions in England and Scotland, whereby certain classes of patients might enjoy a change in the yearly routine of asylum life, such as well people are accustomed to seek and take each year, if it can be afforded.

The proposition met with immediate favor; and Dr. Rockwell was authorized by vote of the Board to negotiate for the purchase of the property, if practicable, at a cost not exceeding $7,500.

At the November meeting the Trustees confirmed the negotiations of Dr. Rockwell for the Miles place, at the sum stated at the previous meeting. (Deed executed November 12th, '81.)

In the spring of 1882 the Trustees secured a plateau of six acres of land on the Putney road immediately above and adjoining the garden plateau, known as the Waite lot, for the sum of $2,400. This purchase was made by the superintendent the preceding year under the direction of the Trustees, and after the straightening of the line upon the side next Dorman B. Eaton, was turned over to the Asylum by deed, dated April 1st, 1882.

In May the Trustees, at their regular meeting, determined upon the amount of land that should be included about the Summer Retreat for its grounds, and directed a paling fence to be erected upon the side next the farm, and decided to remove all that bordering upon the roadside. In remodeling the buildings they decided to raise up the front portion, so as to bring the floor levels of this upon the same plane with those of the wing, and to build a veranda 10 feet wide entirely around the whole, making something more than 500 feet in length.

At the annual meeting the following officers were duly elected :

OFFICERS OF THE BOARD.

Fred'k Holbrook, Chairman.
W. H. Rockwell, Treasurer.
J. Draper, Secretary.
Fred'k Holbrook, Auditor.

RESIDENT OFFICERS.

Joseph Draper, Superintendent and Physician.
*S. E. Lawton, 1st Assistant Physician.
Edward French, 2d Assistant Physician.
———— ————, Matron.
P. C. Spencer, Steward.
Asa Gilkey, Farmer.

*The change in assistant physicians was made in April 1882. Both the outgoing officials had been several years in service, and left to engage in other fields of usefulness.

The office of matron, made vacant by the retirement of Mrs. Phelps, was not filled at this election ; no applicant with the necessary qualifications and experience being at this time available.

The receipts of the biennial period were, $180,381.43

The expenditures,   179,791.52

Leaving on hand, $589.91

The Trustees in their Report call especial attention to the newly inaugurated departures already noted, and especially to the greatly enlarged territory now appropriated to pleasure purposes, as follows:

"There are twenty acres of grounds connected with the newly acquired property, and thirty acres embraced in the new park, which added to the twenty upon the plateau of the main buildings, will ultimately give seventy acres of pleasure grounds. These extensions of facilities for the treatment of the inmates have been entered upon in pursuance of the settled and uniform policy of the Trustees in making such advances from year to year and time to time as the means at their disposal may warrant, and with full faith in the advantages sure to accrue from these added provisions."

The movement of population, as shown by the Superintendent in the biennial period is as follows :

One hundred and eighty-eight admitted, one hundred and ninety-four discharged, and four hundred and forty-one remaining. The new features about to be incorporated into the Asylum as permanent additions to its facilities for treatment are thus explicitly set forth.

THE NEW PARK.

"Two years ago the laying out of a new road by the town authorities, separated a tract of thirty acres from the farm proper, and left in immediate connection with the Asylum upon the west side of the road, a broken hill-side, its summit two hundred and fifty feet above the plateau on which the buildings stand. The top of this is wooded and rocky, but from many points beautiful views are obtained, and delightful shade with free breezes, which are every day enjoyed by the patients to whom it is already devoted. Near a mile of walk has been already made, and a plateau graded for games, the whole in accordance with the plan of a competent landscape gardener, by whom the same has been accurately surveyed and laid out. The completion of this will be the work of years, but it will eventually be one of the most attractive features of the place."

THE SUMMER RETREAT.

"This, so far as we are aware, is the first departure in this direction in the United States. It is not an extension of the capacity of the Institution, but an added provision, calculated, we believe, to enhance the benefits of treatment. It is a movement in the interest of the inmates, and it will necessarily add materially to the current expense account; secondarily, we think it will likewise benefit the Institution by increasing its curative results. The practical working of this adjunct to existing hospital advantages was observed by the writer in connection with some of the best English and Scottish asylums, in the summer of 1881. The testimony of the superintendents of the British institutions where the experiment has been tried, was uniform and outspoken in its favor, and its advantages so well recognized that some asylums have leased ordinary houses or cottages by the sea, or in the mountains, for use in the summer months by such inmates as could be sufficiently trusted, and needed such change. In this country the capacity of some hospitals has been increased by the occupancy of cottages or detached buildings, but it is not this that is here proposed. We wish this point to be particularly noted. * * * * The capacity of this establishment will be for a family of twenty or twenty-five inmates, including the necessary number of attendants, and there will be little in the nature of restraint connected with the arrangements of the building. Its design is to afford to the inmates of the Asylum that change from a wearisome routine that is universally recognized as essential, and where a family of twenty or more inmates may, in the hot season, find that rest which cannot but be as beneficial as desirable. That it will hasten and confirm convalescence in those who are recovering can hardly be doubted, and to all capable of appreciating the change it will be a happy relief from the routine of asylum life. It is believed that the best results will be realized by utilizing it in rotation by successive groups of patients, for two, three or four weeks together."

An inaugural trial of this new summer retreat was made from the 22d of September to the 7th of October inclusive. Sixteen patients, with a chief attendant and three assistants, constituted the family, apart from the man and wife in charge of the domestic department.

The amount expended in remodelling and furnishing this establishment was $6,500.

In the autumn of this year granite gate posts at all the entrances to the grounds of the main Asylum were set, the sidewalk raised and graded, and the brick connecting wall, with granite foundation and coping, between the two north sections of the west wing (determined upon June, '81), was built, separating the court within from the principal one of entrance for carriages withòut.   Upon the inner side of the enclosed court was projected a veranda about one hundred feet long and ten feet wide around two sides, supported by posts twelve feet high upon a granite curbing, the floor being filled in solidly with earth and covered and finished with Portland cement; the same being designed for the exercise of excited male patients in winter or wet weather, thus converting to permanent use a previously useless enclosure.

At the same time à similar structure was extended eastward from the extreme wing of the female department along the front line of the airing court for the excited class of female patients, its ridge line forming the division wall, and the roof being projected upon both the inner and the outer side of the court, supported by posts ten feet high resting upon granite curbing, the floor being filled and cemented as already described.   By this substantial construction, a permanent open air sheltered promenade was secured, the side bordering the inner court for the use of the excited in any weather, and that upon the outer side looking upon the garden and grounds, affording in winter a sunny side, and in summer a sufficient protection to be in both seasons a favorite resort.

THE work detailed in last year's record was resumed as early as possible in the spring, and completed by the extension of a veranda, identical in plan, at right angles to that already described, and surrounding the inner court of the east wing upon two sides, making about one hundred and seventy-five feet altogether of sheltered promenade. The last extension, by reason of the slope of the ground from the buildings, allowed the construction of a basement story beneath for the use of the gardener in which to keep garden tools, and store the vases, lawn-settees, etc., in winter. The veranda floor of this last extension was made of wood and formed the ceiling of the room below. This work was all completed in June of this year. The cost of these permanent improvements was $3,650.

At the April meeting of the Board, 1883, the question of a reconstruction of the chapel was opened, and the superintendent was directed to communicate with an architect and obtain his opinion as to what would be practicable in the matter.

May 18th, the Trustees met to consider the plan of the architect for improving the chapel, and directed other plans to be submitted for comparison, before adopting any.

July 5th, the Trustees *voted*, To adopt the plan submitted by Mr. Geo. D. Rand of Boston ; and on the 11th of the month, at a conference with him in respect to supervising the work, determined that a competent man should be engaged to raise the roof, and that the remainder of the work be done by the day under a foreman and the general superintendence of the architect. The plan adopted changed the pitch of the roof by opening the ridge line and carrying up each side to a point eight feet higher than before, and building out therefrom at the central point large dormers one-third the length of the building, and surmounting the whole with a ventilating cupola eight feet square with pyramidal roof. Interiorly the roof was supported longitudinally, on semi-circular arches, four in number, giving a height of twenty feet from the floor in the clear. The dormers were supported likewise by arches transverse to the main ones, and fifteen

feet in height. The interior was thus broken into a main audience room with transepts, having a long diameter of about seventy feet, and a transverse one of about fifty feet. The space between the arches was finished in panels on the slant of the roof, but leaving an air space between ceiling and roof, by which increased facilities for the ventilation of rooms below were gained by direct communication with the cupola.

No changes were made in the corps of officers at the annual meeting this year. Those of 1882 were all re-elected :

OFFICERS OF THE BOARD.

Fred'k Holbrook, Chairman.

W. H. Rockwell, Treasurer.

J. Draper, Secretary.

Fred'k Holbrook, Auditor.

RESIDENT OFFICERS.

Joseph Draper, Superintendent and Physician.

S. E. Lawton, 1st Assistant Physician.

Edward French, 2d Assistant Physician.

——— ———, Matron.

P. C. Spencer, Steward.

Asa Gilkey, Farmer.

It was *Voted*, To purchase an extension to the park if practicable, and Dr. Rockwell and Mr. Tyler were elected a committee to negotiate for and purchase the same.

At the December meeting the office of matron, which had been vacant since August, 1882, was filled by the advancement to that position of Miss H. E. B. Gibson, who, for five years preceding, had rendered acceptable service in a position qualifying her for the duties to which she was now elected.

Work upon the chapel began in September, 1883, and continued till March, 1884. The cost of this improvement, together with changes involved in the third story of the center building, was $7,500.

On the 10th of May a purchase was effected of 2 3-16 acres of land contiguous to the park, of Joseph Prescott, for $700. This made a straight boundary line between the Asylum Park and that of Mr. Crowell, from Cedar street on the West nearly to Chase street upon the East, and included a very desirable point of view, from which all the village, from Cemetery Hill on the South to the West River on the North, with the mountain on the New Hampshire side of the Connecticut River, is embraced in the outlook.

The Report of the Trustees called particular attention to the lessening of the average number of inmates, due to the removal by the State authorities of harmless chronic cases, which to a certain extent had diminished the insane of the Asylum, and especially to the lessening of the number of self-supporting cases, and increase of the number supported by towns, by which the receipts upon which the Institution solely depends had been still further decreased, and asked an additional allowance of fifty cents per week for those aided or supported by the State. The suggestion that the criminal class have provision made for them in connection with one of the penal institutions of the State was also once more urged, for the reasons fully set forth in 1878.

This second appeal, it may be stated in this connection, did not avail anything ; but the request for additional allowance for those supported at public expense was responded to by an increase in the rate, of twenty-five cents a week, by an Act approved Nov. 26, '84.

The Superintendent's Report shows one hundred and eighty-six admissions, and one hundred and ninety discharges, in the last biennial period, leaving four hundred and thirty-seven in the Asylum at date of this Report.

Open Air Treatment of the Insane is especially dwelt upon, as follows :

"We can safely say that in the past two years we have, more than ever before, made open air exercise prominent in the treatment of the cases committed to our care. We believe much in its curative as well as tranquilizing influence. We go even further, and are disposed to regard fresh air exercise in the treatment of maniacal cases of the sthenic type, as essential as the use of water in the febrile state. It is a natural craving of the patient in both cases, and ought to be indulged and afforded at least to a judicious amount."

The new park, as a means of affording increased privileges in this regard, is especially rejoiced in ; also the Summer Retreat, concerning which the following statement is made :

"The practical working of this newly created adjunct has been all that we anticipated. We have sixteen rooms furnished singly, and these have all been kept full. A chief attendant and two assistants have proved equal to the charge of this number. The suites of apartments designed for those who desire special attendants have not yet been furnished, but will be at any time when occasion demands their use. The public rooms, consisting of a parlor and library connected, and a recreation room twenty by thirty feet, furnished with a parlor organ and table games, are all upon the lower floor; the sleeping rooms above. No doors are locked in the daytime, and only such at night as would be considered essential to the ordinary safety of a sane family. The absolute unrestricted freedom of the grounds is enjoyed by the household, and in addition to this, walking groups are daily made up for a ramble in the adjacent fields, or to some of the surrounding points of view, to one of which a path has been extended and seats placed, beneath a pine grove crowning the summit of a hill which commands to still better advantage the scene already described, stretching eastward from the front of the buildings across the Connecticut Valley."

The abstract of receipts and expenditures for the two years, shows receipts, $178,247.21
Disbursements, 178,214.10

Leaving a balance of, $33.11

The election of officers resulted as follows :

OFFICERS OF THE BOARD.

Fred'k Holbrook, Chairman.
W. H. Rockwell, Treasurer.
J. Draper, Secretary.
Fred'k Holbrook, Auditor.

RESIDENT OFFICERS.

Joseph Draper, Superintendent and Physician.
S. E. Lawton, 1st Assistant Physician.
L. F. Wentworth, 2d Assistant Physician.
H. E. B. Gibson, Matron.
P. C. Spencer, Steward.
Asa Gilkey, Farmer.

At the September meeting of the Trustees, they considered the proposition for protecting the grave of the founder of the Asylum, Mrs. Marsh, (now in a neglected and abandoned cemetery), and appointed Mr. Tyler and the superintendent a committee to ascertain what was practicable, and report at a future meeting. At the meeting in October plans were debated for the re-arrangement of the farm buildings and removal of the piggery thereto, also for further and more radically improving the sewerage.

A T the monthly meeting in April, 1885, it was *Voted,* " To construct the system of sewerage outside the buildings anew to the foot of the bank, and to abandon the old drains whenever the new connections are made ; also, to reconstruct that portion of the engine house which has cracked and settled by reason of defective foundation, and rearrange the boilers upon the west side of the boiler room, where more secure foundation for them may be obtained." The new sewer was laid in accordance with a plan suggested by Mr. E. S. Philbrick, sanitary engineer, Boston, of Akron pipe, eight inch main and six inch branches, with traps just outside the buildings, ventilated through the soil pipes above the roofs, and with man-holes at these, and at every angle in their course, the joints being made close by cement and rings, or by bricks laid solidly around the joints in cement. The working of this has been perfect, and was accomplished at a cost of $2200.

The work in connection with the boiler house was likewise satisfactorily completed according to the plan, at an outlay of $4,500.

The following is the result of the annual election, 1885 :

OFFICERS OF THE BOARD.

Fred'k Holbrook, Chairman.
J. M. Tyler, Treasurer.
J. Draper, Secretary.
F. Holbrook, Auditor.

RESIDENT OFFICERS.

Joseph Draper, Superintendent and Physician.
S. E. Lawton, 1st Assistant Physician.
W. E. Bowie, 2d Assistant Physician.
H. E. B. Gibson, Matron.
P. C. Spencer, Steward.
Asa Gilkey, Farmer.

Cupolas upon the wings, three on each side of the center building, and one upon the Marsh Building, were also this year added for architectural effect and for ventilating purposes, at a cost of $300.

At the December meeting, '85, the Trustees considered the matter of the Willoughby Legacy, the annuity from which had been suspended for five years past by reason of mismanagement and involvement of the funds, resulting in permanent reduction of the income,—and *Voted*, "To accept the same proportionally with the Protestant Episcopal Institute at Burlington, co-legatee, and waive right of priority of mention in the will, under existing circumstances."

At the first meeting of the Trustees in 1886 (Jan. 12,) it was *Voted*, "To repair, reconstruct, and enlarge if practicable, the water reservoir upon the park (now leaky), as early in the spring as possible ; also to build a new piggery upon a new site ; and instructed the superintendent to obtain plans and to submit them to the Trustees seasonably."

The location of the latter involved extended consideration, and was not determined in time to do more than grade the plateau and construct the roads leading to and from it this season.

The reservoir was made perfect in its holding capacity, and doubled in its size, and covered by a roof with dormer windows on each of its four sides, surmounted by a ventilating cupola, the completed structure becoming thereby an attractive feature of the park. In addition to the increased reserve of water thus obtained, arrangements were entered into with Mr. Crowell for extending from his village works a branch pipe for a fire hydrant in front of the main line of buildings, the same being connected and under pressure from his reservoir on Highland Park, which was also completed this year.

At the June meeting, Messrs. Holbrook, Tyler and Bradley being present, "Visited the wards, the domestic departments, the park, and especially inspected the working of the new system of sewerage constructed last year, and now fully perfected in all its connections. The whole establishment was pronounced in satisfactory condition. The general work of repainting during the winter was especially approved, also certain minor changes at the Marsh Building, by which the old furnace room had been converted into a lodging room, and the chimney made to serve a ventilating register in each story.

"The proposition to erect a carriage porch at the rear central entrance, and make a new entrance to the kitchen department, was also indorsed and accomplished.

"In addition to the foregoing, a plan was suggested by Mr. Tyler, looking to the commencement at no very distant day of the work of reconstructing the Asylum upon a modern plan ; by doing it one wing at a time, as it was originally accomplished. This met with the immediate indorsement of Gov. Holbrook and Mr. Bradley. Voted also to change the time of the monthly meetings from the 2d to the 1st Tuesday."

The result of the annual election of officers this year was as fol-lows :

OFFICERS OF THE BOARD.

Fred'k Holbrook, Chairman.

J. M. Tyler, Treasurer.

J. Draper, Secretary.

Fred'k Holbrook, Auditor.

RESIDENT OFFICERS.

Joseph Draper, Superintendent and Physician.

S. E. Lawton, 1st Assistant Physician.

W. E. Bowie, 2d Assistant Physician.

H. E. B. Gibson, Matron.

P. C. Spencer, Steward.

Geo. W. Pierce, Farmer.

The Biennial Report of the Board calls attention to the comple-tion of the first half century of the Asylum, and closes as follows : "The Trustees feel that the work of fifty years, represented by the present establishment as now completed and modernized, is a credit-able monument to those who have had in charge the legacy of the founder, and the development of her cherished wishes. Their plans for the future embrace further efforts at improvement, and other departures in accordance with the ideas and demands of the time, to the full extent of the means they may have for the promotion of the chartered objects of the Institution."

The Superintendent's Report shows the number in the Asylum to be four hundred and fifty ; two hundred and forty-nine men, and two hundred and one women. The admissions for the biennial term were one hundred and eighty-four, and the discharges one hundred and seventy-one. Three cases are especially noted as having recov-ered after unusually long periods of continuous insanity, and are commented upon as follows :

"Two of them, both men, were admitted to the Asylum in 1881. Both labored under melancholia, and both were strongly suicidal—had made attempts upon their lives before their admission to the Asylum, and subsequently thereto on repeated occasions. In neither was there a visible lifting of the clouds until about a year preceding their discharge, and then convalescence was slow but sure. The duration of insanity was in each case over five years, inclusive of the period of convalescence. Both were in middle life.

"Another case, a woman, was admitted in 1880. This commenced as one of melancholia a year preceding admission ; but developed into active destructive mania, which continued without intermission, and without manifest abatement until about six months preceding her discharge, when a decided change for the better took place, and convalescence was thereafter continuous and unmistakably genuine. The duration of insanity in this case, including the period of recovery, was fully seven years. The mental disorder was connected with the climacteric period, and doubtless dependant upon that change. This latter case is especially interesting, as we had come to regard it · a confirmed one, and saw no reasonable ground for, a hopeful prognosis until the close of last year.

"It illustrates the possibility of recovery in cases *dependent upon this cause*, even after the lapse of some years. Physicians engaged in this specialty know that in many cases arising from *other causes*, the friends often look forward to the climacteric in hope of a turn for the better, but in our experience this change oftener aggravates than mitigates the previously existing malady, and no good ground exists, in the experience of the writer, upon which such hope can be confidently stayed.

"The two cases of melancholia are instructive in the confirmation they afford to the theory that the course of melancholia, as a rule, is more protracted than that of the more active phases of insanity, as of mania—in its various forms."

Apart from the analyzation of the statistics of the period, the following discussion of morbid tendencies goes to make up this report, under the head of

DANGEROUS GROUND.

"Commenting upon the liability to insanity is like stepping upon boggy soil ; however carefully one picks his way he rarely escapes missteps. Still it is a territory which can hardly be wholly avoided. The fact shown by statistics in respect to the element of heredity, which enters into so large a percentage of individual cases, is liable to be given undue weight, and the conclusion is too hastily drawn that those born with hereditary tendencies, from their earliest years walk over pitfalls or quicksands by which they are ever liable to be engulfed. Such a conclusion, however, cannot be accepted without much qualification. In the discussion of all questions of social science, hobbies are ridden. Special vices are often greatly magnified in their influence, both upon the individual and the race, as the gross exaggeration of the evils of one in particular, by charlatans, who reap profits from the fears and apprehensions of its subjects, well attests. The heritage of mankind is subject to great variations, and there can be no question but that its drift, undirected and unmodified, would be in many cases towards destruction ; but the course of every man's life is, to some extent, in his own hands. Not only may an inborn tendency be held in check, but it may often be deflected from its original course, and even decided mischiefs that may have been sustained, may be repaired. Human nature is often exhibited to view in its truest colors in a state of insanity. Every psychological student has, doubtless, been surprised in reflecting upon this matter, and, recognizing this fact, at the almost involuntary inhibitory power exercised over mankind in general, by those acquired influences which are the result of educational agencies. The safeguards of society are really much greater than are generally realized. The sway exercised over the masses by the customary conventionalities of life, bears rule over many a wayward prompting, and holds in check very decided tendencies to abandonment.

"'Pride," said a distinguished divine of a generation ago, "is the ruling principle of an unsanctified world ; " and, so far from condemning it, he accredited it with a most salutary power, in the absence of a worthier motive. We might almost venture the assertion that one is safe so long as he is responsive to environing influences, and only in danger when he ceases to be affected by public sentiment, by social dicta, or when he turns within, and preys upon himself. Egotism is usually exalted in the insane, but its manifestations vary greatly. Elevated personal appreciation or conceit is the most harmless and superficial phase of it. It takes its strongest and most baneful hold upon a person when it absorbs everything to itself and sequestrates its rule.

"It is unfortunate to be in the world and not of it. So long as one realizes, and acts in accord with the realization that he is but an individual among the multitude, and that the welfare of the whole is the happiness of each, we may look for healthy activities ; but, when this grand general fact is lost sight of, morbid action begins, and a process is set up which is fatal to the individual. Involution instead of evolution then goes on, and time weaves about him a net work, in which, as a chrysalis, lost to his fellows, he awaits the final transformation. Every life, however modified, is colored by its inborn tendencies.. The sources of happiness or misery spring largely from the constitutional predispositions of individuals. A naturally cheerful person sees the sunny side of life and finds in any environment a prevailing amount of enjoyment, while one of a gloomy cast lives amid forebodings, and, as one without light, gropes silently along life's pathways, half fearing to tread where others have before him and shunning the healthful sunlight which at every turn beams upon him as upon all others. Such natures are most liable to become gradually morbid, and to glide slowly into the realm of delusion and melancholy. In the experiences of asylum life, not a few are seen to have thus drifted into confirmed insanity. The early view of life may have been a cramped one ; the outlook through the narrow window of self-interest, opening out upon a very limited field of observation, and this hedged about by suspicion and envy.

"No greater misfortune can be labored under than that of a childhood passed without opportunities for expansion. As the years move on, the little circle becomes the whole world, and all outside is viewed with vague and incorrect ideas, and with more or less of distrust. To be mentally healthy one must be largely unconscious of self. In the human economy the vital operations go on unconsciously. There is something the matter when we become aware that we have a heart, or a respiratory apparatus, or a stomach. The functions of all these organs go on silently in the normal state and occasion us no subjective anxiety.

"An individual is but a member of the great body of mankind, and his functions should go on as silently as those of the single organs that go to make up the individual organism. There is something wrong when the individual jars against the body politic. A healthy organism, individual or collective, should be largely oblivious to special functions. There is incipient disorder always when the latter rise into prominence, and exact undue attention. It is a fact well known to medical men that it is the minor ills that oftenest occasion anxiety. A grave organic disease usually gives less apprehension than a mere functional disorder. Not unfrequently a hopefulness attends its whole course, while hypochondria connects itself with the merest functional disorder. Then, too, it must be remembered that persons with born peculiarities, and encircled by unusual or abnormal influences, to some extent grow into harmony with them, and adapt themselves thereto. It is not an unusual circumstance for tourists to lose their lives in attempting to scale precipitous points, but much more seldom does such disaster overtake the native mountaineer. His earliest steps being taken amid such dangers, he confidently leaps from point to point, and measures with accuracy not only the distances, but the strength of the supports upon which he ventures.   Born and reared amongst the crags, he realizes not the risks as those, who, ascending from the plains gradually comprehend their grandeur and awful heights, and become appalled, dazed, giddy and lost in the overwhelming environment. The chief element of safety to the denizens of this dangerous territory is their utter obliviousness to its perils.   Precisely in this state is the individual whose life is hedged about with unfortunate predispositions—safe while he dwells not upon this fact; safe if he turns not selfward and broods over the possibilities.   Woe betide him, when he withdraws within himself, and shuts the door.

"By the conditions or accidents of birth, some inhabit unstable ground ; others recklessly or inconsiderately choose perilous paths, and not unfrequently incur greater risks of falling than those whose foundation is to some extent uncertain.   Not every devious and irregular way pursued by such erratic natures should be regarded as morbid, though abnormal as measured by the course of mankind in general ; and it should not be forgotten that those to the manor born may tread a pathway which might not be followed by others with equal safety.

" Besides the mischiefs that result from a bad start in life, there are some incident to an unwise ending of it.   It seems to be a cherished idea with most men who are fortunate in business or professional life, to anticipate a period of restful enjoyment.   To the man of active life, impelled onward by forces he has helped to create, and often crowded by them to the point of weariness and exasperation, it is the most natural thing to look upon rest and freedom from such pressure as the nearest approach to bliss, and ever and anon as the years go by he finds himself longing and planning for a complete surrender of all the activities which for a score or two of years at least have constituted his life.   But, when this is accomplished and he sits down at his ease to enjoy the accumulations of his life labor the situation is not what he expected ; the happiness he had pictured he does not find.   Involuntarily he sighs for his accustomed routine. In his devotion to the one object of securing a competency, he has not forecast the necessity he now feels for some healthful occupation of his energies, and, instead of repose, unrest is upon him.   Soon misgivings come over him, and the realization that he has made a mistake that is irretrievable, and too often the balance of life becomes unhappy and a condition of melancholy beclouds his latter days.   This result is seen in country as well as city life, among the agriculturalists as among the commercialists. ·A hardworking farmer devotes himself to the securing of an estate and its belongings. It is the one idea of his life, and all his energies are devoted to it. He is successful, and, as his sons grow up, ambitious they should continue with and succeed him in the management and care of the farm. Other fields of labor, however, beckon them away. They go, and by the aid of hired laborers he continues his charge. As the waning years of life creep on him, he begins to feel the responsibilities weigh more heavily. Each year increases the burden, until he induces a son to return, on condition that he surrender to him the management and a joint title to the farm, or he disposes of his estate and determines to live upon the proceeds for the balance of his days without work. In either case he soon realizes that he has made a mistake. What he wanted was not the abandonment of all the avocations to which he was accustomed, and which he had most rejoiced in when in the full vigor of his years, but only such modifications of burdens as gradually increasing age demanded; relief short of absolute idleness. In the large proportion of cases the absolute retirement from a life-long engrossing business is fraught with danger, and followed by the wreckage of all anticipated satisfaction. Some of this result is due to too circumscribed ideas of life—too complete devotion to a single object—to habitual neglect of mental cultivation, or of maintaining an interest in the worlds affairs in general, so that when the life-long pursuit is given up there offers no other channel in which the remaining and accruing energies can be employed or become engrossed. It is a serious and too common error to neglect an interest in other things than those connected with one's chosen labor, and tends gradually but ultimately to narrowing and degeneracy.

" To the individual of active temperament *change is rest*. Everything in life is opposed to passive rest. Activity in proportion to strength is as needful to the preservation and enjoyment of life, as is continued breathing. The phlegmatic usually take the whole of life so easily that the evils of nervous exaustion seldom overtake them. It is the sanguine and nervous who break down most frequently ; nevertheless, such, having more versatility, are better prepared to rally and find in varied ways restoration.

" Those of the bilious or motive temperament, who devote themselves to continued physical labor, who have least change in the routine of life and who seek and take fewest diversions, travel the most dangerous road and are most helpless and hopeless when they fall."

One additional mode of diversion for the male patients is chronicled in this report, which was experimental at the outset and designed as an offset to the Summer Retreat, which had from its opening been devoted to the female patients, but which has proved so entirely a success that it may now be regarded as an established thing. It was commenced in the summer of 1885. "One day of each week was set apart for a camping excursion. The party was made up of fifteen patients, with the chief attendant and two assistants who started off in the gray of the morning with portable camp equipage and provision for the day, partly cooked and partly uncooked, with instructions only to remain away all day, and choose for their encampment any place upon the Asylum territory. They pitched upon the highest land of the estate, a mile or more distant from the Asylum, a point commanding beautiful views up the valleys of both the Connecticut and West rivers, and there improvised for themselves, returning in the gloaming, a most thoroughly rejuvenated company.   After two or three excursions of this kind (being obliged to return once prematurely to escape a threatened tempest of wind and rain), arrangements were made for shelter, and two roofed structures with open ends were erected to guard against sudden contingencies.   These recreations were continued late into the autumn and resumed again in June this year with unabated zest. The advantages of this departure were so manifest, not alone in the enjoyment of such change, but in the curative influence evident (two particularly seeming to date their convalescence from these excursions last year), that we have determined to make it a permanent feature, and two acres have been surveyed, enclosed, and set apart for this exclusive purpose.   It is an open field, skirted by a fringe of wood as a back-ground.   Other sheltered structures have been erected ; also a kitchen and store house, and a croquet ground graded for use.   Hereafter the camping ground will be one of the organized features appertaining to the establishment."

The receipts of the biennial period aggregate, $180,245.22.   The expenditures, $165,338.18, leaving on hand a balance of $14,907.04, which the plans for the immediate future will consume.

The following extract from the Report of the Board of Supervisors of the Insane for the years 1885-6, shows the estimation in which the Asylum was held by the State authorities at this period.

The Sanitary Condition of the Asylum.

" It would hardly seem possible that the sanitary condition of the Asylum could be materially improved.   The improvements in this direction, begun two years ago, have all been completed.   The external sewerage of the building has been made to correspond with the perfection of the internal arrangement for that purpose and the entire system is now complete. The sewerage is now conveyed away under ground to some distance from the Asylum, and below it, with little if any possibility of any offensive odor. In order to accomplish this the water supply is abundant in all the wards ; the water closets in the various wards are all flushed at short periods by a patent automatic arrangement and thereby kept free from impurities.

"The ventilation and heating are accomplished by steam power. A large steam engine in the rear of the main building, so far away and so thoroughly protected as to occasion no danger from fire, supplies the power which sends sufficient heat to every ward in the Asylum to make the coldest day in winter seem warm and genial as a summer's day, and at the same time sending through them all currents of fresh outside air, which displaces the peculiar odor which pertains more or less to asylum and hospital life. This perfection of sewerage, heating and ventilation in the Asylum has been specially noticed and remarked by those who have visited it, both citizens and strangers. The culinary arrangements of the Asylum are admirable. The inmates are well provided for in respect to food. It is well prepared and in abundance. Each day has its special service, and each season of the year brings its special luxuries and necessities for the table. Invalids have dishes prepared for them with all the care and forethought of the well-trained nurse. The Board have occasionally heard complaints from the inmates of failure in quality or quantity, but inquiry has not elicited any confirmation of the fact. When it is remembered that a large share of the inmates of the Asylum came from the lower and less luxuriantly fed classes of the community, it will hardly be surprising that complaints should be made, nor that they should not bear inspection. The Board also take pleasure in commending the neatness and cleanliness of the various departments of the Asylum, and the general tidy appearance of the inmates in dress and person. The activity of the laundry and sewing rooms are evidence of the labor necessary to accomplish this desirable result, and the inmates seem to respond well to the requirements in this direction. The dormitories are now nearly all supplied with hair mattresses, with woven wire accompaniments, which have taken the place of the old style of beds. This is a new departure and quite in contrast with the uncouth sleeping arrangements of former days. As a whole, the Board consider the sanitary condition of the Asylum to be all that can be desired, and, as a result, there has been during the past two years but very little sickness among the inmates, comparatively none save that which is incident to this class of people in any community."

The fiftieth anniversary of the opening of the Asylum (December 12, 1886) fell on Sunday, and was not passed without notice.

The religious service was this day performed by Rev. C. H. Merrill of the Congregational church at West Brattleboro, who preached from the text, John iv: 37, 38, "One soweth and another reapeth.   *   *   *   Other men labored, and ye are entered into their labors."

He spoke of the intimate relations which succeeding generations bear to one another, and of the debt of obligation which this present age must owe to the past.   There has been inherited from the past all the *wealth* which has been so rapidly increasing during this 19th century.   Indirectly this wealth, accumulated by individuals, has all gone to benefit the entire community.   But directly in increasing measure it has been applied to the endowment of schools and hospitals, and libraries, and asylums, and "homes."

There has been inherited from the past also, the results of *scientific investigation,* and increase in the *knowledge* of the laws of nature.   The fruits of this appear to-day in the means adopted for the prevention and cure of disease, the treatment of the sick, the relieving of pain, and the marvelous feats of surgery.

A far more precious inheritance appears in the *spiritual legacy* bequeathed.   With the institutions firmly established, and liberally endowed, have come down to this generation the spirit of wisdom that moved for their establishment, and the spirit of liberality that provided their endowment.   These institutions are of value as they are alive to-day with the spirit of the age, and their endowment is of highest importance as it gives them power to secure the largest measure of this spirit in the officers which they can command.

He closed with the following words :   "We are reminded by our surroundings this afternoon, that this is the fiftieth anniversary of the opening of this Institution.   The blessing it has been to those that have been treated here during all these years may be taken as the fruit of the seed sown in a former generation.

"I have no personal knowledge of the life and the character of her by whose act this Institution was founded.   But I know, as you well know, that the act was a Christly act, worthy the approving word, 'Inasmuch as ye have done it unto one of these ye have done it unto me.'   Perhaps in no other way does the truth of the brother- hood of man and the unity of the race find better illustration than by the bestowment of free gifts, by those who are in health, for the endowment of institutions for the care and treatment of those providentially deprived of this blessing.   It is an act done in recognition of this kinship.   Beyond the ties of family and kindred and blood, there is felt to be the tie of a possible fellowship in suffering, and heirship to the same covenant of promise.   Institutions of this kind are Christian institutions, whatever be their name ; and it is because we live in a land where the civilization is of the Christian type, that we find them among us in such numbers and in such excellence. It is fitting then that we turn our thoughts from the gift to its ultimate source, the Master himself, by whose spirit hearts are quickened to acts of devotion.   The immortality of a good deed is to us the type of the immortality of a character formed by good deeds, unselfish service, loyalty to the truth.   To those who have been blessed with the blessing of Christian institutions, there comes the call for the yielding of life to a more perfect obedience to the power of the divine truth, and the divine life."

There was present at this service one patient* who was admitted during the first year, and who had been a continuous resident almost the whole half century.

*Abijah W. Betterly of Newfane, Vt.

CONCLUSION.

BRIEFLY has been reviewed the history of the Asylum and its work from its precarious beginning, and struggling early life, to its full development. Here we rest. It is for the future chronicler to record its coming annals, and note what may henceforth be accomplished in the great cause of humanity, here. Its previous history has been unpretentious. No imposing ceremonies —as in more modern days—attended the laying of its corner stone ; but the hands of the masons were directed by the guiding spirit of philanthropy, and possibly "they builded better than they knew."

The principal object of the foregoing pages will be accomplished if they serve to correct the misapprehensions which have grown up concerning the status of the Institution, and to show how it has been created and developed.

If we mistake not, too, it will illustrate as the history of no similar institution does, the possibilities dependent upon the pursuance of a steady line of policy and prudent financial management. It bears witness too, to the wisdom of that form of government usually denominated "a close corporation," by which vacancies in the managing board are filled by the surviving members. In no other way can a steady principle of management be secured. Had it been otherwise it is more than probable that the story of a deplorable failure, instead of a success, would have been the tale to be told.

Appended to these annals are presented in condensed form the medical, financial, and constructive records of the fifty years. These, with their brief explanatory comments, merit careful notice. The memorial chapter following, it is believed will likewise be of interest as affording a clearer idea of the men who have wrought the results which here appear. The individual sketches are obituaries rather than biographies, and the facts shown are chiefly those affording the record of their labors in connection with the Institution. But without these the record of the half century would be incomplete, and the reader be left to the misleading conclusions of his own fancy in respect to the living character of the individuals here passed in review.

THE MEDICAL RECORD.

The following tabular view of the results of the half century, is compiled from the published reports year by year.

Year.	Admitted. Males.	Females.	Total.	Discharg'd Males.	Females.	Total.	Recovered.	Improved.	Not Imp'v'd.	Died.	Remaining Males.	Females.	Total.
1837........	20	28	48	7	7	14	6	5	2	1	13	21	34
1838........	27	20	47	22	23	45	25	10	8	2	18	18	36
1839........	36	35	71	19	19	38	25	8	3	2	35	34	69
1840........	36	37	73	30	31	61	33	13	9	6	41	40	81
1841........	40	44	84	38	32	70	41	13	12	4	43	52	95
1842........	50	51	101	41	42	83	49	14	14	6	52	61	113
1843........	55	56	111	44	44	88	51	13	13	11	63	73	136
1844........	47	49	96	38	36	74	51	11	5	7	72	86	158
1845........	97	107	204	49	50	99	59	12	8	20	120	143	263
1846........	95	102	197	78	91	169	94	34	16	25	137	154	291
1847........	71	64	135	62	60	122	74	13	12	23	146	158	304
1848........	74	82	156	62	86	148	84	18	10	36	158	154	312
1849........	69	67	136	67	63	130	74	22	12	22	160	158	318
1850........	78	72	150	65	75	140	79	16	19	26	173	155	328
1851........	63	74	137	67	63	130	73	11	11	35	169	166	335
1852........	79	82	161	73	72	145	78	20	16	31	175	176	351
1853........	70	89	159	62	76	138	72	10	13	43	183	189	372
1854........	77	86	163	72	74	146	80	12	14	40	188	201	389
1855........	78	86	164	81	78	159	79	13	15	52	185	209	394
1856........	80	92	172	75	84	159	82	21	18	38	190	217	407
1857........	64	83	147	62	79	141	74	19	11	37	192	221	413
1858........	89	68	157	74	81	155	80	17	19	39	207	208	415
1859........	80	76	156	75	65	140	67	17	16	40	212	219	431
1860........	78	65	143	73	65	138	58	22	21	37	217	219	436
1861........	83	57	140	70	68	138	56	29	21	32	230	208	438
1862........	71	75	146	69	52	121	47	15	17	42	232	231	463
1863........	47	51	98	71	48	119	41	16	24	38	208	234	442
1864........	64	64	128	54	58	112	52	12	9	39	218	240	458
1865........	82	62	144	59	63	122	55	14	11	42	241	239	480
1866........	77	84	161	77	71	148	58	27	20	43	241	252	493
1867........	85	58	143	61	64	125	48	21	18	38	265	246	511
1868........	74	61	135	75	56	131	46	22	21	42	264	251	515
1869........	76	48	124	73	55	128	49	19	16	44	267	244	511
1870........	61	59	120	60	53	113	35	18	20	40	268	250	518
1871-72.....	140	101	241	158	106	264	99	48	43	74	250	245	495
1873-74.....	109	95	204	136	92	228	48	87	37	56	223	248	471
1875-76.....	125	97	222	108	96	204	56	69	25	54	240	249	489
1877-78.....	108	59	167	124	73	197	52	49	32	64	224	235	459
1879-80.....	105	72	177	96	93	189	36	49	55	49	233	214	447
1881-82.....	111	77	188	104	90	194	36	49	23	86	240	201	441
1883-84.....	117	69	186	118	72	190	52	51	26	61	239	198	437
1885-86.....	112	72	184	102	69	171	44	36	20	71	249	201	450
	3200	2876	6076	2951	2675	5626	2398	995	735	1498			

The foregoing, summarized, shows of the whole number *discharged*: recovered 42.6 per cent.; improved 17.7 ; not improved 13.1 ; died 26.6,; and of the whole number *received* (barring fractional percentages), out of every one hundred (100), thirty-nine (39) were discharged recovered, sixteen (16) improved, twelve (12) not improved, twenty-five (25) died, and eight (8) remained under care.

This is compiled from the abstracts of the current receipts and expenditures contained in the annual and biennial Reports, and affords the basis for some approximative conclusions and generalizations.

Year.	Average No. of patients.	Average per capita cost per week.	Rate all'w'd for pauper insane.	Total receipts per year, including cash to begin with.	Total expenditures per year.	Surplus from private patients insurance, etc., in excess of the amt. computed at pauper rate.
				$ 324.02		
1837...........	19	$3.527	$2.00	1,866.73	$ 3,484.71	$ 214.75
1838...........	35	2.731	2.00	5,045.46	4,970.10	1,405.46
1839...........	52	2.815	2.00	7,926.54	7,612.68	2,518.54
1840...........	75	2.429	2.00	9,926.86	9,473.67	2,126.86
1841...........	88	2.524	2.00	11,839.26	11,549.13	2,687.26
1842...........	104	2.333	2.00	12,935.36	12,615.54	2,119.36
1843...........	124	2.024	2.00	13,498.61	13,050.15	602.61
1844...........	147	1.844	2.00	14,673.19	14,092.05	- 614.81
1845...........	210	1.531	1.50	17,341.29	16,721.45	961.29
1846...........	277	1.596	1.50	23,758.40	23,148.05	2.152.40
1847...........	297	1.712	1.50	26,720.09	26,445.80	3,554.09
1848...........	308	1.934	1.50	31,295.34	30,975.93	7,271.34
1849...........	315	2.144	1.50	35,825.09	35,110.23	11,255.09
1850...........	323	2.017	1.50	34,240.12	33,868.93	9,046.12
1851...........	331	1.996	1.50	35,423.54	34,349.66	9,605.54
1852...........	343	2.224	1.50	38,290.88	39,673.96	11,536.88
1853...........	361	2.231	1.50	40,305.73	41,877.18	12,147.73
1854...........	380	2.287	1.50	44,492.33	45,194.20	14,852.33
1855...........	392	2.498	1.50	49,805.11	50,924.42	19,229.11
1856...........	401	2.550	1.75	53,609.03	53,161.59	17,118.03
1857...........	410	2.638	1.75	55,745.43	56,238.12	18,435.43
1858...........	414	2.736	1.75	58,663.44	58,890.58	20,989.44
1859...........	426	2.746	1.75	59,433.70	60,408.76	20,940.70
1860...........	433	2.568	1.75	59,270.28	57,809.68	19,867.28
1861...........	437	2.720	1.75	59,704.75	61,797.24	19,937.75
1862...........	451	2.544	1.75	60,381.02	59,653.59	19,340.02
1863...........	453	3.755	1.75	85,788.51	88,451.81	44,565.51
1864...........	450	2.749	1.75	61,744.27	64,335.14	20,794.27
1865...........	469	2.762	2.25	66,164.93	67,358.37	11,291.93
1866...........	486	3.043	2.25	76,289.19	76,904.17	19,427.19
1867...........	502	3.005	2.25	78,938.29	78,450.11	20,204.29
1868...........	513	2.960	2.25	79,554.28	78,943.72	19,533.28
1869...........	513	3.054	2.25	80,028.63	81,472.07	20,007.63
1870...........	515	3.105	3.00	85,281.72	83,163.49	4,941,72
1871-72.........	506	2.960	3.00	160,708.51	155,771.73	2,836,51
1873-74.........	473	4.349	3.00	213,810.66	213,929.11	66,234.66
1875-76.........	477	3.640	3.00	180,818.55	180,584.06	31,994.55
1877-78.........	472	3.810	3.00	187,261.96	187,036.16	39,997.96
1879-80.........	452	3.581	3.50	168,493.28	168,352.06	3,965.28
1881-82.........	443	3.902	3.50	180,381.43	179,791.52	19,129.43
1883-84.........	434	3.948	3.50	178,247.21	178,214.10	20,271.21
1885-86.........	436	3.646	3.75	180,245.22	165,336.18	10,205.22
	368.74	$3.036		$2,926,098.24	$2,911,191.20	$604,701.24

The foregoing table shows that the current receipts of the Asylum for the fifty years of its operations aggregate $2,926,098.24.

Apart from the resources thus collated, there has been received and expended on separate account :—

1.   The Marsh legacy, received, October 3, 1835, $10,000, which was expended in the purchase of the original site of six acres, with buildings, together with forty-five acres of meadow for farming purposes, and for remodelling and enlarging the house for the reception of patients, to which it was opened Dec. 12th, 1836.

2.   The appropriations made by the State for enlargements of the buildings, aggregating $23,000. The several appropriations making up the above amount were received and expended as follows :—

January 13, 1837,	Received of State Treasurer,					$1,500
" 27,	"	"	"	"	"	2,500
Decemb'r 11,	"	"	"	"	"	2,000
April 9, 1838,	"	"	"	"	"	4,000
Decemb'r 14,	"	"	"	"	"	2,000
February 15, 1839,	"	"	"	"	"	2,000
March 11,	"	"	"	"	"	2,000

These appropriations were expended in the construction and furnishing of the original center building and first wing west.   The last three drafts were discounted and cashed by the State treasurer before they fell due, the Trustees having urgent need of the funds to meet the pressing demands of the Asylum extensions.   The foregoing sums include the first appropriation of $10,000 (Nov. 9, 1835) payable in five annual instalments, also the individual appropriations of $2,000, Nov. 15, 1836, and of $4,000, Nov. 1, 1837, due April 1, 1838.

In January, 1841, the appropriation made Oct. 29, 1840, of $2,000 annually for two years, was discounted and cashed, and expended in the erection of the first wing east in 1841-2.

The final appropriation, Nov. 1, 1843, of $3,000, payable Oct. 1, 1844, was discounted and received of the State Treasurer Aug. 15, 1844, and was expended in the extension of the west wing that year.

3.   The amount of the Marsh legacy, $10,000, and of the State appropriations, $23,000, added to the aggregate of the current receipts as per table, gives a total received and expended in the half century of $2,959,098.24, save the balance on hand at the close of the last fiscal year of $14,907.04, which latter is offset by liabilities exceeding it by $4,477.46.

The current receipts of the Institution, as shown by the table have been derived almost exclusively from the care of the patients, save what has been received at three different times from insurances.

In 1858 the receipts include $1,448.63 from this source, on account of the burning of the stock-barn the December previous.

In 1863 $25,300 was received and expended in the rebuilding of the center building and west wing, burned in December previous. This, in the table, has been added to the ordinary receipts and expenditures of that year. Again, in 1877, insurances to the amount of $7,837.62 are included in the current receipts and expenditures. The entire resources derived from sources other than the care of the inmates therefore, aggregate in the whole fifty years $67.586.25 to wit:

From the Founder,		$10,000.00
" " State,		23,000.00
" " Insurances,		34,586.25

4. Calculations based upon the average number of patients for the whole time, show the average cost for each patient per week, for the whole fifty years, to have been $3.036.

From the opening of the Institution to 1845, the pauper rate was $2 per week. From 1844 to 1856, it was $1.50 per week. From 1855 to 1865, it was $1.75 per week. From 1864 to 1870, it was $2.25 per week. From 1869 to 1879, it was $3 per week. From 1878 to 1885, it was $3.50 per week, and subsequently to 1884, it has been $3.75 per week. The average rate paid for those supported at the public charge for the whole half century is $2.30 per week.

5. Had all the patients from the beginning been of the dependent classes, and been supported at the rate allowed by the State, the total resources derived, as shown by the table, would have been less than the actual receipts by $604,701.24.

The Construction Record shows the whole cost of the Asylum estate* and buildings, to have been $383,197.36. Add to this the personal estate $56,683.00, and a total property valuation is represented of $439,880.36.

It is clear, therefore, that the establishment has been developed out of the receipts over and above the income derived from the rate allowed by the State; and upon striking the balance there appears

---

*The landed estate proper embraces a little over seven hundred acres. There are also outlying lands—principally mountain tracts—of about the same area, originally purchased for the fuel upon them, and of little value for any other uses.

still a surplus of $164,820.88.   Taking from this all that has been derived from sources other than the care of the inmates, there still remains $97,234.63, which has been swallowed up in making the financial ends meet from year to year.

The conclusion inevitably reached respecting the financial relations of the Asylum to the State is, that the latter has been largely the gainer.   In any view possible, the Institution has been the loser by so much as the average rate per week paid by the State falls below the average expended per week.

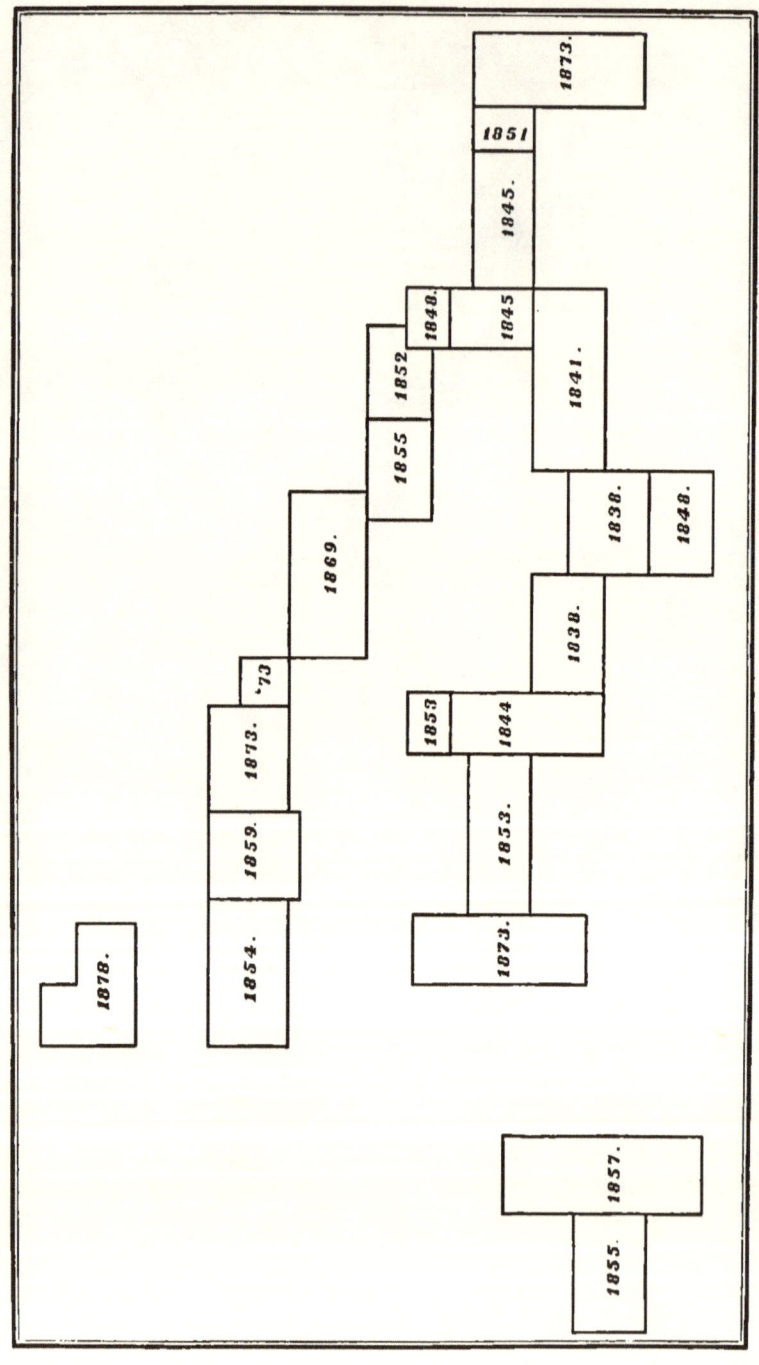

BLOCK PLAN, CHRONOLOGICALLY CONSTRUCTED.

THE CONSTRUCTION RECORD.

1836—1886.

Compiled from the preceding annals, deeds, etc.

1836.	Land and buildings of N. Woodcock,	$3,500.00
"	of Eben Wells,	2,700.00
"	" Houghton Pike,	8.00
	Remodeling and extension of buildings,	3,560.65
1838.	Spring of Houghton Pike,	150.00
	Cost of original centre building and first wing west,	12,399.67
1841.	Cost of first wing east,	7,769.87
	Aqueduct shares of J. Minott, and pipe,	250.00
1842.	" " " A. Greene,	150.00
1844.	Extension to west wing,	4,654.82
1845.	" " east "	6,325.66
	Spring of Eben Wells,	200.00
1846.	Cemetery plat of A. Brown, and construction of tomb,	150.00
1847.	Land of John L. Dickerman,	1,000.00
	Aqueduct and right of way of N. Allen,	340.00
1848.	Land of A. and A. Bennett,	800.00
"	" Chas. Chapin,	150.00
	Extension of centre building, and east wing (north),	6,485.99
1849.	Land of John R. Blake,	3,500.00
"	" Newman Allen,	180.00
"	" Samuel Thomas,	250.00
1850.	" " Nelson Crosby,	100.00
"	" Newman Allen,	482.00
	Cost of meadow barn and horse shed,	1,100.00
1851.	Addition to east wing,	2,000.00
	Cost of iron aqueduct pipe from Wells Spring	1,436.04
1852.	Cost of laundry building,	2,500.00
	Cost of laundry machinery and fixtures,	1,500.00
	Land of Houghton Pike,	5.00
	" " David W. Miller,	600.00

	Land of Addison Brown,	$150.00
	" " Chas. Chapin,	500.00
	" " W. H. Rockwell,	4.800.00
1853.	" " W. E. Eason,	300.00
	" " Wells Heirs,	3,700.00
	Cost of piggery,	500.00
	" " west wing extension and addition (north),	8,000.00
1854.	" " brick storehouse in rear of west wing	4,000.00
	Land of the Wells Heirs,	5,185.00
	" " Nelson Crosby (including quarry),	90.00
1855.	" " W. H. Rockwell,	450.00
	" " John L. Sargent,	210.00
	Cost of male infirmary,	5,000.00
	" " female "	5,000.00
	" " wood storehouse appended to Marsh Building,	400.00
1857.	Land of P. B. Francis,	300.00
	" " Martha, Elizabeth and Harriet Crosby,	600.00
	" " Prouty & Sampson,	2,010.00
	Cost of Marsh Building,	10,000.00
1858.	Land of Shepard Rice,	20.00
	" " Newman Allen (farm),	10,500.00
	" " John L. Heywood and others,	840.00
	Cost of rebuilding meadow barn,	2,000.00
1859.	Land of Mary A. Knowlton,	30.00
	" " W. H. Rockwell,	100.00
	Cost of brick stable,	2,500.00
1860.	Land of Keith White,	1,700.00
1861.	Cost of raising roofs of wings on main line,	12,000.00
1862.	Land of Farnsworth and Colburn,	200.00
	" " Colburn and Cobleigh,	400.00
1863.	" " Fred'k Holbrook,	1,700.00
	" " J. F. Stearns, Sally Nurse and others,	1,752.00
	Cost of rebuilding centre, and west wing,	41,000.00
1864.	Land of Wells Goodhue,	1,800.00
1865.	Cost of barn at farm house,	2,500.00
1866.	Cost of large wood-house (now stable),	1,500.00
	Land of Henry F. Smith,	250.00
1867.	Spring of James H. Capen, (by exchange of land).	
1868.	Land of Francis T. Green,	1,800.00
	" " Mary A. Knowlton,	1,800.00
	" " William Knowlton,	300.00
	" " Willard Edwards,	1,500.00

1869.	Cost of new laundry wing and furnishing,	12,000.00
1870.	" " new farm house,	2,500.00
	Land of H. H. Rice,	3,500.00
1871.	" " D. W. Miller,	2,600.00
	Water right of C. J. Weld,	500.00
	" " " I. B. Taft,	250.00
	" " " J. H. Capen.	
	" " " Executors of James A. Chase,	50.00
	Land of Executors of James A. Chase,	2,575.00
	" " Lavinia C. Chase,	500.00
	Cost of iron pipe from Capen Spring,	3,375.44
1873–4.	Cost of east and west extensions to wings,	43,214.18
	" " boiler house, tunnels, boilers and engine,	13,000.00
1875–6.	" " steam works and reconstructive work,	17,313.54
1877–8.	" " completion of heating and ventilating,	8,888.21
	" " rebuilding burned line of rear buildings and reconstructing wood-house into stable,	23,449,29
	Land of R. N. Hescock, and house,	775.00
	Cost of shop and ice house,	5,000.00
1879–80.	Cost of radical alterations and extensions of rear wards, six new bath rooms, etc.,	4,853.00
	Land of George Person and wife,	1,800.00
1881–2.	" " J. Draper,	2,400.00
	" " C. A. Miles,	7,500.00
	Cost of park survey, plan and fencing,	1,169.00
	" " reconstructing Miles house,	5,500.00
1883–4.	" " constructing verandas, brick connecting wall and granite work,	3,650.00
	" " reconstructing chapel with alterations in third story of centre building,	7,500.00
	Land of Joseph Prescott,	700.00
1885–6.	Cost of new system of sewerage,	2,200.00
	" " reconstructing engine house, and relocating and reconnecting boilers, etc.,	4,500.00
	Cost of cupolas on wings, (7)	300.00

	$383,197.36
Personal estate as per appraisal Aug., 1886,	56,683.00
Total valuation,	$439,880.36

IN MEMORIAM.

A T the close of a fifty years' record few remain who at its beginning were instrumental in its initiatory work. It is our
purpose now to roll back the cloud of oblivion which year
by year has settled down upon its history, and catch once again a
glimpse of those figures which in the early years came and went,
and finally passed out of the sphere of earthly activities into the
mists which we cannot lift, and which are beyond our following. Of
the four to whom was committed the bequest of Mrs. Marsh, and
who were charged with the trust, one alone is yet living.—

SAMUEL CLARK.

Judge Samuel Clark, the first named member of the original
Board, died in April, 1861. At the date of his appointment as Trustee he was 57 years of age, and he presided over the meetings and
deliberations of the Board for eighteen years, resigning his trust at
75. His characteristic traits are well set forth in a biographical
sketch of his life by Rev. Joseph Chandler, as follows :

" He was, in his sphere, a strong man ; fitted by nature and by
the wise and diligent use of his energies, to exert an influence in
society. Though possessed of strong feelings, his judgment was
sound and his opinion was much valued by his neighbors. Prudence
and sagacity were marked traits in his character. Another pleasing
trait was his readiness to make amends for anything done under the
impulse of excited feeling, which he was led afterward to look upon
as wrong. He was not one of those men of assumed infallibility,
who make it a point never to take back anything, and never to
acknowledge themselves mistaken. In many instances when he was
called upon to express his opinion and to give his vote, he seldom
hesitated to declare himself faithfully and frankly upon the point in
question ; and almost as often would express his willingness to
acquiesce in the decision of the majority against him. In all matters, however, involving moral principle, or that seemed to him of

superlative importance, he was firm and unyielding ; and he brought all the energies of his strong and impetuous nature to bear upon the business of maintaining and carrying out his convictions."

This sketch doubtless correctly.estimates Mr. Samuel Clark, but from other sources we have evidence more to the point, illustrative of the strong elements of his character, showing his marked individuality, keen observation, unusual executive ability, and withal his strong religious convictions, his sense of the humorous, his position on questions of the day, and especially his systematic business habits. His private affairs often led him to make journeys from home of days and even weeks together, and letters written to his family during these absences from home have been preserved and bear testimony to his positive qualities. On one occasion, writing from Hampton, Washington Co., N. Y., he speaks of attending a fair, and says, "'Those who went to see fine horses, handsome cattle, great sheep, ten thousand people, abundance of dirt and a great scarcity of water, must have come away satisfied ; but [I] heard so much talk about Black Hawk and Morgan, that it became sickish as abolition[ism];" by which latter remark his politics may be inferred.

Again, writing from Saratoga Springs, (Aug. 8, 1833), he describes the inconveniences incident to the crowded hotels, and says, "Very few people here from Vermont, none from our own county,—chiefly from the South and New York," adding humorously, "no very great characters here, except Mr. Van Buren and myself."

Under date of August, 1836, he writes to his son at home, concisely, in regard to business accomplished, which doubtless typifies his method of doing it : "I think I have put a quietus on all our boys in Troy, and they will all be easy with their business and places one year. Have advised S. to keep his store and go on alone, J. to keep his place and be easy, E. to be a good boy—to which they all agree." Of Saratoga he says, " Twenty-four hours is long time enough to be at the Springs merely to see what is to be seen, but three weeks or more is necessary in order to form agreeable acquaintances and enjoy them. Everything seems to go by steam, and at high pressure, too."

In the autumn of 1837 he was commissioned by vote of the Trustees of the Asylum to go to Montpelier and urge further aid on the part of the State, in extending the capacity of the buildings. Writing from there (Oct. 21st) he says, "Our Insane Report was presented this morning and 500 copies ordered to be printed. Those whom I converse with speak favorably of the project, but can give no opinion of its final result. I am preparing myself to make my statement before the committee, when perhaps half the Legislature will be present. Many agree to assist me in my business, but it will be a hard thing to get $12,000. I shall go home when my business is done if a kind Providence permits. They all like the Institution for the insane—they like my report, but have no money to give away. I do not think we shall succeed, but as long as there is any chance I will not leave. I attend no caucuses whatever, but have been to one anti-slavery meeting quite as bad. The great Birney is here. I appeared before the temperance committee and made my little speech when our petition was under consideration."

In 1843, writing to his son, then member of the General Assembly of Vermont, he says: "You will have much to do for your constituents—the railroad, bank, insane, temperance, etc., for which I hope and presume you will do all you can. I think very little of the railroad, but the East village is all engaged in it, and they must have an act of incorporation. I think the railroad will never come to B., and if it does the stock will be worth nothing."

He lived to see the iron track laid, and Brattleboro thus held in connection with the rest of the world; but his prediction in respect to the value of the stock, up to the date of his death, had been fulfilled.

A subsequent letter in reply to one from this son, so well shows his strong common sense that we quote the bulk of it :

"Yours by Mr. Keyes is received, read twice, shown the family, and laid on the table. We, the people, as yet approve of what our servants are doing at the seat of government, and think we shall if you will follow our directions, and

1st. As a general thing let existing laws alone.

2d. Have a short session.

3d. The law of last year respecting capital punishment ought to be repealed ; so says the sound part of the community.

4th. Let the usury law alone.

5th. We are satisfied with the present organization of our courts, and doubt if you make them any better,—but care little about it.

6th. Pay the State debt if you can get time, and the laws will let you.

7th. Get the bills for the banks and insane through if possible, as they are right and just.

8th. In order to satisfy your constituents pay a little attention to the railroad.

9th. All come home next week.

10th. We, the people, think well of Judge Williams. Maj. Smith thinks you will leave him out of office."

His views relative to Asylum management nowhere individually appear, but the foregoing quotations sufficiently indicate his abiding interest in the Institution. There seems, indeed, to have been no conflicting views in respect to practical management between either Trustees or Superintendent. The only individual expression in respect to policy is gleaned from a letter to a son under date of August, 1847, in which, among other matters of mention, he says, "It was our annual meeting at the Insane [Asylum] yesterday. The books show 330 patients. We hope there will not be any more."

JOHN HOLBROOK.

Dea. John Holbrook, the second member of the original Board, died in office in 1838, when the Asylum was in its infancy, or had but just been set upon its feet. He was 73 years of age when appointed to this trust, but his life had been second to none other in prominent connection with the development of this village in growth and prosperity. Like Samuel Clark, Mr. Holbrook was a man of the most sterling character, and of marked personal peculiarities.

The historian of Brattleboro says of him : " Difficulties, dangers, obstacles such as discourage common men, act, if they act at all, on such men as Mr. Holbrook merely as stimulants to their progress;" and again, "Some idea of Mr. Holbrook's peculiar style of expressing his emotions can be seen by the following : Mr. Holbrook sent his man-of-all-work some distance from home to get some early potatoes for planting. The man returned with the potatoes and informed him of the price charged. Mr. H. said, ' Jacob, return the potatoes immediately, and say to Mr. W. I would as soon die by famine as by the sword.' "

This incident serves to indicate the self-reliance and independent action of the man, and the manner he would have been likely to meet any attempts in those early days that might have been made at exorbitant exactions upon the meagre funds which had been left to found so great an enterprise upon, and which the result shows were so religiously husbanded and so judiciously appropriated by the Board.

Another anecdote is related of Mr. Holbrook illustrative of his true catholicity of spirit, which, notwithstanding his identification with the Puritan church and the dogmas of the time, asserted itself on occasion. An old clergyman, and distant relative, once drove up to his hospitable door, and being welcomed and made comfortable, entered soon into a discussion and advocacy of the doctrine of infant damnation. Mr. Holbrook listened until his patience was exhausted and his indignation swelled beyond endurance, when he broke forth declaring in no uncertain language that " he would not entertain one who held such damnable˜views," and literally driving him from the house.

In person Mr. Holbrook was above six feet in height, strong and well proportioned, of swarthy complexion, and of unusually commanding presence, so much so that a stranger observing him in a crowd would look at him a second time.

Col. Crocker, late of Fitchburg, Mass., when a young man and clerk in the Kendall Manufacturing Company's establishment, in Leominster, used to relate the circumstance of his first interview with Mr. H. in substance as follows: It was toward the close of a summer's day that Mr. Holbrook, then on his way to Boston, and covered with dust of travelling, entered unannounced the counting-room of the manufactory, and approaching young Crocker, inquired with a voice and manner never to be forgotten, " Is Col. Kendall within?" Being politely informed that he was not far off, Mr. H. supplemented his inquiry by the command, " Young man go and find him, I wish to see him immediately," which he lost no time in doing. The naturally swarthy complexion of Mr. Holbrook, made more so by the heat and dust of travel, and his remarkably commanding air and voice, left the most abiding impression upon young Crocker, and as he was wont afterwards to say, he " could not have gone much quicker had he been shot out of a gun."

Notwithstanding this character of authority, however, he was as remarkable for tenderness of feeling, and for benevolence of the most spontaneous and generous kind.

His death, which occurred in the second year of the operations of. the Institution, cut off the opportunity for the exercise of his strong individuality in the direction of the work thus newly inaugurated, but there is evidence showing that the selection of the site was largely determined by him.

EPAPHRODITUS SEYMOUR.

The third member of this first Board was Epahpro' Seymour, who at the time of his appointment was cashier of the Bank of Brattleboro, and 51 years of age. The following testimony to his general character is given by Hon. Charles K. Field :

"Mr. Seymour was eminently practical in all his views and opinions, and of most excellent judgment. The public, particularly those who were about to engage in new enterprises, reposing great confidence in his superior financial ability, uniformly consulted him in relation to their proposed investments, and were always controlled by his opinions. His advice was always eagerly sought and adopted. He constantly warned all who were inclined to engage in speculations, against the folly and danger which was so alluring to a man with a greed for wealth, and so dangerous to him when the money of others is under his control. He begged of his friends to make no investments but those that were perfectly legitimate and promised a safe return. The community reposed the most implicit confidence in his integrity. Before the adoption of Savings Banks and Trust Companies in this State, large sums of money were intrusted to his care and keeping, and in many cases with a simple minute noting the amount, yet for the period of more than forty years not a whisper was ever breathed against his fidelity in the discharge of any fiduciary engagement he had assumed. He was a generous-hearted man to the poor and unfortunate, and kindly aided young men who were struggling against adversity and poverty to obtain an education, and qualify themselves for professional pursuits."

Such was the man who was elected treasurer of the Asylum funds, and who filled the office from the organization of the Board in 1835, till the election of Mr. Williston as his successor in 1841. He was a man of positive character and strong in his likes and dislikes. He often gave to young men sound and cautious advice.

An instance is related in which he sought an interview with one since distinguished, and after referring to a recent event in the line of his advancement, and remarking that "this, in his view, was but the beginning," said, "I am an older man than you, and have perhaps considered some things you have not yet had occasion to. I want merely to say that when you meet a man and converse with him on any subject, you can say anything to his face that it is proper to say to a gentleman, and he will understand you just as you mean it; the circumstances attending contribute to his correct understanding of you; but if you go and write it, it may turn out that an entirely different construction is placed upon it from what you intended. Therefore, I would advise you *to be very careful what you put on paper.*"

JOHN C. HOLBROOK.

John C. Holbrook was the fourth, and now only surviving member of the original Board, and to him I am indebted for much of early history in detail.   Under date of March 11, 1885, he writes: "You are aware of the difficulties connected with the founding of such an institution with so small a beginning as was provided for in Mrs. Marsh's will, and especially when three out of four of the original Trustees were somewhat advanced in life, and all very *cautious* business men.   We had many long and anxious meetings, and the fact that one of the Trustees was comparatively a young man [26 years], and of a sanguine and hopeful disposition, probably had an important influence in deciding the case."

Again, under date of Nov. 3, 1886, he says, " The announcement by Mr. Keyes of our appointment took the four original Trustees by surprise, and caused us to hesitate to undertake the founding of an institution for the insane, as none of us had had any experience in such work, nor had ever studied or thought on the matter.   The task of correspondence with persons abroad who were experienced and interested in institutions for the insane, to gain information and advice, devolved upon me, and involved considerable labor.   My father also [John Holbrook] and myself spent considerable time in searching for the best location for the Institution, and we personally examined many sites.   Then the question of a superintendent for the Institution was a perplexing one ; but I believe we were providentially guided in securing Dr. Rockwell, whose careful management and enthusiastic devotion to the enterprise, under God, secured its remarkable success."

John C. Holbrook, during the period of his trusteeship, was a prominent business man as well as public-spirited citizen.   No man was more prominent than he in all public enterprises, and at all gatherings he was active and apt to seize and forcibly present the strong points, which he grasped as by intuition, and with a ready flow of language gave full and strong expression to.   After his retirement from the Board he went west, settling in Iowa.   Here he buried his wife and two remaining children (four in all) within a brief period, which turned his thoughts toward the ministry for which he prepared himself, and in which he has since distinguished himself as a preacher, and now bears the title of D. D.   He was largely instrumental in the founding of Iowa College, of which he was one of the original Board of Trustees.

ASA KEYES.

Judge Keyes was elected to fill the first vacancy in the original Board, succeeding Dea. John Holbrook upon his decease in 1838.

He was 51 years of age at this date, and held the office till 1874, when he resigned on account of age and infirmities. He was longer identified with the Institution than any of his colleagues, having drawn up the will for Mrs. Marsh who founded the Asylum, and been subsequently employed by the original Trustees to procure the charter as the testatrix stipulated should be done.

By profession a lawyer, his standing is thus attested by an eminent colleague, Charles N. Davenport :

"Though not eminent as a jury advocate, he was a successful practitioner, a good draughtsman, a skillful pleader, and the best equity lawyer in Southern Vermont, if not in the whole State. His Supreme Court briefs are models for other practitioners. He was always listened to attentively by the courts, for he never talked unless he had something to say. He was studious and painstaking, faithful to his clients and honest with the Court. He was a good husband, a kind father, and always faithful to every trust. He never attained wealth. The income arising from the practice of his profession he spent freely in his family, and gave generously to the church he attended, to public objects, and to the poor and needy, as many among them can testify."

As a Trustee of the Asylum it is difficult to see how he could have been more judicious in counsel or more devoted in his interest. He died in 1880, passing away at the close of a summer's day (June 4th) without illness, while quietly seated in his chair, at the advanced age of 93.

NATHAN B. WILLISTON.

Mr. Williston came upon the Board in 1839, as the successor of Mr. John C. Holbrook, who then resigned and removed from the State. Mr. W. was all his life identified with the town of Brattleboro as a business man, and filled the office of treasurer at the Asylum for thirty-four years. He resigned in 1875, and died in 1883, at the age of 86. He was very useful upon the Board as one of its building committee for many years and in connection with the financial interests of the Asylum, from the practical view he habitually took of all business affairs.

An obituary by Rev. Dr. Geo. L. Walker (his son-in-law) says, "Mr. Williston was a man of retiring and modest disposition, though of somewhat curt and brusque manners. He had a tender heart, and many more were the recipients of his generous kindnesses than ever the history of this world will know. In his religious life he was a man of naturally doubting, and even almost skeptical tendencies, though a member of the Congregational church and one of its most loyal supporters for over fifty years."

Jonathan Dorr Bradley.

J. Dorr Bradley, Esq., was elected to succeed Mr. Seymour as a Trustee of the Asylum in 1847. Born in 1803, of an old Vermont family (he was grandson of Stephen R. and a son of Wm. C. Bradley), a graduate of Yale College in the class of 1822, and a lawyer by profession, he entered upon this trust at the age of 44, and for the remainder of his life served upon the Board with great efficiency, and with both wisdom and zeal. Tributes to his memory, and expressive of the estimation in which he was held by his co-trustees and the superintendent, will be found in the record of 1863.

The estimation in which he was held throughout the State is indicated in the following obituary notice from the pen of Hon. E. P. Walton of Montpelier:

"It is with great sorrow that we record the death of this distinguished gentleman, at his residence in Brattleboro, Sept. 8, 1862. We learn that he was taken severely ill with fever some three weeks since, and that his disease made rapid progress until it quenched one of the most cultivated intellects and genial hearts that our State has produced. He had a discerning, rapid and comprehensive mind, an elegant and varied culture. He was quick and ardent in his sympathies, a lover of truth and justice, and a fervid hater of all shams and hypocrisy. He was a member of the House of Representatives for two years, in which the State House controversy was waged, and and distinguished himself as a leader in debate in that most brilliant conflict. If it had not been for his deafness, which prevented his hearing all points of a discussion, no man that Vermont has produced would have surpassed him in debate in the halls of legislation. But whatever might have been the qualities that fitted him for a public career, he was most eminent in social and private life. His rare store of information and culture was open to his friends, and he had few equals in the genial exchanges and conversations of social life. His reading was extensive and recherche, his memory was retentive, his style of conversation was playful and captivating and always appropriate to his theme. His perceptions were quick and vivid, his illustrations apt and beautiful, and his whole air and manner reminded us of the school of elder times in which he had his training.

The death of such a man is a public calamity, and in common with his nearer associates, neighbors and friends, we would lay a small tribute of our high appreciation of his worth upon his fresh-made grave."

DANIEL KELLOGG.

Hon. Daniel Kellogg was elected the successor of Mr. Bradley in December, 1863. He was advanced in life at the time of his election to this trust, but held the office until May, 1874, when he resigned. He died the following year, May 10, 1875, at the age of 84 years. A lawyer by profession, and a resident of Windham County for more than sixty years, the esteem in which he was held is indicated in the following record of his public services :

He was for a few years State's Attorney for Windham County, and Judge of Probate for the District of Westminster, Secretary to the old Governor and Council of Vermont during the administrations of Governors Butler and Van Ness, U. S. District Attorney for the State of Vermont for twelve years, during the administrations of Presidents Jackson and Van Buren, Adjutant and Inspector General of the State, Representative for the town of Rockingham in the General Assembly, and State Senator for the County of Windham for two years. In 1843, he was chosen President of the State Constitutional Convention, and elected Judge of the Supreme Court of the State from 1845 to 1852. After his retirement from the bench he moved to Brattleboro, where he resided until his decease. His wide and varied experience and extended acquaintance throughout the State was of service to the Institution, and his connection with the Board added to its strength, while his leisure enabled him to interest himself actively in the mission and work of the Asylum. Few men more fully sustained in personal appearance and bearing a character for dignity, courtliness and integrity, than he; he looked all these, and commanded everywhere unreserved respect. In religion he was an Episcopalian; in politics a Democrat. But his patriotism, like that of the founders of the Republic when its existence was contested, governed his action to the exclusion of all other considerations. The following ringing utterances are ascribed to him in the dark days of the civil war : "I know of no other way but to stand by the old flag ; come what may, all else is, with me, of secondary consideration—my party, my church may perish, but save the country."

THE PRESENT BOARD.

EX-GOVERNOR Frederick Holbrook, the chairman, is now the veteran Trustee, having been elected to succeed Judge Samuel Clark, the chairman of the original Board, in 1852, and having already had a continuous service of near 35 years.

Dr. William H. Rockwell was chosen to succeed Judge Daniel Kellogg in 1874, and has been upwards of twelve years upon the Board.

Hon. James M. Tyler was elected at the same time, as the successor of Judge Asa Keyes.

Richards Bradley, Esq., was chosen to succeed Mr. Nathan B. Williston, who resigned in 1875.

SUPERINTENDENTS.

DR. Wm. H. Rockwell, the first superintendent and the presiding genius of the establishment for more than the average period of a generation, was born in East Windsor, Conn., Feb. 15, 1800. He was a graduate of Yale in its collegiate course in 1824, and in the medical department in 1831. The history of the Asylum for the first thirty-six years of its existence, is the record of his life-work ; and so far as the chronicler of these annals has been able to do it, is faithfully portrayed. He came to the charge of the Asylum with an experience of some seven years at the Hartford Retreat as the assistant of Dr. Todd, and after the death of Dr. T. was for a number of months in charge of the Retreat, and wrote the Report of the Institution for 1834.

It is difficult in this place to enlarge upon his signal career without repetition. He entered upon his work in connection with the Vermont Asylum with a determination to make it a success, that was invincible. Throughout these annals the work of each year, and the salient points in connection therewith illustrative of his strong self-reliance and individuality, are set forth. His great financial and executive ability require no enlargement. Many were the incidents connected with the "days of small things" which he was fond of recalling and relating in his later life. A single anecdote may here be mentioned.

It was in the winter of the opening ; all the funds had been used in the purchasing, remodeling and furnishing of the establishment, and when the snow fell there was no suitable vehicle in which the patients could be taken out to ride. The Doctor found where a second-hand two-seated sleigh could be obtained at the moderate price of $12. He stated the want to the treasurer, but that official was out of funds, and advised that "the outlay be avoided that season." The Doctor solved the problem by making the purchase on his own account, and carrying it till the funds of the Asylum warranted the treasurer in lifting it from the hands of the superintendent.

A single case illustrative of the Doctor's professional sagacity and judgment seems worthy of special mention. When, in 1859, the writer became an assistant to Dr. R., one of the earliest cases falling under his medical care was that of a gigantic Scotchman,* then in a decline, and suffering from dropsical complications of which he soon after died.

This man had been an inmate of the Asylum nineteen years. He had been previously for several years kept in a cage, and cared for by the lowest bidder annually. His insanity was originally caused by bathing in cold water when overheated. He was brought to the Asylum chained. It is related that on his arrival in Brattleboro he particularly attracted the notice of a medical man from New York, then stopping in town, from his immense stature and the strong manner in which he was bound ; that he followed him to the Asylum and saw with astonishment that the Doctor at once had his irons removed, and manifested no apprehensions as to the risks. From day to day he came to the Asylum to learn of the condition of the madman, and when, after a month had elapsed, he saw him working in the garden, his astonishment and admiration of the management of the case knew no bounds. He returned to New York saying, "he had found the place in which to treat lunatics, and the man to do it." It may be added that from the time the patient commenced working in the garden. it is a matter of record that he continued a steady worker until stopped by his last illness. In the management of this case we see a repetition of the act which made the name of Pinel famous ; but no one who knew Dr. R. would venture to charge him with having aped the distinguished Frenchman. The motives leading to the apparently venturesome risk, if closely sifted, we apprehend would be found identical. That a condition warranting restraint had existed, would hardly be denied ; and in those days chains were the approved means of restraint. But both recognized

*Duncan McDonald, Ryegate, Vt.

that a stage had been reached in these cases, when the harshness and unrelenting rigor of such restraint might be safely dropped, and other controlling means and influences be substituted and depended upon.

By reference to the events of the year 1873, it will be seen that the Doctor died at the Institution he had been so largely instrumental in creating. A biographical sketch of his life was presented to the Association of American Superintendents and published in their transactions of 1874. Another was read before the State Medical Society of Vermont, and published the same year.

A third was published in the History of Brattleboro, 1880, prepared by Dr. E. R. Chapin, whose family relationship to him qualified him most faithfully to compile.

I quote from this sketch that which refers especially to his personal characteristics, domestic relations, and the closing scenes of his useful life:

"In person, Dr. Rockwell was much above the ordinary height, but of erect and well-proportioned figure. His head was large and of fine shape, features regular, and countenance pleasing in expression. On May 10, 1872, as he was starting from his door, he was thrown from his wagon with such force as to cause a fracture of the neck of the thigh ; this, together with internal difficulties consequent upon the shock to his nervous system, confined him to his bed until his death, Nov. 30, 1873. Every day until his death, during his long and painful illness, some of his patients came to see him, and it was most interesting to witness them leaning over the form of the prostrate physician, and in their turn speaking words of encouragement and sympathy. Encouraged and sustained he indeed was by their presence and kind words, but in a way they knew not of, and cheered by the thought that he had been of service to them, to humanity, and to his adopted State, he died, as since early manhood he had lived, in the hope of a blessed immortality beyond the grave.

"Of Dr. Rockwell's family, his wife, daughter and one son survive him. His second son, a graduate of the U. S. Military Academy at West Point, died in the service in 1868. Largely indebted for his success to the Trustees of the Asylum, from whom he ever received unswerving sympathy and support, and to the harmonious co-operation of those immediately associated with him, he was also in many ways efficiently aided by his wife, who, though holding no official position, devoted the greater part of nearly every day of her long residence in the Institution to efforts to promote the comfort and welfare of the insane."

Mrs. Rockwell's interest in the Asylum and affection for all connected with it, continued through her life. Her rare qualities of amiability, tact and culture were ever recognized, and among those who were members of her own family by virtue of their official connection with the Asylum during the long term of her husband's superintendency, are still the common theme when in their subsequent meetings old-time reminiscences come up. Alike do all thus related to the family recognize the wonderful individuality, sagacity and energy of the Doctor, and the rare combination of force and influence the two together embodied and wielded.

She died at the residence of her son, in New York, Aug. 30, 1885. Her funeral took place from the Asylum, whence she was borne to her last resting-place in the village cemetery.

Dr. William H. Rockwell, Jr., was elected superintendent Aug. 19, 1872, but tendered his resignation Dec. 11, the same year, to take effect whenever his successor should be secured, and be ready to assume charge.

Dr. Joseph Draper was elected Dec. 11, 1872, and entered upon service Feb. 16, 1873.

ASSISTANT PHYSICIANS.

DR. Chauncey Booth, acting assistant physician at the opening of the Asylum (being then a medical student), filled the position until 1841. He was born in Coventry, Conn., Sept. 21, 1816, and died at Somerville, Mass., Jan. 12, 1858. At the time of his decease he was in charge of the McLean Asylum, with which he had been connected some fifteen years, succeeding Dr. Bell in the superintendency in 1856. Between his service at the Vermont Asylum and that of the McLean Asylum, he filled the position of assistant physician in the Maine Insane Hospital for near three years, making a continuous service of about twenty-one years in the specialty.

A memoir by Dr. Luther V. Bell, his predecessor and friend at the McLean Asylum, was published in the American Journal of Insanity, Vol. XIV, p. 394. All who knew him bear uniform testimony to his rare fitness for the position he filled.

Dr. Samuel B. Low, the successor of Dr. Booth as the assistant of Dr. Rockwell, filled this position for three years, 1841-2-3. From the Asylum he went to Suffield, Conn., where—as the successor of Dr. Sumner Ives—he was held in high esteem. He was elected a

Judge of Probate in 1849, which office he held for one year. He was also postmaster of the town for one year. In 1853, he sold his home in Suffield and went west, to Ohio or Illinois, where he died about 1860.

Such are the facts gathered from a citizen of Suffield, who adds, "His success here as a doctor was most marked, and his standing excellent; but he held an itching ear for the great West, and left here an excellent practice."

Dr. Henry M. Harlow succeeded Dr. Low at the Vermont Asylum. He was a native of Windham County, Vt., and a graduate of the Berkshire Medical College, Mass., in the class of '43. He served as an assistant to Dr. Rockwell in 1844, and was then appointed to a similar position in the Maine Insane Hospital, of which he subsequently became superintendent. He is now living in retirement in Augusta, Me.

Dr. David T. Brown, of Massachusetts, followed Dr. Harlow in 1845. He was a graduate of the College of Physicians and Surgeons, New York, and on leaving the Vermont Asylum filled for a time the position of assistant physician at the Utica Asylum, subsequently being appointed Physician in Chief to the Bloomingdale Asylum, which position he held for many years. He is likewise still living.

Dr. Francis A. Holman succeeded Dr. Brown in 1846. Dr. H. was from Massachusetts, and was appointed to the Asylum service from the Massachusetts General Hospital. He was four years connected with the Asylum, and much liked by the inmates, and appreciated by the management. On leaving the Asylum he engaged in the service of the Pacific Mail Steamship Company between New York and San Francisco, and ultimately settled in the latter city, where he had an extensive and successful practice, and where he died in 1884.

Dr. Oliver S. Lovejoy was the successor of Dr. Holman. He was likewise a native of Massachusetts, graduating in medicine at the college of Physicians and Surgeons, New York, in 1849. He entered upon service at the Asylum at the close of that year, and remained three years, when he married and engaged in general practice in Haverhill, Mass., where he has since resided, with the exception of three years (1871 to 1874), when he was superintendent of the State Farm, Work House and Insane Asylum, at Cranston, R. I.

Dr. Barton W. Chase, of Springfield, Vt., succeeded Dr. Lovejoy, and filled the office in 1853. He was a graduate of Dartmouth in the collegiate course, class of '47, and of the Vermont Medical College at Woodstock in 1850. He is now a resident of Detroit, Mich.

Dr. Henry M. Booth (a younger brother of Dr. Chauncey Booth, the first assistant connected with the Asylum), followed Dr. Chase in 1854, and remained two years. He was a native of Connecticut, born in 1826, and a graduate of the Woodstock Medical College, Vt. He died at Garden Plain, near Albany, Ill., where he had lived for twenty-five years, and acquired a wide reputation as a skillful physician and wise counsellor. The following tribute to his personal character is transcribed from a published obituary notice :

"A born gentleman, of commanding presence and pleasing address, singularly affable and polite in his intercourse with others, refined and cultivated in his manner and expression, he moved with grace and ease in any work of life, readily adapting himself to any circumstances or condition where professional duty called him. His very presence in the sick chamber, so kind, gentle and unobtrusive, with his acknowledged skill and ability as a physician, gave him a large and lucrative practice. Few physicians ever so fully retained the affections and confidence of their patients as Dr. Booth. Their faith in his skill and medical knowledge was unbounded, and so long as he could be reached no other was sought or accepted save on his recommendation."

Dr. Edward R. Chapin was officially connected with the Asylum as an assistant physician during the years of 1855–6–7. The son of Mrs. Dr. Rockwell by her first marriage, he came to the Asylum as a member of the family, at the opening of the Institution in 1836, being then a youth of fifteen years of age. He was born in Salisbury, Conn., Jan. 1, 1821, and died in New York Dec. 7, 1886. An incident connected with the opening of the Asylum was always remembered by him and often told. Dr. Rockwell had secured an attendant of experience from the Retreat at Hartford, Conn., to be ready on the opening day, but it chanced that the first patient admitted was a female so that service of him as an attendant was not at once required. With some reluctance he made himself useful, however, in the preparations being made for male patients, and in beginning housekeeping on the family scale some potatoes were engaged at a neighboring farm-house, and the attendant was asked to go for these —which he flatly refused to do, saying "he was not hired for that work." Young Chapin at once volunteered the service and soon returned with a bushel basket of them upon a wheelbarrow, the first ever used at the Asylum.

Dr. Chapin entered Yale for a collegiate course in 1838, but was obliged to abandon this after one year on account of some trouble of his eyes. After his graduation in medicine at the Yale Medical College, in 1842, he was appointed assistant physician at the Maine Insane Hospital, at that time superintended by Dr. Isaac Ray, which position he held for one year, 1843. He was then two years in Bellevue Hospital, and subsequently for four or five years located in practice in New York. In 1849 or '50 he went to California as surgeon on a Panama steamer, and remained for two years or more in San Francisco, connected with a city hospital there, during which period he improvised, in connection with the general hospital, the first provision ever made in that State for the accommodation of the insane. Returning, he was for a year or two in service as surgeon upon Atlantic steamships, and in 1855 entered the specialty again, this time permanently. From the Vermont Asylum he was, in 1858, appointed Resident Physician to the Kings Co. Lunatic Asylum at Flatbush, N. Y., which position he held for upwards of fifteen years. In the winter of 1871, he was seized with pneumonia and barely survived. Convalescence was protracted and the following winter was spent by him in Europe. He returned improved in health, but resigned the following year, married, and henceforth retired from professional life, usually spending the summer seasons in New England, but seeking in winter the more genial climes of the Southern States or California. In the Autumn of 1885, he went abroad with his wife to spend the winter in Torquay. She died in Paris, June 1886, after a brief illness of double pleurisy, and the Doctor immediately returned to this country with her remains for burial in Brattleboro, her native place; but almost immediately after reaching New York where he had arranged to spend the winter with the family of Dr. Rockwell, and to live, he was attacked again with pneumonia, which terminated his life in little more than a week.

Dr. John P. Clement succeeded Dr. Henry M. Booth and was associated as the colleague of Dr. Chapin, upon the medical staff of the Asylum in 1856-7. He was born in Chester, N. H., March 2, 1825. He was educated in Dartmouth College, class of '48, and took his medical degree from the Vermont Medical College at Woodstock in 1854. After leaving the Vermont Asylum in the spring of 1858, he married and settled in practice in Wisconsin. He was appointed to the superintendency of the State Hospital for the Insane at Madison, in 1860, resigning the charge in 1864, by reason of ill health. He died June 19, 1873, having returned to Vermont with the purpose, had his life been prolonged, of engaging again in his profession here.

A member of his family writes, "Such is the brief record of a life which was long in suffering and struggle, for he was never well after leaving college, and only those who knew him best realized how manfully he bore up under difficulties and discouragements which would have crushed a less brave spirit. After leaving Madison he was never idle, although obliged to make many changes on account of his health. He went frequently to Panama as surgeon on a steamer, and more than once went to Europe in the same capacity. During the war he was surgeon of a Western regiment for a few months."

Dr. Franklin C. Weeks was an assistant physician for four years, from the spring of 1858 to 1862. He was born in Chester, N. H., November 1, 1835, and graduated at Dartmouth Medical College in the class of '58. After leaving the Vermont Asylum he filled for a few months the like position at the Bloomingdale Asylum, when he · enlisted as assistant surgeon in the Fourteenth New Hampshire Volunteers. In this service he continued until his decease, which resulted from diphtheritic disease or malignant tonsilitis, at the Hospital of the N. E. Relief Associations in New York, March 28th, 1864. He was attacked with the fatal malady as he was returning from a furlough, to New Orleans, and his illness was of but a few days' duration.

Dr. Weeks was remarkable for his affability, and by his obliging disposition endeared himself to his patients. The writer, from an official association with him of two and a half years, can bear testimony to his devotion to professional duty, and his fondness for the work of the specialty.

Dr. George M. Buffum, a native of Monroe, N. H., and graduate of Dartmouth Medical College in '58, was associated with Dr. Weeks as a co-assistant from the spring of 1858, till the autumn of 1859. He was born January 18th, 1834, and died March 15th, 1862, in his native town, of consumption. He was of good professional ability, and had he lived, would doubtless have distinguished himself as a successful practitioner.

Dr. Joseph Draper, a native of Massachusetts and a graduate of the Jefferson Medical College, Philadelphia, succeeded Dr. Buffum and filled the position of an assistant physician for five years.

Dr. William H. Rockwell, Jr., graduate of the College of Physicians and Surgeons, New York, in class of '62, came upon the medical staff of the Asylum upon the retirement of Dr. Weeks, and held the position of an assistant physician until his election to the superintendency in 1872.

Dr. Nelson D. Rumsey followed Dr. Draper and was a colleague of Dr. Rockwell, Jr., during the year 1865. Dr. Rumsey came from Goshen, Orange County, N. Y. He was born in Monroe, N. Y., March 13th, 1828, and with the exception of the year of his connection with the Vermont Asylum, always lived in his native county. He graduated at the Castleton Medical College, Vermont, in 1853. He engaged in general practice after taking his degree, but a frail constitution and consumptive tendencies obliged him to seek a more regular and indoor life, and for several years preceding his appointment at the Vermont Asylum he was engaged in the drug business. After leaving the Institution he travelled for a year or two for his health, then married, and resumed his former business, until his failing health obliged him finally to relinquish it. He died in his native town February 7th, 1885. The testimony of those who knew him best is, that "for one of such delicate physique, he was notable for force, push, indomitable will and ambition, successful in business and professional life, which was only laid aside when his bodily strength failed him."

Dr. Edward B. Nims, of Sullivan, N. H., a graduate in medicine of the University of Vermont in 1864, was appointed the successor of Dr. Rumsey, and entered upon service at the beginning of 1866. He was the colleague of Dr. Rockwell, Jr., until the end of 1868, when he was appointed assistant physician at the Northampton Lunatic Hospital of which he is now superintendent.

Dr. Daniel H. Lovejoy of Rindge, N. H., a graduate of Bowdoin Medical College, Me., followed Dr. Nims, and was associated with Dr. Rockwell, Jr., in the years 1869-70. He was born October 16th 1838, and died at Concord, Mass., February 17th, 1881. He was a man of good professional acquirements, winning address, and possessed of some brilliant qualities, which, had he lived, would have insured for him distinction in his profession.

Dr. Charles H. Tenney of Hartford, Vt., was selected to succeed Dr. D. H. Lovejoy as second assistant physician in the early part of 1871. He was born February 21, 1830, and graduated from Dartmouth Medical College in 1858, also at the New York Medical College in 1859. Besides a number of years' experience as a general practitioner, he had a year's army experience in the civil war. In

August, 1872, upon the election of Dr. Rockwell, Jr. to the superintendency, he was promoted to the first assistancy, which position
he held to the time of his death at the Asylum April 23d, 1874, of
apoplexy.

A short memoir was published in the Transactions of the Vermont
Medical Society, 1874, from which I quote the following: "In
my inquiries I have failed to ascertain any specially notable
incidents in his life, but as one has expressed it 'the *whole* was so
made up of kind and worthy acts that no one prominent deed out-
shone all others.' His was the exemplification of a thoroughly
useful, consistent, Christian life. Governed in everything by high
and uncompromising principle, yet painfully sensitive to the opinions
of others, no man was more truly benevolent and humane in his
feelings and no one more charitably disposed in his judgments of
others than he Firmness was a prominent trait, and conscientiousness a ruling principle of action. He was the last man to be
approached or influenced by sinister proposals in any way, and in
all his fraternal relations scrupulous and mindful of his obligations.
To the Institution with which he was connected as a medical officer
he brought superior qualifications. To his professional acquirements were added mature judgment and social qualities of a high
order. In music he delighted, and many an hour was passed in
this indulgence with those under his professional charge, and many
in this way were undoubtedly drawn into nearer relations with him,
and realized more fully that he was in sympathy with them than
otherwise they might have supposed. He saw clearly the great
power of moral agencies in the treatment of the disordered mind,
and exerted himself to aid in every possible way in the diversions of
the inmates even at the cost of personal convenience and comfort.
Especially was this manifest during the last winter of his service,
when, notwithstanding his growing indisposition, he relinquished no
effort, but more than ever before studied the wants of those under
his care, and ministered to them with ever increasing assiduity and
conscientiousness."

Dr. John M. Clarke, a native of Vermont, and a graduate in medicine of the University at Burlington, was chosen to the position of
second assistant after the promotion of Dr. Tenney to the position
of first, in 1872, and upon the death of Dr. Tenney he was advanced
to the place of the latter, which he held until 1882. He has since
continued in the specialty, receiving and treating insane persons in
his own house at Burlington.

Dr. Henry T. Whitney, of Lunenburgh, Mass., and likewise a graduate of the University of Vermont, filled the position of second assistant in 1874-5. He has since had charge of the Opium Asylum and Medical Missionary Hospital in Foochow, China, in which service he has been engaged for the past ten years.

Dr. Frank W. Spaulding, of Bingham, Me., a graduate' from Bowdoin College in 1872, and at the medical department of the University of New York in 1875, followed Dr. Whitney and filled the position in 1876-7. He has since resided and practiced in Epping, N. H.

Dr. Olney W. Phelps, a native of Waitsfield, Vt., a graduate in the Chandler Scientific course at Dartmouth College in 1873, also of the Medical Department in class of '77, succeeded Dr. Spaulding at the close of the year 1877, and held the office till the spring of 1882, when he resigned to enter into general practice, and has since resided at Bellows Falls.

Dr. Shailer E. Lawton, a native of Connecticut and graduate in medicine of the University of Vermont, was appointed to succeed Dr. Clarke in the spring of 1882, and still holds the position of first assistant.

Dr. Edward French, a native of Iowa, and graduate of Dartmouth Medical College in 1881, was appointed to succeed Dr. Phelps in 1882, and held the office until the spring of 1884, when he left to accept a similar position in the New Hampshire Asylum for the Insane.

Dr. Lowell F. Wentworth, of Bridgewater, Mass., graduate from Dartmouth Medical College, class of '83, was elected the successor of Dr. French in 1884, and held the office till the spring of 1885, resigning to accept an advanced position in the Kansas Insane Asylum at Topeka.

Dr. Willis E. Bowie, a native of Maine, and graduate in medicine of Dartmouth, class of '84, succeeded Dr. Wentworth, and is still in service.

APOTHECARIES.

THE office of apothecary, it will be seen in the foregoing annals, was but irregularly filled and was practically abolished after 1856, a second assistant physician having been added to the medical staff, also a business clerk.

Many of the early assistants commenced as undergraduates in medicine, and performed the duties connected with this office. Dr. Henry M. Booth was the last of these, and held the position in 1845-6-7.

Jacob Catlin was elected apothecary in 1855. He was an elderly man, in broken health, and died at the Asylum after about a year's service. He was born and buried in Connecticut.

James Hunt was elected to succeed Jacob Catlin, in 1856, and was the last incumbent of the office.

MATRONS.

MRS. Ann F. Wilkinson, the first matron, came from Connecticut in the opening year of the Asylum, having had a previous experience in the care of the insane, with Dr. Rockwell at the Hartford Retreat. The following tribute to her faithful service is taken from the Report of the Superintendent for 1842:

"It was a source of great regret that we must part with our matron, Mrs. Wilkinson. She had devoted her energies to the best interests of the Institution, with a zeal and prudence that is rarely equalled. Being at once kind, humane, prudent, assiduous and untiring in her efforts to promote the welfare of those committed to her care, her resignation was much to be regretted by the friends of the Asylum."

Mrs. Deborah K. Baker succeeded Mrs. Wilkinson in 1842, and filled the office seven years, resigning in 1849. She was born in Peru, Vt., but was a widow and living in West Brattleboro at the time she was elected to her official position in the Asylum. On her retirement she married the farmer of the Asylum, Mr. Shearer, who likewise resigned his position at the same time. They went to Michigan, where both are still living, she at the advanced age of 84 years.

Miss Abigail Rockwell, of East Windsor, Conn., was elected to succeed Mrs. Baker, and held the office upwards of seventeen years. She was a sister of Dr. Rockwell, and like him possessed of rare executive qualities. She died in service, after a short illness of pneumonia, Jan. 11, 1867, at the age of 68 years. Her decease is very briefly chronicled in the Report of the Superintendent of that year, and may be read in the annals of '67. Her lengthened period of labor deserves further mention and comment. "Anything I could say concerning her faithful service would very likely be misconstrued or misinterpreted," said Dr. Rockwell at the time, to the writer of these pages, who can now speak from his personal official relation with her from 1859 to 1865, and out of the full appreciation of her rare qualities of mind and heart, and in the fullness of time.

It is indeed a grateful privilege to bear testimony to the worth of a friend whose virtues have faded not in the lapse of a score of years. It requires no effort of memory to bring her once more into our living presence, and no stretch of imagination to see her again in the steadfast performance of her unfailing round of duties. Few persons were ever better fitted by natural endowment for the useful position she came to fill. She embodied all the elements of a strong character. To a sympathizing heart and ready hand were added the Christian virtues, and the spontaneous promptings of humanity were guided and governed by her religious convictions—strong and puritanic, without bigotry. Hers was emphatically a Christian life, in which precept and practice were ever consistently joined. She commanded both respect and affection. In person and presence she exemplified the ideal matron. In figure somewhat stout, in countenance benevolent, in good sense and efficiency never wanting. Dressed in matronly garb, lace cap and kerchief of spotless white, and with the habitually worn spectacles, no one who ever knew her can fail to recognize her. To this day her memory is cherished by many of the older inmates of the Asylum, and it is no disparagement to those who have succeeded her in office, if they have failed fully to fill in the hearts of these, her place. No one's work was ever more unostentatiously performed. While the day lasted she was at her post. When she lay down for her long rest, she had no cause to reflect upon unperformed duties that might have been done. Hers was a lifetime of duties each day fully rounded out.

Miss Frances M. Palmer, of Putney, Vt., succeeded Miss Abbie Rockwell in 1867, and filled with efficiency the duties of the office for nine years. She was for six years previously in service as an attendant.

Miss Mary Draper was elected matron in 1878—having been advanced from the position of superintendent's clerk—and held the office for four years, making altogether a more or less continuous service of nine years.

Miss H. E. Blanche Gibson, at present in office, was promoted from the position of chief attendant January 1, 1884, having had a previous connection with the Asylum of near five years.

FARMERS.

M R. James M. Shearer, of Coleraine, Mass., was the first elected farmer under the By-Laws of 1845. He held the office four years.

Warren E. Eason, of Leyden, Mass., was elected the successor of Mr. Shearer in 1849, and held the office eight years.

Alanson Weatherhead, of Guilford, Vt., succeeded Mr. Eason in 1857, and held the office about five years, resigning on account of failing health. He was born in Guilford March 27, 1824, and died in Vernon April 9, 1862.

Ira X. Haywood, of Ludlow, Vt., was appointed to succeed Mr. Weatherhead. He entered upon duty early in 1862, and gave near twelve years of faithful labor, resigning in 1873. He died at Ludlow Dec. 23, 1884, where he was born April 13, 1823.

Asa Gilkey, of Plainfield, N. H., was elected upon the resignation of Mr. Haywood, and held the office for thirteen years.

George W. Pierce, of Westminster, Vt.—the present farmer—entered upon duty in August, 1886.

All the farmers, without exception, have been advanced from less responsible situations in which they had proved themselves faithful and capable.

STEWARDS.

T HE office of steward, as will be seen by the Record of 1879, is of recent creation.

Porter C. Spencer, of Brattleboro, was elected to this position in August, 1879, having previously for two years and upwards been employed as a business assistant or clerk.

It is impossible to pass in review those who, in the fifty years past, have for longer or shorter periods filled non-official positions in the Asylum. They number many hundreds, and constitute an ever-changing throng, who, as they move in their orbit within this little world, impress upon it—at least in a general way—a character that from time to time is reflected upon the outer world in light or shadow, as the case may be. The record of the six thousand patients treated, affords material for much elaboration which cannot be entered upon here. It embraces all grades of social status, and all forms of mental disorder. As in the world at large there are individual celebrities, so here there are notables—a few of whom have found mention in the annals here recorded.

With the close of the first fifty years, we lay down the pen, but there is no pause in the work ;—already we have passed into the second half-century, the story of which will be told by another chronicler.

"Like shadows gliding o'er the plain,
　Or clouds that roll successive on,
Man's busy generations pass ;
　And, while we gaze, their forms are gone.

"'He lived,—he died :' behold the sum,
　The abstract, of the historian's page !
Alike in God's all-seeing eye
　The infant's day, the patriarch's age.

"O Father, in whose mighty hand
　The boundless years and ages lie !
Teach us thy boon of life to prize,
　And use the moments as they fly ;

"To crowd the narrow span of life
　With wise designs and virtuous deeds :
So shall we wake from death's dark night,
　To share the glory that succeeds."